SCOTCH J&B WHISKY
RARE

THE BOOK OF
The Woodcock

Debrett

BY APPOINTMENT TO HER MAJESTY THE QUEEN
RARE
J&B
SCOTLAND
A.A. BROWN & SONS

SCOTCH J&B WHISKY
RARE

THE BOOK OF
The Woodcock

Colin Laurie McKelvie

ISBN 0 905649 83 4

Published by Debrett's Peerage Limited,
73–77 Britannia Road, London SW6 2JR.

Represented by:
Michael Joseph Limited
27 Wright's Lane
Kensington
London W8

Distributed by:
TBL Book Distribution Services
17–32 Nelson Way
Tuscan Trading Estate
Camberley
Surrey

Designed by:
Vic Giolitto

Typesetting:
P&M Typesetting Ltd, Exeter

Printed and bound by:
R. J. Acford
St. Ives Group Plc, Chichester, Sussex

CONTENTS

Richard Robjent

To the Memory of

J. C. Harrison

Alec Perceval

Brian Stronach

– an artist, a sportsman and a scientist –
who loved woodcock and their ways

FOREWORD

BY THE RT. HON. THE LORD MARGADALE TD JP DL

FONTHILL HOUSE
TISBURY
WILTSHIRE

This is an unusual and important volume, for it is the first British book solely devoted to the woodcock.

In other books this delightful bird has been dealt with in no more than a chapter, and sometimes only a few pages. This is surprising, since many woodcock books, good, bad and indifferent, have been published in Europe over the years. The excitement which a woodcock causes when it appears on a shooting day; the bird's mysterious and secretive life; and the many questions which remain unanswered about it – all these show the need for a thorough individual study of the woodcock.

Artists, like sportsmen, have always been drawn to the woodcock, with its rich plumage and unusual shape, unique among the birds of the British Isles. In the pages which follow are some of the finest studies of woodcock, in colour and black and white, from the brushes of past masters like Archibald Thorburn and of modern artists like Rodger McPhail and Richard Robjent. Some splendid photographs give intimate glimpses of the private life of this very private bird.

Colin Laurie McKelvie has made a special study of woodcock, in the field and by searching through old sporting books, obscure foreign publications and modern scientific papers, including important recent studies by The Game Conservancy. The result is a lively and well-informed study of the woodcock and its ways.

All my life I have enjoyed watching and pursuing woodcock. Two woodcock can be seen as Supporters in my Coat of Arms. I hope this book will give pleasure and food for thought to all who, like myself, love this wonderful little bird.

June 1986 Margadale

INTRODUCTION

Woodcock are very memorable and very special. To the ornithologist they are elusive and mysterious. The game shooter looks on them as special treats whose unexpected appearance, usually on pheasant drives, quickens the pulse and enlivens the scene in a unique way. A woodcock shot and brought to hand is cause for delight and comment by the lucky Gun and his companions. To modify a remark of W.C. Fields, "A pheasant is only a pheasant – but a woodcock is an *event*!"

This book is a personal attempt to celebrate in words, pictures, sketches and engravings some aspects of a very remarkable sporting bird. Its reclusive and silent ways make it especially difficult for the naturalist to study it fully: only recently have modern scientific techniques enabled game biologists to make real headway in uncovering the private life of the woodcock, bringing it out of the realms of sportsmen's anecdotes and into the more objective and soundly based world of scientific understanding. Much remains to be discovered about the woodcock and its ways: like most research, recent woodcock studies have raised as many new questions as they have answered. Meanwhile, the perennial enthusiasm and interest of the sportsman continues undiminished.

It seems extraordinary that the woodcock, which is so widely known and is such a constant focus for anecdotes, tales, legends and endless sporting gossip, has never had a full-length book to itself in English. At most it has usually been given little more than a short chapter in general books on game birds and game shooting. A half volume in the Victorian *Fur, Feather & Fin* series and another in the *Sportsman's Library* of 1936 went further, but still denied the woodcock the more detailed consideration it deserves, and which sporting writers of other nations have given it. No fewer than nine books on woodcock are currently in print in France, with others in German and Italian, and its smaller cousin the American Woodcock has also been the subject of several important books.

This book is intended to appeal to all who take an interest in this most elusive and fascinating bird – the sportsman, the naturalist and the general reader. It is not a scientific study, although I have tried to discuss some of the principal findings of important recent research in Britain and Ireland. But the layman is often baffled and dismayed by the scientists' delight in technical jargon, graphs and all the complex apparatus which is appropriate in a biological monograph. Similarly the scientist may be unimpressed by the wealth of anecdotes, sporting traditions and historical lore which has accumulated around the woodcock – from the plays of the Elizabethan dramatists to the scribblings of amateur sportsman-naturalists in successive generations. Perhaps this book is only an indulgent compromise – but I hope it may be an enjoyable and informative one.

I have tried to draw together many aspects of our perceptions of the woodcock – old and new, scientific and anecdotal – in a general survey of the species. A thorough discussion of all the scientific data, the historical records and the many unanswered questions about woodcock would call for a much larger book – and, dare I say, a duller one for the general reader. Like every woodcock shooter I have my personal beliefs and theories, but I have tried to present as fair and wide-ranging a picture as possible. Only a fool would be dogmatic about woodcock: we have still so much to learn. But repeated reservations and qualifications become irritating for the reader. T.C. Kingsmill Moore – whom I knew when he was the *eminence grise* of the Irish field sports world and also of Trinity College, Dublin while I was a mere Freshman – felt the same when he wrote his angling classic *A Man May Fish* (1960), and expressed it aptly when he begged: "May I ask, then, that conclusions which appear to be stated too positively should be read as if introduced by the words – 'As far as my limited experience goes, and as a provisional hypothesis...?'"

My main aim here has been to share something of the pleasure and delight I have found in the woodcock – pursued like a Grail in a prolonged quest with dog and gun in the coverts of Britain and Ireland; through dozens of game books from generations past and present; in the pages of scores of old sporting books; and in a hundred and one scientific papers and reports.

I must begin by thanking the Rt. Hon. the Lord Margadale for his kindness in writing an enthusiastic and encouraging Foreword. His wealth of knowledge of woodcock and their ways, and his life-long interest in the species, makes this especially appropriate. His family's property on Islay in the Inner Hebrides has long been a by-word among woodcock enthusiasts, and it is no accident that, when he was ennobled in 1964 as the first Baron Margadale, he chose two woodcock as heraldic supporters in his coat of arms.

This book – the first British book ever devoted exclusively to the woodcock – would never have appeared in its present form without the co-operation of the *Shooting Times* and its recently formed Woodcock Club, and the Club's sponsors, J&B Rare Scotch Whisky. In particular I must thank Henry Lorimer of J&B, a generous sporting host and an enthusiastic supporter of this book from its conception. Tony Jackson, formerly editor of *Shooting Times*, and his successor Derek Bingham were equally unflagging in their enthusiasm. Without their tangible support and whole-hearted commitment to the publication of this book the tasks of the author and the publisher would have been much more difficult.

Everyone, it seems, is fascinated by woodcock – sportsmen, wildlife artists, ornithologists and country-minded people. I had always believed this to be so, but it was not until I began gathering information and illustrations for this book that I realised the full extent of the fascination the woodcock holds. Those I turned to for advice and help were, with very few exceptions, generous to a fault in their enthusiastic support for a new book about the woodcock and its ways.

To have included all the information, anecdotes and illustrations I was offered would have swelled this volume to many times its size. It is difficult adequately to express my thanks to so many friends and fellow woodcock enthusiasts, throughout the British Isles, Europe and further afield. Without their help, advice and encouragement the writing of this book would have been much less enjoyable and I should have missed a good deal of material.

Much of the appeal of this book lies in its illustrations. I have been especially fortunate in securing the help of my friends Rodger McPhail and Richard Robjent, two of Britain's foremost sporting artists, who undertook commissions for watercolour studies of woodcock, reproduced here as full-page colour plates, and also many less formal sketches and drawings which are published here for the first time. Jane Brewer and Neil McReddie have also provided some delightful illustrations specially for this book. The enthusiasm of all the artists for the woodcock and its ways is evident in their work, which has greatly enriched the pages which follow.

The work of these active modern artists is complemented by pictures and sketches from some of the "old masters" of British sporting art. Archibald Thorburn, George Lodge and Philip Rickman were all practical sportsmen who returned again and again to the woodcock as a subject for their brushes and pencils. Their studies of woodcock are some of the finest ever done.

William Hollywood's delightful study in oils of a woodcock in the snow is reproduced here with his kind permission, and with that of the owner. John Paley kindly made available his study of a spaniel retrieving a woodcock, and I must thank David Carlisle for his study in oils of winter woodcock.

T.A. Waddell has generously made available to me some of his wonderful collection of photographs, both in colour and black and white, of woodcock at the nest. These are some of the finest ever taken, and give us a unique series of intimate glimpses of the life of nesting woodcock.

I find it difficult to know how to begin to express my special thanks to Robin Knowles of the British Museum of Natural History. His tireless help and innumerable kindnesses during my researches for this book were equalled only by his vast store of arcane and obscure information about woodcock – and almost every other subject!

Dr. Graham Hirons, who studied the breeding biology and wintering behaviour of woodcock as a major research project for The Game Conservancy, has been a source of much vital information, and I also owe a debt of gratitude to him and to many of my colleagues among the scientific and game advisory staff of The Game Conservancy. They and my long-suffering assistant Judy Pittock have patiently endured and encouraged my interest in woodcock. The sporting community and all who care for the future of game and other quarry species should be in no doubt about the importance of the work of The Game Conservancy – the only organisation in Britain and Ireland wholly devoted to the scientific study of game species and the development of practical management techniques to promote game and all the many other forms of wildlife which share the same environment. It deserves the support of everyone who cares for our heritage of game and wishes to see it flourish for future generations.

Countless friends, fellow sportsmen and correspondents have helped me in many ways, with information about woodcock, shoot bag records, anecdotes and illustrations. I am especially grateful to the following:

The late Mario Abbiattico
Ken Aldridge
James Archdale
Mervyn Archdale
Col. Glenn O. Baker
Sir Derek Barber
Peter Bickford-Smith
The Hon. D.E.H. Bigham of the Tryon Gallery
Derek Bingham (Editor – *Shooting Times & Country Magazine*)
Mrs. D. de B. Bingham
Major Brian Booth of the Tryon Gallery
James Booth (Director – Sporting Guns & Firearms at Sotheby's)
Eugene and John Brazil
The British Trust for Ornithology and T. & A.D. Poyser Ltd.
Jane Brewer
Ewan Brodie of Lethen
The late Viscount Brookeborough KG
John Buckland
The Lord Buxton of Alsa
Arthur Cadman
Nigel Cardwell
David Carlisle
V. Clarke
B.J. Crichton
The Viscount Coke and the Trustees of Holkham Estate
Edward and Charles Cooper of Markree Castle
Moffat Crockard
Major Lionel Currie
Howard Cutliffe
Geoffrey Dashwood
Mrs Ann Datta and the staff of the library of The British Museum (Natural History)
R.J. Deterding
John Fergusson
Colin Foote
Veronica, Lady Gainford
Godfrey Gallia
Caesare Giovanelli of Brescia
Miss Aideen Gore-Booth of Lissadell
Capt. R. de Cl. Grant-Rennick
R.D. Gregory
Major Charles Hamilton
Capt. James Hamilton of Brownhall
Dr John Harradine of the British Association for Shooting and Conservation
The late J.C. Harrison
Robin Harrison and the Trustees of the estate of the late J.C. Harrison

The late Major R.O. Hermon
Michael Hicks MH and Mrs P.M. Hicks
Dr. David Hill
Dr. Graham Hirons
William Hollywood
Ian and Dorothy Holman
Billy Hosick
G. Humble
Charles Jardine
Robert Jarman
Simon Jervis-Read
Oscar and Peter Johnson Ltd.
Peter Keyser of The Keyser Gallery
Robin Knowles of The British Museum of Natural History
Dr. P. Lack
Peter Lapsley
David Lea of Messrs Longmans (publishers)
Christopher Lees
Crawford Little (Editor – *Countrysport*)
The Trustees of the estate of the late G.E. Lodge
Henry Lorimer of J&B Rare Scotch Whisky
Rodger McPhail
Neil McReddie
Pal Mariassy
Brian Martin
Drummond Nelson
His Grace the Duke of Northumberland KG
John Paley
Brian Peake
The late Maj. Alec Perceval of Temple House
Mr & Mrs A.R.H. Perceval of Temple House
Lord Ralph Percy
Mrs Judy Pittock
Talbot Radcliff
Brian Redfearn
The Philip Rickman Trustees
Dr. Peter Robertson of The Game Conservancy
Richard Robjent
Kevin Ruff of Messrs. Ruffs (Jewellers), Gosport
R.G. Schaub
The late Brian Stronach
The late Sir Norman Stronge Bt.
Mike Swan of The Game Conservancy
Sergio Treves
The Hon. Aylmer Tryon
Merlin Unwin
Henry Vyner
T.A. Waddell
Bjorn Waktare of Gunmark Ltd.
Adrian Weller of Sotheby's
Sam Wilson
Wilson Young

With such a wealth of expertise, this book has been enriched enormously.

Robert Jarman (Managing Director of Debrett's) has been a source of advice and encouragement at all stages in the preparation and production of this book. Any errors and omissions are mine alone.

It is a great sadness to me that the three woodcock enthusiasts to whose memory this book is dedicated did not live to see it published. Their wisdom and experience taught me a great deal about woodcock and their ways. I like to think that in reading this book they might have found even a fraction of the pleasure I would have felt in giving them a copy.

Although I was only privileged to get to know J.C. Harrison shortly before his death, his enthusiasm for woodcock and his knowledge of the bird and its habits was unbounded. He was eager to make some of his many wonderful pictures of woodcock available for this book, and they are reproduced by kind permission of his son, Mr Robin Harrison, and the trustees and executors of his estate. (I am also indebted to the Tryon Gallery, and especially to David Bigham and Brian Booth, for their help and guidance with copyright matters.)

Alec Perceval was fortunate to have one of Ireland's finest woodcock shoots, and took delight in sharing his sport with a host of friends, old and young. An invitation to shoot at Temple House was something to be savoured in anticipation and enjoyed to the full – woodcock shooting at its best, in the best of company. Alec's sudden death in February 1986 was a great shock to his many sporting friends. But it came as he would probably have wished, at the end of a full and successful shooting season, and one in which he had enjoyed his first woodcock shoot in the company of his son and grandson – three generations shooting together on a day of sparkling January sunshine and frost, when the coverts were full of 'cock and the bag was good.

Brian Stronach was that rare individual, a thoroughly professional game biologist with the zest and enthusiasm of a true sportsman. His especial interest in woodcock was as evident in the field with dog and gun as it was in the laboratory. His studies of woodcock in Ireland were carried out with the fullest co-operation of Irish sportsmen, who respected his scientific expertise and relished his company on shooting days. His untimely death in 1984 was a great loss to the world of game biology, and woodcock research in particular.

Colin Laurie McKelvie

Broad Chalke
Wiltshire
June 1986

So life-like it might fly off at any moment – Linda Heaton-Harris' full size sculpture of a roosting woodcock, modelled in clays. (From the collection of Mr & Mrs I. H. Holman.)

CHAPTER I

INTRODUCING THE WOODCOCK

"No man who has ever carried a gun forgets his first woodcock to the day of his death. You may forget your first salmon, or even 'the first kiss at love's beginning', as the poet hath it, but never your first woodcock; and you may fish, shoot and hunt in any and every land, and have the best of sport, but of many days **creta notandi** *in your sporting diary, the good days with the woodcock will be marked with the whitest pencil and be for ever fraught with the pleasantest recollections.*

J.J. Manley: ***Notes on Game and Shooting*** **(1880)**

As you take a shot woodcock from the mouth of your retriever, which is how most people have their first sight of a woodcock at close quarters, you will be in absolutely no doubt about identifying the species. It is distinctive and immediately recognisable. Quite simply, it looks so unlike any other bird. And, as we shall see, it behaves in a unique way too. All in all it is an extraordinary bird, which inspires more enthusiasm, affection and curiosity among shooting people than any other species we normally encounter.

As regards its appearance, on first impressions we would probably be tempted to draw comparisons with the Common Snipe (*Gallinago gallinago*), which is familiar to most sportsmen. In fact, we often talk about woodcock and snipe in the same breath. Another superficially similar-looking species is the Great Snipe (*Gallinago media*), which has much the same compact and rather rounded body, but is smaller and has more elongated and pointed wings than its larger cousin. But this comparison is of limited value to the practical sportsman or the average field naturalist in the British Isles. Few of us have ever seen a Great Snipe, which is a scarce winter visitor for which many ornithologists will have to wait years before they can tick it off on their "life-list". It also enjoys total protection, so it is not fair game for the shooter

even when it does put in an appearance. And there should be very little excuse for the accidental shooting of a Great Snipe, which has a distinctive white tail, unlike a woodcock, and normally rises in straight flight, unlike the zig-zag departure of the Common Snipe.

It is incorrect, strictly speaking, to introduce the woodcock as a gamebird, although that is how most sportsmen, naturalists and ornithologists regard it. In Britain woodcock and snipe have never been accorded the same full legal status as "game", which the pheasant, the partridge or the grouse enjoy. But they have been deemed to be game for the purposes of raising revenue through game licences. This was first introduced by the Chancellor of the Exchequer in April, 1808, and a sporting versifier of the day immortalized the change of status of "the longbills" in some lines of doggerel:

The Woodcocks and Snipes t'other eve met together,
To talk o'er the news of the day,
When the President, shaking indignant each feather,
Cry'd, "List, friends, to what I've to say –

"By the Chiefs of this land, we've been deemed a rich prize,
We have flown far to pamper their wills;
A, year after year, when they wanted supplies,
We were all on the wing with long bills.

"... But now they may cry up a crow or woodpecker,
Their owls and their pies, great and small,
For the Chancellor vile, of the British Exchequer,
Has fairly made Game of us all."

By this story depress'd, they all slowly took wing,
For to fly fast, they seem'd quite unable,
And each took his oath – *"By the clear water-spring*
I'll be ***shot****, if I e'er grace his table."*

The Game Act of 1831, the basis of all present-day game laws in Britain, continued to deny full gamebird status to the woodcock, but the law still requires the sportsman to have a Game Licence to shoot woodcock or snipe. So when is a gamebird not a gamebird? When it is a snipe or a woodcock! This

is an example of the anomalies which exist in our game laws, and just one of the many oddities of this very unusual and mysterious sporting bird.

Whatever the strict *de jure* status of the woodcock may be, it is *de facto* every inch a gamebird in the sportsman's eyes, and it is to the sportsman that the woodcock is best known and most important. Few general naturalists or ornithologists share the shooting man's intense interest in woodcock, and almost all of what we know about this bird is due more or less directly to what sportsmen have seen and recorded over the centuries.

The European woodcock (*Scolopax rusticola*) belongs to a large family of species which includes most waders and shorebirds and also comprises the gulls and the auk species, like puffins, guillemots and razorbills. From the sportsman's point of view its most obvious close relatives are the various species of snipe. Technically speaking – and I have made a special effort to avoid being too technical – the woodcock belongs to the *Scolopacidae* family, part of the larger Order of *Charadriiformes*. For the British and European sportsman it is the most familiar member of the genus *Scolopax*, which also includes other species of woodcock found in eastern and south-east Asia and in North America.

Most of the woodcock's closer relatives, like the curlew, the sandpiper, the godwit and the snipe, are to be found along coasts and by the margins of lakes and rivers. They tend to be gregarious, usually quite active during the daytime, and are often very conspicuous by their movements in flocks and by their calls, whether it be the piping and whistling of coastal waders or the *scaape-scaape* alarm cries of a wisp of snipe as they rise from a bog or flooded meadow. The woodcock, by contrast, is an altogether more secretive and solitary bird, living and breeding mainly in woodland, feeding actively under cover of darkness, especially in the winter months, and flying back swiftly and silently at dawn to spend the daylight hours roosting in cover, until the coming of dusk gives the signal for it to flight out again at last light to its night-time feeding grounds. The woodcock is a webless-footed wader, with shorter legs than most of its wading relatives, and is adapted to life in temperate woodlands, living its quiet life close to the frost-line. Its distribution and migratory movements are intimately linked to the climate in general, and to the prevailing weather conditions at particular times.

The Germans call it the *waldschnepfe,* "the snipe of the woods", which is a good name for a wading, probing bird which favours wooded habitats. The French, too, emphasize the woodland connection, calling it *la bécasse des bois*, the "longbilled bird of the woods".

In describing the physical appearance of the woodcock a great many writers have used the words "squat" and "bulky", and a woodcock roosting in cover or on its nest does indeed present a rather rounded and compact shape. But most of us rarely if ever see a woodcock on the ground: indeed it is one of the most notoriously difficult of all birds to spot until it is flushed and on the wing. That is what makes it such a very difficult bird to study fully, and largely explains why we still know so relatively little about it. But once it is in flight the woodcock's shape and movements give us an impression for which the word "squat" could hardly be less appropriate.

The woodcock's overall length is about 14 inches, including the bill which accounts for some 2¾ inches (*c.* 72 centimetres) and is the bird's most prominent physical feature. A more practical guideline for its size would be to say that it is roughly the size of a partridge or a pigeon, and its weight generally averages 11–12 ounces, based on many weighings of shot and live-caught specimens in the British Isles and abroad. However, weight and size can both vary considerably from individual to individual, and weights in particular are known to vary depending upon the bird's stage in its life cycle,

The fast, swerving flight through low cover which is typical of woodcock flushed from their roosting sites on winter days.

its breeding behaviour and the availability of food, especially as it is affected by severe frosty weather.

Before we look closely at the woodcock and its size, shape and colouring, let's consider those parts of the world where the sportsman and ornithologist can expect to find it.

The European woodcock *Scolopax rusticola* is found across a surprisingly large geographical range through the year, from the Atlantic islands of the Azores, Madiera and the Canaries, through Ireland and Britain and their offshore islands and eastwards throughout Scandinavia, western, central and eastern Europe and across Siberia to the Pacific coast. It is rarely found north of the Arctic Circle, but large breeding densities are to be found in summer in northern Europe and Asia, in places where winter conditions would be impossible for a bird which feeds by probing in unfrozen ground.

The southern extent of its breeding range includes the Pyrenees and northern Spain, eastwards across the southern Alps and northern Italy and through the Balkan countries and southern Russia, continuing eastwards across the northern foothills of the Himalayas and through Mongolia and Manchuria, as far as the Pacific coastline. It is also known to breed on some of the Pacific islands, particularly in the northern Japanese archipelago.

In winter, however, the southern extent of the species' range is much greater. Woodcock are very migratory in their behaviour, and birds which breed in the unfrozen summer woodlands of northern Europe and Asia will winter down through the Mediterranean countries and into North Africa, through the Atlas Mountains, Morocco, Tunisia, Libya and Egypt and into northern Iraq, Iran, Afghanistan and the southern Himalayas and south as far as Assam, the hill country of southern India and into Sri Lanka.

The British in India and Ceylon loved their sport and left detailed accounts of the game and other wildlife they encountered. However, the extensive sporting literature of British India in the eighteenth and nineteenth centuries is almost silent about woodcock. While snipe and many species of waterfowl provided superb sport on the *jheels* and marshes of the sub-continent, the very existence there of the woodcock was sometimes hotly disputed. The Rev. William Daniel's *Rural Sports* (1801), which is an important book for tracing the history of the woodcock, especially in Britain and Ireland, also records a woodcock shot at Chittagong, which caused so much comment that it was sent to Bengal to be mounted and preserved in a museum. *Wild Sports of the East*, another early nineteenth century work, mentions "several brace" being seen "near Huzaribagh", at a time of extreme frost.

But the earnest correspondents to *The Oriental Sporting Magazine* in 1829–32 continued to dispute the woodcock's presence in India, though there were claims for occasional individuals being shot "in the Neilgherri hills and near Madras". "Snaffle" [Robert Dunkin] wrote about the Nilgiri woodcock in 1894, but did not believe they occurred in Ceylon, where he had lived and shot regularly for many seasons. A more recent scientific account, in 1969, reported that numbers of wintering woodcock in the hill country of Nilgiri and Assam have decreased in recent years owing to habitat changes, principally the clearance of woodland to make way for the cultivation of potatoes and tea.

In south-east Asia and Indo-China the "European" woodcock is found in Malaysia and as far east as Taiwan and the Philippines, but other and as yet little-studied species of woodcock also exist there.

As with many long distance migrants, woodcock have also been recorded as rare sightings far outside their normal wintering range. Since the mid-nineteenth century there have been occasional reports of European woodcock in the eastern USA, where it does not normally occur, its niche being taken by its near relation, the smaller American woodcock (*Philohela minor*). On 9 January, 1862, a woodcock was shot near St John in Newfoundland. It was close to an unfrozen spring and the preceding weeks had been cold and stormy with strong easterly winds. This specimen was apparently in good condition, weighing 12¾ ounces, well above the average for the species in general. By 1912 the US Department of Agriculture's Biological Survey was able to record other instances throughout New England and the eastern USA, including Virginia, Pennsylvania, New Jersey, Rhode Island and to the north in eastern Quebec. More recently there have been accounts of stragglers as far west as Ohio and also in Alabama in the south. These birds' origins are a matter of conjecture; they may have come from the most westerly breeding population in the Azores. But the woodcock of the Azores are generally regarded as sedentary, so it is just possible that these

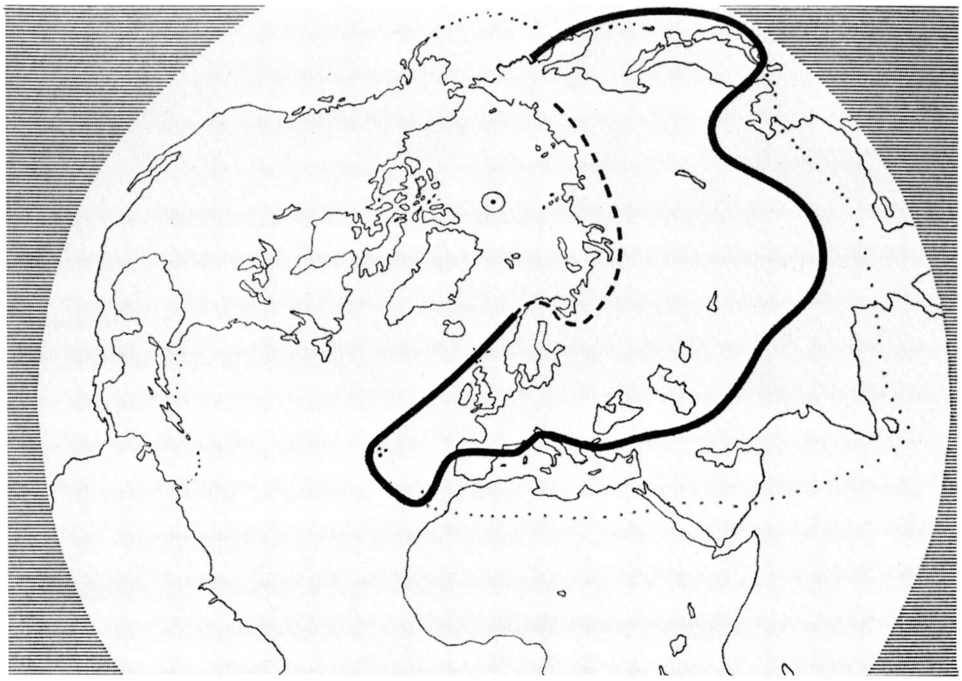

The breeding and wintering range of the European woodcock. The solid line marks the southern limits of the woodcock's breeding range in Europe and Asia, while the dotted line shows the approximate limits of its wintering range.

North American recoveries may have been migratory birds from Scandinavia or western Europe, driven far off their normal range by extreme easterly winds and freezing conditions.

The Faeroe Islands do not have resident or breeding woodcock, but migrants have been seen there on passage in spring and autumn. Greenland is far to the north-west of the woodcock's normal breeding or wintering range but woodcock have turned up there on rare occasions. Two confirmed specimens from Greenland are now preserved as skins in the natural history museum at Copenhagen: one was shot in eastern Greenland on 5 October, 1906, while the other was found in western Greenland in the early 1940s.

Iceland is closer to Europe and to the woodcock's normal range, and a report published in 1949 said that about fifteen woodcock had been seen there in as many years. It has been suggested that Iceland's climate has become progressively milder since the 1930s and that this may have made it more attractive to woodcock, but they remain very rare and occasional visitors.

While Spitzbergen is an impossible place for woodcock in winter there have nevertheless been several summer records from the west of the island, although it is not on a normal woodcock migration route. These birds must be regarded as stragglers, perhaps driven off course by contrary wind and weather. There are four possible records from 1907 to 1954 and a more detailed account of a positive finding in July, 1964, when an ornithological expedition found the partially eaten remains of a woodcock close to an arctic fox's earth in western Spitzbergen.

As you might expect, more is known about the habits and distribution of woodcock in western Europe than in other areas to the east. Russia, central Asia, China and the East have vast areas of potentially good woodcock breeding and wintering habitat which are still virtually unstudied. Russia, for instance, is especially important for the woodcock shooter in mainland Europe, for most of the birds he bags may originate there. There is enormous potential for further research, but political considerations and the sheer difficulty of getting there often mean that these areas are inaccessible to visiting ornithologists, and likely to remain so for the foreseeable future.

The woodcock's plumage is a wonderfully rich combination of russets, buffs, creams and greyish-browns, highlighted with lines, flecks and bars of dark brown and black and with occasional subtle lavender-hued hints among the feathers on its back. The underside of the bird is much paler, a soft and intricate pattern of light creamy buff and brownish-black barring which can still give a degree of camouflage even to a shot bird which falls on its back, quite unlike the startlingly prominent white of the underparts of a Common Snipe. But the superb natural camouflage of the bird's upper parts, especially the wings, back and head, is particularly striking and unsurpassed by any other European species.

Although the precise details of colouration can vary considerably from one individual woodcock to another, the overall effect always succeeds in making the bird blend discreetly and almost invisibly into its surroundings of dead leaves, rough grasses, brambles, heather and all the other types of ground vegetation in which it may be found, either during the winter months or in the course of its spring and early summer breeding season. "Cryptic" is the biologists' term for this variegated colouring which breaks up the bird's outline and helps it to melt so successfully into its surroundings, and we apply the same principles of "disruptive patterns" to our human attempts at camouflage for the soldier and his equipment or, among sportsmen, the woodland deer-stalker.

If you compare a number of woodcock, perhaps when the bag is laid out after a shoot, you will probably see that there are considerable differences between individual birds, both in general colouration and in the more minute aspects of the plumage colour and patterning. The woodcock is a species which displays a very wide range of individual colour variations. This has been interpreted in the past as signs of different races and "breeds" of woodcock. Some Victorian and Edwardian woodcock enthusiasts became quite obsessively interested in these plumage variations, and collected them avidly. Often agents were employed to search among the game dealers' racks and in the poultry markets to find odd or unusually coloured woodcock to swell the cabinets of collectors like Joseph Whitaker of Nottinghamshire. He claimed to have a personal collection of no fewer than twenty-four different-coloured types of woodcock. In fact he was dealing with a bird which is simply very variable in its colour, although he did acquire some extremely unusual albino and semi-albino woodcock, and some that were exceptionally dark.

If you read what sportsmen wrote about woodcock a generation or two ago you will find endless references to "grey birds" and "red birds". Often we are told that the reddish-brown woodcock tends to be smaller and also to be the home-bred resident, while the larger greyish woodcock is an immigrant from Scandinavia or some other part of northern Europe. Or you can find another theory which is quite the reverse. An experienced gamekeeper in County Galway, who knew his woodcock well, both on winter shoots and when he found their nests around the fringes of the heathery "red bogs" of the west of Ireland, thought of the home-breeding residents as "them big reddy fellows" and the winter migrants as "the little grey fellows".

J.W. Seigne, who was the most important and active student of woodcock

Roosting in cover on a wet autumn day, this woodcock clearly shows the prominent barring on its head and the two lines of lighter coloured feathers running down the bird's neck.

and their ways in Ireland between the wars, and who wrote extensively about them, shared this keeper's view. His impression was that the woodcock he found nesting in Ireland were big and boldly marked, "of a rich chestnut colour". The winter visitors, by contrast, he described as having an "ashen grey hue and paler brown mottling of the plumage.... Besides, on an average, these winter migrants are smaller."

He compared his Irish birds, both those which he saw on the nest and those shot in winter, with others he had seen on some very big shoots in the eastern Mediterranean, and concluded that the resident woodcock was definitely red, averaging 11¾ ounces, while the overseas visitor was greyish and averaged 11 ounces. This was such a firm conviction that he made a point of shooting some specimens of both alleged types which he sent to the artist Philip Rickman, who used them as models for a watercolour which forms the frontispiece to Seigne's *A Bird Watcher's Note Book* (1930).

This theory was an unwise conclusion, based on a comparatively small sample of specimens, and Seigne was too quick to assume that an individual was a resident or a visitor without firm evidence for his assumptions. When he found a grey-type woodcock on a nest he fitted this into his theory by concluding that it must be an oddity, perhaps a migrant which was injured and did not re-migrate but remained to breed – the exception which proved what he believed to be the rule.

It is possible that woodcock originating in certain geographical areas may develop a tendency towards a certain plumage colouration, but this is an aspect of the woodcock which has not yet been properly studied. The true

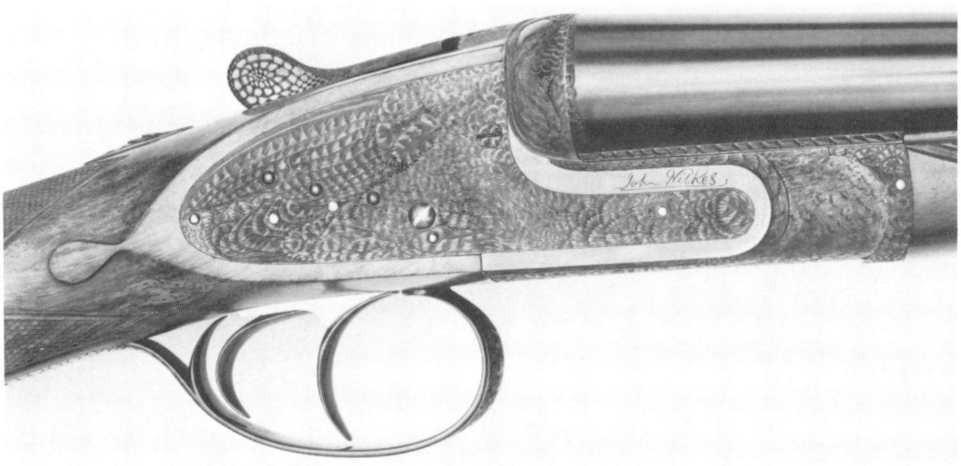

Engraver Malcolm Appleby has worked some exceptionally fine detail into this "woodcock gun" by John Wilkes. Note how the lockplate surfaces show the woodcock's primary feathers and coverts, while the top lever and the bottom strap behind the trigger guard are engraved with the scaling of the bird's legs. (Photo: Sothebys)

position is certain to be much more complex than the rather simplistic "grey" and "red" categories for migrants and residents (or vice versa!) that have often been propounded on very slender evidence. And the whole subject dissolves into absurdity when an otherwise serious woodcock enthusiast suggests that perhaps Irish resident woodcock tend to be reddish for the same reasons that a good many Irishmen have red hair!

And yet there are interesting indications, drawn from recent scientific research, that woodcock colouration may hold some clues to the birds' origins. In 1971 the French woodcock biologist Charles Fadat pointed out that Morocco and adjacent parts of North Africa appear to receive two distinct waves of winter migrants moving south from France – one greyish and the other redder in colour; and one wave tending on average to be larger than the other. Only further research, based on sound scientific principles and not on pleasing but ill-founded conjecture and sporting anecdotes, will provide the real answer.

"Fools are known for looking wise,
As men find woodcocks, by their eyes."

That comes from *Hudibras*, a satire on religious controversy by the seventeenth-century poet Samuel Butler. He chose a metaphor which tells us two things about the woodcock and men's attitudes to it, its behaviour and appearance. Woodcock have historically been thought of as stupid, foolish birds – a view which few modern sportsmen would share, since 'cock are regarded as the most elusive and erratic of targets for the sporting shooter, with an almost uncanny ability to jink round a tree or hedge and escape. But in the days when woodcock were taken principally by netting and the use of snares or "springes" it was a different matter. A skilled "fowler" found woodcock relatively easy to lure into the area of the trap or snare and thus to catch, and so woodcock became synonymous with gullibility and dim wittedness.

But the woodcock's eye, so prominent, shiny and richly lustrous, has never been an object of contempt but always of admiration. When you spot a woodcock on the ground, perhaps roosting by day or on her nest, it is almost always that big eye, as bright and shiny as polished jet, which you see first. Next to the woodcock's long bill the eyes are its most prominent physical feature. They are set high up on the side of the head and recent studies of the structure and position of the eyes suggests that the woodcock has binocular vision around almost 360°, with perhaps a small blind segment along the axis of its bill, and also immediately behind its head. These large eyes and their positioning give the woodcock certain obvious advantages, which include good low-light vision at dawn and dusk, when it is often most active, and a good field of view for potential predators while it is probing in a head-down attitude. (Curiously, in Ireland the woodcock's gaelic name is the *crowour keough*, "the blind cock".)

As a probing bird the woodcock needs to be able to thrust that long bill deeply and powerfully into the earth, and the whole structure of its head has evolved so as to allow this. The neck is powerful and the position of the bird's

"Men find woodcock by their eyes." Roosting on a winter's afternoon among brashings on the woodland floor, this woodcock is superbly camouflaged. Only that large and lustrous eye is immediately obvious.

Those large, prominent eyes set high on the sides of its head mean all-round vision for the woodcock. Its only blind spots are along the axis of the bill and a narrow segment to the rear.

brain is almost literally upside down. The ear opening is unusually placed too, being below and just forward of the eye.

If the intricate pattern of the woodcock's plumage is reminiscent of the snipe family, as also are the eyes, though these are not so large nor so prominently placed as in the woodcock, the most obvious common feature is the long bill. This is clear evidence of a very high degree of adaptation and specialization in the woodcock's feeding habits, and there are major implications for various other aspects of the bird's physical appearance and its way of life. The bill is long, strong and dagger-like – indeed various European hunters' terms refer to it as "the stabber" – and it is specifically adapted to a style of feeding which involves probing and thrusting deep into the soil in search of animal material. This consists principally of earthworms and other similar invertebrates such as insect larvae, which the woodcock can reach at a depth of almost three inches below the soil surface.

The woodcock's bill combines considerable strength with great sensitivity, especially towards the tip of the mandibles. These are packed with highly sensitive nerve endings, visible as a honeycomb structure if a section of the bill is examined under magnification. This is a highly developed feeding instrument, which can thrust deep into mud, ooze and any reasonably soft earth, can detect the presence of potential food items by their movements and vibrations, and can grasp, extract and swallow even large insect larvae and vigorously wriggling earthworms. If you examine the bill of a freshly shot woodcock before it has time to stiffen and dry out you will see it is surprisingly soft and flexible. The upper mandible in particular can flex along about a third of its length and this allows the bird to grasp its food under ground, and quite large items can be swallowed without the bird even having to withdraw its bill from the earth. The woodcock's long, slender tongue and the insides of the mandibles have rough, almost barbed surfaces which help grip its food firmly.

The woodcock's oddly shaped head has been compared by various early writers to an inverted tobacco pipe. In its feathering, the most obvious feature is the distinctive barring across the top of the woodcock's head. This barring, the bird's long bill and its generally reclusive habits are the subjects of a delightful legend from Spain and southern France. This tells how the woodcock got its long bill, its secretive ways and those three broad black bands across its head.

Looking curiously like a frog from this angle, the woodcock seems to have eyes in the back of its head. Set high on the sides of that curiously shaped head, those large and prominent eyes give it all-round vision. This bird was photographed on its nest in a Hampshire wood. (Photo: T.A. Waddell)

Woodcock are specialised feeders, probing deeply in soft ground to find earthworms and other invertebrate and insect life. Woodcock are slow and deliberate in their probings, unlike some waders. This detail from an engraving after a picture by Archibald Thorburn shows how deeply the bill can be thrust into mud and ooze.

"Once upon a time, very long ago, a covey of partridges hatched out. One of the chicks was small and weak, and began to pine. An outcast from the covey, he was bullied by his stronger brothers and sisters, who ate all the best grains of corn, seeds and insects. He had to make do with their left-overs and was reduced to searching for insects among the cracks and crannies among the stones. Alas! His bill was too short for him to be able to reach even this meagre food.

"From heaven, the Blessed Virgin looked down, saw his plight and had pity on him. She called softly to him, and he flew to her and nestled securely in her hand. She said, 'Little bird, I am going to change you, so that you too can delight in life. An outcast from the other birds, you will live quietly and alone, in the depths of the forests. There you will find lots of rich and nourishing food. You will be the beautiful mistress of the shady woods, admired by all

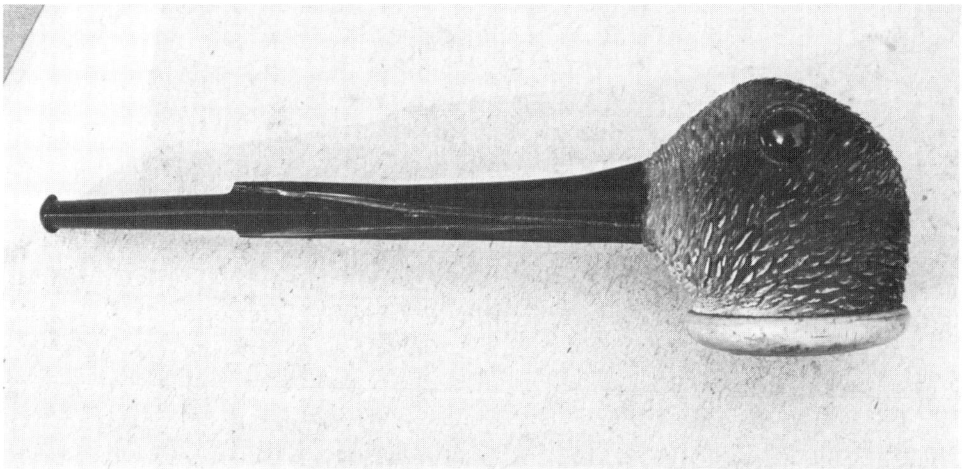

A Victorian meerschaum pipe, delicately carved in the shape of a woodcock's head and bill, and given to the Perceval family of Temple House by a grateful shooting guest. The bird's mandibles hold the mouthpiece, and the feathering and other details have been accurately picked out. Similar pipes are in Continental collections. Elizabethan writers described early tobacco pipes as shaped like woodcocks' heads.

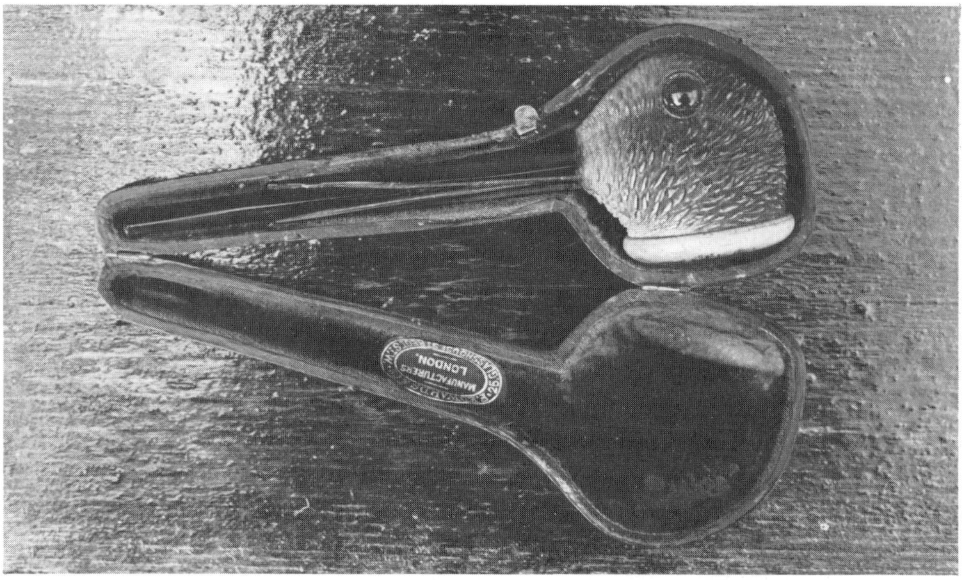

"The Woodcock Madonna". This unusual picture shows the infant Jesus holding a woodcock in his right hand while the Virgin and some cherubs look on. The central figures are flanked by two old-style sporting dogs. That on the left looks like a rough-coated *braque* while the other is more like a pointer. A litter of puppies can be seen in the foreground, surrounded by game of various sorts.

who love the beauties of nature. Your clever disguise and unpredictable flight will save you from danger. I will protect you.'

"And so saying the Blessed Virgin laid three fingers in blessing upon his head, making three blackish-brown marks which are still called 'the Virgin's fingermarks'. His bill immediately grew longer; his feathers took on a beautiful mottled reddish-brown colour, and the bird flew off joyfully to his new home in the forest.

"And that is how the woodcock was created, and it is still known to its admirers as 'Our Lady of the Woods' or 'the beautiful mottled-brown one'."

It is not surprising that the woodcock should have become the subject of many legends, myths, strange beliefs and a host of sportsmen's tales, if we look in more detail at the bird and its mysterious ways – its silent and secret life; its unusual breeding-season behaviour; its migrations and its life in winter; some of the unusual oddities it can produce from time to time; and the wonderfully exciting sport it provides, usually in winter but sometimes in spring, too.

This winter woodcock, roosting among the leaf litter in an oak plantation, shows the distinctive transverse barring on the head ("the Virgin's finger-marks" of the Spanish legend), the prominent eye-stripe and the lighter lines running down the bird's back. (Photo: T.A. Waddell)

CHAPTER II

WOODCOCK RODING

"As early as six or seven o'clock, they begin to fly,
uttering their curious cry, which resembles more
the croak of a frog than anything else;
varied, however, by a short shrill chirp."

Charles St John: *Wild Sports* (1845)

Although he often wrote sensitively and observantly about wildlife, Charles St John's writings also afford one of the most decadent and cynical descriptions of woodcock in the breeding season to be found anywhere in the British literature of woodcock shooting. St John was one of our most interesting and shrewdly observant sportsmen-naturalists of the last century, but he had a distressingly over-developed belief in the contemporary adage that "what's hit is history and what's missed is mystery". For him, close observation in the field was often not enough: birds and beasts in the bag were better. In his *Wild Sports and Natural History of the Highlands* (1845) he tells how he "rather astonished an English friend of mine, who was staying with me in Inverness-shire during the month of June, by asking him to come out woodcock-shooting one evening. And his surprise was not diminished by my preparations for the *battue*, which consisted of ordering out chairs and cigars into the garden at the back of the house, which happened to be just in the line of the birds' flight from the woods."

Roding woodcock are a familiar sight to the woodland deer stalker, who is out and about in the coverts at dawn and dusk in spring and summer. Rodger McPhail has depicted a woodcock as it passes a stalker on his solitary vigil up a high seat in a conifer plantation.

Instead of sitting quietly over cigars and port, or amusing themselves with some conventional after-dinner activity like billiards or cards, St John and his guest calmly shot several woodcock as they flew around his lodge in the long Highland gloaming. "After he had killed three or four from his chair, we stopped murdering the poor birds, which were quite unfit to eat, having probably young ones, or eggs, to provide for at home, in the quiet recesses of the woods, along the banks of Loch Ness, which coverts afford as good woodcock-shooting as any in Scotland."

Anyone who spends a few hours after dawn, or better still towards dusk, in the vicinity of suitable woodcock nesting habitat during the months from March to early August is sure to see and hear signs of woodcock activity and breeding display. This is the time of year when the presence of woodcock in the coverts is more obvious than at any other season. Instead of their secretive wintering routine of quiet and solitary daytime roosting, with a quick and silent flight out at last light to feed on wet pastures through the dark hours, before flighting back to their roosts at dawn, woodcock in spring and summer are conspicuous both to the eye and to the ear. The coming of early spring marks the start of the roding season, when the birds can be seen flying about in an apparently slow and unconcerned fashion, and uttering their distinctive breeding season calls-deep and almost frog-like croaks punctuated with a high-pitched squeaking *twisick* or *twisk*. These are particularly familiar sights and sounds to those who enjoy stalking roe deer in and around woodlands. The woodland stalker's senses are alert to every sound and movement, and his stealthy pursuit of the roebuck can result in a good many sightings of roding woodcock as they fly and call overhead.

Until quite recently this aspect of woodcock breeding-season behaviour was not properly understood, and there are still many aspects of it which remain to be clarified by further research. But we do know that the birds which perform these prominent and audible displays at dawn and dusk are always male woodcock advertising their presence to any females which may have taken up their nesting sites in the area.

Roding is therefore an especially important aspect of woodcock behaviour in the breeding season. And since the woodcock is at its most conspicuous, both to the eye and to the ear, when it is roding, in contrast to its generally silent and secretive life during the rest of the year, and because of the importance of the springtime shooting of roding woodcock in many central and northern European countries, it seems worthwhile to devote a separate chapter to an examination of some aspects of woodcock roding.

European naturalists and sportsmen have always been particularly interested in the spring roding flights of woodcock. Indeed, in many central and northern European countries this was the only time when the shooters there could be fairly sure of getting a shot or two at woodcock during the course of the entire season, since the coming of the first frosts of their hard winters have always meant the wholesale migration of woodcock, which are not seen again until the following spring. Consequently, in countries like Sweden, Finland and much of European Russia, woodcock shooting as a sport was only feasible during the spring and summer months, when the birds had returned from their milder wintering gounds far off to the south and west to breed in these northern and eastern European regions. It is interesting here to note that one recent estimate of the total number of woodcock shot annually in Norway, Sweden and Finland, with their large spring populations of breeding woodcock, amounted in all to only 11,250 birds, compared with an estimated 150,000 or more woodcock shot each season in Britain and Ireland and some 1,500,000 shot each year in France.

To shoot a sporting bird in the breeding season seems anathema to us in Britain and Ireland, where our sporting traditions and the law have given long-established close-season protection to gamebirds in spring and summer. Surely the shooting of adult birds when they are mating and nesting can only be counter-productive, resulting in fewer young and a reduced shootable surplus the following winter? And yet, paradoxically, we have never had the slightest qualms about stalking our Highland stags at the height of their noisy and frenzied rutting season, which for many of us is the most sporting and exhilarating time to be on the hill. We also stalk our roebucks during the rut, often one of the most interesting and exciting times in the woodland stalker's year.

However, the spring shooting of woodcock is now more restricted in many European countries than it used to be: some have banned it altogether, and in others there is pressure both from shooting and non-shooting organizations to end it. The important and influential French *Club National des Bécassiers* strongly opposes the shooting of roding birds, not only in France but throughout the species' breeding range, despite the fact that this form of shooting has always held a special appeal and romance in French sporting traditions. In 1960 the French ornithologist Geroudet angrily proclaimed that "the wanton springtime destruction of woodcock is a practice which is more truly stupid than the unhappy victims are proverbially said to be".

Opinions are still quite sharply divided in sporting and game biologists' circles about the value to woodcock-breeding success of banning the spring shooting of roding birds. It has been argued that the shooting pressures on woodcock in the roding season, when the bag comprises almost all male birds, have never made any significant impact on the total population. This view has been strengthened by recent research which shows that woodcock do not pair up in spring, and that one male bird can mate successfully with several females during the species' prolonged breeding season. On the other hand, roding birds are now known to be the dominant males: when shot, their place is soon taken by sub-dominant birds which have probably not hitherto been roding. Does shooting roding 'cock mean the elimination of some of the better individuals, leading progressively to genetic deterioration in the woodcock population? More of that anon.

It is, of course, quite illegal to shoot woodcock in Britain or Ireland outside the statutory seasons, and spring shooting has never been any part of our sporting traditions, despite occasional lapses like the post-prandial amusements of St John and his friend. He also related an extraordinary account of an old poacher in Sussex who claimed once to have killed three woodcock with one shot while the birds were engaged "in an aerial tournament" in April. This is presumably a reference to roding, and woodcock will occasionally have brief and sometimes rather excited skirmishes, especially during the early part of the breeding season, often chasing one another in twos and threes at high speed and with shrill calls.

Things are different on the continent, however, Central and northern Europe have long traditions of spring shooting, since it was the only time of year when the birds were around and shootable. Robert Dunkin was a Victorian sportsman with wide experience of game shooting in northern and central Europe. He wrote under the pen-name "Snaffle" (not to be confused with the artist "Snaffles") and he describes in 1894 how the spring shooting of woodcock began in Germany, with the poulterers' shops "crowded with the toothsome longbills". According to Dunkin the period from 10 March to the beginning of April was considered the best for shooting roding 'cock, and there was a tradition that the arrival of the migrants which came north-eastwards from their wintering haunts – the *schnepfen strich* – was

marked by the third Sunday in Lent. This was known as "Occuli Sunday", from the opening word of the Latin Collect for that Sunday, and woodcock in spring in northern Germany were colloquially referred to as "occuli" – and what term could be better for a bird with such large and conspicuous eyes? But Easter is a moveable feast, and it was much wiser to take the fixed date of 10 March as the time to expect the woodcocks' return.

In passing, it is interesting to note that some British sportsmen may have had their own equivalent of "Occuli Sunday", not in spring but in autumn. J.J. Manley, writing in 1880, says of an old Devonshire sporting parson: "In the month of November, on a certain Sunday after Trinity, he used to make his way after the afternoon service to a favourite covert, just inside which he concealed himself, gun in hand, to have a shot at the woodcock, knowing from experience year after year that an arrival would take place about twilight. It is said that he never failed to get his first cock of the season. He called that particular Sunday 'Woodcock Sunday'."

France, which has large numbers of wintering woodcock and has always been able to offer some of Europe's very best woodcock shooting, especially in the relatively frost-free western regions along her Atlantic coast, has an equally important tradition of shooting woodcock during *la croule*, the roding period. This has always been most prevalent in the central and eastern parts of France, and, in the best traditions of French sporting life, the practice acquired its own special mystique and rituals. French *bécassiers* have rhapsodised in the purplest of prose about the amorous conjugal flights and aerial love dances of the woodcock, which they contrast so strikingly with its silent, secretive and solitary life in winter. In a great deal of classic French sporting literature the roding woodcock is seen as the *genius loci* of the woods in springtime, the epitome of the season.

This European tradition is beautifully expressed in Rebecca West's novel of the last years of Tsarist Russia, *The Birds Fall Down* (1966). Old Nikolaievitch, exiled from Russia and his beloved estates, describes the excitements and the symbolism of the annual spring woodcock shoots in the Russia he knew as a young man:

"... among the greatest pleasures any man could know.... We shoot

woodcock when the snows are melting, when the spring has come, when the birds are courting.... The foresters used to send word when they had seen them coming up from the south, in their three-cornered flights, and we would make up a party, and drive out into the forest about midnight.... We had to be at the trysting-place about half past two or three in the morning. Then we would go into the brushwood shelters the foresters had built on the side of a clearing, for each Gun a shelter. There was something holy about sitting there alone, looking at the dawn.... Then we would hear the swish of many wings, and a croaking call, and a curious double whistle, and the woodcocks came dropping down into the clearing.... A woodcock shoot is for men, and it is beautiful with more than its own beauty. There is an indescribable fascination in what is happening."

To be fair, the Europeans have not always been alone in taking this romantic view of woodcock in spring. J.W. Seigne, who made an enthusiastic and important study of woodcock in Ireland in the 1920s, and had shot them as far afield as China and Greece, described some roding flights as "playing ...an expression of *joie de vivre*, and both sexes take part in them. At this time of the year the birds are full of energy and this is how they let off steam, and, at the same time, express their delight at the coming of spring and all that it means to them."

He really ought to have known better. To superimpose his own pleasure at the coming of spring upon his interpretation of the breeding behaviour of a wild creature was engaging but fanciful. More accurate was his statement that roding birds intended "to show off before each other, and perhaps at times the birds may do a little flirting". We now know that roding is an aerial display by males advertising their presence to females, which is an important form of "showing off". There is also some suggestion that woodcock, while not flirtatious in quite the way that Seigne intended, may indeed be quite selective in their choice of mates. Receptive females have been seen with two or sometimes more males in attendance, from which a choice is made and mating with that selected bird then takes place.

A more hard-headed view of woodcock breeding behaviour is taken by today's new generation of game biologists and sportsmen-conservationists. Spring shooting has been studied in some depth by European scientists in recent years, especially to clarify its effects upon breeding success, the genetic strength of woodcock populations and the wider implications of spring shooting for a species which is also subject to shooting pressure on its wintering grounds throughout the autumn and winter months.

European traditionalists have tried to cling tenaciously to their spring shooting, waiting for the birds at dawn, like Rebecca West's Nikolaievitch, or in the gathering dusk, and bagging perhaps two or three woodcock on outing after outing in prime roding areas. One of the few British sportsmen who did this regularly and wrote about it was "Snaffle" (Robert Dunkin), who has left a good description of it in his *Gun, Rifle and Hound in East and West* (1894). But the practice had already begun to fall into disrepute more than a century ago. French dictionaries of the 1860s defined *la croule* as "woodcock shooting carried out during the mating and nesting season in spring", and that definition seems to carry an implied condemnation both on ethical and biological grounds. Several eminent anti-*croule* French sportsmen and naturalists went on record as having actually witnessed woodcock mating at the same time as Guns not far away in the same woods were shooting roding birds. This, they claimed, made *la croule* an unacceptable sporting practice. Even died-in-the-wool *bécassiers* of the old school like Georges Benoist, whose classic book *Bécasses et Bécassiers* was first published in 1921, were unhappy about spring shooting – though that did not prevent him printing a photograph of his friend Prince Albert of Monaco shooting roding woodcock in spring in the Rambouillet forest.

Whatever the effects of the shooting of roding birds in the spring on the species' breeding success and later wintering numbers, this traditional practice has yielded some fascinating insights into their breeding-season behaviour. Scientific examination of woodcock shot in West Germany at dawn and dusk during the spring and summer months in the period 1962–1981 showed that the vast majority of birds shot were males – well over 90%. And where the shooter reported that the bird shot had been calling with either the croaking or whistling (i.e. *twisick*) sound, all the birds involved were found to be males. This study showed that only males are able to croak, and that a whistling female is exceptionally rare, if indeed it actually happens at all.

I have noticed on a good many occasions that some wounded woodcock will utter a low, croaking sound which is not dissimilar to the roding croak. This seems to happen when the bird is picked up in the hand or, more usually, in a gundog's mouth. On a few occasions I have set these birds aside and examined them carefully when cleaning them before cooking, and in each case the bird has been a male. I do wish I had made a point of sexing every bird which had croaked, as my sample size would have been bigger and thus more reliable. But it may be that the female woodcock actually lacks the physical means to make the croaking call. As is so often the case, only more research will give us the answer.

The German naturalist Otto Steinfatt, who made some careful studies of breeding woodcock in the pre-war period and whose statements cannot be dismissed lightly, claimed to have shot a number of birds which were on the wing at roding time which had made the high-pitched *twisick* call (rendered by him as *pssiep*) and which proved on dissection to be females. But we know from recent studies that, even when the bird shot was quite silent, the mere fact that it was flying at that time of the day and at that season of the year meant that it was six times more likely to be a male than a female. These findings from Germany have been reinforced by other information from studies in Sweden and Finland, where nearly 99% of the spring-shot woodcock were found to be males – conclusive proof that these dawn and dusk flights are confined almost exclusively to the male birds.

A roding woodcock shot at dawn in central Europe. Short spring shooting seasons are permitted in some European countries. Since the 1930s, the use of pointing dogs like his Hungarian Vizsla to find woodcock in spring has been banned in Germany.

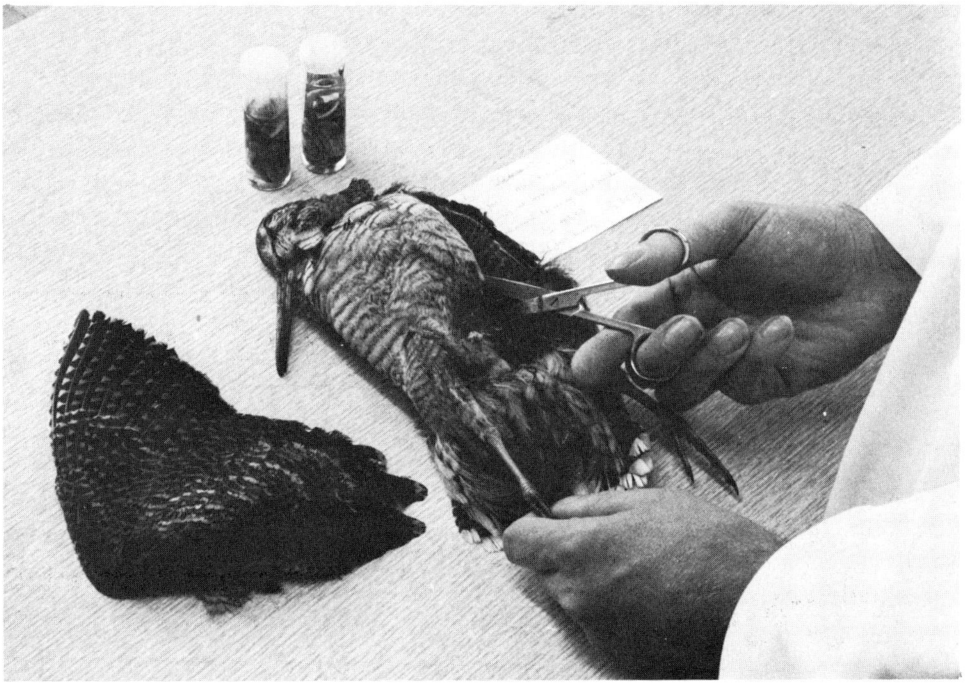

Sexing a woodcock accurately calls for dissection. Laboratory examination of specimens also allows study of internal parasites, trace elements in the feathers and accurate weighing and measuring of the bird.

But arguments about the acceptability of spring shooting still continue. On the island of Bornholm spring shooting was banned in 1931 and has remained so ever since, despite which there was no significant increase in the numbers of breeding woodcock during thirty years' monitoring of the population. Sweden, which banned springtime shooting in 1961 and thus reduced the estimated total annual bag of woodcock shot in Sweden from 25,000 to 4,500 in one year, re-introduced spring shooting in 1977, allowing shooting up to July. Hungary and the USSR have extended their spring seasons through March and April, but banned autumn shooting. West Germany, however, banned all spring shooting in 1977, although there had been some restrictions since 1937.

Hermann Goering was probably as grossly selfish in his framing of the Third Reich's hunting laws as he was in every other aspect of his public life, but he left his mark by some very enlightened, if self-interested, policies and decisions. While he did not stop spring woodcock shooting altogether, he made it illegal to hunt woodcock over pointing dogs in spring, or to beat out the coverts in spring for 'cock. An important study of the woodcock in Germany, published in 1867, had shown that walked-up and driven woodcock shoots in spring combined with the shooting of roding birds could produce up to 38% of females in the bag. The thinking behind Goering's law was that the *Jäger* should take up a static position, usually in a clearing or along the woodland edge, and shoot only at those roding birds which passed within range overhead. This is the European purist's style of spring woodcock shooting, and various studies have shown that this results in a bag consisting almost exclusively of males, especially if only those birds which give both the *quorr* and *twisick* calls are shot.

The main argument against spring shooting used to be based on the mistaken belief that woodcock paired off in a conventional way and that the home life of the woodcock, like the grey partridge, was a model of conjugal fidelity. From this premise it was argued that spring shooting of males was breaking up the pairs of breeding woodcock and removing adult birds which were believed to play an important role in incubating, brooding and caring for the young chicks. We now know that male woodcock are not monogamous but will mate successively with several females, and that they take no further interest in the female or her eggs once the clutch is complete. That basis for opposing spring shooting is therefore not a valid one.

The most recent research, based on studies in West Germany from 1962 to 1981, concluded that spring shooting of males did not result in fewer birds roding, for those shot were quickly replaced by other woodcock from the reservoir of non-roding males which seems to exist in most breeding areas. These less dominant males do not seem to be any less effective in contributing to the breeding success of the population. These observations have been largely corroborated by those of Dr Graham Hirons in his Derbyshire studies of breeding woodcock. On the basis of this research, it would be very difficult to show that the shooting of dominant, conspicuously roding birds results in any reduction in the productivity of the woodcock breeding population or leads to progressive genetic deterioration in the species.

The meaning of these flights and how they relate to the woodcock's general breeding behaviour were among the main questions investigated by Dr Graham Hirons in his major woodcock research project for The Game Conservancy in the late 1970s. Various earlier writers and game biologists had commented on the gaps in our understanding of the woodcock's breeding behaviour. It was not even clearly understood whether the birds paired off in a monogamous relationship, or if some form of polygamy prevailed. The roding flights and their functions in relation to breeding were a matter for speculation and debate, and little was known of how the feeding habits of woodcock in spring and summer compared with those in winter. Since effective conservation and management of any game bird can only proceed from a thorough understanding of its private life, research was called for.

Graham Hirons' studies of breeding-season behaviour began in 1977 at Wytham Woods near Oxford and continued over the next four years on a study area at Whitwell in north-east Derbyshire. This consisted of an area of 171 hectares of woodland, comprising chiefly deciduous species of trees.

From 1978 onwards these studies involved the extensive use of radio-tracking, a god-send to the modern field biologist who can place miniature radio transmitters on individual creatures whose movements and

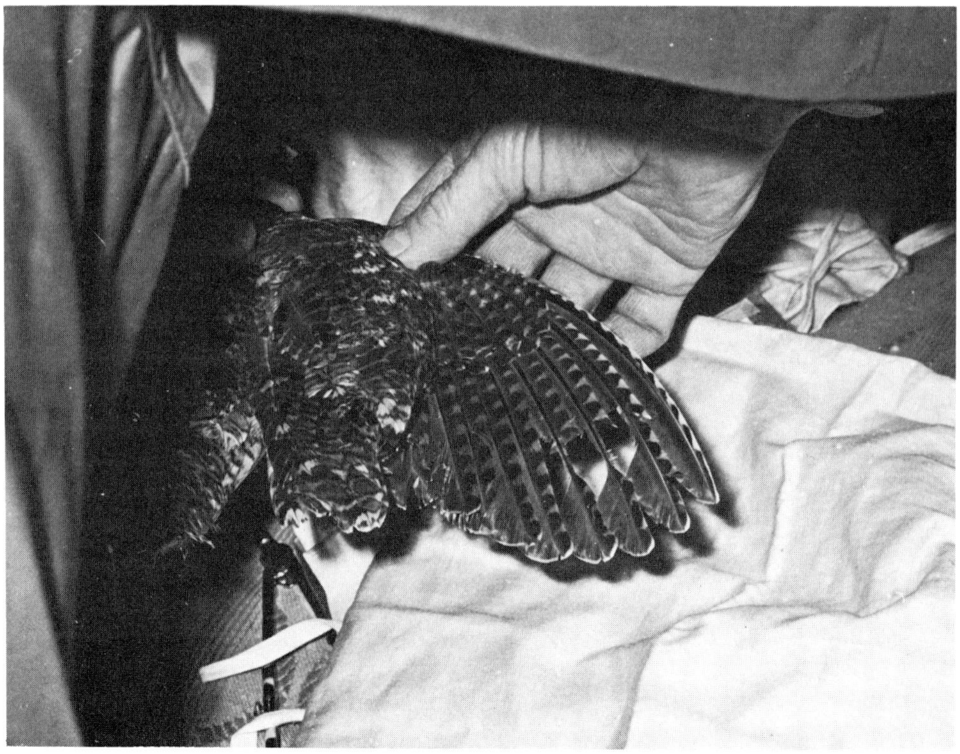

Shaving the wing feathers of a male woodcock caught in a mist net while roding give it a distinctive silhouette when in flight, enabling that male to be identified and its subsequent roding flights recorded.

activities can then be monitored more or less continuously, even when that individual cannot be seen. Automatic recording of the stream of tell-tale high-frequency transmissions, on a separate frequency for each individual, even allows the scientist to keep a round-the-clock record of what his radio-tagged specimens are doing while he is working elsewhere, writing up his notes, or even snatching a few hours' well-deserved sleep.

But first catch your woodcock. In fact a great many were caught during the course of this study, and a total of 144 fully grown woodcock and 48 chicks were ringed and released with those familiar leg-bands issued by the British Trust for Ornithology. Some woodcock were also marked with small metal tags, numbered and colour-coded, pinched into the *patagium* or fleshy part of the bird's wing joint. This is a form of tagging which is widely used by gamekeepers and shoot organizers who release numbers of pheasants and partridges and who want to keep a record of the proportions of reared and wild birds in the bag throughout the shooting season. But wing tags and coloured leg bands are rarely visible when a woodcock is flying, and radio-tracking is quite the best way of placing an individual marker on each caught and released specimen. Clipping and shaving the wing feathers of woodcock to give individual birds a distinctive and recognizable silhouette when seen in flight has been done with some success by researchers in Europe, but this cannot compare for effectiveness with the tiny radio transmitter which plays an active role from the moment it is fitted to the bird.

A tiny radio transmitter fitted on its back turns this woodcock into a source of important information about how woodcock live and behave. With a weight of only a few grams these radios enable the birds to readjust to normal life very quickly. Some have even migrated across the North Sea carrying their radio tags.

The first transmitters used in this work weighed between seven and eight grams, with a battery life of some 50 to 80 days, although a much lighter 3½ gram radio became available later in the study. Slender whip aerials were fitted, either five or ten inches long depending on the wave-length involved. The whole tiny package was attached by bands of elastic passed around the bird's body and tied at the breast, with the radio held in position in the centre of the woodcock's back. This was found to work better than the latex rubber harnesses which other researchers had used in America on the American woodcock. These had an inconvenient tendency to disintegrate after a few weeks, resulting in a loss of data and of a valuable piece of miniaturised transmitting equipment. In all telemetry studies, the longer the transmitter stays in place and continues to send out its stream of data the better. The best of all fixing methods is a dab of "super-glue" to attach the radio to the feathers on the woodcock's back, a quick and easy business which minimises stress, since the bird need not be handled for more than thirty seconds, and keeps the radio firmly in place without harnesses or other encumbrances, until the feathers moult out in the normal way.

Graham Hirons caught his woodcock in various ways, some reminiscent of the methods used by poachers, "birders" and "fowlers" for centuries. Mist-nets, similar to the "cock-shuts" that Shakespeare and Ben Jonson knew about, were set across clearings and rides at intervals of about 20 yards, and these accounted for a good proportion of birds caught in spring and summer. The majority of these were males, which spend more time on the wing than the females, and which were often intercepted on their roding flights. Some low fliers flew straight into the nets, while others were lured down by a remarkably simple technique. A concealed observer waited in a hide along a ride, and when a roding bird came within sight a small hand-tame bantam was tossed up. This invariably resulted in the roding male dropping straight down to join what it obviously believed to be a female giving an attracting "flutter flight", so becoming entangled in the mist net's meshes.

Graham Hirons' bantam method of attracting roding males has been carried a stage further by a French scientist. Using small, dark-coloured hand-tame ducks thrown out at the critical moment, he has been able to bring roding males down into rides and clearings, and some have alighted and actually tried to mate with mounted specimens of female woodcock placed on the ground.

Females are more difficult to catch by this method and at this time of year, but good results have been achieved by setting live-traps on the ground and creating lead-in "funnels" to guide the walking bird towards the trap. This is another ancient technique which was used here in the interests of science but which the old woodcock trappers and "springe setters" knew all about centuries ago. These were especially effective when set in those parts of the woodland which offered the best feeding and nesting habitat. Trapping females on the nest, though not particularly difficult, was quickly abandoned as the disturbance and stress usually caused the hen birds to desert, even when the eggs were close to hatching. This contrasts with the reaction of other birds like partridges, which will stay faithfully with their eggs, despite considerable disturbance, once incubation is well established.

Like some other scientists in Europe and North America, Graham Hirons recorded and analysed the calls of roding male woodcock, using a directional microphone of the sort used by television film crews. The croaking and *twisick* calls were recorded on tape and later traced out in visual form on paper as sonograms. These show the sound-profile of the woodcock's calls much as a strip of paper on a barograph traces the fluctuating levels of barometric pressure. Comparison of the sonograms of different individual male woodcock shows that each has its own distinctive pattern, an individual "tone of voice" or auditory fingerprint which the unaided human ear cannot detect but which the tracings of the sonogram's lines clearly reveal. These "voiceprints" were useful in identifying certain actively roding and particularly vocal woodcock, but the benefits of the radio-tag are much greater.

In addition to this individual tone of voice which the sonograph can detect and which another woodcock may be able to hear, there is some evidence that roding woodcock can give individual physical gestures as they fly. Rodger McPhail, while fishing on the Findhorn in Morayshire, has seen woodcock roding there, and noticed how one bird tended to drop its legs in a half

Dr. Graham Hirons of The Game Conservancy used a directional microphone and a portable tape recorder to record the roding calls of individual woodcock. When traced out as sonographs, these recordings showed that individual displaying males have distinctive and identifiable "tones of voice".

Its radio-tag securely in place, this woodcock is about to be released. Its movements and behaviour will be tackled and monitored by an automatic receiving station, adding to the biologists' understanding of the private life of the woodcock.

dangling position at a certain point in its croak and twisick callings. I have seen other birds which had individual habits, such as flicking or flirting the tail in a certain way and at a specific point in the calling routine. Perhaps this plays an additional role in enabling the bird, especially if it is a particularly dominant one, to indicate "This is *me*!" to receptive females, and perhaps also as an extra warning to other males.

After being caught and fitted with a radio-tag the woodcock tends to fly off and lie low for some hours, an understandable reaction after being subjected to the stress of capture and handling, albeit very briefly, and while it is getting used to the feel and weight of its new burden. Eight grams represents roughly 2½–3% of the average total body weight of a woodcock; in human terms, this is comparable to adding a back-pack weighing about 6 pounds to a man of twelve stone. That is not a huge additional burden but sufficient to be both noticeable and uncomfortable – or so one might think. But it is always unwise to try to put oneself in the place of an animal or bird. Anthropomorphising is an unsound approach to the scientific study of any wild creature.

In fact the birds seem to accept their new radios remarkably quickly, and have often been found to have resumed active roding within less than a day of being caught and having the transmitter fitted. With the ultra-light 3½-gram transmitter it was confidently expected that males caught and tagged at dawn would be roding again by dusk that evening. In every respect they seem to resume their normal patterns of movement, feeding and behaviour within a day or so; and the final proof of their full acceptance of the radio-tag must surely come from the fact that they will migrate for many hundreds of miles in spring and autumn with their radios still in place.

Once any radio-tagged creature has been liberated the first and most obvious benefit to the scientist is that he can pinpoint that creature's position fairly easily. This is done by "triangulating", which involves plotting two or more "fixes", using a directional aerial to get a bearing on the transmissions. Where the lines of the bearings intersect marks the position of the radio and of its bearer. This has enabled Graham Hirons and other woodcock researchers to plot the positions of their radio-tagged birds, but modern radio-telemetry brings other benefits too.

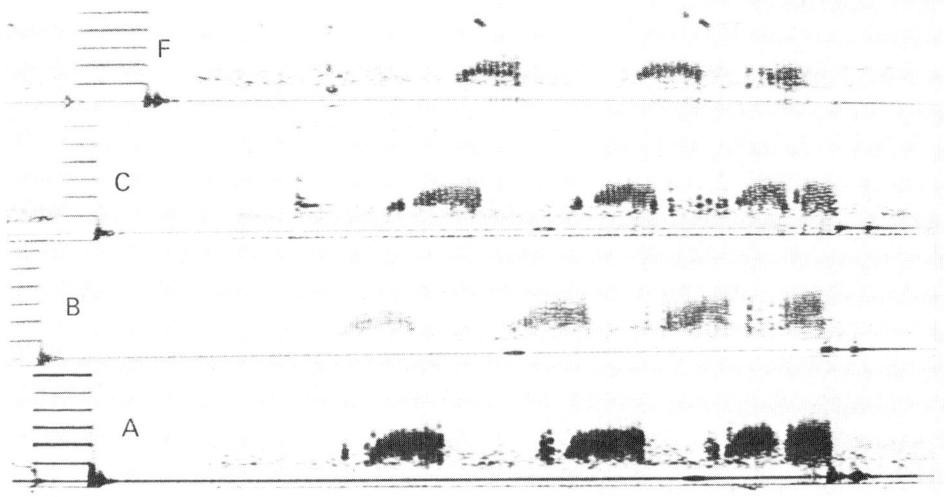

The roding call of four male woodcock were recorded and traced on this sonograph. The different patterns show how each individual bird has a separate "voice-print."

The radios used in the studies at Whitwell were linked to a thermistor, a tiny temperature sensor under the woodcock's wing. This detected the drop in temperature caused by the airstream when the bird was flying and caused the pulse rate of the radio signals to slow down. A faster pulse rate from a male therefore indicated the bird was on the ground, perhaps feeding, roosting or with the female at the nest, while a slower pulse meant it was on the wing. This refinement in transmitter design was linked to an automatic scanning receiver with an omni-directional aerial capable of picking up transmissions from a number of radio-tagged birds simultaneously and continuously. The result was a remarkably detailed picture of how several woodcock undertook dawn and dusk roding flights of varying duration. This was later compared with those birds' success in finding and mating with females, and some important conclusions were drawn about the relationship between the amount of roding activity a woodcock undertakes and its success as a breeding male.

The dawn and dusk display flights of nesting woodcock can begin as early as February and often continue into July and even August. This is generally seen as a comparatively slow and deliberate flight in which an individual bird passes on a roughly oval or almost triangular circuit just above tree height, calling repeatedly with the deep, frog-like croak sound, often represented as *quor, quor, quor, quor* followed by a single or double high-pitched call (*twisick* or *twisk*). The latter seems to some listeners to be clearly a two-syllabled call, while others will hear the same bird's call as a definite single note. Perhaps this depends upon the acuity of the individual's high-tone hearing. The sonographs traced from recordings of calling woodcock clearly show that the *twisick* call is a single sound which rises and falls in pitch. At the top end of the frequency perhaps it is inaudible to most listeners, who only pick up the beginning and end of the call, resulting in an impression of a two-syllabled sound. Others with better high-tone hearing may tend to register a single-syllabled call.

Conventional roding behaviour has been seen as early as the first days of February when conditions have been mild. Snipe have also been heard to drum in mild weather as early as January, but these are both quite exceptional and untypical. They are certainly not good grounds for pressing for an end to the shooting of snipe or woodcock after the end of December, and some important research from Ireland, which is discussed later, has shown that woodcock there do not come into breeding condition until late February.

The alert field observer who is out and about in suitable woodcock breeding habitat after mid-February will probably see the first signs of breeding activity, not in the form of conventional roding behaviour but when

"Woodcocks tilting" – Charles Whymper's stylised representation of the noisy and aggressive chasing flights, often involving several male woodcock, which can be seen at dawn and dusk in early spring.

two or more males chase each other in close, fast flights at last light. Typically, these flights are accompanied by a series of calls, excited, high-pitched and more raucous than the usual roding *twisick*, and the birds dash about in close formation, often only a few feet above the ground. It is slightly reminiscent of an aircraft dogfight, and seems to be some form of territorial aggression between the males which will later undertake those more familiar and deliberate roding flights. Some observers have seen as many as seven or eight birds chasing in a group, and these have been seen as late as May or June in the north of Scotland.

My own sightings of these early-season chasing flights have mostly taken place while I have been stalking deer in late February around the fringes of woodland, mainly in southern England and also in parts of Ireland. The birds have always appeared just as the last of the evening light was going and when conditions were much darker than in later months, when roding begins several hours before last light. For eight successive seasons since 1978 my first such sightings have always been in the period 20–25 February, and often the conditions have been wintry in the extreme, such as in February, 1979, and again in 1982 and 1986.

On 20 February, 1986, I was stalking in north-east Dorset, waiting by a woodland edge in the gathering dusk for roe does to appear. A bitterly cold east wind was blowing and the thermometer showed around −2°C. While watching for emerging deer with a pair of 8×56 binoculars I clearly saw a woodcock fly fast and low out of a patch of several acres of ash and hazel scrub some sixty yards ahead of me, followed within a few yards by another bird which called repeatedly with a loud and rasping squeak and followed every twist and turn of the leader's flight. The same performance was re-enacted at the same spot five evenings later, when it was still freezing hard with a chill wind. On other occasions in earlier years, while I have been waiting quietly with my rifle along the edge of a hedgerow or a copse, I have had chasing woodcock pass suddenly within inches of my head, almost taking my hat off, those squeaking calls sounding startlingly loud and harsh.

These early season chasings have often and understandably been interpreted as a male chasing a female or, where several birds are involved, a group of rival males in jealous pursuit of a female. In fact it seems always to be a sparring session involving males only, and the bird which is giving chase is the dominant male chasing a sub-dominant one. A recent French study showed that 85% of chasing flights involved males only, although the sub-dominant male tended to behave like a female in his attempts to avoid his pursuer. When one or both birds in a "chasing pair" were shot, they almost always turned out to be males. One biologist shot five right-and-lefts of chasing woodcock and also bagged seven single birds out of chasing "pairs", and every bird was male.

As the weather gets warmer and the days longer woodcock gradually take up a regular pattern of roding at dusk and also, to some extent, at dawn. The roding period and the number of roding flights seen gets longer as spring advances and seems to reach a peak in late May and June, as the longest day approaches. Graham Hirons' Derbyshire studies showed that roding activity increased very noticeably in intensity during March and early April, from a roding period of around 20 minutes in early March to over three-quarters of an hour by mid-April, and over an hour by early June. Roding begins progressively earlier in relation to sunrise and sunset, but the shorter pre-dawn display period ends when the light intensity is still much less than at the end of the evening displays. Most males display for about twice as long in the evening as in the early morning, and most individual male woodcock indulged in roding flights for about one-third of the total period during which roding could be seen in the Whitwell study area. From Graham Hirons' study of individual birds at Whitwell the roding record was held by one male which roded for a total of 64 minutes during one 24-hour period, with a single continuous roding flight of 43 minutes in the evening.

Although the low temperatures and chilly winds of February do not seem to deter woodcock from their shrill and aggressive chasing flights, finer and warmer weather combined with longer hours of daylight in later weeks does seem to promote more roding activity. This was evident from Graham Hirons' Derbyshire studies, especially in early spring, when temperatures at dawn and dusk varied considerably from day to day. Later in the spring and early summer, when temperatures are generally higher, roding activity was apparently unaffected. There was an old tradition at Baronscourt in County Tyrone, seat of the Dukes of Abercorn and a favourite place for woodcock in winter and also as springtime breeders, that in spring and summer the estate workers would keep on working in the woods and around the park until the first roding woodcock was seen and heard each evening. That signalled "quitting time" – a charming tradition, but one imagines it was rather too haphazard to please any clock-watchers on the work force.

My own experience of regularly watching woodcock roding in central southern England, in parts of north-east Scotland and in Ireland tends to make me believe that weather can have quite a marked effect on the timing, extent and duration of the roding period, especially at dusk. Warm, overcast and rather sultry weather with little or no breeze seems to promote the highest levels of roding activity, with birds on the wing comparatively early in the evening and several hours before last light. Cooler, breezy weather appears to result in a somewhat reduced amount of roding, but continuous rain, high winds and sudden unseasonable drops in temperature can signal a virtual end to this displaying until the weather improves. Some other observers, especially in Europe, disagree and claim that while misty conditions can reduce roding activity and heavy rain can halt it temporarily, moderate rain and even snow and a considerable variation in temperature seem to make little difference.

The wingbeat of a roding woodcock is shown by a photograph to be stronger and deeper than it often appears to be.

Roding normally ceases when darkness descends, but I have seen a woodcock roding and heard it give both calls as late as midnight. This was on 24 April, 1986, with a full moon and a silvery sky, and the temperature was rather lower than average for the time of year. I was giving my dogs a late-night walk by the western edge of Lough Melvin in County Leitrim, and the 'cock's croaking and *twisick* calls were quite distinct. I saw the bird clearly silhouetted against the moonlit sky as it flew past about eighty yards away and at a height of about sixty feet.

Many writers have commented on the distinctive style of flight of the roding woodcock. Often it is described as owl-like, with a slower and shallower wingbeat than usual. There is no denying that a roding woodcock can give this general impression, and its flight seems much more relaxed and ponderous than the fast and twisting movements of a bird flushed by beaters or dogs in the shooting season. But photographs taken of roding woodcock clearly show that the birds' wingbeats carry the wingtips well above and below its body, much more than we seem to see with the naked eye or through binoculars. A deceptively powerful, deep wingbeat tends to make the observer underestimate the bird's speed, and roding woodcock are usually flying faster than they appear to be. Among the sportsmen of northern and central Europe, where spring shooting of males as they rode is the traditional norm, it is generally agreed that their flight is deceptively fast, and an inexperienced shot is likely to miss behind, having given insufficient "lead" to a bird which seems to be flying much slower than it actually is.

Deceptive though the roding flight speed may be, it is still considerably slower than the getaway flight of a shooting-season bird, and it is also very much straighter. While the twists and turns of woodcock in those early spring chasing flights is very reminiscent of the birds' evasive tactics in winter, the

normal spring and summer roding flights tend to follow a much more direct and undeviating flightpath. This is often oval or almost triangular in shape, and the bird may make repeated flights following almost precisely the same route, at much the same height and speed, without resting. If the observer has a suitable vantage point it is sometimes possible to see the whole of these circuits without losing sight of the bird, and this obviously makes that individual a very rewarding subject for study – and very vulnerable too, if one had shooting in mind. By taking up a position before dawn or dusk in an area where woodcock are known to rode and nest, where one is not unduly conspicuous to the displaying birds but still able to see and hear their movements and calls, one can often have several roding birds pass quite close overhead, usually just above the height of the woodland canopy. The same bird may make pass after pass over you, and on evenings when roding is at a peak the concealed watcher can count as many as forty or fifty passes over or close to his position. I have found this to be true not only on warm summer evenings among the deciduous woodlands of Dorset and Wiltshire but also around plantations of conifers in the long, lingering gloaming of midsummer evenings in Ross-shire and east Inverness-shire.

It used to be thought that woodcock took up and maintained individual territories, and roding was believed to be the bird's way of "beating the bounds", asserting its rights and warning off potential intruders. In fact, recent research has shown that male woodcock do not have specific individual territories, either for feeding, roosting or even for their display flights. Some radio-tagged males in Graham Hirons' study were found to spend the main part of the day roosting or feeding very close to one another, sometimes within thirty yards or less.

The area over which a displaying male rodes seems to vary, depending on the degree of dominance of that individual compared with other males in the area. A very dominant bird may fly more or less regular circuits over an area of 250 acres or more, and some have been recorded roding on the same evening over points as much as a mile and a half apart.

Some males are especially dominant and have been known to rode throughout the four months or so of the normal breeding period, normally reckoned in Britain to last from mid-March to mid-July. Some also spend a great deal of time on the wing during the course of an evening or series of evenings, and a single dominant woodcock can often account for a very high proportion of the total number of sightings made. In the Derbyshire research, one bird was seen to make 13 roding passes out of a total of 22 seen on that occasion, which represents 59% of the total.

However, in contrast to these very conspicuous and active individuals, it seems that a high proportion of males do not rode much, if at all. In particular most first-year males seem not to display. Consequently there may be quite a large reservoir of non-roding males present in an area of good breeding habitat without one's knowing they are there. Some of these may be mature birds which are simply not as dominant as others, but a high proportion will be males hatched the previous spring. These tend not to rode or mate, and are not believed to make any significant contribution to breeding until another year has passed. Females will breed in their first year, however, but more research is needed before we know if they all attempt to nest, and how their reproductive success compares with older females.

A final aspect of roding which still remains to be fully explored and explained is the two apparent peaks of display activity which have been noticed by many woodcock enthusiasts. One occurs early in the season, which in Britain probably means around March to late April, with some subsequent falling-off in roding activity before it picks up again in late May and June. This

A steady flight around a regular roding circuit, just about level with the tops of the trees, is typical of the male's dawn and dusk display in spring. Neil McReddie has shown a roding woodcock over a plantation of older hardwoods and younger conifer trees.

pattern requires further investigation, but has been cited along with other aspects of woodcock behaviour as pointing to the conclusion that woodcock can rear two broods of young in a season. Double-brooding is still unproven, though many experts strongly suspect that it can and does occur occasionally. But even if it does happen it must be very uncommon, and cannot be the only explanation of the two apparent roding peaks. Perhaps the second wave of activity is created by males which have previously not been roding, as sub-dominant individuals take over from the more dominant individuals which display so vigorously and vociferously in the early part of the season. Like so many other aspects of the woodcock and its ways, more research is needed to provide the answer to that question.

CHAPTER III

WOODCOCK AT THE NEST

"Woodcocks are never seen with us save in the winter, wherefore I have naught to say about their young or mode of nesting."

William Turner: *Avium Praecipuarum* (1544)

Turner was wrong, of course. Woodcock do stay and breed in Britain, and some undoubtedly did so even in his day, although the intervening 450 years have probably seen an enormous expansion of the woodcock's breeding range, including the British Isles, especially in the last 150 years and in western areas.

The BTO Woodcock Inquiry of 1934–35 asked its correspondents throughout Britain and Ireland to say whether or not woodcock bred in their particular part of the country, how long woodcock had been known to breed there, and to notify any marked increases or decreases in the population. The replies given to these questions still form the most important single body of information about the distribution and spread of breeding woodcock in the British Isles, and the picture revealed when W.B. Alexander published the Inquiry Report in 1945 was found not to have changed significantly when the BTO's important survey of breeding birds in Britain and Ireland took place in the early 1970s.

Systematic and thorough surveys of bird distribution are a modern phenomenon, and there is little evidence to guide us prior to the mid-nineteenth century. Scattered records can be found from the seventeenth and eighteenth centuries of woodcock breeding in southern, western and northern England, and there are a handful for Wales, Scotland and Ireland too. By the mid-1850s the records began to fill out the details of the overall picture, with records of nesting in almost all counties of England, and most parts of

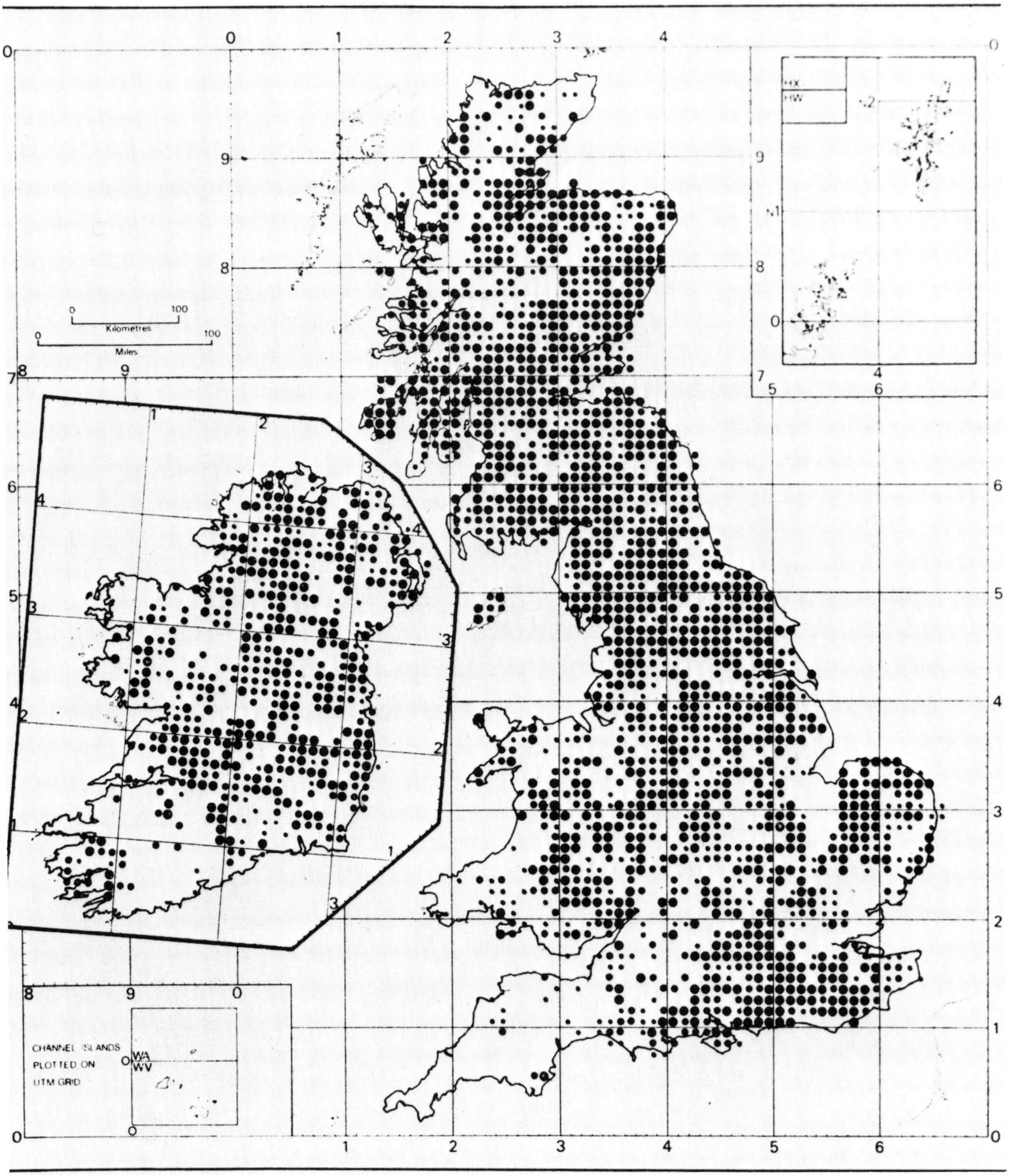

The three sizes of dots on the map signify: largest dots = confirmed breeding, medium dots = probable breeding, small dots = possible breeding (Bird(s) present in breeding season in possible nesting habitat but no further evidence). Roding birds will have been shown as medium dots.

The distribution of breeding woodcock in Britain and Ireland, as revealed by the 1968–72 survey conducted by the British Trust for Ornithology and the Irish Wildbird Conservancy.

Scotland. By the turn of the century there was some evidence to suggest that woodcock had bred in every county of England, Scotland and Ireland, and in many parts of Wales, although data for there remained sparse.

Today we have a countrywide network of keen amateur ornithologists and the woodcock's breeding distribution and density can be stated with much more certainty. Nests can be found in suitable habitat in almost every part of Britain and Ireland, but they remain a rarity in south-west Devon and in Cornwall, in the treeless landscapes of the fenlands of the eastern counties, and in parts of south-west Ireland. Even in otherwise well populated areas breeding can be patchy where habitat and soil type are unfavourable. Chalky soils with dry woodlands hold few nesting woodcock, though there may be more in wet summers, and the high moorlands of northern England and Scotland are unsuitable. Nests will be found in most of the glens and river valleys of Scotland, especially among the birch woods so characteristic of those parts. Woodcock will also nest in open heather on low blanket bog and on off-shore islands to the west of Scotland and Ireland.

From the scanty evidence available, it would appear that the woodcock has gradually extended its breeding range westwards and northwards throughout Britain and Ireland, and that the last fifty years have been a period of consolidation rather than of further expansion. Densities have often increased, and where few woodcock bred a century ago they may now be plentiful. Better and more extensive habitat for wintering woodcock and also for resident breeding birds now exists in many parts of the west and north, chiefly owing to extensive afforestation with large acreages of softwood trees. However, these have usually been planted in acidic soils, though often close to worm-rich feeding areas. These suit wintering woodcock very well, but their feeding patterns while nesting in these plantations is still something of a mystery.

The woodcock has a prolonged nesting season, and in Britain nests and newly hatched young have been found as early as mid-February and as late as the beginning of September. (The bird shot in County Tipperary in late November, 1904, and found to have an egg in its oviduct can only be described as a freak.)

The woodcock is an unco-operative bird for anyone who wants to study it at close quarters. That is both a nuisance and a challenge. In particular the nesting habits and behaviour of woodcock have never been easy to study, even in those parts of Europe where they have always bred in good numbers. It is such a secretive and retiring bird and that its breeding biology has been as difficult to establish as all the other aspects of its life and ways, and more difficult than most. But sportsmen and naturalists have always had their theories, and some recent research in Britain and Europe has revealed a lot of new information, thanks to modern techniques of bird study in the field and the wonderful advantages conferred by radio telemetry.

Radio-tagged birds can now be tracked, their nest sites located and the whole business of mating, incubating, hatching and the birds' behaviour during the nesting period can be followed more precisely than ever before. This has dispelled many myths about woodcock and clarified our understanding of what actually happens. But, like so much successful study, it has posed almost as many new questions as it has answered.

It used to be thought that woodcock paired up in a monogamous breeding relationship. Some writers even went so far as to suggest it was a lifelong bond. This latter view was held quite firmly by some people, despite the fact that woodcock are almost always solitary, even in spring and summer, and it is very unusual to find two together. It would be even more unusual to expect lifelong pairing between members of a species which is not particularly

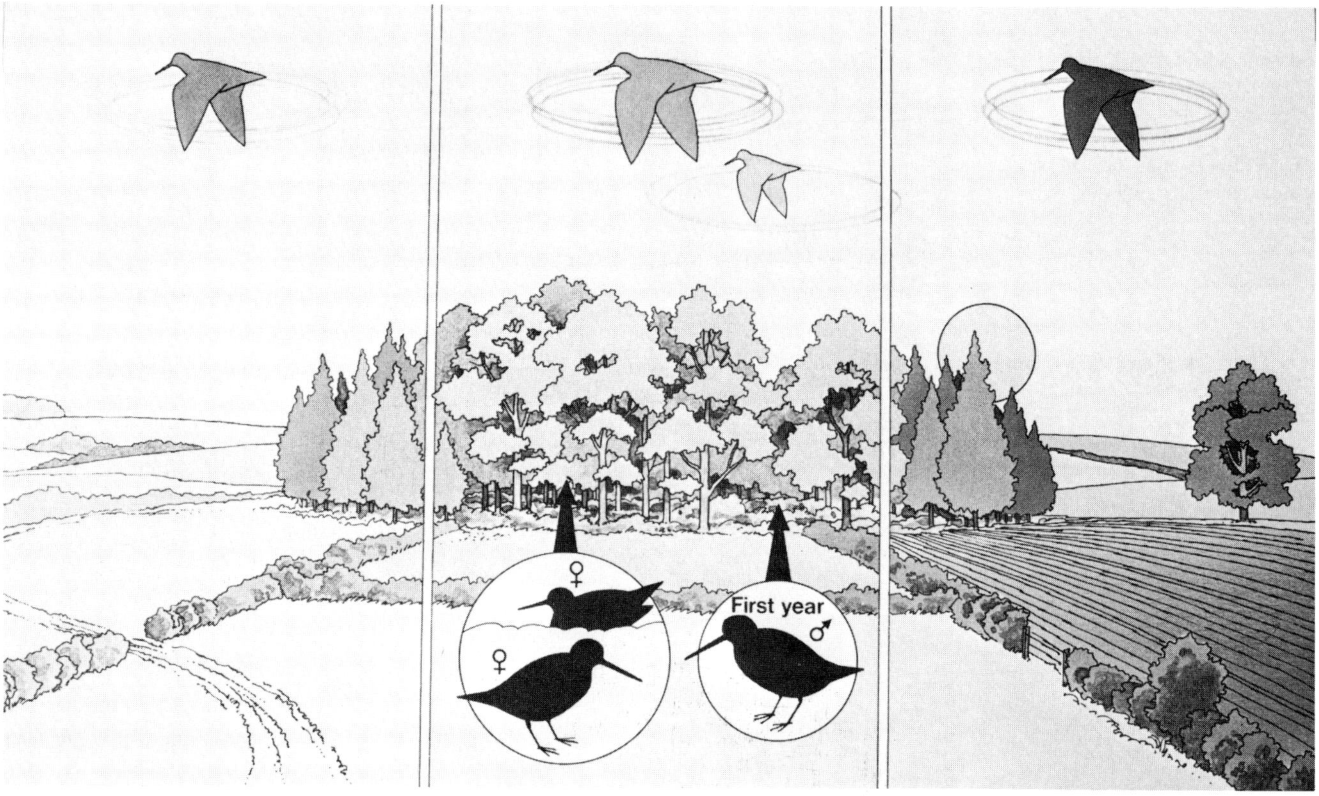

long-lived, and which is so very migratory in its habits, with the constant likelihood of pairs being split up in bad weather, or one party succumbing to bad weather or predation en route. In the European tradition this view of the woodcock's breeding-season life as one of cosy domesticity is closely linked with the romantic interpretation of the roding flights.

Among British writers, De Visme Shaw was in no doubt that woodcock paired in the third week of February and that the pair-bond lasted during incubation, with the dawn and dusk roding flights of the male no longer intended to attract a female but to assert the bird's possession of a nesting territory. He also believed that, when resting between these crepuscular flights, the faithful male bird roosted close to his mate, "never more than a few feet away from the nest", and that both parents would give a distraction display to lure an intruder away from the eggs or young.

A generation later, J.W. Seigne was sure that the male played at least some part in the incubation of the eggs, and in 1936 he wrote a detailed eye-witness description of how he saw one woodcock fly down and relieve another of her incubation duties, whereupon she promptly flew off into the sunset. He also describes how, on another occasion, he saw a sitting woodcock react with apparent anger and "a queer high, squeaking note" at the appearance of another 'cock, which flew low over her. "As if by magic her mate, never far away, appeared beside her to protect her from the intruder, who then flew away." There is no reason to doubt the accuracy of these accounts, for Seigne was an experienced and perceptive field observer, though he has described very untypical behaviour.

Other ornithologists have reported females with eggs or broods with the male bird usually to be found fairly close by, but these incidents are unusual and probably very untypical, especially in the light of recent findings in various European studies and in particular Dr Graham Hirons' five-year study of woodcock for The Game Conservancy.

From the behaviour of his radio-tagged individuals, both male and female, it was clear that the male only stayed with the female until the clutch of eggs had

Graham Hirons' studies with The Game Conservancy showed that woodcock rode extensively and breed successfully in areas of mixed hardwood and broadleaved woodland. The best habitat will be occupied by breeding females and a non-breeding reservoir of first-year males. Dominant males will display over these favoured habitats. Open farmland is unsuitable breeding habitat, but high levels of roding are often seen around some plantations of conifers, especially in northern and western parts.

This wonderfully camouflaged woodcock on her nest would have been hard to find, had she not previously been caught and fitted with a radio-tag. The slender antenna can just be seen curving up over the incubating bird's back.

been laid and was complete, after which the female alone took charge of the business of incubation and brooding, the male taking no part whatever in hatching or rearing the young.

Seigne and many earlier writers maintained that woodcock began to pair up in January and advocated an end to January shooting as one of the best ways to encourage more woodcock to nest in Britain and Ireland. "Undoubtedly many more woodcock would breed at home if these birds were not shot at all in January...", but he acknowledged that "this would mean that some years there would be little or no 'cock shooting". His compromise solution was that there should be no shooting of woodcock "after 20 January or the end of the month at latest. The man who disobeys this rule will find many of his nesting sites unoccupied."

The late Viscount Brookeborough (formerly Sir Basil Brooke) shared this

One of many classic woodcock studies by Archibald Thorburn shows two woodcock roosting in sparse birch woodland, with just a hint of the onset of spring. It used to be thought that woodcock paired in February, prior to migration.

Colebrook House in County Fermanagh, where Sir Basil Brooke (later the first Viscount Brookeborough) experimented successfully to improve the coverts for wintering woodcock and for resident breeding birds. Chicks ringed here were invariably shot within a few miles of the nest sites.

view, and exchanged ideas about woodcock with Seigne in the 1920s when he made a special and very successful attempt to build up the woodcock shooting and the numbers of nesting 'cock in his coverts at Colebrook in County Fermanagh. "I never shoot 'cock after 20th January. I have found eggs on the 10th March, which shows that they pair up before the end of January and should not be shot late in the season." Payne-Gallwey, like most of his generation, thought that woodcock paired up before leaving on their return migration northwards in March.

To try and determine when woodcock come into breeding condition a very interesting piece of research was carried out in Ireland in 1972–74. This was at the instigation of Ireland's National Association of Regional Game Councils (NARGC) which co-ordinates and represents the interests of the majority of those who shoot game in the Irish Republic, and who are organized in local gun clubs and a network of Regional Game Councils established on a county basis.

Traditionally Ireland's shooters had been able to shoot woodcock up to 28 February. By general agreement the period from December to the end of the season was regarded as the prime time for sport with woodcock, the months of October and November being much less productive, chiefly owing to the later arrival of the main wintering migrants. Inevitably there was a good deal of dismay and disappointment when the law was changed and woodcock shooting had to end on 31 January. Although feelings ran high among Irish sportsmen generally, particular concern was expressed by the Federation of County Cork Gun Clubs. Cork and adjacent parts of Munster, Ireland's south-western province, attract large numbers of wintering woodcock. That most celebrated of "big shots", the Marquess of Ripon (formerly Earl de Grey), had some big bags there at Muckross, one of Ireland's finest woodcock shoots at that time, as Lord Kenmare's guest in the 1870s, and the Munster sportsman relies upon woodcock for his sport as much if not more than other Irish shooters.

What began in 1967 as a local attempt to estimate woodcock densities in Munster and arrive at an informed view of the proportion of home-bred woodcock to migrants from overseas later changed direction and grew into a countrywide research programme to find out when woodcock begin to breed. Under the co-ordination of James Cummins of the NARGC and the scientific direction of the late Brian Stronach, a regional order permitting the shooting of woodcock for scientific study during the period 1–15 February was granted to selected sportsmen in County Cork in 1972 and extended to County Donegal in 1973. In this way birds were collected and made available for examination from Ireland's most southerly and northerly areas.

Several hundred woodcock were collected as part of this research. Measurements were taken of each bird's bill, wings and tail, but particular interest focused on sexing the birds and looking closely at the extent to which they showed signs of coming into breeding condition. The ovaries of the females and the testes of males undergo important changes with the onset of breeding, and these organs were measured and categorized on a scale of 1 to 6, stage 6 indicating that a male was capable of being fully sexually active. Only one bird was found to be in a stage 6 condition, and only 11.1% of the total were at stage 4 or 5.

This tends to confirm what Irish woodcock shooters had argued, that woodcock do not come into breeding condition until several weeks after the end of January, and that birds shot in February are not paired up and in breeding condition. This is not unexpected, since one would not expect a predominantly migratory population to undergo the stress of coming into breeding condition before they first undertake the very major stresses and hazards of a long migration back to their breeding areas in Scandinavia. Resident woodcock might be expected to come into breeding condition sooner than migrants, and perhaps it was residents which comprised most of the small percentage of birds which showed the first signs of breeding season development. However, despite the hopes of many Irish sportsmen who felt that the evidence vindicated the shooting of woodcock at least in the first fortnight of February, there has not been any extension of the woodcock shooting season in the Irish Republic, and woodcock shooting ends on the same date – 31 January – throughout Great Britain, Northern Ireland and the Republic of Ireland.

But in any event it is rare to find a woodcock's nest in Ireland before late March, and the period from late April to June is believed to be the main nesting time. Other conditions may prevail elsewhere in the woodcock's breeding range, and it would be unwise to suggest that no woodcock are ever ready to breed until late February. Similarly, in some northern parts of its range, the woodcock may not generally begin to breed until much later than British and Irish birds. A comparison of the dates of ringing week-old chicks in Britain and Scandinavia points to the northern birds breeding on average a month or so later than British Isles woodcock.

Neither the sportsmen nor the biologists involved in this Irish research saw any sign of woodcock being in pairs in February, which is in keeping with the later findings of Dr Graham Hirons that woodcock do not "pair" in the conventional sense, but that male woodcock will mate with a succession of females – "successive polygyny".

These findings suggest that De Visme Shaw, Seigne and Brooke were all mistaken in believing that woodcock numbers would increase if "paired" birds were not shot after the first week or so of the new year. Increased numbers of breeding woodcock at Colebrook and on Seigne's "sanctuary" were more probably encouraged by better habitat management and reduced disturbance when females were taking up their nesting sites. In particular the remarkable success of the late Lord Brookeborough in building up breeding and wintering numbers at Colebrook was mainly due to careful tunnelling and trimming of his extensive rhododendron plantations, with rides and gaps at frequent intervals.

Rabbits, once present in tens of thousands, caused intolerable disturbance, but their numbers were ruthlessly reduced and the coverts were kept quiet throughout the year. No releasing of pheasants was an additional bonus, and

A winter woodcock roosting by day and wonderfully camouflaged amid a litter of dead leaves and withered bracken. (Photo: T.A. Waddell)

there was regular breeding and large bags of 'cock at Colebrook over a period of several seasons prior to the last war.

More research, taking a larger sample of birds from a wider geographical area across Europe, would give us a much clearer picture of when woodcock are ready to breed, and of how sedentary populations in temperate climates compare with the long-distance migrants moving in spring from Mediterranean countries to Scandinavia and northern Russia. Meantime, for most of us, the first signs of breeding are those hectic and often vocal chasing flights at twilight in late February and March, followed by the unmistakable sight and sounds of woodcock roding in spring and early summer.

Moist broad-leaved woodlands with plenty of earthworms are more attractive to woodcock in spring and summer than other habitats with less food available on the forest floor. In hot, dry summers earthworms are more accessible to woodcock in woodland than on pastures, where the dryness drives them deeper underground.

Where do woodcock like to nest? The question of breeding habitat has still to be investigated more thoroughly, and is currently the subject of research in Britain and Europe, funded by the *Conseil International de la Chasse* (CIC). Woodcock are ground-nesters and seem to prefer woodlands with low vegetation and a fairly well-developed under-storey of secondary growth. Bare, draughty woods of mature trees seem as unattractive to them as they are to many other creatures.

Food must play a part here, and since woodcock are known to subsist chiefly on a diet of earthworms and other invertebrate life, the attractiveness of an area in terms of the availability of food must be related to various related factors like its geology, the soil makeup and the vegetation which grows there.

Earthworms, which all woodcock studies have shown to be the most important single food item, are sensitive to the acidity or alkalinity of the soil. This is usually expressed as a pH value, a term familiar to anyone who studied elementary chemistry at school. A pH factor of 5-6 is conducive to good numbers of earthworms. Below 5 the soil is too acidic to maintain high worm

At The Game Conservancy's headquarters at Fordingbridge in Hampshire, Dr Graham Hirons demonstrates to an international gathering of woodcock enthusiasts how earthworm numbers within an area of ground can be sampled, using a formalin solution.

populations: over 6 it begins to become too alkaline and numbers of worms drop away. This means that impoverished, acidic soil over blanket peat, as in much of western and northern Britain, is unlikely to encourage woodcock, nor are areas of chalky land. Woodcock may winter in both these types of habitat, but they must be able to find food within easy flighting distance, usually on wet, well-manured pasture land. At nesting-time food should be available within the immediate vicinity of the nest, unless woodcock nesting in places with little or no suitable food available close to the nest can adopt some other system for feeding themselves and their young.

In an area on the borders of south-west Wiltshire, north Dorset and west Hampshire, where I have studied breeding woodcock for several seasons, the levels of roding activity I have seen and the numbers of woodcock nests I have found have been very much higher in woodland on areas of clay soil than on lighter soils over chalk. This confirms the impression given by many of those who contributed to the BTO Inquiry of 1934-35.

Graham Hirons' findings in his five-year Derbyshire study show that trees like sycamore and birch comprise the best breeding habitat, with oak woods not quite so good, and beech woods decidedly less attractive to woodcock. Conifers, especially large acreages of one species like Sitka spruce or Lodgepole pine, are least attractive of all in terms of the food they afford. This can be measured by biologists, using a preparation of formalin to bring worms to the surface within sample areas, perhaps each of one metre square.

The weather and its seasonal variations can also affect food availability. Earthworms are known to "aestivate", which is really the opposite of hibernation. When the warmth of summer heats and dries out the upper layer of soil the worms go deeper, into damper earth and out of reach of the woodcock's probing bill, which cannot reach deeper than about three inches at most. This is more likely to happen to worm populations in fields and open areas, since trees and other large growth keeps the ground moist and shades out some of the drying effects of summer sunshine and dry winds. The dryness of the soil, together with its acidity or alkalinity, has a direct bearing on the availability of earthworms, and of some other invertebrates too, and thus affects woodcock breeding. There is evidence that breeding finishes earlier in dry summers than in wet ones.

Yet we know that woodcock breed in the worm-deficient environments of these extensive new conifer plantations which now cover so much of northern and western parts of Britain and Ireland. Do woodcock nesting there adopt a different strategy for feeding themselves and their young? More research into woodcock nesting habitats and breeding strategies is needed if we are to learn more about how the birds' breeding behaviour varies throughout its extensive range.

Some of the best recent descriptions of woodcock mating come from a French researcher. Vincent Bouckaert has studied the breeding behaviour of woodcock in the forest of Compiégne in northern France since 1976. His observations there have led him to give an exceptionally detailed account of the behaviour of the male and the female from the time contact is established between a roding male and a receptive female until mating eventually takes place.

Although we tend to think of the female woodcock as a silent bird, with only the males calling as they rode, a female woodcock which has chosen her nesting area and is ready to mate will call to a roding male with a gentle, high-pitched call, rendered as *psieopp*. Bouckaert says the male replies with its high *twisick* call, similar to the call made while roding but very much louder and uttered only once, as the male drops down towards the female. What then takes place has been described as a "carousel" movement as both birds swirl around in flight, crossing their bills in a show of apparent aggression and with tail feathers spread widely, known to be an aggressive posture.

The female then disengages from the carousel manoeuvre and flies off with another single, soft call. The male follows, and the birds call to each other in turn, their calls and answers getting faster and louder, before the birds alight, the male making a deep grunting *orrr*, which is apparently only heard in this pre-mating situation.

On the ground the female squats passively while the male stands in an upright posture and pecks at the ground as though feeding, though nothing is actually eaten. Finally the female moves towards the male and the two birds face one another bill to bill, heads pulled backwards. By this stage the various shows of aggression are over, and the female now leads the male off in flight,

Nesting in the open, by a small conifer tree, this woodcock is still beautifully camouflaged, its barred and mottled plumage blending with the shadows among rushy grasses. New softwood plantations may be providing important new breeding habitat for woodcock, especially in northern and western parts of Britain and in Ireland. (Photo: T.A. Waddell)

Twisting like a contortionist, this woodcock was preening vigorously on its nest in a Hampshire woodland when it was photographed by T.A. Waddell.

Woodcock facing bill-to-bill as part of the pre-mating display, from a sketch by M.E. Seigne.

both birds calling in an almost continuous "song", in which it is impossible to distinguish the male's cries from the female's. Finally the birds land and mating takes place, the female having fanned her tail feathers to indicate willingness. The male responds by turning away from the female with his tail upright but the feathers closed. Bouckaert believes the female's final signal is to stretch her neck up to show her white throat before squatting to be mated. He describes the male as gripping the female's nape feathers in his bill, either with the tip or at the base. This has been confirmed by almost everyone who has been lucky enough to see it happen. The woodland stalker tends to be abroad at dawn and dusk, and to be moving quietly and watchfully, or sitting vigilantly up a high-seat, and his stalking may give him more opportunities than most people to see woodcock mating. Brian Booth has twice witnessed it while roe stalking, and both males gripped the female by the feathers on her

Woodcock behaviour prior to mating, as sketched by Philip Rickman at Burnside in Angus. In each case the female stands more erect with her head stretched upwards and back while the male approaches in a crouching posture from behind.
(From *A Bird Painter's Sketch Book* (1931) and *Sketches and Notes from a Bird Painter's Journal* (1941)).

nape. These accounts are in interesting contrast to an eye-witness description given by Brian Peake in 1984, who distinctly saw the male bird's head and bill stretched *upwards* during mating.

Vincent Bouckaert has concluded that mating woodcock make particular play with some aspects of their plumage which are not normally prominent, such as the female's white throat and the attitude and shape of the tail with its white-tipped feathers. He argues that woodcock do form a true, if brief, pair bond and that since a male may go on to mate with several other females during the woodcock's extended breeding season, the birds should be regarded as "successively monogamous" rather than polygamous.

Next time you have a woodcock in your hand look closely at the underside of the tips of the main tail feathers. They are startlingly white, almost as if they had been tipped with a bright gloss paint. This is an unusual departure from the generally sombre and well-camouflaged colour of the woodcock's plumge. What is the purpose of this bright white colouring, which is confined to the underside of the tail feathers and only visible when the bird fans its tail while facing away from another bird?

These white spots reflect light even under dark conditions, such as might prevail in deep woodlands at dawn or dusk, and the naturalist Collingwood Ingram suggested that they may play an important role not only in the nuptial behaviour of the birds but as a distraction and threat mechanism. There are several accounts of woodcock leading chicks away from the nest or towards a feeding area or into cover while the tail is held upright and fanned outwards. Perhaps this gives the chicks a bright marker to follow?

G. W. H. Davison, replying to Ingram's comments, noted that bright tail feather patterns in various birds may represent contact signals between members of the same species, as well as signs of fear or aggression. He pointed out that of all the gallinaceous birds with these distinctive markings, 40% live in woodlands. Can this be a multi-purpose visual signal, adapted to work even when the light is poor? Anyone who has shot a significant number of woodcock will know that a wounded bird will often flare out its tail feathers, possibly the result of a combination of fear and aggression at the approach of the Gun or his dog.

A woodcock's nest is not an elaborate affair. Usually it is little more than a shallow depression which may be from half an inch to two inches below the level of the ground, and with a rim of nest-lining material built up around the edge just above the ground. Typically the nest-lining consists of dead leaves and grasses with a few feathers, and there may also be mosses and ferns, needles in coniferous woodland, forming an indented pad.

A vivid arc of dazzling white points is presented as a woodcock fans its tail feathers. This display has a part in the birds' pre-mating display and can also signal aggression or fear.

The siting of the nest is often close to an "edge", such as the woodland fringe, a path or forest road, or where well-established growth gives way to an open area where there has been clear-felling or windthrow damage. Many woodcock watchers have remarked that nests tend to be found close to the base of a tree, which may be anything from a mature hardwood to a young conifer, although woodcock can also nest well away from trees and bushes. Nests have been made and broods reared successfully by woodcock nesting well out among rough moorland grasses, or in long heather on the almost treeless islands off the west coasts of Ireland and Scotland.

Woodcock sit tight on their nests, which makes them very difficult to find. William Daniel in 1801 said, "They are remarkably tame during incubation; a person who discovered one in its nest has often stood over, and even stroked it, notwithstanding it hatched the young, with which in due time it disappeared." This habit of sitting tight means that unless the adult is flushed off her eggs and their pale colour gives them away, her superb camouflage will usually protect her and her nest from the keenest human eye. But it is the woodcock's large and lustrous eye which can betray its presence, and you may even be able to bend down and stroke an incubating woodcock on her nest. But this is not to be recommended. Woodcock will desert their nests if unduly disturbed, even when incubation is well advanced, and the hen and her eggs should be left quietly until hatching takes place, after which the adult will defend her brood and is not likely to desert.

Incubation takes 22 or 23 days, and the eggs all hatch together, unlike the snipe which has "asynchronous" hatching over a period of several hours, with the male bird often taking charge of the first two chicks. During incubation, which is generally accepted to be the role of the female only, the female will probably only leave her eggs for a few fairly short periods every 24 hours. Most incubating woodcock seem to sit tightly on their eggs all night, but leave the nest to feed for an hour or so before dusk. That is a good time to find nests, when the light-coloured eggs show up clearly, and it must be a vulnerable time too, with a high risk of predation.

During the day woodcock will come off their eggs perhaps three or four times, for spells of up to half an hour each time. They may leave for only 15 or 20 minutes, but are unlikely to be away for longer than three-quarters of an hour. In some cases they seem less willing to leave eggs more than twice a day when hatching is imminent. This has been the general impression of those who have spent time watching incubation, including T.A. Waddell, who has given me some detailed field notes and a series of superb photographs taken

A typical clutch of four eggs laid in a shallow depression among grasses and dead leaves. The eggs are surprisingly pale for such a well camouflaged bird, and are very conspicuous when the incubating female leaves her nest to feed. (Photo: T.A. Waddell)

Despite a spring rainstorm and the water which has beaded up on its plumage, which is waterproofed by natural oily secretions, this bird continues to sit tight on its nest in a shallow scrape among grasses and dead leaves.
(Photo: T.A. Waddell)

during his vigil at a woodcock's nest in Alice Holt forest in Hampshire, at the headquarters of the Forestry Commission. But there are still very few good observations of woodcock behaviour at the nest, and we need to know a great deal more about what goes on during the time between the adults' mating and the fledging of the young.

The chick and its mother can call to each other while the egg is not yet hatched and while the young bird is chipping its way out. The newly hatched youngster is soon dry, active and often moving quite busily around the vicinity of the nest. "Precocial" is the biologists' term for this active behaviour, which is characteristic of the young of many gamebirds. Insects and surface worms can be eaten by the chicks from an early stage and are often found in the grasses and leaf litter around their nests. But although the young woodcock comes into the world with a bill which is already noticeably elongated, it is not yet ready to feed itself by probing as an adult will. In the very early stages it is fed by the adult regurgitating partly digested food, and various observers have seen this at close quarters. "A brown fluid" is how several people have described the regurgitated food, which is probably composed of partly digested remains of earthworms and a variety of other invertebrate matter.

A typical clutch of four eggs, surprisingly light in colour for a species which is otherwise so expert at camouflage. When the nest is unattended the eggs are very conspicuous, making them vulnerable to crows and other predators. When woodcock leave the nest to feed, often just before dusk, the nest-hunter can find his more innocent task made easier too.
(Photo: T.A. Waddell)

The chicks are often led away from the nest site within a day or two of hatching, following their mother away through the undergrowth. There is, however, the intriguing and much disputed possibility that adult woodcock may sometimes *carry* their young to areas where there is better feeding. No one can now doubt that carrying does happen, but is it for purposes of feeding the young? More of this later.

Although they weigh a mere 17 grams or so at hatching, the chicks may weigh over 100 grams by the time they are ten days or so old. Their down will have begun to give way to the first signs of more mature feathering, and the birds are generally able to flutter and fly short distances after two weeks. Complete fledging and fairly powerful flight comes when the young woodcock is about five weeks old, by which stage it should weigh 220-250 grams, which is well on the way to the 300-gram average weight of a juvenile woodcock in its first winter, calculated from the weights of young birds shot during the season.

If more woodcock were ringed as chicks we would build up a much fuller

This sequence of photographs shows a woodcock returning to her nest in a Hampshire woodland, and subsequently standing over her eggs while going through a thorough preening routine.
(Photos: T.A. Waddell)

Woodcock eggs hatch almost simultaneously and the chicks are active as soon as they are dry. This woodcock and her three downy chicks appear to be waiting for the fourth chick to make its appearance from the last egg (at front) which is just chipping.

picture of how populations survive, their movements and lots of other important data. Those who have ringed young woodcock or seen young chicks with the mother nearby have described how she will defend her young from an intruder and try to lure the potential predator away with all kinds of distraction and feigned injury displays. T.A. Coward gave a well-known account of an adult woodcock putting up an exceptionally aggressive display

Newly hatched woodcock chicks already have a noticeably elongated bill. (From a sketch by Richard Robjent.)

which frightened off a sparrowhawk. A fluttering or "broken wing" feigning is commoner, and may be accompanied by signs of extreme agitation and high, squeaking cries.

As a ground-nesting bird the woodcock is obviously vulnerable to predation by ground-hunters like stoats, weasels and foxes, and perhaps the occasional feral cat too. Little systematic study has been carried out on this subject, but there are plenty of records of the remains of woodcock having been found near fox earths and traces of their feathers in fox droppings. Each spring I usually find evidence of two or three sitting birds having been taken in such a way that everything points to a fox as the culprit, including the strong and unmistakable smell of fox lingering in the air in some instances. A Highland stalker once told me how he had been lying out on the hill at dusk, waiting to get a shot at a certain dog-fox which he expected to be coming in to feed cubs in a den in a cairn of rocks. He succeeded in bowling over the fox with his rifle and found him to have a woodcock in his mouth. The bird had the bare brood-patch on her belly which indicates an incubating hen.

Woodcock will adopt the "broken-wing" distraction tactics of many other wader species, when danger threatens her brood of chicks.

Weasels and stoats have also been seen to take small and also quite well-fledged young, and even adult birds, including some winter woodcock which have presumably been caught as they roosted on the ground by day, are known to have been taken by stoats. Rodger McPhail provided a delightful sketch of a stoat in winter pelage carrying a dead woodcock as one of his illustrations for Lord Home's *Border Reflections* (1979).

Birds of prey can take woodcock too, and there are many records of sparrowhawks killing woodcock, both on the air and on the ground, while roosting and nesting. Though predation pressures on woodcock are probably highest in spring, sparrowhawks will also take woodcock in winter, although the birds are not normally on the wing, and thus not conspicuous and vulnerable, except when flighting to and from their feeding grounds at dusk and dawn. When shooting woodcock on driven shoots in the west of Britain I have several times seen a sparrowhawk make a dash at a woodcock flushed by the beaters, and in December, 1981, I saw a female sparrowhawk shoot out of the trees and attempt to grab a high-flying woodcock which had just been shot and begun to fall. I vividly remember the great forbearance of the Gun

Female Woodcock With Young Chicks – a watercolour by Jane Brewer. Very young chicks already have prominent bills and will forage among the leaves and grasses around the nest within a few hours of hatching, but keeping close to their mother.

A twelve day old woodcock chick, whose mother was killed by a sparrowhawk, shows an elongated bill and the quills of its first plumage are beginning to show through the down.

involved, who refrained from firing his other barrel but chased the sparrowhawk off with some colourful imprecations.

Barn owls used to be blamed for taking woodcock, but there is no evidence to show that they take woodcock other than very rarely. The buzzard can include woodcock in its diet, and that of its growing chicks. In looking at buzzard prey remains in 81 nests in the New Forest in Hampshire during the period 1962-70, Colin Tubbs found the remains of woodcock chicks on six occasions, in five nests, and once the feathers of an adult bird. I have twice found remains of woodcock chicks in buzzard nests in the Glens of Antrim in Northern Ireland, and also on three occasions among prey remains at eyries and plucking posts used by peregrines.

Foxes can take incubating woodcock, which are vulnerable as tight-sitting ground nesters. The extent of fox predation on wintering woodcock is unknown, but Rodger McPhail's sketch captures the moment vividly.

However, all my recent information from landowners and gamekeepers who have found signs of dead woodcock and predated nests in spring points to the fox and the sparrowhawk as the principal predators, with various members of the crow family ready to take unguarded eggs and sometimes very young chicks too.

Woodcock rely heavily upon their superb natural camouflage to protect them from predators of all kinds, including man. Perhaps they can even mobilize some special physiological means of suppressing their scent when a predator like a fox or a dog comes near, as I have discussed in the chapter on woodcock and gundogs. But the incubating bird can be more vulnerable than usual when spring is late and the woods are still bare of new growth, even in late April and early May. This happened in the cold and late springs of 1985 and 1986, when I found unmistakable signs of several woodcock being killed on their nests in prime breeding habitat in west Hampshire and Dorset.

Cold, bare woods also afford scant cover for the eggs when the nest is left unattended. Even when spring growth is well advanced the woodcock's pale eggs are often very easy to see. All incubating females, even the most devoted of mothers, must occasionally leave their eggs unattended, sometimes during the day and almost always in the hour or so just before dusk. This is by far the best way of finding woodcock nests in likely habitat where you have seen birds roding, and corvids of all sorts are never slow to spot them too. I have known eggs to be destroyed by carrion and hoodie crows, magpies, jackdaws and even rooks, and jays have been accused of this also.

Incubation continues while the female dozes in the sunshine of a spring afternoon – but with one eye just open a fraction to watch for approaching danger. (Photo: T.A. Waddell)

If the adult hen is unharmed there is a good chance she may re-nest, usually in another site some distance away, mating with another roding male. Graham Hirons saw a new clutch laid within twelve days of the loss of the first eggs, and at a distance of about five miles from the original nest site. This is one of the benefits to the species of the woodcock's prolonged breeding season.

In discussing woodcock migration the question arises of the local movements of woodcock after nesting and before the main autumn migrations. This involves the behaviour both of adult birds and their recently fledged young in the late summer, and it remains something of a puzzle. Where do woodcock go after nesting?

Woodlands which hold good numbers of nesting woodcock in spring and early summer and a further population of wintering visitors from late October onwards are often found to be empty of woodcock in August and September. This has been widely commented upon, and it is not merely a general impression caused by the cessation of roding and the birds leading a less conspicuous life. Various enthusiasts have tried to find woodcock at this time and coverts which held numbers of breeding woodcock from March to June have been systematically worked through with beaters and spaniels in an attempt to try and find woodcock in late summer, all to no avail. In one covert after another the birds are simply not there, or only one or two at most. Where have the rest gone?

J.W. Seigne commented on this puzzle, and the BTO Inquiry considered the question, since a high proportion of its respondents from all over the British Isles mentioned the same thing – coverts empty from mid-July until the first falls of October migrants.

Part of the answer lies in the fact that adult woodcock are moulting at this time of year. The moult begins around late June and can continue until late September. This extended moulting period may be linked to the woodcock's long breeding season. It may be that those which breed early also moult early, while late breeders of birds with replacement clutches or broods may have a delayed moult. Moulting woodcock lie very tight and seem to give off so little scent that even experienced woodcock-finding dogs can miss them. This has been the experience of many practical sportsmen, and Seigne described these woodcock as "very hard to flush. If I had not worked all likely ground very carefully with the dog in all probability I might not have seen many of them."

In western and northern parts of the British Isles woodcock are often reported lying out in rough hill grasses, bracken and heather in late summer. King George VI, while Duke of York, killed his 500th woodcock on 19 August, 1935, as one of three Guns walking up grouse and rabbits on the fringe of the moor at Glamis. Six woodcock were shot by that party, of which four were bagged by the King. Parties of early-season grouse shooters, especially those shooting over setters and pointers, have reported finding and flushing woodcock on the hill. There are well-attested instances of this on the islands of Raasay and Islay in the Inner Hebrides, and in parts of Perthshire and Inverness-shire. I have several times done this myself, when working setters on heather moorland in western Scotland and in Ireland in the days immediately following "The Twelfth".

I have always had the impression that the woodcock I flushed under these conditions were less strong on the wing than an autumn or winter woodcock. This would suggest that they may have been moulting, with their powers of flight impaired as a result, but that is no more than a tentative idea, based on my impressions after seeing it happen a dozen or so times. And a woodcock flushed in the open can often appear to fly slowly, and the absence of trees and cover means that they may give a false impression of slow flight.

If woodcock do in fact move up on to higher ground in late summer it would seem likely that they do so because conditions there are usually cooler and damper than in the warm, dry woodlands of July and August. It would also appear to parallel the behaviour of woodcock in their Alpine and Himalayan

Incubating woodcock leave their eggs periodically to feed, usually on the forest floor within a short distance of the nest. The hen bird may leave her eggs for a final spell of feeding just before nightfall.

The trio of woodcock in this interesting montage are picked out with remarkable accuracy in woodcock feathers against a watercolour background. This unusual woodcock item came from an Irish country house and dates from the 1860s. (From the author's collection.)

Three woodcock are shown against a background of woodland and foliate decoration on the floor-plate of a Browning over-and-under gun. This detailed design in heavy relief is the work of engraver Ken Hunt. (Photo: Sothebys)

A woodcock contentedly asleep in the sunshine among young bracken, as seen on a spring roe-stalking outing by Brian Booth and sketched by Rodger McPhail.

breeding areas, where post-breeding migration seems to take place on the basis of altitude rather than geographical distance. And the woodcock is known in all its habits to be a bird of cool temperate climes, avoiding extremes of cold or heat or dryness.

An interesting additional twist to this question is provided by the fact that some parts of Scotland and Ireland actually experience an influx of woodcock in August and September, often at quite high densities. Such instances were reported to the BTO Inquiry, and I have been given several more recent accounts by landowners and gamekeepers. Two places in particular, in the Findhorn valley in Morayshire and in a long glen in Galloway, are noted for an annual congregation of woodcock around a particular spot of not many acres, in September. These are believed to be home-bred birds and densities are high, to the extent that two or three Guns working through the bracken and heather with spaniels can make a bag of 20–25 birds in a few hours. (In Scotland woodcock may be shot from 1 September.) These woodcock gatherings do not last long, and the place may be deserted within a day or two. If such areas could be mist-netted and some of these birds ringed it would be an important step towards learning more about the movements of our home-bred woodcock.

If woodcock do move to the hills in late summer it is a simple matter for those birds which have bred in the glens of Scotland or the valleys of Ireland and Wales. But what of the birds bred in southern woodlands, where there are no hills nearby? Seigne asked this question in the 1920s and there still seems to be no clear answer. Yet southern observers have remarked on the scarcity of woodcock at this time of year, and especially in dry summers like 1976 and, to a lesser extent, 1983. This suggests that drier conditions and a shortage of earthworms may force birds to move away. But where they go remains a mystery. If they migrate overseas, which seems unlikely, they must presumably return by the autumn, since ringing returns show that very few British- or Irish-bred woodcock winter abroad.

CHAPTER IV

DO WOODCOCK CARRY THEIR YOUNG?

"... it carries its chicks in its bill when fleeing from danger"

G.A. Scopoli: *Annus Primus Historico-Naturalis* (1769)

"Do woodcock carry their young?" The answer is yes, some woodcock undoubtedly can and will do so on some occasions – though probably *not* in their bills! There is no longer any serious doubt about that fact. So why have I devoted one of the longest chapters in this book to this question? Quite simply, it is an issue which has taken up a vast amount of space in woodcock literature. Thousands of words have been written about it and countless hours of discussion and argument have been spent by generations of woodcock-minded sportsmen in debating it. It is also an aspect of woodcock behaviour which is particularly charming and fascinating. Many eye-witness accounts are very interesting and worth considering for that reason alone. The fact that woodcock sometimes behave in this way also raises many other questions about precisely how, why and when the adult bird airlifts her chicks.

The question "Do they or don't they carry their young?" must have brought smiles of delight, and perhaps an occasional look of horror, to the faces of the editors of many a sporting magazine – horror at the prospect of starting yet another endless and probably inconclusive correspondence in their "Letters" pages; or delight at the re-emergence of one of those perennial topics of discussion and dispute which can usually be guaranteed to catch the imagination of readers and correspondents for issue after issue.

This much-disputed aspect of woodcock behaviour has been aired by

Archibald Thorburn's picture of a woodcock carrying its chick is probably the best known depiction of this much disputed aspect of woodcock behaviour. The chick is shown as clasped against the adult's belly, supported between the bird's lower legs and its toes.

British and Irish sportsmen and naturalists for at least two hundred years, and it can still provoke a spirited discussion today. Although I merely mentioned the matter in passing in an article in *Shooting Times & Country Magazine* in 1984, it sparked off a lively spell of correspondence and discussion. A minor deluge of letters, many with accompanying sketches, came through my letter box and the telephone rang regularly for several weeks afterwards. Almost everyone who contacted me wanted to pass on their personal accounts of seeing a woodcock airlift a chick. But several people – some of them experienced and observant sportsmen, wise in the ways of woodcock – expressed doubts about the possibility of woodcock carrying their young. Most of them admitted that they were sceptical primarily because they hadn't seen it with their own eyes, but there remained a hard core of determined sceptics who resolutely refused to believe that it ever happens. No doubt they will continue to do so, whatever others may say they have seen.

At this point I should say that I have never personally been lucky enough to see a woodcock carrying a chick. Perhaps I have had less opportunity than some, having lived most of my life in areas which are more noted for the numbers of wintering woodcock than for big nesting populations. But I am quite prepared to accept that woodcock will carry their young, and most sportsmen and naturalists now recognize it as an aspect of woodcock behaviour, although its purpose is not fully understood. Those who remain sceptical seem almost wilful in their refusal to credit the hundreds of eyewitness accounts of the woodcock airlift, many of them from the most experienced and knowledgeable observers one could wish for. Those descriptions and the accumulated weight of evidence are good enough for me, and in this section I have tried to include a number of those which seem to me to be the most interesting and closely observed.

But if we do accept that woodcock carry their chicks, as I think we must, there are other interesting questions which still remain to be answered. How does the adult bird support the chick in flight? Is carrying always a response to a threatening intruder, or will woodcock also carry their young to feeding grounds or into a more congenial habitat, or for some other reason?

Some of the answers to these supplementary questions begin to emerge if we look in detail at the whole woodcock-carrying controversy, and consider some of the fascinating eye-witness descriptions of it.

"Whether or not woodcock carry their young at other places, I dinna ken; but this I dae ken, they dinna carry them at Bowhill!" That was the uncompromising view of Andrew Warwick, one of the Duke of Buccleuch's under-keepers at Bowhill estate in the Scottish Borders at the beginning of this century. He took a very special interest in woodcock, which have bred in good numbers at Bowhill for decades, and while doing his rounds in the woods and coverts he had often seen adults and their young during the spring and summer months. But he had never seen a woodcock carrying its young, and he communicated his sceptical views on the matter in those terms to Tom Speedy, a celebrated Borders keeper and the author of two books on Scottish sport and wildlife at the beginning of this century.

Further south and 150 years earlier, Gilbert White, the great chronicler of the natural history of his beloved Selborne, took much the same view as Andrew Warwick, but characteristically he expressed it in rather gentler and more philosophical terms. On 14 September, 1770, he wrote, "Candour forbids me to say that any fact is false because I have never been witness to such a fact". White had just been reading the account of woodcock carrying their chicks given by the great Italian naturalist Giovanni Antonio Scopoli in his *Annus Primus Historico-Naturalis*, published in 1769: "... *pullos rostro portat fugiens ab hoste*" – "it carries its chicks in its bill when fleeing from an enemy". Although he had never seen woodcock carry their chicks by this or any other means, White was especially and understandably sceptical about Scopoli's account of the use of the bill alone: "The long unwieldy bill of the woodcock is perhaps the worst adapted of any among the winged creation for such a feat of natural affection."

Almost everyone who has claimed to see a woodcock carrying a chick or chicks has described the adult as using its thighs, legs or feet to clasp the youngster, but occasionally the bill has been mentioned as giving additional support to a chick held between the adult's legs, the adult apparently pressing its bill backwards beneath its breast to hold the youngster in position. Sir Ralph Payne-Gallwey spoke to Irish gamekeepers in the 1870s who claimed to have seen woodcock carrying their chicks "one by one, supporting them with both feet and bill, which a Cock could well do, as he always flies with down-pointed bill".

The woodcock, as we saw when considering its physical make-up and feeding habits, has a sensitive bill which can flex along part of its length and take a firm grasp of food items like worms and insect larvae. But it seems extremely unlikely that this prehensile ability could be used to carry a chick, or only very exceptionally and if the youngster was very small and light. As for the downward-pointing attitude of the woodcock's bill when in flight, descriptions of this are often exaggerated. A woodcock flushed into flight rises with the bill in a depressed position which has led some people to think, quite mistakenly, that the bird uses its long bill as a lever or vaulting pole to help it spring into the air. Once on the wing, the downward angle of the bill is rarely more than about 30° below the horizontal when the bird is in level flight. The bill would have to be pressed downwards and backwards at considerably more than 90° if it was to afford support to the chick – a very ungainly, uncomfortable and aerodynamically awkward position for a bird in flight.

Let's begin our exploration of the eye-witness evidence by looking at one of the best-known descriptions, an account written by Charles St John in his *The Wild Sports and Natural History of the Highlands*, first published in 1845. St John has achieved a latter-day notoriety in our conservation-conscious age for his depredations among some of the rarer creatures of the Highlands in the middle of the last century, and especially for his relentless pursuit of the last Highland ospreys, which were already on the verge of extinction when he sought their eggs and shot the adult birds wherever he could find them.

But Charles St John was, by any standards, a very acute and observant field naturalist who kept detailed written notes of much of what he saw. Were it not for his books, based on his sporting notes and game records, our knowledge of the natural history and wildlife of the Highlands in the era just prior to the coming of the railways would be very much poorer. Whatever his shortcomings may have been in the matter of osprey shooting – or in his shooting of woodcock in spring, as I have described in the section on roding – he was an accurate and gifted practical naturalist. This is his 1845 account of the woodcock airlift:

"It is a singular but well-ascertained fact that woodcocks carry their young ones down to the springs and soft ground where they feed. Before I knew this, I was greatly puzzled as to how the newly-hatched young of this bird could go from the nest, which is often built in the rankest heather, far from any place where they could possibly feed, down to the marshes. I have, however, ascertained that the old bird lifts her young *in her feet* and carries them one by one to their feeding-ground. Considering the apparent improbability of this curious act of the woodcock, and the unfitness of their feet or claws for carrying or holding any substance whatever, I should be unwilling to relate it on my own unsupported evidence; but it has been lately corroborated by the observations of several intelligent foresters and others, who are in the habit of passing through the woods during March and April."

In this account St John specifically mentions the carrying bird's use of the feet and claws, though with some misgivings about its viability. It is interesting to compare this with his later account, drawn from some breeding season observations he made in 1848. By then he had concluded that the chicks were not carried in the feet but between the thighs, and one at a time:

"From close observation, however, I found out that the old woodcock carries her young, even when larger than a snipe, not in her claws, which seem quite incapable of holding up any weight, but by clasping the little bird tightly between her thighs, and so holding it tight towards her own body."

By general agreement among those who have seen carrying or analysed the various accounts of it, this is by far the commonest method by which the adult bird supports the chick in flight.

Two years after Charles St John's experience, which caused him to dismiss any ideas about woodcock using their feet to carry the young, the eighth Duke of Beaufort saw a sight which he later described in a personal footnote to Sir Ralph Payne-Gallwey's chapter on the woodcock in the Badminton Library volume on *Shooting: Moor & Marsh* (1889).

"In the New Forest, in the year 1850, I came upon a female woodcock watering her three young at a rivulet. She picked up one in each claw and flew off with them. I hid in a high gorse brake close by, and saw her return in four or five minutes and pick up the remaining bird also in her claw."

Here we have two important and experienced observers giving different accounts, and the picture is further complicated by a description given by De Visme Shaw. In the 1890s he made an important contribution to the *Fur, Feather & Fin Series* half-volume on woodcock, and stated that "the way a woodcock starts is ... to grasp, say, the left wing of the young bird near the body with, say, the left foot and then to spring off the ground with the free foot, afterwards using the free foot to grasp the young bird's other wing".

While those who believed that carrying does happen continued to disagree about *how* it happens, there were eminent and adamant non-believers. J.G. Millais, son of the Pre-Raphaelite painter John Everett Millais and himself a celebrated sporting and wildlife artist, spent a great deal of time roe stalking in spring in parts of Scotland which were familiar to Charles St John, especially the Findhorn valley in Morayshire. Woodcock breed there in large numbers, but Millais was very sceptical about the carrying of chicks.

"I have disturbed hundreds of woodcocks, and on several occasions when they were squatting beside their young. In no case have I ever seen a woodcock carry, or attempt to carry, its young. Being especially alert as to this point, I have watched woodcock very carefully at close range, and have frequently seen them rise and go through all their usual tricks of the anxious parent. What the woodcock seems to me to do is to rise and fly in a halting and zigzag flight. It utters low croaks and hangs its legs over the much-inflated vent feathers, which to untrained observers may appear to be a young one. The tail itself is broadly spread and held in a forward position, and this heightens the appearance that the bird is carrying something.... Even if these birds do perform such an act it is at all times very rare, and in most cases the so-called carrying of a young bird has been mistaken for the peculiar way in which the

vent feathers are held in movements of fear or alarm on the part of the parent bird."

Those who have studied woodcock at the nest confirm that woodcock will exhibit various types of distraction behaviour when danger or a potential predator threatens. Low flutterings and "broken wing" displays are common, as with many other waders and plovers, and the woodcock will also sometimes depress its tail and trail its legs while rising with a laboured flight off the ground in the vicinity of the nest or young. This has certainly given rise to a great many mistaken sightings of woodcock which the observers genuinely believed to be carrying a chick. It does not, however, explain away what some writers have dismissed as the myth of woodcock carrying their chicks.

Tom Speedy, who was not only a writer but a practical gamekeeper of great experience, was one of the most vociferous sceptics. He asked a keeper friend, Sandy Fraser, who worked on an estate on the Isle of Mull where woodcock bred in good numbers, to shoot every woodcock he flushed which appeared to be carrying something. "At my request he shot three birds in the supposed act of carrying a young one, but in no case found the chick. As this was a cruel experiment, he discontinued it and adopted different tactics. When one rose in the usual labouring fashion, he told his retriever to 'go fetch it.' The bird quickly drew up its legs and elevated its tail, and flew off in its normal fashion, but nothing dropped from it. Is it not strange that after five-and-thirty years' close observation in the Isle of Mull he should never see a young woodcock carried by its parent?"

Strange perhaps, but not impossible. And Tom Speedy was making the mistake of extrapolating from the comparatively limited experiences of himself and some friends while dismissing a large body of eye-witness evidence from many other people. He lacked Gilbert White's gentle open-mindedness.

Before looking in further detail at some of the many eyewitness accounts of chicks being carried between adults' legs or thighs, it is interesting to examine some more descriptions of the birds' alleged ability to grasp and carry their young in their *feet*. These seem very ill-adapted to gripping or carrying anything substantial, as Charles St John remarked, and by 1848 he was satisfied that chicks were in fact carried between the adult bird's thighs. Nevertheless, some very reliable observers have claimed to see chicks carried in the adults' feet, including some of St John's "intelligent forester" friends.

An especially full account was given by those extraordinary neo-Jacobite sportsmen, the brothers Charles Edward and John Sobieski Stuart, in their two-volume *Lays of the Deer Forest* (1848). Like St John and Millais, the Stuart brothers knew the Findhorn valley well and this is a description of what they saw there:

"Without any search, and merely in the accidental occasions of roe-hunting, we have found, in one season, nineteen nests with eggs [in the Darnaway area].... As the nests are laid on dry ground, and often at a distance from moisture, in the latter case, as soon as the young are hatched, the old bird will sometimes carry them *in her claws* to the nearest spring or green stripe. In the same manner, when in danger, she will rescue those which she can lift.... Various times, when the hounds, in beating the ground, have come upon a brood, we have seen the old bird rise with a young one *in her claws*, and carry it fifty or a hundred yards away; and, if followed to the place where she pitched, she has repeated the transportation until too much harassed. In any sudden alarm she will act in the same way.

"Upon a dry bank, half-way down the brae, I almost stumbled over a bird which rose at my feet; and as it darted through the trees I saw that it had something in its claws.... As soon as I followed, she led me away, hirpling and halting like an 'old wife', taking little flights, which became longer as she drew me farther; till at last, thinking she had sufficiently succeeded, she took a turn down the brae, rose over the trees, and wheeling back dropped on the spot where she had left her charge.... I ran forward, and she rose with him *in her feet*, her long legs dangling and swinging with her little burden like a parachute. She lighted at no great distance, and as I again came upon her she got up, and in her hurry dropped the young bird. I instantly stopped, for she came to the ground almost at the same time with the little one, and she ran back and sat upon him, and rose again with him *in her claws*."

The Welsh Quaker Llewellyn Lloyd was another of those remarkable sportsmen and amateur naturalists of the same generation as the Stuart brothers and Charles St John, although he chose to live not in Britain but in Sweden, from where he inspired and assisted Sir Thomas Fowell Buxton's successful re-introduction of Scandinavian capercailzie to their former haunts in Scotland in the early 1830s. Writing about woodcock, which he often saw on their Scandinavian breeding grounds, he said, "If in shooting you meet with a brood of woodcocks, and the young ones cannot fly, the old bird takes them separately *between her feet*."

Lloyd's friend Anders Oterdahl described how he once "shot a woodcock, flushed by the dogs, and when flying at about six feet from the ground, that was bearing an unfledged young one *in her claws*. It seemed to me she grasped it with her feet, one foot having hold of one wing and the other foot of the other." This is similar to De Visme Shaw's account, quoted earlier, of the adult grasping the chick with one wing in each foot.

The BTO Woodcock Inquiry 1934–35 included in its questionnaire, as Question 13:

"Have you ever seen parents carrying their young? If so, describe how they do it, under what circumstances, for what apparent purpose, and any other points that may be of interest."

Over 300 respondents answered this question, and 150 claimed either to have witnessed it, or to have reliable second-hand accounts of it. Thirty-eight of these described the chick(s) as held "in the feet or claws"; a further two merely described the chick as being carried "underneath", with no additional details. Seven described the chick as being carried on the adult's back – but this must surely be the most insecure and improbable position imaginable. If a woodcock does ever intentionally carry a chick on her back it must be a very rare event indeed, and almost certainly unsuccessful except over the shortest distances. (In passing, however, it is interesting to note that in parts of eastern England the goldcrest (*Regulus regulus*) is known among countrymen as the "woodcock's pilot". This name seems to stem from an old belief that goldcrests migrating to Britain from mainland Europe in autumn travelled on the backs of the migrating woodcock and helped with their navigation in exchange for this piggy-back transport!)

Most importantly, however, the carrying of woodcock chicks between the legs or thighs was described by no fewer than ninety-seven correspondents in the BTO Inquiry, and the chicks were apparently carried "between the legs, or between legs and breast", while a further nineteen said the chick was "partly supported by the tail" and thirteen that it was "partly supported by the bill".

The BTO Inquiry remains the most comprehensive broad study of the species ever carried out in the British Isles, and it is clear from the data it

Woodcock will distract intruders near the nest by flying off with depressed tail feathers and dangling legs, as depicted here by J. G. Millais. This behaviour may have given rise to some of the mistaken sightings of woodcock apparently carrying a chick, but it does not explain away the carrying phenomenon, which some people still refuse to accept.

gathered, and from many subsequent accounts, that the "between the legs" position is by far the commonest. But, despite the apparent unsuitability of the woodcock's feet for gripping and carrying anything, one cannot lightly dismiss these detailed descriptions given by very observant people, although they are the minority. Undoubtedly some must have been confused by the dangling legs of the adult bird, which many correspondents describe as similar to the appearance of a hawk carrying off its prey. Trailing legs and a laboured flight, often with tail feathers depressed, are part of the woodcock's distraction display at the nest, and it may be that well-grown chicks carried between the bird's thighs will force the lower legs of the adult to hang down. It is not totally impossible that an adult woodcock might just be capable of using its feet to grasp very small, recently hatched chicks, and those who have seen it tend to emphasize that the chicks thus carried have generally been very small. The "one wing in each foot" style of carrying, as described by De Visme Shaw and Oterdahl, may be a particularly uncommon variation of this, perhaps where an adult is dealing with a well-grown chick.

So on the basis of the available evidence, the majority view is that the chick is held between the adult's legs or thighs, with some claims that the bill and possibly the tail may sometimes also be used to give additional support to the chick.

The evidence for woodcock carrying chicks is so extensive that several volumes could be filled with good eye-witness accounts. It is worth singling out just a few of these, especially the more detailed ones, some of which are fascinating.

Two Irish maiden ladies, the Misses Fairholm, had a remarkable sighting in 1900:

"My sister and I were standing in a field here one day in May last, and our two dogs were hunting in a small oak-wood on the other side of the fence near us, when we heard a noise close behind us, something like the cry of a kestrel, but not quite so loud. On turning round we saw a woodcock crouching on the ground, fluttering her wings and crying. On going a step or two towards her, to see if she were hurt, she gathered up two little ones; one clasped to her breast by her head and beak, and the other between her feet. She flew on slowly a few yards to the top of a very low bank where she let down the young ones, and crouched over them, fluttering her wings and crying as before. We waited to see what would happen, when the dogs came out over the fence of the wood. The bird immediately raised up the two young ones as before, and flew back into the oak-wood. Both flights were short, and she flew heavily and near the ground, so that we saw the whole proceeding perfectly."

This remarkable account also added that the adult bird's bill was not visible in flight but reappeared in the forward position when the chicks were set down. So here we have a detailed description of two chicks being carried simultaneously by a single adult, one between the feet and the other tucked under the bird's throat and held in place by the depressed bill. And evidently the Fairholm sisters saw it all at very close quarters and the bird performed this two-at-once carriage twice in quick succession. There is absolutely no reason to doubt this, unless we suspect downright fabrication, deceit or hallucinations.

In late 1985 another account of two-at-once carrying was published. Angus Nudds, a gamekeeper of long experience, describes in *The Woods Belong To Me* how, during his time as keeper at Clarendon Park near Salisbury, he clearly saw woodcock carry their young off quite bare ground.

"From about twenty-five yards range, we saw the two young run to their mother; after a few seconds she flew heavily away, with her legs half-dangling *and what appeared to be a lump on each thigh*. There was no possible way those chicks could have been moved off that bare ground without them being carried. There is no doubt in my mind that woodcock do carry their young when danger threatens."

The BTO Inquiry heard of several claims like this of two young being carried simultaneously, and in a variety of positions, but descriptions of the carrying of several chicks singly and in quick succession are much more common. Nevertheless, credulity is strained to the limits by an account given in 1921 by the French woodcock enthusiast Georges Benoist. He had been

The unstable, lurching, labouring flight of a woodcock carrying a chick – Rodger McPhail's sketch shows what many observers have reported.

Neil McReddie's sketch shows a tiny woodcock chick gripped between the adult's legs and held up against its body.

told by a forest ranger from the Arville area of how he had flushed a woodcock which he knew to have a nest in the vicinity and which *"rose with all four chicks at once!* ...but one chick, which was probably not gripped properly, fell and called out and the hen bird gathered it up again and carried it off with the others. Next day I looked for her again and flushed her, *and she again carried off her four young together.*"

Whatever we may make of this extraordinary account, Benoist does make an interesting point when he suggests elsewhere that the woodcock chick may help to make its transportation more secure by using its bill and feet to hold onto the adult when she picks it up.

A much more typical account of several chicks being carried off one by one was given in these terms by a retired gamekeeper from the New Forest, who described what he saw there one day in June, 1931:

"I was walking through the wood when I saw a woodcock with four young ones. I saw the old bird carry away one of the young ones by pressing it between its thighs, which it took for about 100 yards. It then returned again to another one and, after making a croaking sound and fluttering round on the ground, it took up a second young one and carried it away."

Another observer, a Wiltshire parson, wrote that he once "put up a woodcock which flew carrying a young bird under her thighs. On looking very carefully where she rose, I saw two more tiny chicks and, close by, what had evidently been the nest. I walked away a few yards and sat down and waited. She soon came back and took away the two chicks I had seen."

A Berkshire gamekeeper who knew of a woodcock's nest containing four chicks described how, on his approach, the adult flew off, leaving only three chicks on the ground. He waited nearby in hiding and "after a few minutes the woodcock returned and pitched on a bare patch about a foot from the nest, and then waddled on to the nest like a broody hen. She snuggled down and immediately spread her wings on the ground (as a wounded bird will) and rose from them about a yard and flew off. As she went away I could distinctly see a chick between her thighs. The chick's head was pointing backwards under her tail. It appeared as if the chick was sitting on the bird's feet and held in position by her thighs. She flew away into a patch of bracken and came back for the next chick in about five minutes. I watched her pick up each of the three chicks, and she went through the same performance in each case."

Similar accounts also come from Scotland and Ireland. Patrick Synnot, a gamekeeper on an estate near Ballinasloe, County Galway, described how he found a brood of three recently hatched woodcock chicks.

"The old bird came behind the chick and, with fluttering wings and shuffling squat, took one after another chick from the open space in the wood to the high heather on the edge about sixty yards away. She did not drop them all in the one place, but about ten yards apart, and on taking the third she disappeared into the heather. She showed no fear of me, but took the three almost at my feet."

A landowner in Ross-shire, who had his keeper and a ghillie as additional witnesses, "saw a woodcock rise with a young one and saw the bird return for the other three ... and carry one each time away and deposit it and return for the next."

One of J.W. Seigne's most valuable and closely observed descriptions is of the only occasion on which he personally got a really close look at a woodcock carrying a chick, though he often saw woodcock flying at dusk and apparently carrying a chick, perhaps to the feeding area.

He explains how he was watching a goldcrest's nest in May when "suddenly a woodcock flew past and alighted about thirty yards away. On looking closely at the spot I saw a young woodcock on the ground beside her. Both birds ran about for a few minutes, then the parent suddenly rose with the young one. Owing to the distance away I could not see how she was carrying it. When about ten feet in the air, to my surprise, the woodcock hovered for a second, with rapid wing-beats, and let the chick drop. After a violent fluttering the little fellow landed, head first, on the soft moss. My impression is that the mother was giving her offspring a lesson in confidence and flying. She again alighted beside it and both started running about in the prettiest way imaginable. By this time they were quite near me and the old bird must have been aware of my presence, for she uttered a low croaking note and the chick immediately ran underneath her. She gave it a few light taps with her bill, as if to make sure it was properly in position, then rose without difficulty, passing right over my head and carrying the young one between the thighs, pressed close to her breast and clasped firmly in her claws. The bird was flying well and did not seem embarrassed by the extra load it was carrying.

"In this case, the woodcock's bill was only used to get the chick into position before rising from the ground; it was certainly not used at all as an aid in carrying it. The old bird held her head in the normal flying position and could move it at will. The neck was not arched and the whole bill was clearly visible, pointing straight downwards. The chick's bill was just discernible protruding from the parent's breast."

This is a remarkably detailed and very important account of a woodcock airlift, although I have doubts about Seigne's statement that the adult bird's head "was in the normal flying position" if its bill was indeed "pointing straight downwards". A woodcock flying in the normal way does not point its bill vertically downwards at an angle of 90° to the axis of its body. The bill is usually held at a shallow downward-pointing angle in normal flight.

Seigne was in regular contact with a number of other woodcock enthusiasts in the inter-war period and had a number of eyewitness accounts from reliable observers. These included a number of instances where the adult bird was "carrying two chicks away at the same time, one in each claw", but he believed that this was a rare event, and that woodcock would probably "only perform this feat when danger threatened the family, and for a very short distance, just far enough to get them into safety."

Especially interesting are the reports he gathered in which "the bill is undoubtedly used in some way as a prehensile organ". From his analysis of these sightings he concluded that "first of all on the ground the chick is lifted by its [i.e. the bill's] aid in a series of short, quick, hitching movements until it is under her neck. The bird then rises, carrying her young one in this position with her head bent and the bill used as an additional support." He had received a particularly detailed description of this from Sir William MacEwen who described the carrying bird's attitude in this way:

"The neck is arched, the head stiff and the eyes look downward. Even when turning to look at anything it keeps the head fixed and turns the whole body like a person with a 'crick' in the neck."

Allan Allison, the well-known taxidermist and naturalist, has given me details of the successive carrying of several chicks, a sighting made by his mentor and friend, the late Ernest Blezard, a noted Cumbrian taxidermist and a particular authority on the birds of north-west England. Blezard was fortunate to see events at the closest possible distance, which further rules out any chances of his having been mistaken. In a small wood near Dalston he came upon a woodcock brooding four small chicks, and the adult bird rose and "immediately departed, obviously carrying one chick. Remaining standing quietly near the remaining three – *they were actually crouched between his feet!* – he was treated to the experience of the adult bird returning, shuffling down on the three chicks and then departing with another one."

When a naturalist or sportsman has lived for years in an area where woodcock are known to breed, has watched them roding and often found their nests, eggs and young, but has never actually witnessed the "woodcock airlift", he may not unnaturally be rather sceptical about it. Every time this topic is aired it is clear that there are a great many enthusiasts who fall into this category, but most of them are ready, like Gilbert White, to accept that it can and does happen, even though the sight may so far have been denied to them.

Arthur Cadman, a professional forester and a sportsman-naturalist of enormous experience, is one of those fortunate people whose working and leisure time has largely been spent out of doors, much of it in or close to woodlands where woodcock nest. Over half a century of careful observation has resulted in Arthur's having clearly seen a woodcock carrying a chick on four occasions, and he has kindly given me written accounts of each of these events.

The first was in July, 1937, in a plantation of 12-year-old Douglas Fir near Machynlleth in mid-Wales, when he saw what appeared to be a brood of almost fully grown and well feathered young woodcock on a path some twenty yards ahead. "Suddenly one, presumably the adult female, took off carrying another hanging full length between her legs. It could hardly fly and flew heavily eighteen inches above the ground."

Arthur Cadman's second sighting came almost two years later, in June, 1939, when he was accompanied by Frank Best, another well-known and widely experienced sportsman. In a well-grown plantation near Bettws-y-Coed a woodcock rose from the bare forest floor "carrying a small young one between its legs which were outstretched."

Almost thirty years later, while roe-stalking in Ringwood Forest in Hampshire in 1968, Arthur "saw a roe cross the ride and put up a woodcock.

Roland Green's dashing study of a woodcock carrying a chick. The position of the chick held between the adult's legs and pressed against its belly conforms with most good accounts of how woodcock carry their young.

Presently the woodcock returned to the same spot. When, stalking slowly behind cover, I reached the place the woodcock got up some ten feet away with a young chick, perhaps two weeks old, held clearly in her outstretched legs. The chick's legs were also hanging."

Most recent of Arthur Cadman's sightings was in 1970 at Novar in Ross-shire, when he was driving in a Land Rover through a young plantation of five-year-old conifers at an altitude of about 1000 feet. Twenty yards ahead of the vehicle a woodcock rose from the bare forest track "carrying a young one, adult's legs dangling". Here we have four clear sightings, and it is interesting to note that in three cases the adult bird was flushed from ground which was virtually bare of vegetation. If we assume that carrying in each of these instances was the adult bird's response to disturbance and a potential threat to her young, it is interesting to consider whether or not she would have gathered up her youngster and flown off had there had been cover close by, in which mother and young could have hidden.

In September, 1984, Mr B. Redfearn, a gamekeeper living near Preston in Lancashire, wrote to me describing how, in the course of his rounds, he came upon a well-grown brood of four young woodcock, three of which took flight "from almost under my feet... and then to my right, no more than a few feet away, I saw an adult bird carrying a fourth bird. The young bird was being carried between the legs of the adult, but the sheer size and weight of the young bird enabled it to be carried no more than twenty-five yards. At this point both birds landed rather clumsily. Standing quite still, my eyes fixed to the point of impact, the adult bird became invisible almost at once, but then the young birds commenced to raise both wings and walk about in circles, becoming increasingly vocal. The best way I can explain this is that they were like young pigeons demanding attention from their parents. The voice, however, was quite different, more like that of young jays."

Mr Redfearn was unsure if the cries of the young were intended to attract the adult bird's attention or were an alarmed reaction to his own presence, but he eventually saw one of the young woodcock making towards the spot where the parent bird had landed. At this point he withdrew to allow the family group to re-assemble.

The European woodcock's range extends right across Asia as far as the Pacific coast, and Colin Foote is a widely travelled sportsman who has regularly watched woodcock in India and the Nepalese highlands. But his sightings of woodcock carrying their young have all been much closer to home. All three incidents took place in Argyllshire in the late 1970s, and included one particularly clear and close view of the adult and the chick it was carrying, silhouetted against a clear sky between the trees. In each case the

chick was seen to be carried between the adult's thighs, with the adults' legs hanging straight down and their flight slow and much more awkward than normal. One of these sightings was in a relatively clear and open area. The adult landed with the chick, which scuttled quickly into cover, and she then flew on for a further twenty-five or thirty yards "where she proceeded to squeal and shout, wings beating as if in its death throes. The adult bird then got up, fluffed her feathers and ran into cover.... I saw a woodcock do the same 'dying bird' stunt when inadvertently we flushed her from a nest close to a track.... There were three newly hatched chicks and an egg in that nest."

My friend Major Lionel Currie has given me a written account of his own experience of the woodcock airlift, witnessed some years ago when he was based in Co. Offaly in the Irish midlands. "My English setter froze at the base of a birch tree. As I approached the spot a woodcock rose from the ground with a very laboured flight and flew about thirty yards before dropping into cover. The bird flew across my line of vision and at one time was not more than five yards away. I clearly saw the chick which appeared to be grasped by the claws of the parent. It was held quite close to the breast of the parent and was not dangling from the legs, as I have heard sometimes happens. The bird I saw was not suddenly startled as, I suppose, is often the case, which may account for the pretty firm grip which the parent appeared to have on the chick. After seeing the phenomenon I examined the spot where the bird had left and saw three woodcock chicks in a nest." Here, once again, we have an unequivocal eyewitness account of a carrying incident from someone whom I know to be a most meticulous observer.

Birch trees were also the dominant vegetation in a wooded area in Sutherland where Sir Derek Barber, now Chairman of the Countryside Commission, saw a woodcock carry off three chicks in succession. This was in May, 1962, and he saw the bird rise within a few yards of where he stood, on each occasion clearly grasping the chick between her thighs, and returning to airlift all three chicks one after another.

This is only a small selection of the many accounts, historical and recent, of adult woodcock carrying their chicks away from disturbance and potential danger. So many excellent eyewitness accounts by reliable observers build up a quite incontestable body of evidence that woodcock can and will, on occasion, resort to carrying their chicks when danger threatens.

Carrying is also known to be one means by which adult woodcock manage to get their chicks across or over obstacles which the flightless chicks could not negotiate by themselves. Woodcock nests have been found in walled gardens and other areas surrounded by high walls or wire-netting fences. Walls have been overcome by the adult airlifting her chicks, but wire netting seems to represent a more difficult problem. The BTO Inquiry received several reports of woodcock trying in vain to find a gap in the mesh of wire netting through which to lead their chicks, and making no attempt to airlift the chicks out over the top of the wire. The sceptical Tom Speedy used a long roll of wire netting to try to confirm his stubborn conviction that no woodcock *ever* carries its young.

Knowing that the Buccleuch coverts at Bowhill held a good number of nesting woodcock, Speedy went there, located a nest with the hen bird incubating her eggs, and surrounded the spot with a fifty-yard roll of small-mesh wire netting eighteen inches high. He thoughtfully placed fronds of dead bracken along the top of the wire to minimize the chances of the adult bird colliding with the wire if she flew off the nest in poor light. For the last ten days before her eggs hatched the adult was seen to fly in and out of the enclosure to feed, but when her chicks hatched she made no attempt to carry them over this barrier. She was seen to walk round and round the enclosure with her youngsters for two days and on the third the chicks were found to be still inside the wire, apparently not starving but nevertheless obviously dying of cold and exposure, while the adult bird "was observed outside the netting sitting disconsolate-looking and gazing inwards" at her languishing brood. The comparatively low barrier of wire netting, only eighteen inches high, had been too much for the chicks and Speedy concluded with some satisfaction that, while this did not prove that no woodcock ever carries its young, it at least proved that this particular individual did not do so!

Another confirmed sceptic, and a man out of the same mould as Tom Speedy, was Dugald MacIntyre, a highland gamekeeper of long experience and author of several books, including *Nature Notes of a Highland Gamekeeper* (1960). He too knew Alex Fraser, who was head-keeper on the Allan family's Aros estate near Tobermory on the island of Mull for a period of some fifty years from 1872. MacIntyre met and got to know Fraser in 1925, when the former had just retired from keepering. Like Speedy, he too was told of Fraser's experiment in which a woodcock's nest was surrounded by

One of the greatest sceptics about woodcock carrying chicks, Alexander Fraser was head keeper on the Aros estate on Mull; and despite a lifetime's experience of watching breeding young woodcock he remained adamant that they never carry their young.

two-foot-high wire netting and cites that adult's failure to airlift its young out of this enclosure as evidence that carrying *never* happens. MacIntyre mentions seeing a lapwing rising with a young chick which it quickly dropped, and also describes how a cock grouse was once seen to rise from brooding some chicks and to fly some distance with a tiny chick clinging to it – both mere accidents, in his view, and indeed this was probably so in the case of the grouse. The lapwing, however, may have had a more positive intention than he attributes to it, but his adamant conviction is that "woodcock do not carry their young as of *set purpose*" but only by accident.

In his uncompromising dismissal of chick-carrying, Dugald MacIntyre also invoked the experiences of a head-keeper on a Ross-shire estate where woodcock nested in large numbers. He had ringed woodcock chicks each year, and "used to chase the old birds to make out whether they really had a young bird between their legs, but never had any success".

Very interestingly, MacIntyre records a number of sightings of cock grouse, when suddenly disturbed, flying off with a chick clinging or sticking to it, and accounts for this by reminding us that chicks "are wet and sticky when newly out of the shell, hence the occasional quite unintentioned carrying of a chick". The undoubted wetness or stickiness of the very recently hatched chick may perhaps cause it to adhere briefly and insecurely to the plumage of an adult bird, but that can only apply for a very short time after hatching. Woodcock are precocial as chicks, fairly quick to dry out after hatching and soon busily on the move around the nest site. MacIntyre's argument certainly does not explain away the many very detailed accounts of well-grown and almost mature woodcock chicks being carried, nor does it explain away the sightings of adult woodcock carrying off several young in succession.

Apart from admitting the possibility that a damp and sticky youngster might have sufficient adhesion to cause it to be lifted into the air by a rising adult, MacIntyre's conviction is that all sightings of alleged carrying can be accounted for by distraction displays, and particularly by the depressed-tail and trailing-legs postures, combined with slow and apparently labouring flight. He describes these displays and movements in some detail in his attempts to dispose of what he believed to be the woodcock-carrying heresy, and has thus left us very valuable descriptions of the ways in which woodcock will try to distract a potential predator when danger threatens the young ones.

But will woodcock carry their chicks on other occasions, and for other reasons? What about that firm claim made by Charles St John that woodcock will carry their young from the dry vicinity of the nest down to damper ground to feed?

Like many Scots and Irish woodcock enthusiasts, Charles St John found some nests in long heather growing on dry ground. He naturally assumed that woodcock feed in damp, muddy areas and concluded that in some instances chicks could not reach marshy or boggy feeding grounds at some distance from the nest without being transported there by the adult bird. His ideas were supported by a number of correspondents to the BTO Inquiry, including several who claimed to have seen woodcock carrying chicks regularly from dry daytime nesting sites to boggy areas at dusk, and back again at first light.

These reports came from Inverness-shire, Sutherland and Argyllshire in Scotland, and County Fermanagh in Northern Ireland. There, at Kesh on the north-west shore of Lower Lough Erne, Colonel Clifford reported to the Inquiry that a woodcock was seen carrying a chick at about 9 pm on a June evening in 1933 and transporting it to an island in the lough a quarter of a mile or so away, where the ground was soft and boggy. Another contributor, a land agent at Killarney in the extreme south-west of Ireland, wrote that the adult birds there moved their chicks to damp areas, and if necessary moved them repeatedly if areas dried out and became unsuitable for feeding.

Recent research has confirmed that woodock feed primarily on worms and other invertebrates, including insect larvae, but it is difficult to reconcile this dietary preference with the fact that many woodcock regularly nest, in increasing numbers, in conifer forests on blanket peat and other acidic soils, which support only very low levels of invertebrates. Often these plantations are comparatively close to areas of permanent pasture and heavy, wet soil rich in worms and other suitable food, and it is common for the sportsman to find good woodcock shooting along the fringes of these woodlands, where the birds roost during the daylight hours and flight down to the pastures and boggy meadows to feed by night. When young woodcock hatch out in nests in these woods there can be little or no suitable food in the immediate vicinity of the nest site. In the first days after hatching the adult probably provides sufficient food for her chicks by regurgitating material which she has found and eaten at some distance from the nest. Various observers have seen woodcock regurgitate pre-digested food for very young chicks. But young woodcock grow quickly and are greedy feeders, and carrying may be one means whereby the adult bird gets its young to areas where they can probe in mud and ooze and feed freely for themselves, which may be a less labour-intensive way of ensuring the young are adequately fed.

Perhaps this was what prompted a woodcock to carry her chick at dusk from a copse in Surrey, as observed by Mr R.G. Schaub some years ago. After an evening's pigeon shooting he was leaving a small wood and, looking back, saw a woodcock flying out of the copse towards him, "not ten yards from the ground. She flew over my head and headed for a wood two fields distant. The adult bird carried her chick with ease between her thighs, tucked closely and snugly to her underneath. The chick was not concerned and moved its head from side to side in a nonchalant manner."

The distribution of breeding woodcock in Britain and Ireland has expanded steadily during the past century, and in many parts of Wales, Scotland, Ireland and northern England there is a direct link with the extensive planting of vast areas of new conifer forest. These have created large acreages of suitable daytime roosting habitat for wintering 'cock, and the proximity of wet pastures and hill grazings provides ample food for birds which flight out, in the usual manner, at dusk to feed during the night. Graham Hirons' breeding season studies were carried out in predominantly broadleaved woodlands, where woodcock in the breeding season tended to feed in the immediate vicinity of the nest site during the day, and to sit tight on the nest during most or all of the night. But woodcock are not only wintering but also breeding in large numbers in coniferous woodlands planted on impoverished soils which simply do not sustain adequate numbers of worms and the other food items which woodcock need. In habitat like this the birds must adopt some alternative feeding strategy, perhaps along the lines of what Charles St John described in the early part of the last century.

In the 1920s and 1930s the late Major J.W. Seigne took a particular interest in woodcock breeding around his 400-acre property in the midlands of Ireland. His notes and observations are very important, and there is no denying his accuracy as a field naturalist and an acute observer of wildlife – although he occasionally drew some rather muddle-headed conclusions from what he saw. Seigne corresponded widely with others interested in woodcock and snipe, including the artist Philip Rickman who provided a watercolour frontispiece and two fine pencil sketches of woodcock for his *A Bird Watcher's Note Book* (1930).

Seigne's own observations made him quite certain that it is "a very common thing for woodcock to carry their young to adjoining feeding grounds, although, owing to the difficulty of observing these birds, not many people have actually seen it done". He often noticed that "when woodcock pass over my house in June, they are carrying something. They usually fly very low, but in the twilight it is impossible to make out what it is. Last June [1929?], not far from my place, a keeper fired at what, in the half-light, he took to be a hawk swooping into the dark firs, and killed a woodcock. He noticed that in falling the bird dropped something and, on searching the ground carefully, he picked up a dead woodcock chick."

In observing breeding woodcock around his own property Seigne came to the firm conclusion that the adults fed their young by carrying food to the vicinity of the nest for a period after hatching, but then changed tactics and carried the youngsters to the feeding grounds. After watching the woodcock which flew over his garden, heading from the coverts to the open fields, he remarked that "the birds are certainly carrying something, probably their young ones".

One has only to spend some time along the fringes of conifer plantations on acidic soils in the northern and western parts of Britain and Ireland towards dusk on spring or summer evenings and observe the levels of roding activity to appreciate that breeding woodcock are present in good numbers. High levels of roding activity can be seen where large expanses of even-aged growth have been broken up, perhaps by a clear-felled area, a replanted block, an area of wind-throw or simply along the forest edge – in fact, wherever an "edge effect" occurs. Only the highest forests and those planted on huge expanses of blanket bog far away from marshes, wet grassy fields, hill grazings or "white ground" will show little or no signs of woodcock breeding activity. Otherwise, where these sorts of worm-rich feeding areas are accessible, the forests will sustain breeding woodcock. There are few earthworms or other

Woodcock make extensive use of conifer plantations in northern and western areas, both in winter and as breeding grounds. Much has still to be learned about the ecology of woodcock in this type of habitat. (From *Under the Moon,* a watercolour by Richard Robjent.)

invertebrates for the adult birds or their chicks on the bare and almost sterile floor of these conifer plantations. Do the adult birds feed by flighting out at dusk, like wintering woodcock? Do they move their chicks to better feeding grounds, and, if so, how? Do they airlift them, as Charles St John and J.W. Seigne have described? This is just one of many woodcock mysteries which remain to be answered by future research.

Despite the sceptics – and anyone who remains sceptical must have a quite wilful determination to ignore all this evidence and accumulated testimony – we can be sure that certain woodcock will carry their chicks on certain occasions, apparently in response to frightening stimuli, of which the disturbance caused by the approach of the observer or his dog is probably the commonest. But this, the simplest explanation of most of the sightings of woodcock carrying chicks, does not account for incidents of chicks being carried by undisturbed adults. Were these birds moving their young away from other forms of danger – perhaps a fox, or a wandering dog or other predator – or are there other "natural" reasons for the chick-carrying phenomenon? Only further research can provide the answers to these questions, and the whole puzzle of how young woodcock chicks hatched out in food-deficient areas such as blanket peat and deep heather find their way to suitable feeding grounds may be a good starting point for more study.

CHAPTER V

WOODCOCK MIGRATION

As woodcocks, when their plumes are grown,
Borne on the wind's wing and their own,
Forsake the countries where they're hatched,
And seek out others to be catched.

Samuel Butler (1612–1680)

"'Here today and gone tomorrow' is a woodcock's motto", according to those two pre-eminently successful "big shots" of the last century, Lord Walsingham and Sir Ralph Payne-Gallwey. Writing in the *Badminton Library* in 1889, they urged anyone finding his coverts suddenly full of 'cock to write to his shooting friends instantly: "Come without fail *tomorrow morning*. One of my woods is *now* full of 'cock, but may not be the day *after tomorrow*." That example of how to phrase your invitation was dated "Sunday": had the fall been discovered on any other day of the week, invitations would certainly have been sent by urgent messenger – "*Come this afternoon*"! The letter ends, "P.S. We once hit off a flight of cocks in this wood some years ago, and got eighteen couple; and though we went again to it on the next day we got none!" That Victorian advice will strike a chord with most of today's woodcock enthusiasts, who have probably experienced something similar.

Some populations of the European woodcock are largely sedentary, breeding and wintering in much the same places throughout the year. But over most of the bird's enormous range in Europe, Asia and northern Africa woodcock are very migratory in their habits. This is reflected even in the way we talk about them: we refer to "a *fall* of woodcock", an ancient term first

recorded in print in 1486 in *The Boke of St Albans*, the first book about field sports to be printed in English. A "fall" is an apt and vivid word to describe the sudden and unheralded arrival, often during the night, of large numbers of migrant woodcock which literally drop into an area where none may have been seen for weeks or months previously. These mass migrations are typical of woodcock behaviour over much of Europe. Shooting literature is full of references to gamekeepers and landowners who have walked out one morning to find the woods, hedgerows and coverts full of 'cock, where there had been none the previous day.

In Britain and Ireland such falls of woodcock have usually been seen first each autumn along the eastern coasts, often around the time of the full moon in late October and again in November. To many shooters the full moon in November is "the woodcock moon", "*la lune des bécasses*" to French sportsmen, indicating the arrival of the largest falls of woodcock which annually come south from their breeding grounds in Scandinavia and northern Europe to spend the winter in the milder and predominantly frost-free climates of the British Isles, the Atlantic provinces of France and the countries around the Mediterranean.

Large and sudden falls of woodcock, especially when these occur on our eastern seaboard, may mean that the birds are only passing through, resting and probably feeding greedily to recover their energy before flying on with only a few days stop-over, eventually to disperse widely across the country – hence the enthusiastic haste of generations of woodcock shooters to make a bag before the birds move on. Some of the largest bags of woodcock in England (with the notable exception of the specialized woodcock shoots of Cornwall) have been made on the great shoots of north Norfolk and also in parts of Lincolnshire and in Northumberland. These are primarily pheasant shoots, where no particular effort is made to manage the coverts specially for woodcock: nor is that necessary, for the woodcock come annually in large numbers in any case. The east coast is their first landfall after crossing the North Sea, and big falls of 'cock can be counted upon each season. Woodcock show very rapid powers of recovery after an exhausting migration flight and, with mild weather and given access to plenty of food, they will be as plump and fast on the wing as ever within a day of arriving. That is when shoots like Holkham, Melton Constable and the other celebrated East Anglian hot-spots for woodcock have traditionally been able to enjoy some superb woodcock shooting.

Several good accounts exist of woodcock being seen arriving on the eastern coast of England, especially in Norfolk. Robin Scott, editor of *Sporting Gun* magazine, told me how he was once fishing by night for cod on the north Norfolk coast, with a paraffin pressure lamp giving a bright light all night. It was a dark, moonless night, overcast and with a light breeze, and close to the time of the full moon in November. Robin was aware of various birds passing low overhead in small groups throughout the night, and their shapes could just be distinguished in the light of the pressure lamp. They were flying quite low and silently, and he was eventually able to see that they were woodcock. Most seemed to pitch down into a large marshy area just inland, a short distance from the beach.

Some woodcock enthusiasts could not contain their excitement when the first falls of 'cock arrived. The redoubtable Colonel Hawker is said to have seen a woodcock land near his house while he was dressing one morning. Half-dressed and half-shaved, he grabbed his fowling piece (one imagines he always had it, ready loaded, at his side) and rushed out and shot it.

Sir Samuel Hoare (later the first Viscount Templewood) tells in his delightful account of his family's generations of life and sport, *The Unbroken*

Woodcock will make a landfall, often by moonlight, and rest close to the coast when they arrive after a prolonged migration flight across open sea. (From watercolour studies by Richard Robjent and Philip Rickman.)

Thread (1949), of how his ancestor Gurney Hoare was taking a bath when a woodcock alighted on the lawn of his house at Cromer in north Norfolk. Without pausing to dress he rushed out, gun in hand, and shot it. He was eventually buried in Beeston churchyard close to the cliff edge, so as to lay his bones as close as possible to the point where migrant woodcock first alight on the coast after crossing the North Sea.

The big days at 'cock in the eastern counties are almost always made when the woodcock population, though big, is transient. In this important respect they differ from the woodcock shoots of Cornwall, west Wales and Ireland. There the birds have come to the end of their south-westerly progress and settled down to a more or less sedentary life in coverts which were traditionally managed with woodcock shooting in mind, and sometimes still are. The Victorian shoot owners found that, once arrived in their westerly winter quarters, woodcock would not co-exist in any numbers with lots of pheasants, and many projects to run western estates as pheasant shoots were quickly abandoned. The biggest landowners, who were usually absentees, felt it was better to keep their western estates for woodcock and concentrate their pheasant shooting in eastern and southern England.

Broadly speaking, there are two sorts of woodcock migration – "distance migration" or the regular annual movements of whole populations of birds over long distances from breeding areas to suitable wintering areas, in which they will remain more or less sedentary until return migration takes place in early spring; and "weather migration", when wintering woodcock are forced by changes in weather, usually uncharacteristically severe frost and snow, to move to milder parts if they are to survive. There may also be a third type of movement by woodcock, which might be called a form of migration, which is the dispersal or relocation of adults and their young in late summer, after nesting and before the autumn migration proper begins. But this is really best considered as an aspect of the woodcock's nesting behaviour and has been discussed in the chapter on woodcock at the nest.

"Weather migration" may be a very short-range affair, perhaps involving nothing more than a movement of 'cock from exposed plantations or other cover at a moderate altitude, down to lower and more sheltered areas, where the frost is less severe and the ground sufficiently unfrozen to let the birds feed more freely. It can also mean the large-scale movements of huge numbers of woodcock and wetland birds across much of Europe and the British Isles, as happened in the prolonged freeze-ups of 1963 and 1981–82. But here we are concerned primarily with the birds' longer and more regular annual movements.

Most of the woodcock you flush on a winter's shooting day in Britain and Ireland have come here on migration from Scandinavia, the states of the eastern Baltic and other parts of northern and central Europe. That seems like stating the obvious: it has been common knowledge among sportsmen and naturalists for centuries. Richard Mant, in his excellent doggerel poem about woodcock written in the 1800s, describes them as coming "from the Baltic's sounding shores" and his contemporary, John Gisborne, described the migrant woodcock as:

> ... she, who in Norwegian dells,
> Or birchen glades Lapponian, near the swamp,
> Sucked from the spongy soil the prey, to cheer
> Her russett young; till winter's icy car
> On summer's step close pressing, from her realm
> Warned her.

Despite the poetic tone, too over-blown for modern tastes, these sporting versifiers were on the right lines.

Until the woodcocks' breeding range in western Europe expanded from the late eighteenth century onwards to include most parts of the British Isles, almost all our wintering 'cock were migrants. Indeed, some country folk and sportsmen actually believed that all woodcock seen and shot in Britain and Ireland were *males*. (That curious belief, if true, would at least have explained why woodcock allegedly did not breed here!) But however obvious and well known the Scandinavian migration may have been, it was not until quite recently that the hard scientific evidence existed to prove it.

Many aspects of bird migration are still a mystery, and the whole affair was often totally baffling to earlier generations. In the 1770s Gilbert White of Selborne solemnly considered whether swallows might perhaps spend the

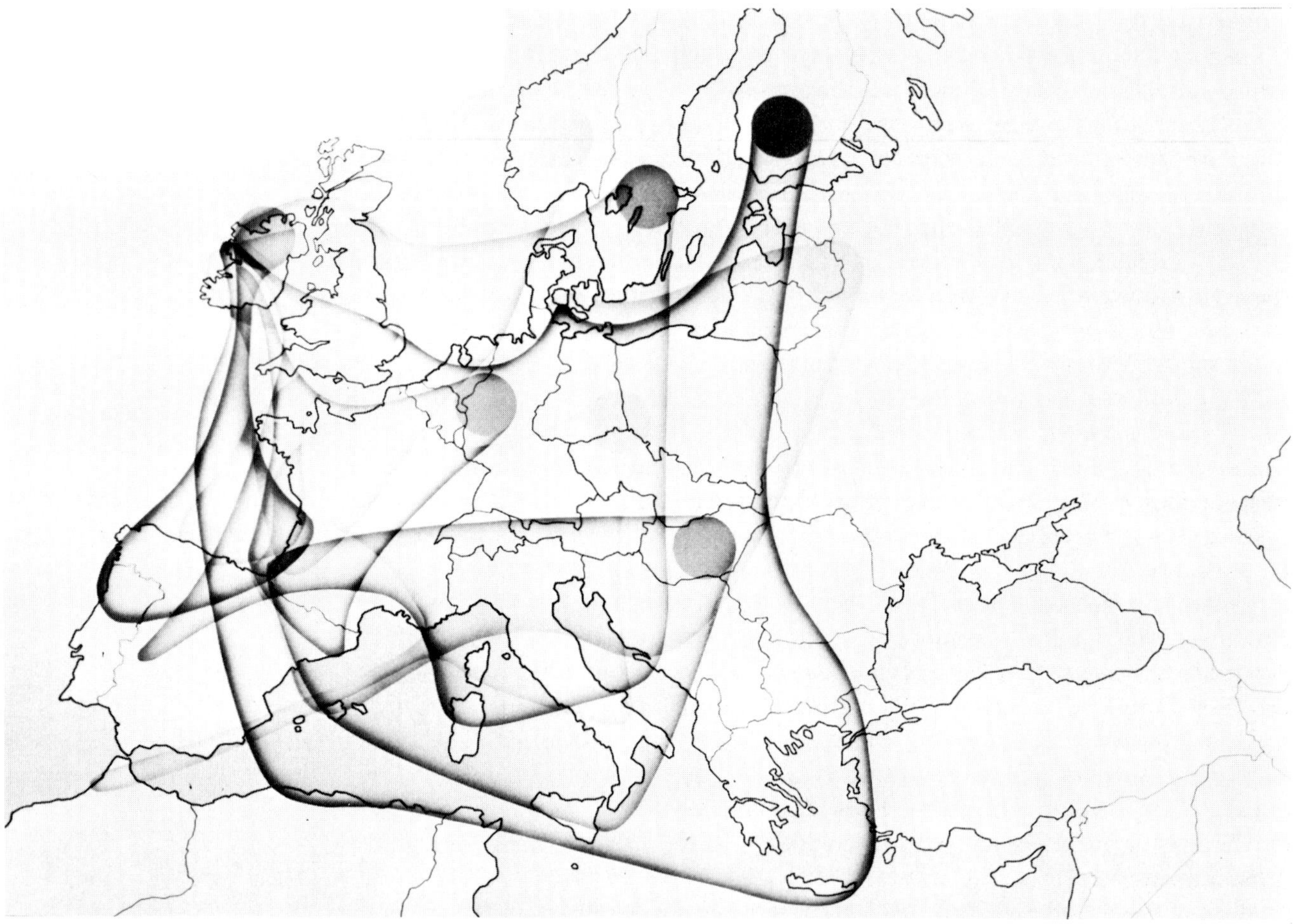

The circles indicate woodcock breeding grounds and from these flow the winter recovery areas of woodcock ringed in each area. Woodcock bred in Finland appear to disperse more widely than those from other breeding areas. (Diagram after H. Kalchreuter.)

winter on the moon, or on the bottom of ponds and lakes. Of woodcock, the Augustan poet John Gay (1685–1732) was more on the right lines, but was equally prepared to consider that woodcock flew off to the moon in summer, when he wrote:

> Some think to northern coasts their flight they tend,
> Or to the moon in midnight hours ascend.

Ambrose Philips (1675–1749) was another sporting-minded poet of the same period, who gave quite an accurate description of how woodcock come to milder winter climates before returning to breed in northern Europe, rightly regarding the woodcock as a bird of the "frost fringe" of Europe and, unusually for that period, he even credits the proverbially stupid bird with some brains:

> ... he, of times
> Intelligent, the harsh hyperborean ice
> Shuns for our equal winters: when our suns
> Cleave the chill'd soil, he backward wings his way
> To Scandinavian frozen summers, meet
> For his numb'd blood.

Gilbert White's friend and correspondent, the Hon Daines Barrington, did not believe in migration, and wrote an essay about it. The whole question of bird movements aroused interest among intelligent men of the time, and even the great Dr Samuel Johnson pronounced on woodcock migration – with characteristic bluntness – in a conversation recorded by Boswell on 7 May,

1773. At a dinner given by some London booksellers, Johnson and Boswell found themselves in the company of several other well-read and eminent men on the London scene. This strangely assorted company included the Rev Augustus Toplady, whose famous hymn "Rock of Ages" was published in 1775, and another *alumnus* of Trinity College, Dublin, Oliver Goldsmith. We tend to think of him as primarily a playwright and poet, but he published an encyclopedia of natural history and "animated nature" in the following year, just before his death, and was hard at work on it at this time. Perhaps it was Goldsmith who turned the table-talk to birds and their migrations, and we know that Johnson had already talked to Boswell five years previously about woodcock migrating across the North Sea.

"I think we have as good evidence for the migration of woodcocks as can be desired," pronounced Johnson. "We find they disappear at a certain time of the year, and appear again at a certain time of the year; and some of them, when weary in their flight, have been known to alight on the rigging of ships far out at sea." Someone interposed the remark that woodcock had been found in Essex in summer, but Johnson was not to be gainsaid. "Sir, that strengthens our argument. *Exceptio probat regulam*. Some being found shews that, if all remained, many would be found. A few sick or lame ones may be found." His last comment summed up the British sportsman's opinion for some time afterwards, and it was generally believed that only those birds too weak, ill or injured to migrate would remain in the British Isles in summer.

The Rev William Daniel, writing in 1801, said that "the time of their appearance and disappearance in Sweden coincides exactly with that of their arrival in and return from Great Britain" and refers specifically to the annual falls of migrant 'cock seen on the coast of East Anglia. "Their autumnal and vernal appearances on the coast of Suffolk has been accurately noted.... A similar abundance is found (at the same periods of their approach and retiring) upon the Essex coast, especially in the large woods at St Osyth.... When the redwing appears in autumn on the Suffolk coast, the woodcocks are certainly at hand.... Between the twelfth and twenty-fifth of March, they throng towards the coast, to be ready for their departure; the first Law of Nature bringing them in Autumn; the second carrying them from us in Spring."

Those are very precise dates, but the reverend writer was not sticking his neck out any further than Dugald MacIntyre who, writing in the 1950s, gave 20 October as the key date each year to watch out for migrant woodcock in Kintyre, in south-west Scotland. So confident was he that he had set out that morning to shoot a bag of 'cock for dispatch to England. The morning did not reveal a sign of a bird, but they dropped in right on cue that afternoon "and, going over the glens which had been empty of cock in the forenoon, I bagged my complement of six in an hour". MacIntyre felt these were long-range migrants from Scandinavia, but the evidence from ringed birds suggests this is usually too early to expect Fenno-Scandian woodcock that far west.

William Daniel, though he committed himself to those return migration dates, covered himself by adding that, however, "the sportsmen on the coast, for some years together, know not precisely the time of the woodcocks departing.... If the wind be propitious, they are gone immediately; but if contrary, they are detained in the neighbouring woods, or among the ling and furze on the coast." This apparently signalled a seasonal 'cock shooting bonanza for the local sportsmen, legitimate and otherwise, and "the whole country around echoes with the discharge of guns.... The instant a fair wind springs up, they seize the opportunity, and where the sportsman has seen hundreds one day, he will not find a single bird the next."

The waiting guns of east coast sportsmen were not the only hazard for migrant birds. Adverse weather, especially contrary gales from the west and

south-west, sometimes combined with the disorientating effects of thick snow or fog, could cause woodcock "wrecks". There are scattered reports of sailors seeing "an acre of woodcock" floating on the sea, dead or dying from exhaustion. A severe storm in the autumn of 1928 resulted in a major woodcock wreck, described by J.W. Seigne: "There were literally thousands of woodcock drowned off the Lowestoft-Yarmouth area, and, where they lay thick on the ebb-tide, one fishing boat alone picked up 470 and sent them to the London market." Lord Margadale has told me that his uncle, the late Lord Granville, saw several woodcock wrecks involving large numbers of birds at migration time, while he was serving on naval patrols in the North Sea in wartime. He also saw a large migratory party of woodcock flying westwards over the North Sea at a height of six or eight feet above the waves, and using his ship's navigational instruments he was able to estimate that those birds would make their landfall in England within about three hours and close to Scarborough.

When woodcock migrate they seem to travel quite low, often only a few feet above the sea or the ground. How they take their bearings and the extent to which they travel in small groups or family parties and in larger flocks is not fully known.

There do seem to be some well-defined and well-established flight lines, however. Aylmer Tryon told me of an interesting instance of woodcock migration he once saw. He was shooting in Cambridgeshire in the 1930s and there was a thick mist, giving a maximum visibility of not more than a couple of hundred yards. He saw two or three woodcock flying low and in a straight line, passing between two prominent trees in an otherwise flat and featureless landscape, and disappearing into the murk, to be followed a minute or two later by another small party of 'cock, flying at the same height and speed, and apparently using the same trees as a bearing. Several more groups of two or three woodcock did the same thing over a period of some minutes, and the poor visibility was such that no group could have been following another, which would have been well ahead and far out of sight in the mist.

Even in fairly good weather migration must be an exhausting business. Charles St John wrote of how he heard from the captain of a merchant vessel plying between Britain and Scandinavia, who had "seen them, tired and exhausted, pitch for a moment or two with outspread wings in the smooth waters in the ship's wake; and having rested themselves for a few moments, continue their weary journey." There are also accounts of woodcock resting in mid-sea in the rigging of sailing ships, on the decks of cargo vessels and, more recently, on oil-drilling rigs in the North Sea.

At the beginning of the last century, like most sportsmen of his day, William Daniel knew from personal observations, general sporting lore and some exchange of ideas with European shooters that woodcock migrated in large numbers to Britain and Ireland from Scandinavia and northern Europe each autumn, returning in the spring. But he gave an unusual amount of intelligent and careful thought to the whole question of woodcock migration, how it happened and what routes the birds followed – questions which have still not been fully answered today. He accepted that a flight across the North Sea could bring woodcock from Norway and Sweden to England's eastern coast, and that migrants from "Polish Prussia, Russia" and "Kamtschatka" could come via the nearest points on the Scandinavian mainland. "But whence to Ireland, where they are much more numerous than in England? Do they first alight in Ireland, and then come to us? Or do they pass over from us to Ireland, and there continue as their *ne plus ultra*?" He goes on to dismiss the possibility of immigration from the west, with American woodcock coming to Ireland, since "our species of woodcock is unknown in that country; a kind is there found that has the general appearance of it, but which is scarce half the size".

We can tentatively answer some of the questions about migration which Daniel raised, thanks to information gathered in recent decades by the simple and familiar method of fitting markers, usually a metallic leg-band, on to individual woodcock. In bird-ringing, whatever the species, the date and place of marking and release are recorded, together with any other details which may be relevant or ascertainable, such as whether the individual bird is a chick, a juvenile or an adult. The sex of each bird ringed is normally noted, but this cannot be done with woodcock, owing to the lack of any reliable way of telling the sex of a woodcock from external physical characteristics.

With luck the band or ring may one day be recovered, to indicate the bird's movement from the point of ringing to the point of recovery, and revealing

A woodcock in the hand – what can we learn from it? This bird flew croaking into a mist net at dusk in March, so it is a male. Before it was ringed and released its bill (70mm) and wings (187mm) were measured, and its weight noted (265 grams). Recoveries of ringed woodcock are the best means of learning about the species' movements.

also how long the bird has been flying free since it was ringed. Not surprisingly, since it is a very sought-after sporting bird, the overwhelming majority of ringed woodcock are recovered by shooting, but there have been some instances of successive live recoveries of the same woodcock, usually in mist nets.

There is nothing new about the principle of ringing or marking a bird. Aristotle knew about it; the medieval falconers did it, both to hawks and quarry released alive; and one obscure Worcestershire parson in the 1680s actually used to amuse himself by catching partridges and "letting them go withe ringes". But organized, systematic bird-ringing or bird-banding in the developed nations is really a post-war activity, which is organized on a national or regional basis by about twenty-five different organizations in western Europe alone.

In the past different countries and organizations have adopted different methods and systems of recording and publishing their data from ringing recoveries. This can cause confusion and obscures the general picture of how birds migrate. There are obvious advantages in having a uniform international system to co-ordinated bird-ringing, and this was the intention behind the setting up in 1969 of the European Union for Bird Ringing (EURING), based in the Netherlands. This system has already helped to create a more uniform approach to ringing, and in time it should help to iron out many of the anomalies and biases which exist in the confused data drawn from past ringing schemes. The importance of this is obvious, when one realizes that a woodcock ringed as a chick in southern Belgium, for example, and shot that autumn a few miles away across the French border has in the past probably been recorded as an example of "international movement", while another chick, hatched near Paris and shot on the Mediterranean coast near Marseilles will not have been listed as a foreign recovery, although it has evidently made a major migration of hundreds of miles southwards.

A woodcock caught by accident in a rabbit net in Clenston Wood in Dorset in February, 1798, was marked with a brass ring and released from Whatcombe House, to be recovered the following December by the proprietor, Mr Pleydell, when shooting in the same wood. Another 'cock was caught in the same wood in February, 1802, and released with a date-engraved band of tin on its leg, to be shot the following December near where it was caught. These are early and interesting recoveries, but serious large-scale ringing of woodcock did not begin quite as long ago as that.

Probably the earliest and most important woodcock ringing programme in Britain began in Northumberland in 1891. Lord William Percy arranged for the keepers on the Alnwick estates, seat of the Percy family, Dukes of Northumberland, to make a point of looking for woodcock nests. Woodcock bred extensively in the Alnwick coverts, and a total of some 600 woodcock were ringed there between 1891 and 1921. These Alnwick rings were simply marked, bearing the letter "N" and the year of ringing – e.g. N 1891.

The pattern which emerged from recoveries of ringed birds from this estate in the extreme north-east of England came as a surprise to many people, who had expected these birds to move off southwards after fledging. In fact, the bulk of the recoveries were made locally, on shoots at Alnwick, and some were made after quite a few years had elapsed. One bird ringed in 1913 was shot in 1921, while another, shot in 1920, had been ringed near the same spot five years previously. (As regards woodcock longevity in general, if we dismiss one unconfirmed report of a ringed woodcock recovered after twenty years, the record age for a ringed bird seems to be thirteen years.)

Between 1898 and 1908 nine birds ringed as chicks at Alnwick were recovered on shoots in Ireland, mainly in the south and south-west, and in

The lower legs and feet of eight woodcock caught and ringed as chicks on the Duke of Northumberland's estate at Alnwick in the 1890s, and later shot nearby. This was one of the first and most important private woodcock ringing programmes in the British Isles. Most birds recovered were shot locally, but some were shot as far afield as Wexford and Cork, as recorded in the notes on this page of the Alnwick game book. (Photo: Lord Ralph Percy)

1907 four Alnwick birds were shot elsewhere in England, in Durham, Oxfordshire, Somerset and Cornwall, and single birds were also shot in the same year in Wales and in France. Over the years a handful of Alnwick birds were also recovered in Scotland, as far north as Angus. In general, however, the recoveries of Alnwick-ringed woodcock showed that the population was sedentary. In his 1945 Report, W.B. Alexander showed that of 128 woodcock ringed in northern England (including the Alnwick birds) and later recovered, 73% were found locally, 25% at some distance but still within the British Isles, and ony 2% abroad.

In Ireland in the 1920s there was an upsurge of interest in woodcock and their management and migration, thanks largely to the enthusiasm of two men, Major J.W. Seigne and Sir Basil Brooke Bt, later Prime Minister of Northern Ireland and the first Viscount Brookeborough.

Before his death in 1973 Lord Brookeborough told me about his efforts to build up the numbers of breeding and wintering woodcock at Colebrook, which had always been a good, though not outstanding woodcock shoot. His work included a systematic private ringing scheme which began in 1924, and 65 woodcock were ringed in the period 1924-28. Out of a total of 120 young woodcock ringed at Colebrook during the period 1924-33, 14 were shot on the estate, four on neighbouring properties up to ten miles away, and two others were recovered at distances of 50 and 60 miles respectively. Thus one bird in six ringed at Colebrook was recovered, a very high proportion and roughly double the general recovery rate of 7.9%, or about one bird in twelve, given by the British Trust for Ornithology. All the evidence points to the Colebrook birds as being predominantly sedentary.

Seigne, though he was the moving force behind several Irish ringing schemes, only ringed comparatively few woodcock on his small property in the midlands of Ireland. Of seven nestlings ringed, one was recovered a few miles away three years later, and there was another unconfirmed sighting of a live bird with a ring nearby. This is too small a sample to be statistically significant, but what evidence there is suggests that Seigne's birds may also have been sedentary.

Sir Basil Brooke's near neighbour, the Duke of Abercorn, had begun a ringing programme at his Baronscourt estate in County Tyrone as early as 1905, with rings marked "BC" and giving the date of ringing. Of these some were recovered as far south and east as Cornwall and Middlesex, and ringed birds from other estates on Ireland's Atlantic coast travelled still further afield.

Lissadell, the seat of the Gore-Booth family, was a top-class woodcock shoot, one of Ireland's best in the days before large-scale afforestation with conifers. Classiebawn Castle, owned by the Ashley family and later the summer home of the late Earl Mountbatten of Burma, is only a few miles to the north of Lissadell and both estates carried out some ringing in the period 1910-1936. Birds from both estates were recovered some distance to the east, in central Ulster, and two Classiebawn woodcock chicks were shot later the same year in Spain and France. But two other Classiebawn birds, both ringed as nestlings, went not south but north-east, one being shot in Midlothian in south-east Scotland, and the other falling to the gun of a Norwegian sportsman shooting roding 'cock at Frederickstad, south of Oslo. These are just two of several instances of Bitish-ringed nestlings being recovered to the north and west of the ringing point, which is untypical and unexpected, but "abmigration" has happened often enough to make it a significant aspect of British-bred woodcock movements, and still unexplained.

Further south and west from Classiebawn and Lissadell are the notable woodcock shoots of Temple House, County Sligo, and the Ashford Castle estate near Cong, County Galway, formerly the most famous and successful woodcock shoot in the world. Birds at both places were ringed, the Ashford birds bearing a simply-marked ring with the letter "G" (the Guinness family owned the estate) and the year. A nestling ringed at Cong in 1910 was shot that December in Portugal, while a Temple House bird was shot in Spain. Like two of the Classiebawn birds, these had evidently travelled far to the south to over-winter.

Last of these enterprising and remarkably widespread independent Irish ringing schemes are two ventures of which I have only been able to discover a little. One involved the activities of two army officers serving in Ireland, who jointly ringed 121 young woodcock during the period 1904-1910, 34 in Limerick and 87 near Clonmel, County Tipperary. In keeping with the general pattern for British- and Irish-bred woodcock, most of those recovered were

Temple House, County Sligo – seat of the Perceval family and a notable Irish woodcock shoot since early last century, when extensive planting and intensive keepering were implemented to encourage wintering woodcock.

shot locally. However, it is interesting that the eighteen birds recovered in Ireland were all shot before 10 September. No others were ever seen locally again. Far to the south and east, however, one was shot in October in the Netherlands and two of the Clonmel birds were shot on the same November day near Gibraltar. Clearly some Irish-bred woodcock are not sedentary but migrate south and south-east in autumn, while a few defy the normal pattern and actually move north-east.

The *Gamekeeper* magazine for February, 1903, carried a detailed report from a gamekeeper on an Ulster estate. He signs himself simply "R.T." and the estate is not identified. However, it must have been both sizeable and well known for its woodcock, for "R.T." talks of abundant woodcock – "hundreds breed each year" – and "over 400 were killed on the place" in a season. (I suspect, but cannot prove, that this estate may have been Tynan Abbey, on the Armagh-Monaghan border, formerly the seat of the Stronge family.)

But wherever it was, "R.T." asserts that "all home-bred birds go away, but where I cannot say. One year an experiment was tried here. About 150 young woodcock were got before they could fly, and rings were put on their legs, just to see if they stopped in the country. Strange to say ... not one with a ring was got or ever heard of."

The British Trust for Ornithology, which oversees official ringing of birds in the United Kingdom, looked in some detail at existing ringing records in its woodcock investigation carried out by W.B. Alexander and completed in 1939, although the war delayed publication until 1945-47.

Like centuries of sportsmen and naturalists before them, Alexander's respondents confirmed that the first immigrant woodcock arrived in October and November, with tendency for arrivals in the early part of October to be reported from England and Wales, while Ireland and Scotland recorded their first arrivals in late October and early November. The general pattern pointed to two principal flights, coinciding with the full moon in October and a month later in November, with some evidence of a further top-up immigration of some woodcock in December.

The bright lights of lighthouses and lightships attract migrant birds of many species, and records kept by lighthouse keepers and lightship crews have added enormously to our knowledge of bird migration. Woodcock reports from lighthouses and lightships over the period 1879-1912 showed that numbers of migrant woodcock peaked around Great Britain, especially along the eastern coast, in the period 21-31 October, tailing off markedly after 20 November. This was in line with reports from generations of countrymen and sportsmen living along the east coast, and the accounts of sailors on the North Sea who had seen woodcock heading in a westerly or south-westerly direction from mainland Europe towards Britain.

Bright light can evidently have a disorientating effect on migrating woodcock. J.W. Seigne describes how the lights of Kilkenny, near his Irish estate, seemed to draw woodcock close to the town during a migration, and *La Mordorée* published an interesting account of woodcock which flew into the brightly lit bowl of a football stadium in France, where a game was in progress during a snow-storm. The unfortunate bird flew round and round, evidently quite disorientated by the combination of bright lights and flurries of snow within a semi-enclosed area. It is not difficult to understand how this can happen. Next time you are out on a snowy night, look up though the flakes and you will appreciate how the movement of the snowflakes disrupts your sense of distance, direction and perspective.

To the well-established attractions of lightships and lighthouses we must now add the bright flares of many oil-drilling platforms, which are strung out across the North Sea from Scotland towards Norway. Woodcock are a common

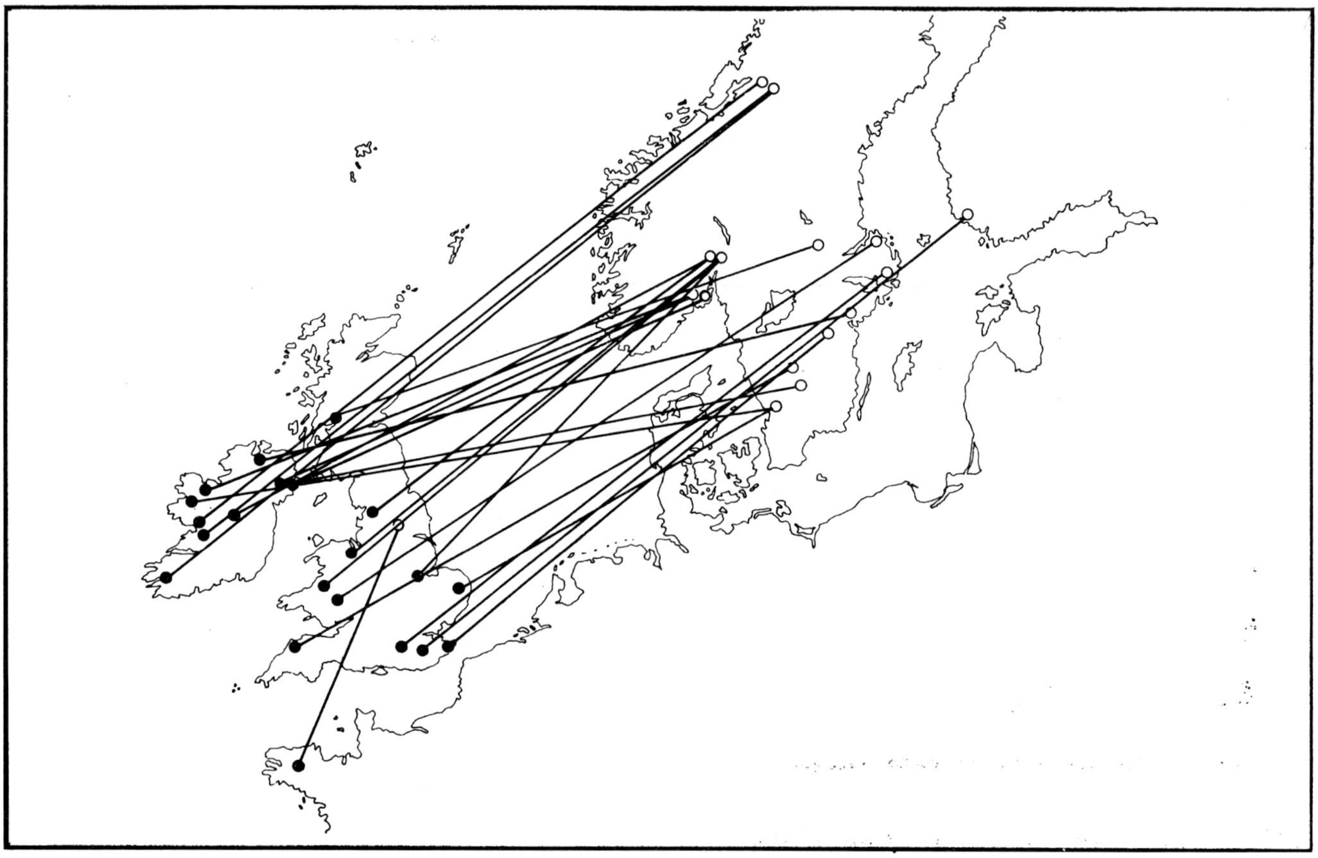

The autumn migration of young woodcock. This diagram is based on ringing recoveries during the period 1927–1970, and all these birds were ringed as chicks.

occurrence around these rigs at migration time in spring and autumn, often dropping down to rest on the platforms. Two such birds achieved brief fame when they were found, tired but otherwise intact, on the "Shell Esso Fulmar Alpha" drilling platform off north-east Scotland on 17 November, 1985. These lucky birds were treated as VIPs and conveyed by Chinook helicopter to be released at Aberdeen. The event was recorded with a snapshot which was later published in *Shooting Times.*

Records from Irish lights showed a different pattern from those around Britain, with two distinct and later peaks occurring from 11-20 November and again from 1-10 December. It is interesting to note that while England's eastern seaboard has always been noted for large falls of 'cock in autumn, it was Ireland's western lights which recorded by far the greatest numbers of migrant woodcock, much more than those at northern, eastern or southern lights. These birds were apparently making their landfall in Ireland by coming in from the west, rather than along what would seem to be the direct route from the north-east.

There have been a number of other reports of large falls of woodcock arriving in western parts of Ireland and Britain from a westerly direction, including various instances in Cornwall and the Scilly Isles, and the Atlantic coasts of Ireland and Scotland. In 1889 Payne-Gallwey wrote of how he had seen migrant woodcock arrive "during a westerly gale in large numbers and quite exhausted". This he attributed to the birds' having overshot the British Isles and flown back, assisted by a westerly gale into which they had previously been battling, or perhaps to some migration flight-line along the western coasts, with birds reluctant to fly further out over the ocean where there was no destination in prospect.

Many aspects of woodcock migration remain a mystery, both in western Europe and elsewhere in the species' wide range. Only more extensive and more co-ordinated ringing will fill the gaps in our knowledge and give a

clearer picture of what actually happens. Meantime, all the evidence seems to point to some sort of general pattern of migration by birds which have been breeding or have just been hatched in Scandinavia or the eastern Baltic south-west in autumn towards Britain and Ireland. In this outward migration the birds appear to move on a broad front, sometimes singly or in small groups and on other occasions in large parties of a hundred or more, following the western coast of mainland Europe before swinging westwards across the North Sea or the English Channel. Their return journey in spring seems to be much more direct, but to take place without particular signs of large numbers of birds collecting together, although this has been seen occasionally along the east coast.

Although ringing remains the principal way of determining woodcock movements, there may be alternatives, or at any rate it may be possible to use additional techniques to supplement ringing returns.

Woodcock, like most birds, carry internal parasites, including various types of worms in the gut. The types and relative proportions of these endoparasites may be influenced by the birds' area of origin. For example, a woodcock hatched in Finland and shot in Cornwall may have a different endoparasite burden from a woodcock hatched in northern Germany and shot on the same shoot on the same day. Robin Knowles of the British Museum of Natural History has already made a preliminary study of the various endoparasites which can be found in woodcock. If this can be developed further so as to give some indication of the parasites typical of woodcock from various specific geographical areas, it may be a useful extra technique in the biologists' studies of woodcock migration.

A further way of achieving the same thing may lie in a minute study of the chemical trace elements in the feathers of woodock. The plumage is known to contain tiny traces of various minerals which will have entered the birds' systems with the food they consume in the areas where they hatch and fledge. As with the internal parasites, the patterns may vary from area to area, and it may be possible to devise a method of distinguishing woodcock from specific breeding areas.

Additionally, it may be possible eventually to examine the genetic makeup of woodcock as indicated by slight differences in blood proteins and body tissue. If this can be done we may be able to answer the old and still unresolved questions about different alleged races and strains of woodcock, rather than relying on the unreliable "greyish/reddish" theory.

CHAPTER VI

THE WOODCOCK IN WINTER

"...they prefer for their haunts woods near moist and marshy springs. They hide themselves under thick bushes in the day... A laurel or holly bush is a favourite place for their repose."

R. Blakey: *Shooting* (1854)

Woodcock shooting is a winter sport, especially for the shooter in Britain or Ireland. Although the season opens on 1 October, and even earlier, on 1 September, in Scotland, woodcock are simply not present in these islands in sufficient numbers to justify organising a day's shooting in early autumn with woodcock as the primary quarry. The only exception to this is when local concentrations of home-bred woodcock occur at this time of year, as happens sometimes in certain parts of northern Scotland and Ireland. Not until after the first wave of immigrants in late October and the main influx a month later, on the November "woodcock moon", do numbers of wintering woodcock reach high levels. Even then, if the weather is mild and open, the birds may be scattered thinly over the countryside and some may roost and feed out on the open hill or the fringes of the moor.

But the onset of real winter weather, and the coming of chill winds, icy sleet or snow and the first hard overnight frosts finally brings the woodcock into their eventual winter quarters in the lower, more sheltered coverts. (This was well described by T.H. White in his essay "Snow in Erris" in *The Godstone & The Blackymore* (1959).) Once there, if there is suitable daytime roosting cover and nearby feeding grounds, preferably unfrozen pastures and boggy ground with a rich supply of earthworms, and unless severe weather forces them to move on still further, or an icy drip from the trees pushes them out into more open cover, they tend to stay put until early February. But there is always the possibility of an unpredictable movement of birds out of these

A winter woodcock by a forest spring, among dead bracken and birch trees, from a watercolour by Archibald Thorburn.

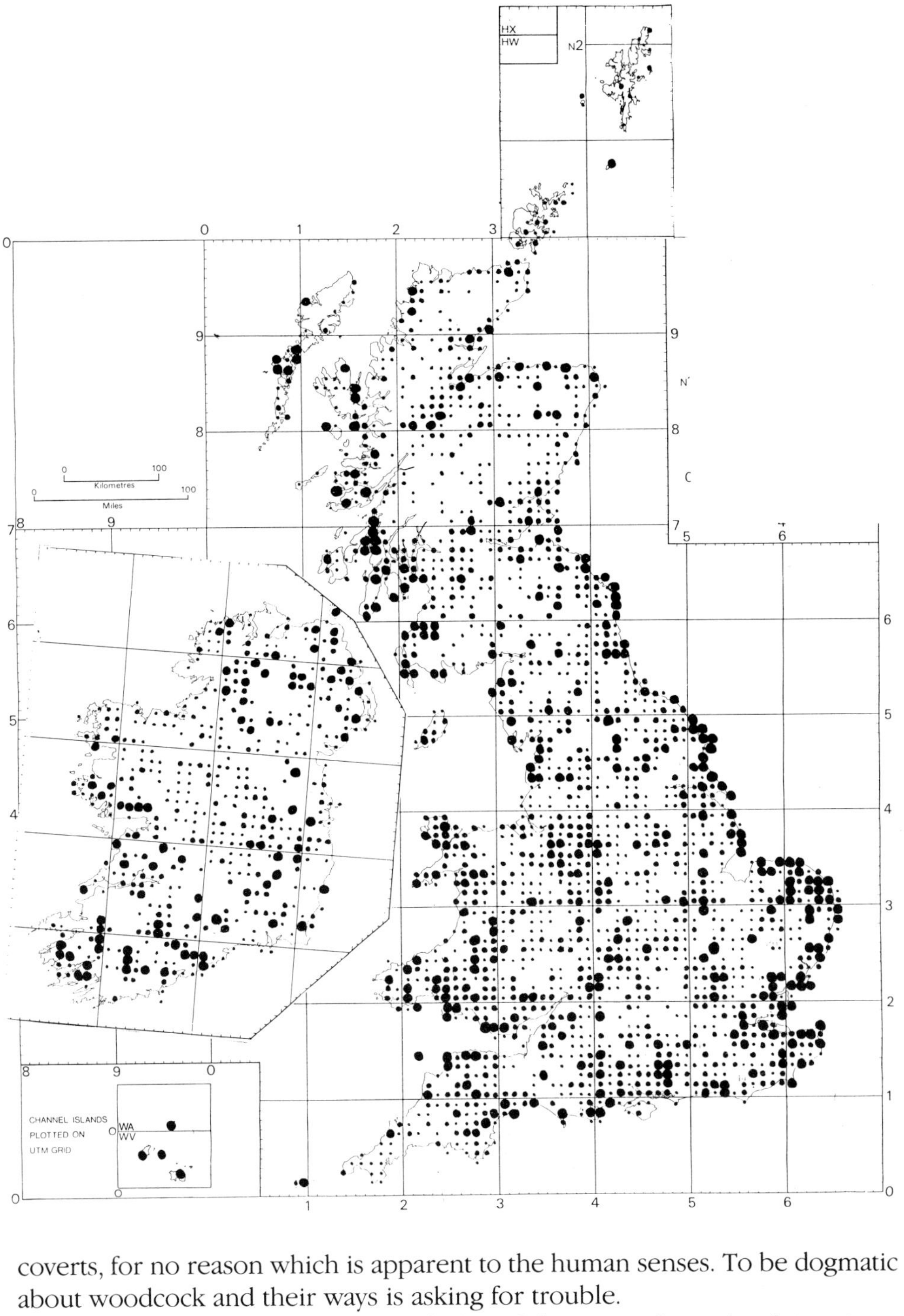

The winter distribution of woodcock in Britain and Ireland, from provisional data supplied by Dr. P. Lack of the British Trust for Ornithology *(data taken from the BTO/IWC Atlas of Wintering Birds* (Poyser, 1986)).

Small dots = 1 bird seen in a day
Medium dots = 2–3 birds seen in a day
Large dots = 4 or more birds seen in a day

coverts, for no reason which is apparent to the human senses. To be dogmatic about woodcock and their ways is asking for trouble.

In the past the sportsman's knowledge of the ways of woodcock in winter was based on the accumulated observations of generations of sportsmen and observant country people. This built up into a generally accepted view that woodcock remain in cover during the day and fly out at dusk to feed. Beyond that, little was known for certain. How far do the birds fly to feed? Do they return night after night to the same feeding areas? Do they feed steadily all night or have one or two big feeding sessions? What does their food consist of? When do they fly back into cover; and does a woodcock tend to return to the same spot to rest during the day?

Woodcock shooters have had their theories about the answers to all of these questions, but to be sure about the ways of winter woodcock something more systematic is needed than random observations. Woodcock, like all our

Winter snow and frosts drive woodcock down from the hills into the shelter of the lower coverts.
(From *Glen Esk – Winter,* a watercolour by Richard Robjent.)

sporting species and other wildlife, are far too important for their future management to be based on vague, unsubstantiated beliefs. In fact, the sporting community has a pretty shrewd understanding about sporting creatures and their habits, but nowadays that is simply not enough.

Increasingly our sport, like so many aspects of our lives, is regulated by laws and rules drawn up by remote legislatures in Europe and administered by equally remote bureaucrats. It is essential that governments and law-makers should be presented with unimpeachable evidence, scientifically based, and the future well-being of all our wildlife deserves nothing less than thorough scientific understanding. Beliefs and convictions, however sincerely they are held or how accurate they may actually be, simply do not carry enough weight if they are based on nothing more than anecdotes, conjecture and

Tail cocked and about to flush at any moment – a roosting woodcock among the litter of dead leaves in a winter covert.

unsystematic observations. It is in achieving this important degree of scientifically based understanding that professional scientific game research organisations like The Game Conservancy, and its counterparts in other countries, have such a vital role to play.

The wintering biology of woodcock in Britain was the other side of Dr Graham Hirons' five-year research project with The Game Conservancy in the late 1970s. After his breeding season studies in Derbyshire woodlands, his efforts were switched to woodcock wintering in Cornwall, where he and Peter Bickford-Smith undertook a joint study of the diet and wintering behaviour of woodcock.

This was a good study area to choose, for a variety of reasons. Firstly, Cornwall has always been known as one of the most important areas in the British Isles for woodcock. Although few breed there, the county affords an extremely important wintering area for very large numbers of migrants. Its position in the far south-west, with prevailing winds off the Atlantic and the warm current of the North Atlantic Drift mean a predominantly frost-free environment. And on those estates where low cover is still maintained and managed specifically for woodcock, winter densities can be very high indeed.

Radio-telemetry and the ringing of individual birds played a vital role in this study too. Radio-tagged woodcock were monitored and their movements noted. In addition, birds shot on normal shooting days were examined to see what food items their stomachs contained, and other birds were shot under licence at various times of the night and early morning, outside the normal legal shooting times, to see how their stomach contents compared.

A woodcock shot during the daylight hours on a normal shooting day will be found to have little or nothing in its stomach or digestive tract. Hence the long-established tradition of not drawing woodcock (or snipe) before cooking them, but instead allowing their "trail" to melt in the cooking and to soak down with the other juices into the traditional slice of toast on which a woodcock is served. The resulting natural sauce or gravy has always been regarded by gastronomes as the crowning glory of a much-prized bird.

Gilbert White, the inquiring amateur naturalist of Selborne, was puzzled by the woodcock's feeding, and wrote in January 1770 to his friend Daines Barrington:

"Many times have I had the curiosity to open the stomachs of woodcocks and snipes; but nothing ever occurred that helped to explain to me what their subsistence might be: all that I could ever find was a soft mucus, among which lay many pellucid small gravels."

Some writers of the eighteenth and nineteenth centuries were less persistent in their inquiries, and simply concluded that woodcock and snipe, like other wading, probing species, were simply "birds of suction", somehow drawing sustenance in liquid form from the mud and ooze in which they probe.

White's description of mucus and small gravels is a good account of what one would expect to find by taking a cursory look at the stomach contents of a woodcock flushed from his daytime roosting spot and shot in late morning or during the afternoon. In normal, mild winters the woodcock is a night-time feeder, and its diet of earthworms and other invertebrates like insect larvae is quickly broken down by its rapid digestive system, leaving little residual matter in its gut by the time it is shot several hours after its last meal.

The modern biologist can make a more careful examination, however, using a microscope and employing various methods of identifying food species from fragmentary remains. Not surprisingly, its diet varies according to the availability of foods, which in turn is affected by the season of the year, the weather and the birds' migratory movements through various different types of habitat.

Traces of animal, vegetable and mineral material have been found in woodcock stomachs, the minerals chiefly consisting of those gravels Gilbert White mentioned. It is not surprising that a bird which feeds by probing in soil, mud and other soft patches of ground should pick up and swallow some particles of sand and grit. There is an old tradition, still adhered to on the Continent, that the woodcock moves after feeding to a rivulet or other water to wash the mud and soil off its bill. In fact there is no evidence for this, and the birds seen in this position have probably been feeding in a fairly normal way by probing in the soft mud along the edges of springs and ponds.

In the Lizard peninsula in south-west Cornwall woodcock roost by day in low cover such as gorse, rhododendron and sallows. Graham Hirons' radio-tagged woodcock were found to be feeding principally on earthworms, which were found in a remarkable 88% of all woodcock stomachs examined. Various sorts of beetles, earwigs, fly larvae, woodlice and millipedes made up the remainder of these birds' winter diet, with fly larvae figuring prominently, in no less than 55% of cases, while beetles of various types comprised a further 61%.

Some of the birds examined were shot at conventional times on normal shoots, between 10 a.m. and 4 p.m. on a winter's day, and about one bird in six showed some signs of having fed recently. But in each case the stomach contents were very small by comparison with birds shot under licence at night. Sixty-four woodcock stomachs were examined and those shot in daylight during normal sporting hours had on average less than half a millilitre of stomach contents – a tiny amount. Even allowing for the fact that woodcock have rapid digestions and some of their favourite foods can be broken down and digested very quickly, this shows that woodcock will not normally feed much during the daytime in winter. But several birds shot an hour or so after sunset presented a totally different picture, with stomach contents averaging over 5ml, and some very much more.

There are various accounts of woodcock shot or caught at night and being found full of food, usually earthworms. On rabbit shooting expeditions after dusk in Scotland, where powerful lamps were used, I twice saw farmers shoot feeding woodcock on the ground by mistake, and have also seen several 'cock

caught at night by lurchers when their handlers were lamping for rabbits. In all cases the birds showed signs of having fed recently, and in particular there were three birds killed shortly after sunset and crammed almost to bursting with large numbers of earthworms. This is in keeping with the findings of the Cornish study.

The radio-tagged birds' movements were tracked, and it was found that during settled, mild weather the birds flew out to pasture fields after sunset and returned to cover well before sunrise next morning. If the sky was overcast and conditions therefore darker, these birds would flight out earlier and return later than when there was little or no cloud cover, the sort of conditions which make dusk seem later and dawn earlier. Some of these radio-tagged birds flew less than 200 yards to feed while others ventured up to three-quarters of a mile, but the average distance from daytime roost to feeding place was estimated at just over a quarter of a mile.

This important Cornish study showed that these woodcock were very faithful both to their daytime roosting spots and to their favourite feeding grounds at night. No bird spent less than 60% of its time at the same roost, while others returned from feeding to roost at the same spot day after day. There was a similar pattern of fidelity to their night-time feeding areas. But nothing in this study suggested that woodcock are territorial about their feeding or roosting places. Several woodcock would feed close to one another and three 'cock were found roosting within a radius of no more than five or six yards. Woodcock shooters and specialist woodcock keepers are all familiar with "the bush that always holds a woodcock". Certain spots seem to have a particular attraction for roosting woodcock, and these "desirable residences" are rarely unoccupied, season after season and even when the previous occupant has been flushed and shot a day or two previously. It is one of the unexplained mysteries of woodcock shooting that a certain spot should have some special attraction for woodcock, winter after winter, while another bush

Studies of wintering woodcock by The Game Conservancy and others has shown that birds will roost by day in many types of cover including the shrubby under-storey of broad-leaved woodlands, in low gorse, laurels and rhododendrons and among conifer plantations. From there they will flight out to feed by night on nearby wet pastures and meadows where earthworms abound.

or corner which seems to human eyes to offer the same conditions rarely holds a roosting 'cock.

Woodcock are known to be faithful both to their place of birth and their wintering grounds. Ringing and radio-telemetry experiments have shown this clearly. But there were early indications of this long before formal ringing was begun and before miniature radios were dreamt of. The white woodcock of Penrice of Glamorgan, first seen in 1791, disappeared each spring and was seen again in the two succeeding winters before it succumbed to the hard weather of 1793. This bird was evidently a migrant, since it was never seen around the Penrice coverts in spring or summer, nor was it reported from any neighbouring estates.

Early this century a remarkable event occurred on a woodcock shoot at Tynan Abbey in County Armagh in Ireland. The late Sir Norman Stronge told me how a shooting party was returning to the house at the end of a long January day when an errant spaniel rushed under a bush close to the house and flushed two woodcock. A beater (who would surely have been an asset to any cricket team) threw his arms out and actually caught both birds, one in each hand.

They were taken uninjured into the gunroom and a council of war was held to discuss what should be done. Eventually it was decided to mark and release the birds. A message was sent for the local goldsmith to come, and he engraved the date and the name of Tynan Abbey on two small, light strips of gold, which were bent into position around the birds' legs. They were then released. In the spring of the same year a letter arrived at Tynan Abbey from Russia, bearing the postmark of St Petersburg. Inside was one of the gold bands and a letter explaining how the bird had been shot while roding in a wooded area not far from the city.

The following December there was another shooting party at Tynan and a

Game Conservancy research in the 1970s confirmed that wintering woodcock roost in cover by day, flighting out at dusk to feed on adjacent areas of worm-rich pasture. The manure of livestock keeps areas of permanent pasture rich in earthworms and other forms of invertebrate food.

Against the wan glow of a winter sunset, a woodcock flights out from the birches to feed. From a watercolour by J.C. Harrison.

woodcock was flushed and shot from beneath the same bush close to the house. It was found to be the other banded bird, back again and roosting under the same shrub from which it and its companion had been flushed and caught the previous winter, a really remarkable instance of fidelity to wintering haunts.

As you might expect, woodcock seem to be very hungry after a day spent roosting in cover without feeding. All the evidence points to active and greedy feeding by the birds during the first three-quarters of an hour or so after they reach their feeding areas. The radio-tagged Cornish birds showed a regular pattern of active and vigorous feeding for 40 minutes or so after flying out from cover, followed by a rest period and the remainder of the night was spent in shorter spells of feeding and resting. Birds shot after the first feeding spell and having their first rest were found to be full of food, chiefly earthworms. They had probably stopped feeding for the simple reason that they couldn't eat any more. Various writers have described woodcock as gluttonous, and those who have successfully kept captive woodcock and fed them on earthworms have commented on how the birds devour large amounts of food very quickly.

Some Cornish birds rested on or close to their feeding areas, but some chose to fly off to nearby moorland. The stream of radio signals from their transmitters showed that, once there, they did not move about very much and were presumably roosting quietly after a hearty meal.

Low cover like gorse, laurels and rhododendrons are attractive as daytime roosting habitat for woodcock, but large, unbroken plantations will not hold many birds, except around the fringes. The most important single duty of a woodcock keeper was to keep the cover broken up by rides, glades, tunnels and clearings. This increases the proportion of "edge" and allows the woodcock to flight out to feed and back again easily. Some West Country shoots still maintain this pattern, which continues to be highly effective in attracting and holding large numbers of woodcock in winter. Maintenance of this broken-up pattern needs to be carried out regularly, rather like the rotational burning of heather on a grouse moor, if conditions are to be kept at the optimum.

In addition to giving woodcock easy ways to flight in and out of good

Where low cover is broken up with rides and tunnels it enables wintering woodcock to flight in and out and easily and make maximum use of the roosting cover available. Chris Minchin, a senior Game Advisor with The Game Conservancy, stands in an area of rhododendron in the Isles of Scilly where habitat is specially managed for woodcock.

roosting habitat, if cover is well broken up it means easier and more thorough coverage of the ground by the beaters and their dogs. Fewer roosting 'cock are likely to be missed or to flush behind, and Guns can be placed along rides and in clearings so that a high proportion of the birds go over them. In large, unbroken coverts it can be difficult to place Guns effectively and birds can break in all directions, with only a proportion of them shootable.

Between the wars the late Viscount Brookeborough, who worked hard and successfully to run the coverts at Colebrook as a woodcock shoot, had rides and tunnels cut to break up some large areas of rhododendrons and other evergreens. This resulted in ideal wintering and, to a lesser extent, nesting habitat for 'cock. Although woodcock still winter there, Colebrook is now run primarily as a pheasant shoot, and the rhododendron rides and gaps have grown in again, although the estate's herd of Japanese sika deer still use some of the old rides and tunnels as deer paths.

These recent researches have tended to confirm many of the beliefs held by generations of sportsmen about how woodcock behave in winter. The vital difference between the received wisdom of sporting tradition and the biologists' findings is that the latter have been proved by rigorous and objective methods. However accurate the shooter and the amateur naturalist may be, only formal scientific evidence is good enough to help guide those who frame the laws and made the major management decisions which affect game and other wildlife.

However, it is interesting to note how generally accurate is this picture of the woodcock's winter life, as given in an obscure poem by an obscure poet of the 1830s. Richard Mant was a Bishop of the Church of Ireland, whose diocese of Down in the north-east of Ireland contains some fine woodcock shoots today, as it did 150 years ago when he wrote this rather florid but perceptive piece of verse:

The marsh his nightly haunt, the wood
Within its secret solitude,
Which on the kind their name bestows,
Supplies their place of day's repose,
Where moss-grown runnels oozing well

Through bushy glen or hollow dell;
There rest they, till the closing day
The signal gives to seek their prey,
Where the long worm and shrouded fly
Close in their marshy burrows lie;
Then issue forth by Nature's power,
To banquet through the midnight hour,
Till the grey dawn their ardour daunt,
And warn them to their woodland haunt.
Mysterious power! which guides by night,
Through the dark wood th'illumin'd sight,
Which prompts them by unerring smell
The appointed prey's abode to tell,
Bore with long bill the invested mould,
And feel, and from the secret hold
Dislodge the reptile spoil!

It is difficult to find fault with that as a brief summary of how woodcock behave and feed in winter.

Although we expect to flush a woodcock on a winter day from its customary daytime roosting site on the ground, woodcock have also been known to perch, sometimes at some height off the ground. The sporting and scientific literature contains several references to this, and the French woodcock club magazine *La Mordorée* has published occasional correspondence on the subject.

Among my own friends and contacts I have had eyewitness accounts from several parts of the country. Derek Bingham, formerly the Editor of *Shooting Times,* has twice seen woodcock perched on low branches of conifers growing on sandy heathland in east Suffolk. In each case the bird was about a foot off the ground and there had been heavy rain for a time beforehand. During the 1982–83 shooting season, at Dengie near Burnham-on-Crouch in Essex, Robin Knowles shot a woodcock which he had flushed from a perching position in a spruce tree, about four feet off the ground. George Emm, my neighbour in Broad Chalke, west of Salisbury, remembers seeing a woodcock perched some 10–12 feet off the ground in a thorn tree on the south Wiltshire downs. This was in early August, and the bird's perch was on a small platform which had been placed in the tree many years before, probably to hold a pole trap or poisoned baits in the bad old days of 'keeping. There is no doubt that woodcock can and will perch, but it is very unusual. Their feet are ill adapted for it, and lack the gripping ability of other perching birds.

"Woodcock Alighting" and "Roosting Woodcock" – two fine bronzes from a limited edition of twenty-five by Hampshire sporting sculptor Geoffrey Dashwood.

The biggest bags of woodcock in Britain and Ireland have generally been made in four clearly identifiable areas - Norfolk and adjacent parts of the east coast, Cornwall, the Inner Hebrides and the west of Ireland. Norfolk has large numbers of woodcock passing through each winter on migration and large bags have been made from populations which are largely transient, pausing for a time before dispersing westwards. The other three areas attract and hold large numbers of birds which tend to remain sedentary during the winter months, and especially in December and January.

Lord Margadale, whose family's woodcock coverts on Islay have been some of the most consistently well populated anywhere in the woodcock's entire range, believes that four factors should coincide to bring woodcock into the coverts on Islay in large numbers. These criteria are a good breeding season in Scandinavia and the eastern Baltic; a good migration assisted by a favourable wind from the east or north-east; hard weather in continental Europe; and hail-storms in the hills and glens of mainland Scotland to bring

A good bag of hard-earned 'cock and only one brace of pheasants – typical sport in rough country in the west of Ireland, with hard work for beaters and dogs and some testing shooting for the Guns. Woodcock are the staple sporting bird in mid-winter in many western areas of Britain and Ireland.

the woodcock down off the open hill and westwards to congregate in the milder areas of Islay and the other isles of the Inner Hebrides.

All these factors play their part in producing high densities of woodcock and consequently plenty of birds for the Guns. But the last point – mild winters – is the real key to the great importance of Scotland's western fringes, Cornwall and Ireland as winter haunts of woodcock. All three areas enjoy predominantly frost-free winters, the result of mild westerly winds off the Atlantic and the warm current of the North Atlantic Drift. If conditions were not mild the woodcock would go elsewhere. They simply cannot feed where the ground is totally frozen.

If you search through the sporting literature of the last 200 years you will find that, when woodcock are mentioned, Ireland is invariably hailed as the 'cock shooter's Mecca. There is no doubt that Cornwall, parts of west Wales and Cumbria, and many areas in Scotland have always held large numbers of wintering woodcock, but perhaps they quietly kept their good sport to themselves. For it is Ireland which keeps cropping up, time and again, as the woodcock area par excellence. The woodcock is given special prominence in Ireland, as the emblem on the head of the 50–pence piece. Since Ireland has been such an important focus for the discussion of woodcock in winter, it is worth looking in some detail at Irish conditions past and present, and noting the changes which have taken place.

When Thornhill wrote his important *Sporting Directory* (1804) he extolled the virtues of Ireland for the woodcock shooter:

"If a sportsman is fond of cock shooting, it will repay him well for his trouble to take a trip to Ireland; it is not material what part to recommend, as it is impossible almost to go to a bad place for sport. As to asking leave, it is needless; as the only cause of jealousy that can subsist between the visitor and the owner of the ground will be for not acquainting him of his coming, in order that he might have it in his power to receive him in the usual hospitable manner, by providing beaters to show him sport, giving him the best of fare, a bottle of good claret, a sincere and hearty welcome, assuring his guest, the longer he stays and honours him with his company, the more welcome he is, and the happier he will make him."

That is still a very fair assessment. Most of Ireland can provide good woodcock shooting, but the western parts tend to be better than the eastern counties, and the warmth of the hospitality is undiminished. But the days of Thornhill's *laissez faire* approach to "asking leave" have gone. There is no free shooting in Ireland, although this seems to have escaped the notice of some individuals. Perhaps it was the splitting up of the old landed estates in the 1920s which fostered the impression that every farmer's bogs and fields were a free range for a man with a gun and a dog. Shooting rights are still in private hands throughout Ireland, and it is nothing less than good manners to ensure that you only shoot where you have permission. Transgression of this elementary exercise in courtesy has led to some animosity towards what is referred to in a clumsy phrase as the "out-of-state shooter" – all because of the inconsiderate actions of a few visiting Guns.

A generation after Thornhill extolled Ireland's woodcock shooting, there was another characteristically vivid and rollicking account from William Hamilton Maxwell in his delightful *Wild Sports of The West of Ireland* (1832):

"The cock-shooting... in the west of Ireland is acknowledged to be very superior; and when the flight has been large, and the season is sufficiently severe to drive the birds well to cover, there is not, to a quick eye, more beautiful shooting in the world.... From a copse of not more than thirty acres in extent I have seen fifty couple of woodcocks flushed; and as several excellent covers lay in the immediate vicinity, it was no unusual thing for two or three Guns to bring home twenty, nay, thirty couple."

But while bags were potentially good, Irish 'cock shooting was hard work. "The best cock-shooting cannot be had without a good deal of fag. Like fox-hunting, it is work for hardy spirits. The short day is hardly sufficient for shooting the different woods; and then the same distance must be again traversed, for which the shooter will be a borrower from the night. Then he must reckon on divers delays and sundry accidents; horses will come down, dog-carts capsize, a trace break, or a spring fail....

"But when all this is achieved – when a cover party have fairly encircled the table, after the luxury of a complete toilet – when the fire sparkles, the curtains are drawn, and the wine circulates – why then, without let the storm blow till it bursts its cheeks – and within, Father Care may hang himself in his own garters."

Don't let's forget that those were the days of flintlock-actioned muzzle loading fowling pieces, unreliable by any standards and unbelievably slow, both in lock time and to reload, for us who are accustomed to the amenities of a modern breech-loading ejector. Yet those were the days of the great Irish bags, both on covert shoots and when one or two Guns walked up with spaniels beating out the ditches and the gorse, or followed a setter on the fringes of the hills. There was a keen and elite "Woodcock Club" in Ireland in the 1850s, whose members included Lords Shannon, Riversdale and Doneraile and the Hyde family of Castle Hyde. They shot together in the winter and dined together out of season, and the talk was always of woodcock. Their devotion to woodcock shooting and the bags they achieved were astonishing.

Ireland no longer affords woodcock shooting of the same type as in the last century. The days when a few favoured estates produced 100-plus woodcock to six or eight Guns are gone for ever, and their passing cannot really be regretted. Big bags have less importance and are often distasteful to the modern sportsman-conservationist, though they were once vital to the prestige of famous estates and to the self-esteem of the big-name game shots of Victorian and Edwardian times. That is not to say that any enthusiastic

The Temple House woodcock coverts around the medieval abbey of the Knights Templar, near Ballymote in County Sligo. They were laid out for woodcock shooting and afford some of the most consistently good woodcock shooting in Ireland.

Mel Carney, woodcock keeper at Temple House, County Sligo, photographed about 1865. The coverts were planted and managed for woodcock shooting, though there was a brief period when pheasants were also reared. The specialist skills of woodcock keepers like Carney are now almost forgotten, but Temple House remains one of Ireland's premier woodcock shoots.

woodcock shooter in the 1980s would not give a great deal to travel back in time, say to the 1890s, and to join in one of the Guinness family's big weeks at Ashford Castle – the privilege of being one of a carefully selected scratch team of the best Guns of the era, and to have 400 or more 'cock in the bag at the end of the five days shooting which usually comprised "the Ashford week". What an experience it would have been!

But those days are long gone. Why has Irish woodcock shooting changed? Why, since Ireland's winter woodcock population is probably larger nowadays than ever before, are such bags not achievable today?

The large Irish woodcock bags of yesteryear were the result of a combination of factors. Geographically and climatically, these and the other great 'cock-shoots of Cornwall, the Hebrides, Wales and Ireland were in the right places. They were usually the last areas in the British Isles to get severe frosts. That has not changed, and these areas still offer the mildest winter conditions in western Europe when European woodcock are forced by severe winters to find milder refuges. Other important changes have taken place, however, and not only on the old Irish estates. The whole pattern of winter woodcock shooting has changed in many other parts of the British Isles. Those old woodcock shoots were keepered and managed in a traditional and highly effective way, with tunnels, rides and glades, and absolutely no disturbance was allowed in or around these coverts from October onwards, until the first shooting day. It was as much as an estate worker's job was worth to enter the woods for any reason. Much of the life of the estate was geared towards the few days 'cock shooting in winter – a mere five or six consecutive days in the whole year in the case of Ashford Castle and its famous "week". But that would be gross extravagance today. Modern estate management means that properties must be run with one eye on the account books and the other on current trends in farming and forestry if the property is to pay its way. Labour, once so cheap and abundant, is now costly and the management of woodlands and coverts solely for woodcock and the employment of specialist woodcock-keepers is simply not economically justifiable. The only exceptions are a very few Cornish and Hebridean shoots. Otherwise the old skills and knowledge of the woodcock keeper are dying and almost forgotten.

If coverts are to be managed for game so as to give an economic return from paying Guns, today's landowner or manager will invariably opt for pheasants. Pheasant rearing and releasing and shoot management is quite an exact science. It has few of the uncertainties which go with an unpredictable migrant

Woodcock, Dusk and Deer – a watercolour by Rodger McPhail. The spring roding display flights of woodcock at dawn and dusk are familiar sights for the woodland deer stalker.

bird like the woodcock, and on a sizeable acreage you can plan your shooting season to consist of perhaps ten or fifteen days of good sport spread over a three-month season, with dates set out well in advance and a more or less predictable expectation of birds in the bag at the end of each day. The costings can be made with some exactness, and the whole undertaking can be budgeted in much the same way as other estate activities.

This is turn suits another aspect of the modern approach to shooting. Only a very few people can still afford to run shoots purely for the entertainment of their friends and family. The "let day" and the paying syndicate are here to stay, and very few shoots do not sell at least some of their shooting to visiting parties of Guns, the income helping to offset the ever-rising costs of running a shoot, however modest in scale. And a paying Gun who has signed his cheque for a 100-bird pheasant day generally wants to get his money's worth, and expects to see sufficient birds go over the Guns. (Whether he and his friends are good enough to hit them and make their 100-bird bag is, of course, another matter.)

This is impossible with woodcock. No shooting host in his senses would ever give any guarantee whatsoever about woodcock numbers on his ground, even if his coverts had been seething with 'cock on the previous day. Remember what Walsingham and Payne-Gallwey, who really knew about woodcock, had to say: "'Here today, gone tomorrow' is a woodcock's motto". The man who has dug deep into his pocket to pay for a day's shooting will be exceedingly disgruntled if the birds have flown, which the capricious woodcock are quite apt to do, and will not be consoled by an assurance that the place was alive with 'cock yesterday. (A non-paying guest, if he really understands woodcock and their vagaries, will take it more philosophically and count himself lucky to have been invited at all!)

If commercial shooting is the main aim, it is very much safer for the estate to opt for pheasants. And if you have lots of pheasants in your woods you will never get large numbers of woodcock, except under freak conditions, and then only for a day or two at most. They will not settle and stay. Woodcock simply do not like the disturbance caused by lots of big, noisy pheasants bustling about and feeding actively during the day. There may be some further disturbance where a keeper goes into the coverts to feed the birds by hand, or to replenish hopper feeders, when the woodcock wants to be left alone to roost quietly under his favourite holly bush.

This trend in shoot management is sad, but it has been inevitable. The most radical social changes have taken place since the days of those Victorian landowners and the famous Guns they invited to their woodcock shoots. Money was not a consideration, it never changed hands between sportsmen, and it was *never* discussed. Who nowadays could afford to keep an expensively maintained woodcock shoot, together with a large house and an appropriate domestic staff, to accommodate and entertain a shooting party of five or six guests and their retinue of loaders and "gentlemen's gentlemen", for only a few day's shooting in the whole year? That was the scale of the undertaking when a Victorian or Edwardian shooting party took place, even on quite a modest landed estate. As recently as the 1930s these things went on. I know of one Irish country house where six Guns arrived for a shooting weekend, without their ladies but with no fewer than thirteen assorted loaders, valets and chauffeurs, who also had to be fed and lodged. In those days it could still be done. Who would dream of such a thing nowadays?

There are still a few families which manage to retain good woodcock shooting for their friends; and to be a guest on such a shoot is one of the greatest sporting privileges. You may only fire a few shots in the course of a long day; or you may strike it lucky when "the 'cock are in" and find forty or fifty birds in the bag – or many more, on the best shoots on the best days. But, productive or blank, you enjoy every minute of it and not to accept such an invitation would be unthinkable. Only illness or a death in the immediate family could keep you away – and as for anyone who turns down an opportunity to shoot woodcock and goes off to a pheasant shoot instead, he needs to have his head examined! The only possible exceptions to this I can envisage are when you are invited to shoot pheasants with someone so very important that you simply dare not refuse; or if you have already accepted another shooting invitation. To renege and go woodcock shooting instead, however tempting, would be very bad manners: you must make the best of your day and try not to think of what you are missing.

Finally, there was the appearance of the landscape in those western parts a century or so ago. All the Celtic fringes of the British Isles were virtually treeless in those days. Woodcock roosting habitat outside the coverts consisted of little more than heather on the hills and blanket bogs, rough grasses and low hedges around the farms with their small fields, and the occasional patch of gorse, thorn bushes or low scrub like alder or sallows. But the great houses had their parks and demesnes, with well managed plantations of trees. Often these were planted for a variety of reasons – as ornamental pleasure grounds, for their amenity value, as a source of timber for the estate and perhaps also as a long-term cash crop. Above all, they were planted for game. Throughout Britain and Ireland all the great estates and most of the smaller properties of the minor gentry undertook extensive planting of coverts for hunting and shooting. The extent of this countrywide trend and the enormous and lasting impact it made upon the face of the countryside have been discussed and illustrated fully by Anthony Vandervell and Charles Coles in *Game and the English Landscape* (Debrett's, 1980).

Woodcock moving south-westwards on their customary autumn quest for frost-free wintering grounds were naturally drawn into the seclusion and shelter of the estate plantations, especially where the landscape was otherwise almost treeless and when hail storms, chill winds and sharp frosts drove the 'cock off the open ground with its scant cover. This used to be the case over most of west and south-west Ireland, much of Wales and the Hebrides and large parts of the West Country. The 'cock were concentrated densely in these carefully maintained and well guarded coverts, and that was reflected in the bags which were achieved. The birds simply had nowhere else to go.

The period since the First World War has seen a revolutionary trend in afforestation. Since the founding of the Forestry Commission in Britain in 1919, initially with a view to replacing and increasing the nation's strategic reserves of timber, and the subsequent emergence of many private afforestation schemes, aided by government grants and tax incentives, the once-treeless landscapes of the west and north of Britain and Ireland have been utterly transformed by the planting of millions of acres of trees, chiefly fast-growing, non-native softwood species like Sitka spruce and lodgepole pine.

This has been good for woodcock in many ways. They find these forests congenial for the trees, especially in the younger and middle-aged stages of their growth, afford shelter from the wind and rain, and there is a moist, dark, frost-free micro-climate underneath. If there are wet, worm-rich pastures and boggy areas nearby and the plantations are well broken up with rides, firebreaks and other gaps, it should suit woodcock very well. Often these new forests are never shot over and rarely disturbed by any human activity in winter, which helps too. All in all, these new plantations have encouraged woodcock to winter, in good numbers but rarely at very high densities, in areas where there was little to attract them before. Woodcock simply love these new forests, despite the fact that some "experts" used to say that no woodcock would roost on the ground among conifers because of the sharp needles, like a bed of nails!

Recent planting means the old-established estate woodlands no longer represent the only refuges for wintering woodcock, and 'cock densities and shoot bags have usually fallen in consequence. We are unlikely ever again to find woodcock present at sufficiently high densities in woodlands which can be beaten out systematically, and where Guns can be placed properly, to achieve bags of 100-plus woodcock. That is only possible under special conditions and usually when there is unusually severe winter weather elsewhere, in which case there will probably be a statutory ban on shooting in any case. The Ashford Castle type of shoot is a thing of the past, with the very rare exceptions of a few specialised shoots in the West Country and the Hebrides which still manage to achieve large bags on a very few days each season.

Most modern sportsmen have mixed feelings about the statistics of game shooting in the last century. They are impressive and absorbing – and also slightly embarassing and distasteful. Quite frankly, we feel they overdid the "numbers game" at times. Some of the spectacular pheasant battues of the turn of the century were excessive by any standards, but woodcock must be viewed in a different light. They are migrants, and woodcock shooting has a good claim to be regarded as a true field sport in the traditional sense of the pursuit of an unpredictable wild bird in its natural habitat. A poor or blank day can be followed by a really memorable day's 'cock shooting, and the woodcock shooter takes his sport as and when he finds it.

Above all, in terms of the conservation of the species, there is no evidence that shooting pressure on woodcock anywhere in its natural range has ever had any adverse effects upon numbers. Rather the reverse, since all the signs are that woodcock populations in the British Isles and Europe are steadily increasing. More research may eventually show what effects, if any, shooting does have on woodcock numbers, but I believe that shooting pressure on the species would have to increase very greatly before it began adversely to affect woodcock numbers. And the woodcock does not lend itself to the making of big bags, except where very high densities occur through special circumstances. The bird's solitary and unobtrusive ways mean that its flushing and shooting is almost a matter of chance. This is borne out by the fact that the vast majority of woodcock shot in Britain are bagged on pheasant shoots, when one or two come out of a drive quite unexpectedly. Only a very few specially favoured parts of Britain can count on woodcock in large numbers, and even there one can draw a blank, such as after a sudden change of weather.

The conservationist must concern himself with the welfare of the species in general, and not with the fact that quite a lot of woodcock are shot on a few shoots on a few days each season. As a proportion of the total national bag of woodcock shot each year it is a tiny amount, probably as little as half of one percent. This is not special pleading, although I love my woodcock shooting. There is simply no evidence that woodcock shooting means fewer woodcock. One respects the wishes of those shooting hosts who ask their guests not to shoot woodcock on pheasant shoots. It is a host's prerogative to specify what may be shot, but he is labouring under a misapprehension if he thinks that, by never shooting woodcock, he will encourage more to nest there and numbers will thus increase, Woodcock populations simply do not work like that.

Every woodcock that hatches must eventually die, somehow or other. Even in severe winters when 'cock congregate and big bags can be made, the death toll from "natural causes" like cold, hunger and exhaustion far exceeds the

A Chance of a Right-and-Left –
a watercolour by Rodger
McPhail. Rodger's picture
shows Sergio Treves shooting
over a German Shorthaired
Pointer with the European-
style *grelot* or collar-bell.

numbers shot. A bird which is shot cannot die a second time from predation, starvation or cold! Mortality is therefore "compensatory", to use the biologists' technical term. Shooting pressure on woodcock would have to increase, perhaps to four or five times its current level, before it began adversely to affect numbers. Like every other sporting species, the woodcock's habitat and the availability of the right sorts of food for a bird with very specialised feeding habits are the crucial factors, the most important influences on its abundance or scarcity. And across much of Britain and Ireland that habitat, both for breeding and wintering, has improved and expanded, and woodcock numbers have increased.

However much the shooting scene has changed, and despite the modern sportsman's increased awareness of conservation and sensitivity to public opinion, no book on woodcock would be complete without some consideration of the great bags of seasons long ago.

The second Marquess of Ripon, formerly Earl de Grey, was probably the finest game shot who ever lived. He certainly devoted his energies to shooting on a Homeric scale, even by the standards of the spacious days in which he lived. Between 1867 and 1923 his gamebooks record a total of 556,813 head of game, wildfowl, rabbits and "various". In forty-seven seasons, from 1867 to 1913, he shot a total of 2,771 woodcock. The vast majority of these were shot on winter covert shoots when pheasants were the main quarry. Ripon's lifetime total was 241,224 pheasants, giving a rough ratio of almost 100 pheasants shot for every woodcock he bagged. This pattern has not changed and remains true today throughout most of Britain. We know that most woodcock are shot "incidentally" on pheasant shoots. Only a few shoots in certain specially favoured parts of these islands can afford a worthwhile day's sport for woodcock alone.

But we know from the Ripon game books that he loved his woodcock shooting and went specially to Ireland, usually after Christmas, to shoot 'cock. His lifelong records include a set of fifty-three neat little leather-bound volumes, supplied by Webster and Larkin of 60 Piccadilly and embossed with an Earl's coronet in his earlier years and, from 1909, with a Marquess's coronet and the letter "R". These were sold at auction by Sotheby's on 12 March 1986, having attracted a lot of pre-sale publicity.

This record of an extraordinary shooting career includes an entry for late January 1872, when de Grey was the guest of Sir Henry Gore-Booth at Lissadell in County Sligo. This was one of the finest woodcock shoots in Ireland, and the

Part of the second Marquis of Ripon's unique archive of over fifty-three game-books, sold at Sothebys in 1986, together with one of his Purdey hammer-guns. Most of Ripon's 2771 woodcock were shot on pheasant shoots, but he regularly visited the south and west of Ireland, as a guest of Lord Kenmare at Muckross and the Gore-Booth family at Lissadell in County Sligo.

Earl de Grey on the front steps at Studley Royal. This shooting party includes his bearded father, the first Marquis of Ripon.

Gore-Booth's neighbours elsewhere in the county also has some first-class 'cock-shooting to offer. (Lissadell is also the only place in Ireland where there were ever roe deer, imported from Perthshire by Sir Henry. They developed some of the heaviest antlers ever seen in Europe, and de Grey shot several on covert shoots there). Sir Henry, a keen shot, also travelled to England to shoot with de Grey, and there were two notable days when the two friends shot together, probably walking-up or over pointers, at Norton Heath on 10–11 November 1874.

Those were the days of fiercely competitive shooting, of jealously guarded reputations for marksmanship and what seems to us to have been an undue concern with personal totals and rates of kills-to-cartridges. The two men's personal totals for 10 November were almost level-pegging – 42 partridges for de Grey and, as he noted in his gamebook with apparent amazement, "Gore-Booth *40* partridges". Perhaps there is a note of self-excuse for not having out-shot his companion by a larger margin when he adds, "Shot with concentrators, which did not care for". ("Concentrators" were a patent design of cartridge invented by Charles Lancaster, using a sleeved wadding which was alleged to concentrate the charge, giving a tighter pattern and increased killing range.) Next day was even more nip-and-tuck, with Sir Henry bagging 40 partridges and de Grey 41.

De Grey was a regular shooting guest at Lissadell in the 1870s, and also shot with the Wynne family at nearby Hazlewood, and on the Ashley estate at Classiebawn, a few miles to the north. In County Kerry, far to the south-west, he also shot with Lord Kenmare at Muckross. Some of the bags were impressive. There were 62 woodcock in the bag to six Guns at Muckross on 7 January 1875, de Grey bagging 26 himself. "Shot very fairly" is his modest comment in his gamebook margin. Four days later the same party got 50 woodcock, de Grey accounting for 21 – "Very wet. Shot v. fairly". Next day the total was 61 'cock, de Grey contributing 24 – and then it was off northwards to Sligo to join the Lissadell party.

Day after day he shot far more than the average for the party; sometimes he accounted for over half the bag. On 23 January 1874 he shot at Lissadell with Gore-Booth, and the total bag for two Guns was 24 woodcock, of which de Grey shot 20. Two days later, as one of five Guns, he shot 16 'cock out of a bag of 43. Once he shot 24 woodcock, all but three being first-barrel kills, and nothing was missed. He seems to have averaged four out of five woodcock he shot at.

This is the standard of shooting which de Grey expected of himself, but a

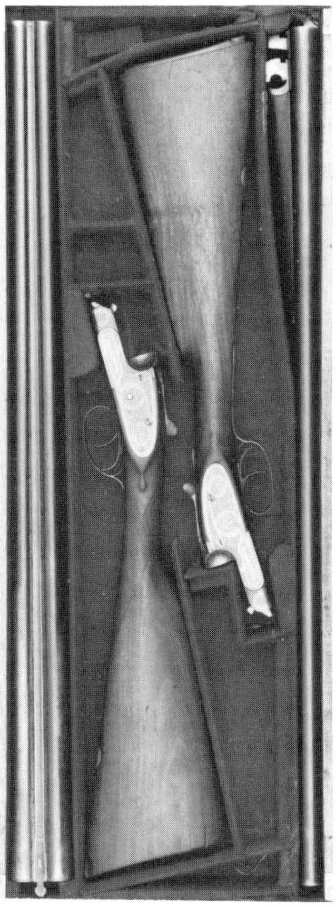

A piece of woodcock history. One of this pair of guns made by William Evans and sold by Sothebys in 1985, was used by a member of the Hamilton family on the record-breaking shoots at Ashford Castle in County Galway in 1929. (Photo: Sothebys, by permission of Major C. Hamilton.)

note of exasperation is to be found on 9 February 1874, when he paid his second visit of the season to Lissadell. Five Guns shot the Wynnes' coverts at Hazlewood bagging 15 woodcock, but de Grey only accounted for one – "not a d....d cock would come near me".

I believe these figures show what a superb shot de Grey must have been – very quick and instinctive. The cynical and the envious have sometimes suggested that he and the other Victorian "big shots" were not really outstanding, but watched as the sky drew dark with clouds of pheasants and only shot at those birds they knew they could hit. But anyone who knows anything about driven woodcock shooting, especially in Irish coverts, knows how very testing and unpredictable the birds are. You simply cannot make the bags de Grey did or shoot his consistently high proportion of the daily totals by choosing only the "easy" 'cock. His performance at woodcock proves he must have been a brilliant shot.

De Grey was not always obsessed with big bags, despite his huge personal totals and the comments of various biographers. There is one rather engaging entry in his gamebook, for 11 February 1884. He and Sir Henry Gore-Booth had a short afternoon's shooting in the "Mountain Plantation" and returned with the grand total of two woodcock – one each. De Grey remarks, "Splendid afternoon's sport". How nice to know that a man who once shot 240 partridges in a single drive could enjoy the sort of pottering which most of us enjoy today. It may have been one of the few occasions when he actually had time to admire the view, enjoy the stroll, and return without a splitting headache!

The Barrington family's Glenstal Abbey coverts in County Limerick were among the best in Victorian and Edwardian Ireland. There were two principal beats, Flavin and Tobermanshill. From 1891 to 1911 Flavin produced not fewer than 53 woodcock and usually between 60 and 105 birds on the only day in the season when it was shot. Tobermanshill was shot several times each season, "where we average about 50 per day", according to Sir Charles Barrington in 1912.

Baronscourt, the County Tyrone seat of the Dukes of Abercorn, was another remarkably consistent and productive woodcock shoot, producing not fewer than 345 'cock and as many as 432 in the seasons between 1905 and 1911. A generation earlier, in 1877, a small party of four to six guns shot at Baronscourt with the Marquis of Hamilton and accounted for 342 woodcock in eight shooting days.

This consistency of bag totals from season to season is also apparent in the records for Eden Vale, a smaller shoot in County Clare. From 1903 to 1911 the season's total was never less than 46 (in 1911 – "our worst year, weather too

"Great windows open to the south . . ." W.B. Yeats wrote evocatively about Lissadell, the home of the Gore-Booth family. Some of Europe's highest woodcock bags were achieved here a century ago, including several seasons when two Guns bagged over 90 birds in a single day. (Lissadell is also famous as the only estate in Ireland ever to have held roe deer. Some of Europe's heaviest trophies were shot here.)

Coastal Landfall on Migration – a watercolour by Richard Robjent. Falls of migrant woodcock occur along the east coast, and the full moon in November traditionally marks the main arrivals of migrants. Exhausted 'cock feed voraciously and soon recover their strength, dispersing across the country to their wintering areas.

mild") and as high as 82, but 55 to 70 woodcock was the usual season's expectation, rarely much more or less.

This season to season consistency in bag numbers on so many shoots has often been remarked upon. Clearly there will be some annual variations according to weather, the success of the preceding spring's breeding season, and losses if adverse weather affects the migration. But if one allows for these factors, which inevitably affect a migrant sporting species like the woodcock, bag sizes seem not to vary enormously even if there are many more shooting days and a consequently higher shooting pressure in one season than in another.

This has led many woodcock enthusiasts to speculate that a given area of good wintering cover will receive a certain annual "dose" of migrants which settle there through the winter, and additional shooting will not increase the bag proportionately. The late Major Dick Hermon, perhaps the most consistently brilliant woodcock shot of the twentieth century (he once bagged 100 'cock to his own gun in three days driven shooting) and an observant student of wintering woodcock, summed up this hypothesis in the form of a neat fable. "King Woodcock" flies over the various parts of the woodcock wintering range, disposing his troops by allocating a hundred woodcock to this covert, seventy to another, twenty to another and three hundred to another. This is necessarily a simplification, but the whole question of the numbers of wintering woodcock which certain areas and habitats will hold and produce for the bag is something worth studying in depth, by scientific methods.

Lissadell in County Sligo, where eminent shots like the Marquis of Ripon shot as guests of the Gore-Booth family, could regularly turn in its 100-bird days, and as early as 1854 a total of 455 woodcock were bagged in eight days – and it is important to remember that the party were using the new-fangled and still primitive early breech loading guns. One astonishing day's bag of 99 woodcock was shot by only two Guns shooting around the coverts with a keeper and some beaters and dogs.

For a single day's bag it is hard to beat the achievement of the party which shot Lord Limerick's coverts in County Down one winter's day in 1842, when 144 woodcock were laid out at the day's end. But that day's total is overshadowed by the truly extraordinary day's sport enjoyed by Lord Claremont at Lord Farnham's property at Donaweale in County Cavan around Christmas time in 1802. Using a flintlock gun (some accounts say he had a pair of French-made flintlock fowling pieces) rather than the more reliable and quicker-actioned percussion gun, he shot 102 woodcock to his own gun in a short day, finishing at 2 p.m. This won him a wager of 300 guineas.

To complete this outline glance at woodcock bag statistics from the great Irish shoots of the past, it is impossible to overlook the astonishing story of the Guinness family and their unique woodock shoot at Ashford Castle in County Galway. The Ashford "week" consisted of five or sometimes six consecutive day's driven shooting for a party of six to eight Guns, usually around late December or in early January. It was a week of sport run with military precision, and an invitation to join the party for this annual sporting ritual was one of the most coveted in Europe. The coverts were never shot or otherwise disturbed from the beginning of October onwards.

In 1879 "the week" resulted in 320 woodcock and during the period 1879 to 1910 the annual average rarely dropped below 320 'cock. The first of the really great years was 1891 with 494 woodcock for the week, and there were 508 in 1895. The Prince of Wales, later King George V, shot as one of the Ashford team in 1905 and the bag was 470. An even greater total came in 1910, with 587 woodcock bagged, and the crowning achievement of the Ashford shoot came in 1929. There were over 100 'cock in the bag each day, and an incredible week's total of 752. The full details, season by season, are set out in detail in Hugh Gladstone's *Record Bags and Shooting Records* (1930) and in the *Fur, Feather & Fin* series volume on *Snipe and Woodcock* (1903).

A more prolonged recital of the bumper bags of the great shoots of long ago would become tedious. But is worth concluding this section by mentioning the real devotees who, after the season's end in the British Isles, set off for foreign shores, often in their lavishly appointed yachts based at the Royal Yacht Squadron at Cowes. Greece and Albania in the 1800s had a magnetic attraction for several British woodcock zealots, including Admiral Sir Hyde Parker – famous for his naval signal to which the aspiring Horatio Nelson turned his blind eye. In 1845 the Parker party shot 1026 woodcock in six days, and still lamented that the cover was so thick that a high proportion of the birds there could not be flushed, and many of those which were flushed did not go over the Guns.

Among notable woodcock shooters we must not forget some members of the royal family, which has a continuing tradition of enthusiasm for shooting. King George V inherited his father's passion for covert shoots, and enjoyed his woodcock shooting, too. This was briefly captured by John Betjeman in his verses on the death of the King:

Spirits of well-shot woodcock, partridge, snipe
Flutter and bear him up in the Norfolk sky...

"A bird fit for a King." King George VI removes the pin feathers from a woodcock on a shoot at Windsor in the 1940s, watched by Queen Elizabeth. The King used red ink to mark up all the woodcock in his game book, and achieved a lifetime total of 1055, almost all shot on pheasant drives.

His second son the Duke of York, who eventually succeeded his father after the abdication of King Edward VIII to become King George VI, was a keen shot all his life, and ritually recorded every woodcock he shot with particular care and in red ink. The King kept a careful record of all game shot, noting both the totals for the day and his own contribution to the bag. Each woodcock was accorded the special honour of the red ink he reserved for them alone, although in his later years snipe were to be recorded in red also.

He shot his first woodcock at Sandringham on 27 December 1911, when there was a day's mixed shooting in Frankfort and (appropriately) Woodcock Woods. That day he actually shot three 'cock to his own Gun, out of a personal total of four woodcock for the season. The party of six Guns bagged 169 pheasants, 25 hares, 167 rabbits, 56 duck, 1 teal, 1 unspecified "various" and 8 woodcock. The King recorded "my first woodcock" in his game book, and showed in brackets after the total of eight 'cock that he had shot three of them himself. For the rest of his lifelong shooting career he always recorded his personal bag of woodcock, as well as the day's total, on each shoot.

On 20 December 1919, when he was one of a party of five Guns at Sandringham, once again in Woodcock Wood, he shot thirteen woodcock out of the party's total of 41 "making His Majesty's score of woodcock 100". His personal total of 500 woodcock was reached not in the cold of a Norfolk covert drive in winter but on a hot day in mid-August at Glamis. It was on 19 August 1935 and an informal day's walking up with two members of the Bowes-Lyon family yielded grouse, hares, rabbits and, oddly for that time of year, six woodcock, of which he shot four himself. (This is an interesting example of the many reports of woodcock found out on higher ground in late summer, after breeding and before the main migrations. Such birds may be seeking a damper environment and adults will probably not have moulted fully.)

The King's thousandth woodcock came on 1 January 1951, when shooting at Sandringham with five other Guns in Wolferton and Dersingham Woods, when he shot six 'cock out of the day's total of fourteen. His shooting career ended with a late-season day in Woodcock Wood at Sandringham on 25 January 1952, when he shot three woodcock, making a lifetime's total of 1055. Of these 928 were shot in Norfolk, and most were shot as single birds on pheasant shoots. On three occasions only did His Majesty bag ten or more 'cock in a day, twice at Sandringham and once in Galloway. He shot one right-and-left, during a covert shoot at Sandringham in the late 1940s.

His impeccably kept game book records that a grand total of 4312 woodcock were shot on shoots when he was present. The average number of Guns per shooting day was six, which would give an average of 718 per Gun, but the King shot 1055 – well above average, and this pattern is consistent throughout his shooting career. He is said to have been a quick and instinctive shot.

What is the best type of gun, cartridge and shot size for woodcock? This is part of the larger and perennially disputed question of what constitutes the best gun and cartridge for game shooting. What hours of discussion and endless reams of writing have been expended on that topic!

First and most obviously, there is no need to buy a special gun for woodcock shooting, unless woodcock (and perhaps also snipe) are going to make up the bulk of your shooting each season. That may well be the case if you live in Cornwall, Ireland or certain parts of Wales and western Scotland, and then there may be a good case for choosing a shotgun specially for those species and conditions. If you have to shoot quickly and at short range, perhaps in thick cover, and if a day's shooting means miles of walking, then the length of the barrel and the weight of the gun can make a difference. No one wants to find his gun becoming a burden half-way through a long day, and

Evening in Glen Esk – a watercolour by Richard Robjent. Woodcock flight out at dusk to feed, and the extensive new conifer plantations of northern and western Britain and Ireland hold many wintering woodcock. Woodcock also breed in these new plantations.

you can't shoot well if the gun feels like a ton weight. A 25-inch barrel of the "Churchill XXV" type may confer some advantage in close cover, although Sir Ralph Payne-Gallwey, who advocated sticking to a familiar gun in which one has confidence, doubted whether a short barrel had ever made the slightest difference. (History does not relate what he thought of the "Pistol Fowling Club" which briefly flourished in Ireland in the early nineteenth century, and whose members shot woodcock in the coverts with flintock and percussion shot pistols. Perhaps they were not as unrealistic and eccentric as one might think: I knew of another Irish woodcock enthusiast who, having lost an arm in the First World War, continued to shoot woodcock and other species with great success with a 20-bore sidelock ejector howdah pistol with 12-inch barrels, made by Westley Richards. His aim was apparently very deadly, although those short barrels meant he could only take fairly close shots.)

Churchill designed his "XXV" guns for a quick, instinctive style of shooting which is often the best for woodcock. A slower, more deliberate style, perhaps with longer barrels, may be better for high pheasants, but good woodcock shooting is a matter of slick and accurate gun-mounting and trusting to one's first aim. Some of the most brilliant performers have achieved this with 28 or 30-inch barrels, but for frequent days of long walking over rough ground and in dense cover a 25-inch barrelled 12-bore will probably save you almost a pound in weight. A 20-bore is worth considering, too. It will rarely weigh more than 5½ lbs. and the standard load of 13⁄16 oz of shot, such as the Eley Grand Prix 20-bore cartridge, is highly effective within all normal sporting ranges, and most cartridge manufacturers can supply a 1 oz magnum load, which gives something closer to a light 12-bore load, though with a greater recoil.

Whatever your choice of gun – and it is best always to stick to your familiar game gun – it should not be too tightly choked. Apart from the fact that few of us are accurate enough to be able to place our patterns so as to be able to make good use of a tightly choked barrel, most woodcock are shot at within 25 yards or less. At that distance a wide, even shot pattern is a decided advantage, while a tight pattern will either mean a miss or a badly smashed bird.

The best shot size for woodcock seems, by universal agreement, to be number 7. This gives a suitably dense pattern for woodcock, even up to 45 yards or so, and it is perfectly serviceable for most other species which may crop up in the course of a day's 'cock shooting. It is adequate for snipe, ideal for pigeon and most inland duck, and is often also the first choice of the pheasant shooter, despite the traditional primacy of number 6 shot.

The shot load need not be more than a normal game shooter's load of 11⁄16 oz, and perhaps the best results in terms of even patterns come from a 1 oz load. Pre-eminent among these is the well known Eley Impax cartridge, available in both paper and plastic cases, and with a fibre driving wad. This gives a very even pattern, especially from an open choked gun, and among specialist woodcock shooters it is usually preferred to the increasingly popular plastic shot-cup or monowad. This can mean a slight tightening of the pattern, equivalent to a little extra choke.

Apart from these simple and rather obvious considerations, woodcock shooting requires no special or unusual gun or cartridge. Much more important is deft and speedy gun-mounting and a refusal to be flustered. Countless thousands of woodcock must have been saved by the way Guns tend to panic on seeing the bird, especially if it emerges without warning from a pheasant covert.

When a woodcock is flushed it usually does not fly very far, and will normally pitch back into cover within a few hundred yards. The woodcock has a particular habit of landing with a sudden drop, almost a collapsing style of

alighting. When the bird has been shot at, this can easily delude the sportsman into thinking that the bird has dropped dead. But a woodcock which has been hit will usually show some signs of a flinch or twitch, especially of the tail, which becomes more apparent the more woodcock shooting one does.

In winter woodcock are normally silent, apart from the click or clatter of wings on rising. But on six or seven occasions I have had a woodcock pitch close to me and give a single high-pitched *chip* call as it touched down. A wounded woodcock will sometimes give a low, grunting croak, not dissimilar to the rather frog-like croak of the roding bird.

It is interesting but rather alarming to see how many old books on shooting encourage you to take long shots at woodcock, for when hit even by a single pellet they say it is bound to come down. G.T. Teasdale-Buckell, an experienced game shot who edited the sporting weekly *Land and Water* from 1885 to 1899, and who ought to have taken a more responsible attitude, said that "a woodcock is nearly always obliging enough to come down when he is hit...". George Lodge, who was a fine and observant shot as well as one of Britain's most outstanding wildlife artists, took a different view: "Although woodcock are generally considered to be very easy birds to kill if hit at all by the shot, I have, nevertheless, seen a woodcock flying strongly with a 'hatful' of feathers left behind him. And such birds are often never gathered".

In fact a woodcock is not a loose-feathered bird and rarely sheds a great puff of feathers when hit, but Lodge was right when he said that 'cock can fly off after being hit. Any sportsman worthy of the name will follow up any bird which he thinks may have been hit, and with woodcock there is a special sign to watch out for. A woodcock flushed and fired at will often give a curious flick or twitch of its tail. This is a sure sign that it has been severely wounded. Watch it carefully, follow its flight and try to mark where it pitches. If you are unsighted, as in a covert shoot where the 'cock disappears out of sight over the trees, follow it up along the line of its flight and work your dogs thoroughly. You will almost always find such a bird dead or dying, and there is something more to put in the game bag.

It is difficult adequately to describe this slight twitch or flick of the tail, but it becomes more apparent and recognizable the more woodcock shooting one does. I have invariably found that the bird concerned is down and dead, perhaps not far away but possibly several hundred yards off. On a good many occasions I have seen a woodcock flushed and shot at by a fellow Gun, and give that subtle and easily overlooked tail-flick, flying on apparently unharmed, and the Gun concerned has shrugged and cursed his bad shooting. But a follow-up and a reliable dog has always meant another bird in the bag – much to the pleasant surprise of the previously disappointed Gun.

There are almost as many theories about woodcock shooting as there are

"Jolly Sir John finds the Missing Article". Sir John Dugdale Astley Bt. of Everleigh in Wiltshire (b. 1823) was a celebrated sporting squire. This unusual 1880s mezzotint shows him on a covert shoot, probably at Everleigh, brandishing one of the new-fangled breech-loading hammerless sidelock shotguns, and in exuberant mood on finding a missing woodcock. Wiltshire's chalky, alkaline soils do not encourage woodcock in large numbers.

woodcock shooters, and to discuss them fully would be a lengthy and probably futile exercise. To lay down the law about how a day's woodcock shooting should be carried out is to invite a chorus of dissent from other woodcock enthusiasts. But there are certain guiding principles based on what we know of the bird and its ways, and we can apply some common-sense as well. Woodcock can generally be found on the sunnier south-facing sides of the coverts, but we can all remember those odd days when we worked the undergrowth all along the southern sides and flushed virtually nothing, while on the trudge back to the cars the dark, northern sides were full of 'cock – for some inexplicable reason.

Whether you shoot woodcock alone over a spaniel or a setter, or in a small group of rough shooters, or on shoots where you take up a more or less static position and the coverts are beaten out, always try to place yourself so as to be in the best position to take a shot if a chance comes your way. Woodcock emerge from cover at all kinds of improbable places, heights and angles, but do your best to give yourself the largest arc of safe fire you can. Safe is the operative word here: woodcock can fluster even the coolest of shots. Always make sure of the positions of beaters and other Guns relative to yourself. This is even more vital if the party is constantly on the move, as is often the case when beating out large woods.

Many of the best woodcock shoots throughout Britain and Ireland call for a team of Guns moving slowly in some sort of open formation, with beaters and dogs in the centre. This calls for great discipline on everyone's part. Keeping a straight line on an open grouse moor can be difficult: close cover and broken ground makes it much more difficult and thus much more important to know where everyone else is, and to take your shots accordingly. I know of one woodcock shoot in the west of Ireland where the coverts were laid out specially for 'cock shooting, in the form of long woods rarely more than 100 yards wide. Here the time honoured strategy is for the Guns to advance in a U-formation, with the leading Guns well forward and a reliable shot hanging back as "rear-gunner". A high proportion of woodcock break back on being flushed, and the tail-end Gun may have some of the cream of the sport. But this all calls for steadiness and a cool head, since your safe arc of fire is ever-changing as you move through the woods, along slopes and up and down hill. Even the best and safest of Guns will occasionally fire a shot which, although it may actually have been perfectly safe, causes him a flicker of unhappiness. That is the sign of a good, safe shot – someone who is constantly aware of the safety factor and critical of his own performance. The over-confident, the exciteable and the down-right careless Guns – and they occur in the best and most experienced circles – are the ones most likely to cause an accident. Every season brings tales of accidents and near misses, on woodcock shoots and in the game shooting world in general. The wise man will always react by reflecting, "There, but for the grace of God, go I!".

When you have shot your woodcock, do take time to admire it. It is a beautiful bird and you should savour the moment – perhaps with a tinge of sadness intruding upon the natural delight at bringing off a good shot. On a busy day in big coverts you may not be able to stop and muse too long over your prize in the way the French *bécassiers* describe in such purple prose. Load up quickly and stay on the *qui vive* – you will curse yourself, and your host will curse you if a woodcock comes over your head while you are gazing in rapt delight at your first bird, the gun lying empty across your arm.

But at lunch or at the end of the day make sure you look at the birds individually and compare them with one another. The pin feathers, once prized by miniaturists and water colour artists as fine, stiff brushes, are the traditional trophy. You may stick them in your hat-band, and some sportsmen have made huge collections of them. In Cornwall and Scotland several big woodcock estates collected sufficient pin feathers to make fans for the owners' wives or daughters. Lord Margadale's grandmother is said to have had a fan made from thousands of woodcock pin feathers.

If you are a woodcock shooter in the mainland European tradition you may take not only the pin feathers but also a tiny tuft of downy feathers from the woodcock's "parson's nose". Together with the pin feathers this makes up the complete trophy, and in German and French gunshops you can buy little brooches and badges specially designed to hold the feathers and the tuft, which can then be worn as part of the panoply of badges and sporting insignia which European sportsmen love.

As you examine the day's bag of 'cock notice too the differences in size and weight, the plumage and colour variations and how the legs can vary in colour too. Look out for short-billed birds, and if possible try to measure *all* the bills. Only in this way will we find out more about the short-billed variants and discover if we have hitherto been missing the less obvious woodcock with bills of intermediate length.

Finally, do make a special effort to keep one wing from each bird shot, as your contribution to the Woodcock Production Survey which has been running in Great Britain and Ireland since 1975. What is this survey, how is it carried out, and what are its aims?

Compared with the American Woodcock, an individual specimen of *Scolopax Rusticola* in the hand of a shooter or taken alive from a mist-net by a ringer reveals very little about its age or sex. Average weights and bill lengths tend to show that females are heavier and longer-billed than males, but the overlap is so great that it does not help us much in telling if the individual woodcock we have just shot or netted is male or female. Reliable sex determination is still a matter for dissection.

Telling the bird's age is another matter. The precise age of a woodcock is difficult to determine, unless of course it has been ringed as a chick. But it is possible to distinguish adult woodcock, whatever their age, from juveniles, i.e. birds hatched the previous spring and summer.

If you shoot a woodcock, especially if it is in the earlier months of the season, it is worth looking for one small but telling physical feature – "the bursa of Fabricius". This exotic sounding term is the biologists' name for a small blind-end pocket or cavity just above the bird's vent, which occurs in young gamebirds, including grouse, partidge and pheasants, and it is also present in juvenile woodcock.

In a fully fledged woodcock aged two or three months the bursa will be quite long, perhaps as deep as 30mm or slightly more. It can be probed with a split match-stick or a fine splinter of wood or strand of wire. As the young woodcock grows and matures the bursa gradually shrinks, until it eventually disappears altogether by the time the bird is about ten months old. It will certainly have gone when the woodcock becomes sexually mature. Thus if the bursa of Fabricius is present you can be in no doubt that you have a young woodcock, hatched the preceding season. Apart from being a very reliable indicator of the bird's youth, the bursa test is a good party piece if you want to show off your expertise!

The bursa test requires a fairly intimate physical examination of the bird, but another and rather more obvious physical feature can be used to distinguish birds of the year from adults hatched in previous seasons. This is done by what woodcock biologists know as "the Clausager method", which takes its name from the Danish biologist who first published his woodcock ageing method in 1973. It involves looking at the wing feathers of the bird, and the principal indicator is the degree of wear to the tips of the primary feathers.

Winter Woodcock – from a study in oil by William Hollywood.

A young woodcock which has fledged in May and been shot in December or January will have had its primary feathers longer and subjected them to more wear than an adult which, after the breeding season, moults its feathers and has new primaries by about September. By the start of the shooting season in the British Isles juvenile woodcock will have primary feathers which are two or three months older than the adults'. Furthermore, there is evidence that adult primaries are stronger and wear more regularly, while young birds' primaries are more fragile and brittle. The individual barbs and barbules which make up the feather can fray and break more easily in a young bird, giving a ragged outline.

The difference shows up in a comparison of the primary feather tips. Old birds' primary tips will usually have a crisp, clearly defined edge with a profile like the point of a butter knife. The young bird's worn feathers will have broken and ragged primary tips. This difference is usually evident in woodcock shot in the peak mid-winter months of December and January, and is even more obvious in spring woodcock caught alive or shot while roding.

However, there can be areas of overlap and some borderline cases. Any sportsman also knows that a woodcock which has been shot and fallen into thick cover or water, been retrieved in a dog's mouth and perhaps carried all day in a pocket or game bag may have had its feathers badly ruffled and crumpled. This militates against total reliance on the state of the wing tips, but there is an important secondary sign to look for, which is the tips of the primary covert feathers. In juvenile woodcock these end with a comparatively wide band of reddish-brown, measuring about 1.5–2.5mm. Adult woodcock primary covert tips end with a much narrower band which is pale buff or almost white and only about 1mm wide. When the degree of wear on the primary tips and the width and colour of the primary covert tips are both taken into consideration it is possible to divide your day's bag of woodock into juvenile and adult with a high degree of certainty.

To be able to distinguish young woodcock of less than a year old from other, older birds is an important aid in assessing the ratio of young birds to

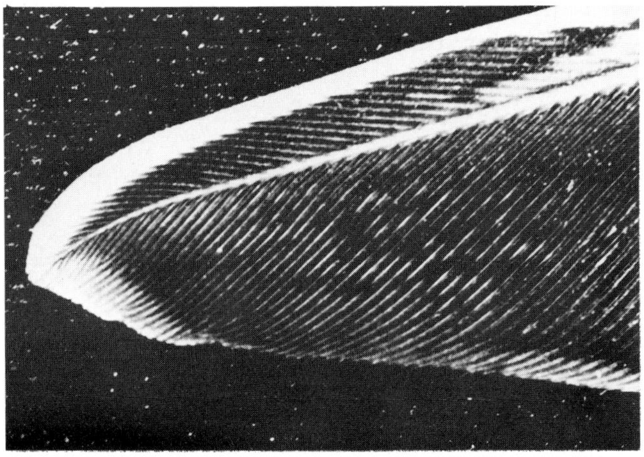

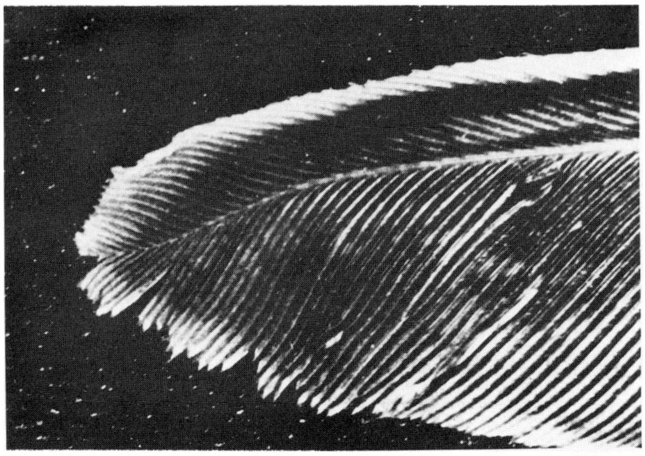

A crisp, rounded tip to the primary feathers denotes an adult bird. A juvenile woodcock, hatched the preceding spring, shows ragged, worn primary tips. This is the principal guideline in wing-ageing woodcock, and a second detail to look for is the narrower, paler band on the tip of the adult bird's primary covert feathers. The woodcock Wings Survey, supported by sportsmen and co-ordinated by the B.A.S.C., is an important long term attempt to monitor the proportions of young and old birds in the British and Irish winter population season by season.

old in the sportsman's bag and thus in the population in general, and so to gauge the reproduction rate of woodcock and the comparative success of each breeding season. This requires co-ordination and cannot be carried out fully without the support of woodcock shooters throughout the woodcock's range. In Britain and Ireland a woodcock wings survey takes place annually with the help of committed sportsmen throughout these islands, under the co-ordination of the British Association for Shooting and Conservation (BASC)

In 1975 the Woodcock Production Survey began as a joint venture between The Game Conservancy and the BASC, then known as WAGBI (the Wildfowlers Association of Great Britain & Ireland). It has continued ever since and is now wholly under the co-ordination of Dr John Harradine of the BASC, based at its headquarters at Rossett in Clwyd. One wing from each woodcock shot is requested to be sent to the BASC, together with details of the date and place where it was bagged. For those who shoot a number of 'cock each season handy cable-tie tags are available on request from the BASC, enabling individual wings to be tagged with this simple information as the birds are shot. A collection of wings can then be sent off to the BASC at the end of the season.

Each wing is examined and classified as "young" or "old" using the Clausager method. This allows each shooting season to be assessed in terms of the proportion of young birds to old, both nationally and regionally, and also in relation to the time of year. These national and regional ratios and timings can then be correlated with other factors like the mildness or severity of the winter, and the dryness or wetness of the preceding spring and summer. Data for Britain and Ireland can then be compared with information obtained from other countries, principally Denmark, where woodcock wings have been collected and examined for many years.

This is an important practical survey, established for over a decade, and one in which the ordinary sportsman plays a central role. That fact alone makes it important. But there are many unknown and imponderable factors and a whole host of variables which add to the complexities of such a survey and make it more difficult to draw accurate conclusions from it. Are young woodcock more likely to be shot than old birds, which may be more wily and elusive? How is the picture altered if a large proportion of wings come from certain parts of the country and few from others? Since migrant woodcock arrive here from various widely scattered parts of Europe and disperse to mingle with home bred birds, what useful conclusions can we draw about the relative breeding success of woodcock in different geographical areas?

The BASC survey for 1983-84 was the biggest and best supported ever, with 3,705 wings from Britain and Ireland, including the Channel Islands and the

Isle of Man. The wings sample for that season, combined with some earlier results, gives some indication of the pattern which has emerged over the years.

Firstly, and not unexpectedly, most wings were from woodcock shot in December and January – 42% and 41% respectively. Less than 1% were shot in October, while November yielded just over 16%. This is wholly in keeping with the pattern of the woodcock shooter's season: December and January are always the best months. The migrants are in and have taken up winter quarters, and there may be a bonus in the form of further late falls if hard weather hits mainland Europe.

Another telling point is the proportion of immature woodcock in the bag in each month of the season. October 1983 yielded wings showing 72% juveniles, which is understandable for a time of year when the birds shot were almost certainly home bred, with a high proportion of young birds hatched in the mild, wet spring of that year. The main falls of migrants always come in November, which in 1983 revealed 56% young birds in the wings received – which may point to a larger proportion of adult birds in the total British and Irish November population following the arrival of adults from northern regions. December and January produced 48% and 46% immature woodcock, which seems to show a continuing of the November trend towards more adults, mainly wintering migrants. But we must bear in mind that the winter of 1983-84 was very mild throughout western Europe and there must therefore have been fewer hard weather migrants than normal, resulting in a higher proportion of home-bred woodcock in the final bag for the season in the British Isles. 0.9 young woodcock were shot for each old bird. Things were quite different in the severe weather of December and January 1981-82, and for that season the wings survey showed a ratio of 1.1 young to each old woodcock in Britain and Ireland.

The ratio of young birds to old, analysed region by region, is interesting. In Denmark, an important wintering area and a jumping off point for woodcock which have come south from Scandinavia, your woodcock is more than twice as likely to be a juvenile than an adult. The Channel Islands in 1981-82 showed 3.8 young woodcock to each adult bird, and 3.9 in 1983-84. South-west England, including the woodcock hot-spots of Cornwall, showed ratios of 1:8 and 1:5 respectively for the same years. Ireland, north and south, showed a preponderance of adult birds in both years, with 0.8 young to each old woodcock in both seasons, which is typical of the general Irish pattern. All the evidence of the Woodcock Production Survey shows that about 56-57% of Irish woodcock in the wing survey sample are old birds, season after season.

So the further west we look in the woodcock's wintering range in the British Isles the lower the proportion of young birds. Why is this?

First, young woodcock may not be willing or able to migrate as far as older birds. Perhaps mortality on migration is higher among the young. Juveniles may also be less willing to cross wide stretches of open water when there is no landfall visible in the distance. Old birds may be stronger on the wing, more adventurous, and some may also have made the long distance migration in previous years. Denmark is an important staging post for Scandinavian and Baltic migrants, some of which remain to winter there while others fly on to the south and south-west. The Channel Islands are not so very far off the French coast, and France's northern and western maritime provinces always tend to have good numbers of wintering woodcock including a high proportion of juveniles. Once you cross the North Sea, the English Channel or the Irish Sea the proportion of young birds becomes very much lower. It is usually not much over 50% for Britain in general, and lower still for Ireland.

The general rule of thumb that "west means old" is not true of Cornwall,

Winter woodcock habitat in Cornwall. An area of low cover, consisting of bracken, gorse and rhododendron, has been carefully broken up with rides and paths to encourage large numbers of wintering woodcock. This layout also ensures that a high proportion of the woodcock flushed pass within range of the standing Guns.

however. In 1983-84 63.6% of wings from Cornwall came from immature birds, compared with only 43.6% on the other side of St George's Channel in the Irish Republic. For the six shooting seasons from 1975-76 to 1980-81 the Cornish wings showed an average of 65% immatures, compared with 43% for Ireland, and a British average of 55%.

Can it be that, once Cornish wintering woodcock have moved down into that funnel-shaped peninsula with its abundance of good wintering habitat, the juveniles are unwilling to undertake a further westward movement across another stretch of open sea? Or perhaps the Cornish woodcock shoots, with habitat specially maintained for woodcock, and Guns and beaters deployed to maximum effect in a very specialized form of shooting, result in a higher proportion of young woodcock in the bag.

The Woodcock Production Survey is affected by many factors including habitat, migration patterns, the possibility that woodcock of differing ages and sex may be more or less easy to shoot, the various types and styles of shooting carried out throughout Britain and Ireland, and the extent to which the sample of wings is truly representative of the woodcock population in general. But it remains one of the most significant long-term surveys of the woodcock in Britain and Ireland, and further study of wings supplied in future seasons will fill out the general picture more fully. It deserves the fullest possible support of all sportsmen, and especially those who shoot significant numbers of woodcock each winter.

It requires no great effort to snip a wing off each woodcock in the bag at the end of the day, to affix one of the BASC's little tags and jot down the place and date of shooting. Store the wings in a dry and moth-proof place until the end of the season, when your collection can be bundled up – preferably in cardboard and brown paper and not in polythene or plastic, which causes sweating and accelerated decomposition, resulting in a damp and smelly parcel. Send it off to Dr John Harradine at Marford Mill at Rossett, and for very little effort you will have made a useful and practical contribution to a greater understanding of the ways of woodcock and to the future of your sport.

Some sportsmen are understandably reluctant to cut wings off, since many woodcock are given away as gifts and no one wants to appear to give someone a mutilated bird. But if you explain that it has been done "in the interests of science", the recipient will usually understand. If more shooting people throughout Britain and Ireland, and especially in northern England and Scotland, joined in this survey and sent in samples of wings we would all know more about a favourite bird. And if the BASC can provide contributors with prompt acknowledgement of their packages and provide a full analysis of each season's wings sample, it helps to sustain the enthusiasm of existing contributors, and encourages them to get their friends to join in and send their woodcock wings too. Supporting the BASC-co-ordinated Woodcock Production Survey is the most important contribution the individual game shooter can make to extending our knowledge of woodcock.

How does really hard winter weather affect woodcock? In recent times this has been one of the most vexed and contentious questions about the woodcock as a sporting species. Does shooting in hard weather seriusly affect woodcock populations? At what point in a long, freezing spell do woodcock begin to suffer? How, if at all, can conservation-minded sportsmen help when woodcock are under pressure from extreme weather conditions? Does it help if we stop shooting woodcock; or will they perish to the same extent whatever we do? How are we to find the answers to these questions and establish proper ways of measuring the effects of freezing weather on woodcock and deciding when we should stop shooting – or even if we should stop at all?

Although we need a Game Licence if we are legally to shoot woodcock, they are not gamebirds in the strict sense. The mainstream game species like grouse, pheasants and partridges are governed by the Game Acts, but the shooting of woodcock and snipe is regulated by other laws, which also apply to duck, geese and other quarry species of waterfowl. In Great Britain the most recent and important of these laws is the Wildlife & Countryside Act 1981.

For some years the bird protection laws in Great Britain and also in the Republic of Ireland have empowered the appropriate government Ministers to introduce statutory bans on the shooting of certain sporting birds, usually when winter weather has been particularly severe for long periods. (For complex constitutional reasons such powers did not exist in quite the same form in Northern Ireland, but the province's major new Wildlife Order in 1985 has brought it more into line with the rest of the United Kingdom.) Bans were implemented in Great Britain and in the Irish Republic in December 1981, and re-introduced a few weeks later in January 1982. January 1985 saw more bans in both countries, and the onset of severe frosts in late January 1986 brought Britain close to yet another hard-weather ban.

On each occasion there was heated controversy among the shooting fraternity, among conservationists in general and in the ranks of the "protectionists" and those opposed to the whole concept of shooting. I have some particularly vivid personal memories of the passionate feelings aroused by the hard-weather shooting ban in January 1985.

I went north from near-Arctic weather in the Home Counties in January 1985 to give a series of lectures on woodcock and other current aspects of gamebird research to meetings of sportsmen and conservationists in various parts of Scotland, including Aberdeenshire and Inverness-shire. I arrived at Aberdeen station off the night sleeper to find the Highlands unseasonably mild and damp, with only a touch of snow on the high tops. The woodcock enthusiasts were, quite naturally, looking forward to some fine sport. There had been a goodly influx of woodcock into their coverts as the birds had moved northwards to those milder parts, and there had been some big falls of woodcock along the coasts of East Anglia and Lincolnshire, too, as Continental birds moved westwards to escape the frosts of mainland Europe.

Just as I arrived to give my main talk to a fairly large audience in an Inverness hotel, the Department of the Environment and the Scottish Office announced that the hard-weather ban, which had already been operating for some days in England and Wales, was to be extended to Scotland. A room full of benign and cheerful Highlanders, most of them looking forward to their

J.C. Harrisons's *First Falls of Snow*. Woodcock will often venture out to feed by daylight in hard frosts and snow. They are often to be found in pheasant coverts, and most woodcock shot in Britain are bagged on pheasant drives. But woodcock will never winter in large numbers where there is disturbance caused by noisy and diurnally active pheasants, and those who go into the coverts to feed them.

woodcock shooting the next day, was instantly transformed into a sort of sportsmen's Slough of Despond. Amid mixed feelings of amazement, incomprehension and scarcely concealed anger, the baffled, rhetorical questions came tumbling out: "Why has this happened?"; "Where is the hard weather in Scotland?"; "Isn't it mild and drizzling outside?"; "Why does some office-bound Englishman stop our woodcock shooting when the birds are in tip-top condition, and our only chance to make a decent bag of 'cock is when it's frosty elsewhere?" – this last from one of Britain's most experienced and respected sportsmen-naturalists.

Having just come from the south of England I found myself, not surprisingly, a focus for the wrath of that gathering of keen sportsmen, who felt cheated of their 'cock shooting by some remote and unthinking bureaucracy based in London – whence have stemmed all of Scotland's misfortunes throughout history. I have no English blood in my veins – proud boast! – and am by ancestry about three parts Scots, but for an hour or two that evening I became a sort of token Sassenach whipping-boy. Anyone who had just travelled up from England must somehow be guilty by association. This, they said, was a bureaucratic nonsense, a daft and unwarranted ban.

Who could blame them for feeling that way, as they looked out on a green and frost-free countryside, knowing that the woodcock, well fleshed and in prime condition, had come in numbers from the cold south and the snowy western glens into the mild seclusion of the woods and bushes along Loch Ness, "which covers afford as good woodcock shooting as any in Scotland", as Charles St John wrote in 1845.

That ban of January 1985 caused a lot of ill-feeling, not only among sportsmen and not only in Scotland. By general agreement the various conservation, environmental and shooting organizations involved felt that the criteria for the ban were not correct, and that the network of weather stations monitoring Britain's winter weather did not give a sufficiently full and fair picture of the countrywide situation. The system whereby a hard weather ban is implemented in Britain also provides for a thorough post-mortem, to review events afterwards and examine the efficacy of the ban, the response of the sporting community and, most importantly, to try and evaluate the benefits of the ban to those species which have been granted temporary protection from shooting.

Confronted as I was in my Inverness meeting with some well-reasoned and cogent arguments against the implementation of that ban, I had a good deal of sympathy with the speakers. But the criteria for that ban had been reviewed and agreed by the principal shooting and conservation organizations as part of the post-mortem assessment of the bans of December 1981 and January 1982. It was therefore incumbent upon responsible sportsmen to abide by the rules for the time being. Any wanton breach of a shooting ban would risk bringing the entire sport into disrepute and play into the hands of those whose avowed aim is to have sporting shooting abolished completely. It was, I could only reply, sad and unwise for responsible and law-abiding people, who would never dream of driving an untaxed motor car or not buying a television licence, to say in a public meeting that they were damned if they would accept the ban, and that they had every intention of going ahead with the next day's woodcock shoots. Just because the game is going badly for them, a team should not suddenly try to move the goal posts!

In the event, most of them slept on the idea, swallowed their anger and wisely decided to play by the rules: inevitably, there were a few who didn't. But the real answer to the problem of wrong-headed bans must lie in a re-assessment of the nature of the problem, the aims and objectives of a hard weather ban, and the devising of a more effective set of rules to guide the Secretary of State's advisers.

In its unhappiness about the 1985 ban the shooting community was not alone. There was general agreement that there was a lot of room for improvement, and so another post-mortem took place in spring 1985, leading to a revised procedure and a more representative selection of weather stations throughout Britain to monitor the conditions which birds may face countrywide. As yet (1986) there has been no occasion for a hard weather ban based on this new system, although we came close to it in February 1986, when bitterly cold conditions threatened to curtail the last few days of wildfowling on the foreshore, which ends on 20 February. In the event no ban was needed, nor would woodcock have been affected by it, their shooting season having ended on 31 January.

However much it may have been in the shooting man's mind in recent years and after several shooting bans, the whole question of the effects of hard and prolonged frosts on woodcock is not a new one. Let's look briefly at this in a historical perspective, from the detailed accounts which some of our sporting ancestors have left us.

Winters in the British Isles used to be much harder than they are today. That is clear from the descriptions we have of skaters on the Cumbrian lakes in the last century, and of huge ox-roasts on the Thames at London Bridge. It was a fairly regular occurrence for the fenland dykes, the Norfolk Broads and even the lochs and loughs of Scotland and Ireland to freeze over for weeks on end, and skating was a common winter activity for cottagers, village children or the guests at grand country house parties. It must have been fun in some ways, and a dangerous and tiresome interruption of normal winter life in others. As regards the effects of these hard winters on field sports, wildlife of all sorts, and on the behaviour, movements and physical condition of woodcock in particular, we can form a fairly good impression from contemporary notes and records.

The winters of 1872–73 and 1878–79 were severe throughout western Britain, extending as far as Cornwall, the Hebrides and the Atlantic coast of Ireland, which are all normally free of frost for most of the winter. The westerly winds off the Atlantic are normally mild and wet, and the warm waters of the North Atlantic Drift help to make these parts of our islands the most attractive and suitable for wildfowl and for probing birds like snipe and woodcock. Woodcock bags were high on shoots throughout western Britain, with reports of major influxes of woodcock along the east coast, and numbers of weak and thin woodcock found in coastal areas of the West Country and Ireland.

It is typical of woodcock that in very hard weather they will eventually resort to the seashore, and when this happens it is a sure sign that the birds are under extreme pressure. This happened in 1878–79, but woodcock shoots reported no apparent falling off in numbers of woodcock wintering in the coverts the following season.

Two years later, in January 1881, another and even more severe winter spell struck western Europe and the British Isles. Its effects on woodcock were carefully observed and recorded by Sir Ralph Payne-Gallwey. In *The Fowler in Ireland* (1882) he tells of "the unexampled frost of January 1881" and how woodcock "positively swarmed on the coast. To my knowledge, peasants out of work and farmers' sons, with old-fashioned muzzle-loaded guns, converted rifles, and Russian muskets [sold cheaply after being captured in thousands in the Crimea] bagged their fifteen couple a day; the best shots among them getting from fifteen to twenty couple. These fellows often ran short of ammunition, or, as they told me, would have accounted for many more. Every hedgeway, every ditch and bundle of furze, held its couple or so of cock; about the cliffs a dozen might often be seen on the wing at once.... This slaughter continued during the greater part of January. For an entire week woodcock might have been bought at between fourpence to sixpence a couple; snipe a penny apiece. One dealer alone in the neighbouring town, though he had two rivals in the trade, forwarded to London a thousand cock a week for three weeks. I counted laid out on benches eight hundred woodcocks in rows – a sight not often to be seen.... From every part of the Irish coast came the same story."

It must have been a remarkable sight, and the birds had evidently been driven quite out of their normal haunts and were to be found at exceptional densities in untypical places. But Payne-Gallwey goes on to tell how these woodcock remained in generally good physical condition.

"It is a common error to imagine that cock, like snipe, will soon lose their condition in frost. The latter in a week will become, if frost be severe, mere skin and bone. Out of hundreds of cock that I examined during the month above referred to, perhaps ony a dozen were small and poor birds, the rest were plump and handsome. I often inspected those shot and exposed for sale, and at the end of the hard weather there was but little appreciable difference in their condition." At a time of severe frost, when woodcock were on the sea-shore and were even being knocked over by countrymen with sticks and stones, Payne-Gallwey was able to look at the huge stocks of woodcock in the dealers' sheds and pick out three birds each weighing sixteen ounces and another of eighteen ounces – far above the normal average winter weight of 11½ ounces.

Payne-Gallwey points out a fundamental difference between woodcock and their cousins the snipe. In a spell of unbroken frost snipe lose condition fast and the wise sportsman will voluntarily stop shooting them after a few days. A really long spell of hard weather hits snipe numbers very hard. The winters of 1941 and 1963 resulted in much-depleted snipe numbers for many years afterwards. Detailed records from some of Ireland's major snipe shoots show clearly that wintering snipe numbers took fully ten years to recover after the 1963 freeze-up. Woodcock do not suffer in the same way. They have repeatedly shown themselves able to adapt to hard weather, to change their roosting and feeding habits, and to maintain good physical condition when many other species are in dire straits.

In 1981–82, 101 years after Payne-Gallwey's observations in western Ireland, the British Isles were hit by yet another unusually hard winter. In December 1981 and again in January 1982 there was severe and prolonged frost over most of western Europe and the British Isles. Woodcock came here in huge numbers from mainland Europe, and the Hebrides, the West Country and Ireland experienced very high densities. In accordance with the agreed criteria, there were two shooting ban periods in Great Britain and in the Republic of Ireland, while sportsmen in Northern Ireland exercised restraint with a self-imposed voluntary ban on the shooting of waders and wildfowl, which reflected great credit on the shooting community.

The birds were restless, were often to be seen on the wing in broad daylight, and could be found feeding by day near open springs and in various patches of unfrozen ground. Corners of fields where cattle had been foddered and had trampled the ground, breaking through the surface ice and opening up slushy, muddy patches, were often frequented by woodcock during the day. Despite weather which killed many snipe, wrens, herons and various other birds, woodcock survived astonishingly well. Conditions were not such as to drive woodcock to the seashore in large numbers, and there were few reports of numbers of weak and emaciated woodcock near the tideline, such as was described in the Poole Harbour area of the Dorset coast during the great freeze of 1963. Woodcock were shot in large numbers on some western shoots in Britain and Ireland in 1981–82, and some bird protection organizations and anti-field sports groups were loud in their condemnation of this. But what were the real effects on woodcock numbers?

As the mildest parts of western Europe, Britain and Ireland were host to countless thousands of woodcock which came here from mainland Europe. Thus fewer woodcock were shot in France and Belgium, where the annual national woodcock bag is normally very high. Although large bags of woodcock were made in some parts of the British Isles, it is questionable whether the total number of woodcock shot throughout western Europe as a whole was any higher than in a more normal, mild winter. Indeed, the total

Frosty weather with a covering of snow means you may see more of woodcock in daytime than usual. David Carlisle's study in oils of a woodcock in the snow shows hints of the influence of Archibald Thorburn.

numbers shot may have been lower than usual. Undoubtedly mortality was high from weather related causes, including deaths by a combination of exhaustion, inadequate food and persistent cold. But these would have happened in any event, with or without shooting. Inevitably the question arises – "Doesn't shooting add to the mortality and make matters worse?"

A clear-cut answer cannot be given to that without more research. Arrangements do of course exist to implement shooting bans on woodcock and other migratory birds and waterfowl in very hard winters, and these are generally observed by sportsmen. Indeed, many will voluntarily stop shooting long before a statutory ban is imposed, especially where snipe are concerned.

But woodcock are clearly a special case, and must be studied further to discover the proper criteria for placing a temporary ban on woodcock shooting. Their obvious ability to adopt alternative feeding strategies and to flourish in conditions which are fatal to many other species means there are good grounds for treating them differently. One suggestion is that woodcock shooting should be permitted for seven days after the banning of shooting of other waterfowl and wader species. However, this or any other delay period must necessarily be rather arbitrary until we actually know much more, from thorough scientific research, about how cold weather actually affects woodcock.

As things stand, hard weather bans apply only to wildfowl and those species which do not fall under the Game Acts in the United Kingdom. Pheasant shoots, where most birds are given large amounts of supplementary feeding, are not affected, and thus there is disturbance to woodlands and other cover which is beaten out for pheasants, and which also holds numbers of woodcock. Woodcock will be disturbed and flushed on pheasant shoots in any event, even if they are not shot, and there would have to be some very persuasive evidence to show that such disturbance is detrimental to woodcock before pheasant shooting could reasonably be banned in hard weather. No such evidence exists at present.

My personal belief is that there is a very good case to be made for treating the woodcock as a gamebird for the purposes of hard weather bans, and in almost every other respect. Indeed, but for a quirk of legislation in 1831, woodcock would already have full gamebird status, and they are certainly every inch a gamebird in the minds of sportsmen everywhere. However, until the scientists can tell us more about woodcock and the effects of hard weather on them, sportsmen must be prepared to bend over backwards to be seen as responsible and enlightened conservationists. Bans applied under agreed criteria must be observed, and the rules can be changed later in the light of new and better understanding of woodcock in hard weather.

I had the good fortune to be able to examine almost two thousand woodcock shot in various parts of north and north-west Ireland during the period from mid-December 1981 to the end of January 1982. Many were examined for wing-ageing purposes and to measure bill lengths, but the birds' physical condition was especially interesting. Out of over 1,800 woodcock which I handled personally, fewer than thirty could have been fairly described as thin. Some were lighter and less well-conditioned than one would have expected, but the vast majority – well over 95% – were plump and in thoroughly good condition. Their good physical condition was reflected in the speed and agility with which they flew when flushed from coverts and hedgerows on shooting days. Somehow the woodcock had been able not only to survive but positively to thrive at a time when other species were suffering dreadfully.

This ability to survive cold conditions is attributable firstly to their positive response to the onset of hard frosts, which means they feed even more

Severe winter weather causes woodcock to adapt their noctural feeding habits. Robin Williams photographed this woodcock probing for food and swallowing an earthworm in broad daylight, amid flurries of snow, during the cold snap in mid-December 1982.

voraciously than usual and thus put on weight and condition. Then when freezing weather has actually tightened its grip the species shows a remarkable degree of adaptability. The normal pattern of daytime roosting and night-time feeding gives way to an opportunistic approach to feeding. Woodcock have a knack of finding out the unfrozen spots and making the most of those feeding grounds which are still usable. There are countless reports of woodcock feeding by day, often close to houses, in gardens and along roadsides. Woodcock have been photographed feeding in broad daylight, often in quite deep snow and amid swirls of fresh snowflakes. The French sporting press, and *La Mordorée* in particular, published several pictures of woodcock feeding successfully by day in some very unlikely places.

In the short but severe frosts of February 1986 Mrs Derek Bingham, wife of the then editor of *Shooting Times*, saw a woodcock feeding by an unfrozen pond in a Suffolk garden in mid-afternoon. It was probing deeply in the mud along the pond's edge, repeatedly plunging not only its bill but its whole head under water. At the same period of hard weather the wife of a prominent Cornish woodcock expert found a woodcock at the back door of their house one evening, presumably driven there in a search for food after blizzard conditions hit the West Country.

Woodcock have come close to houses, and even into them, on several recorded occasions, usually when bad weather has disrupted the birds' normal patterns of movement. One particularly delightful story of a woodcock which came and stayed the night occurred in Argyllshire in February 1984. A blizzard driven by a north-easterly wind brought a woodcock to the window of Lady Gainford's kitchen at midnight. Like Edgar Allen Poe's raven it tapped on the window and when this was opened, it hopped promptly into the house. There it hopped and walked about with apparent assurance, almost as though it knew the layout of the house, finally stopping in a dark corner of the sitting room and settling down to roost on top of the gramophone. There it remained until dawn, when Lady Gainford picked it up and released it through the door into the garden, when it flew off quite happily.

In hard frosts and snow woodcock will fly about by day and are quick to locate and feed at spots they would not normally visit. Muddy farm tracks where passing vehicles have broken through the ice and snow are often used, and the verges of busy roads too. These and other unfrozen places are always worth looking at closely: you may see a woodcock, or perhaps several, in the most unlikely places. But do not disturb them unnecessarily when really severe conditions have made their lives difficult enough already.

All the responses of the European woodcock to hard weather are mirrored in the American woodcock. Some particularly good accounts exist of their unusual behaviour and modified feeding habits in the exceptionally severe North American winter of 1939–40. Mortality was high, but the population recovered fully within a season or two, just as happens with the European woodcock.

CHAPTER VII

"RIGHT AND LEFT" – THE COVETED DOUBLE

"I think it was jolly clever of Les to kill two birds with one stone, or whatever it's called'".

Gerald Durrell: *My Family and Other Animals* (1956)

"Ballistically the equivalent of a hole-in-one", according to one writer, a right-and left at woodcock is one of the most unusual achievements in game shooting. When it does happen – and some enthusiasts with hundreds or even thousands of woodcock to their credit may never manage it – it is cause for personal satisfaction, congratulations all round and membership of a rather exclusive little club.

The emblem of the *Shooting Times* Woodcock Club, showing the four pin-feathers. Anyone who shoots a right-and-left and has two witnesses can apply for membership, which entitles them to a badge and tie bearing the S.T.W.C. emblem, and a bottle of J&B Rare Scotch Whisky.

Providing you have two eye-witnesses who can confirm your "double" you can become a member of the *Shooting Times* Woodcock Club. Membership brings you a bottle of J&B Rare Scotch Whisky to celebrate your feat, and there is a distinctive club badge and a tie, and the emblem on each shows four woodcock pin-feathers. Since 1985 the Club has also held a highly successful annual dinner in early spring, giving members an opportunity to meet after the end of another shooting season, to swap stories about their sport and, above all, to gossip about woodcock.

Why is a right-and-left at woodcock regarded as such a notable achievement? The answer lies mainly in the solitary habits of woodcock, which tend to roost singly in cover on winter days. It is therefore very unusual to flush more than one woodcock at once. To this must be added other factors. Woodcock fly erratically, often twisting off through low cover and rarely flying in a wholly predictable direction. Often when a woodcock is flushed on a general day's covert shooting or rough shooting, normal etiquette and sporting practice is abandoned. A woodcock within range is often regarded as fair game for any of the Guns, and a great many shooters will have had the chance of a right-and-left at woodcock and successfully downed the first bird, only to find that the other 'cock is shot by another Gun before they can fire their second barrel – a very frustrating experience.

This attitude is part and parcel of the excitement which woodcock can cause among some sportsmen when they appear on a shooting day. Guns who would never dream of poaching another's bird, if a pheasant or a partridge is involved, have no compunction about shooting a woodcock which, strictly speaking, "belongs" to a neighbouring Gun. In fairness, this is not always the result of excitement or greedy shooting. Often you must take your chance of a snap-shot at a woodcock while you can, and conditions on 'cock shoots often mean you cannot take an "after you, Claude" approach.

Another problem is the over-excitement which can assail even the steadiest of Guns when two woodcock appear on the wing and in range at the same time. Over-eagerness can mean that even a good shot will fluff it, usually through trying too hard, not shooting in a relaxed and natural way, and already thinking about the second bird before the first has been hit – always a recipe for failure with right-and-lefts of any sort.

One of the most remarkable right-and-lefts I know of happened to a very eminent sportsman and authority on sporting art. It was during his war service, when he was posted to Skye in the Inner Hebrides. A few off-duty hours one September evening meant he and some fellow officers could escape to shoot rabbits, which swarmed among the sand dunes – exciting sport and a welcome source of meat at a time of rationing.

The party was returning by truck at dusk when two woodcock appeared, flighting out together to feed. Quick loading meant two woodcock shot cleanly, right-and-left, by a Gun standing precariously on the tailboard of a bumping, jolting truck on a rough Hebridean track. When you think what that means in terms of modifying the swing of the gun to allow for the forward motion of the vehicle, it is an extraordinary achievement. But it was done by an extraordinarily good shot, who has had several other right-and-lefts over a long shooting career, and whose expertise at knocking down high pheasants still outshines Guns half his age.

Finally, there are many other odd and imponderable problems. Perhaps the two birds flush just as you are getting over a fence or through a gap with an unloaded gun. Perhaps you have just fired a shot at another bird and the pair appear when you have only one barrel left. Perhaps you take two shots to down the first bird, or simply miss them both cleanly. One bird may drop to your first shot while the second has escaped into cover or flicked around a tree in typical woodcock fashion. Perhaps most frustrating of all is when you actually hit both birds and see them fall, but fail to pick one of them, despite a long search.

Wintering woodcock tend to roost singly but if these two, sketched by Neil McReddie, are flushed together the Gun may have the rare chance of achieving a right-and-left.

Even the most straightforward opportunity, as when two 'cock fly out of a pheasant covert and into the open right over your peg, with a steady and undeviating flight, can be missed. Their speed is deceptive, while your eyes, reflexes and swing are attuned to the more predictable speed of driven pheasants – and you may be painfully aware of a gallery of other Guns, pickers-up and beaters all watching you. It is always unexpected, and it is never easy. You may go shooting three days a week for fifty seasons in good woodcock country and still never achieve it; or you may have only a few hours rough shooting on an occasional Saturday and manage to bag a right-and-left more than once. My personal experience is that, if you shoot regularly in good woodcock country, a reasonable chance of a right-and-left will probably present itself once a season, on average. But so often something goes wrong!

In this connection – and this is not being pedantic – what precisely *is* a right-and-left? May the butt of the gun leave the shoulder between shots? (Most shooting school coaches say you ought to re-mount the gun for each shot, to align properly.) Should you actually have two birds dead in the air at once? Does it count if you flush a single 'cock, shoot it, and the sound of the shot causes another 'cock to flush, which you also bag a second or two later with the other barrel? There is scope for lots of heated and ultimately fruitless discussion here – fruitless because I am not aware of any precise definition of what constitutes a right-and-left, nor of any consensus among shooting people. That is one of the charms of game shooting as a sport. There are strict procedures for gun safety and general agreement about etiquette, good sportsmanship and humane practices, but shooting is not hidebound by many other rules. It is essentially uncompetitive: each Gun is on his own, testing his skill against the shots that come his way.

But when you do get your right-and-left – unforgettable day! – and however it may happen, your membership of that exclusive club and the pleasure of broaching that bottle of J&B Rare Scotch Whisky may still be denied you, unless you have the two necessary witnesses. A lot of right-and-lefts have been shot by solitary rough-shooters, or by a Gun shooting with only one companion. Sadly, dogs don't count: if your second witness's signature consists of a muddy footprint inscribed "'Meg' – her mark", it just isn't good enough! I have seen a clean and very skilful right-and-left scored on four occasions when I have been shooting with one other Gun, and the best I could do was to order champagne rather than beer when we got to the pub at lunchtime.

Founded in 1983, the *Shooting Times* Woodcock Club is the British successor to the Bols Snippen Club, set up in the Netherlands in 1949 by the Dutch distillers Bols. For over thirty years this popular club provided lucky shooters with a coveted badge and a handsome tie, with a pattern of four pin-feathers repeated on an attractive dark green background. The tie and the badge became a familiar sight in shooting circles throughout Europe, though it was not surprising that one saw them more often in the woodcock hot-spots like Cornwall, west Wales and Ireland. Your first right-and-left brought you a bottle of Bols apricot brandy, and any subsequent doubles meant a "bar" to your badge and another bottle for your cellar.

In 1981 the Bols Snippen Club was wound up, and Tony Jackson, then Editor of *Shooting Times & Country Magazine*, was quick to establish a new club to succeed it, based in England, co-ordinated by *Shooting Times* and sponsored by J&B Rare Scotch Whisky. A flourishing membership grew up in a season or two, and those whose right-and-left pre-dated the Club's foundation or who had belonged to the Bols Snippen Club were able to become Associate Members. (It is also noteworthy that the predominantly British – and even the Irish – membership of the Club find the taste of J&B's excellent dram more to their liking than a continental apricot liqueur.)

The inaugural dinner of the S.T.W.C. was held on 29 March, 1985, in the impressive civic splendour of the Guildhall in Windsor, just a short walk from the offices of *Shooting Times*. I was privileged to be the guest speaker on that occasion, which was attended by over seventy Club members from Britain and Ireland. Delicious food and the fine wines one would expect to come from the cellars of the Club's sponsors, Justerini & Brooks, made it an evening to remember. As we took our places at table we found two crimson-coloured twelve-bore cartridges, bearing the emblem of J&B Rare Scotch Whisky, flanking each of the crisply folded damask napkins – "for your *next* right-and-left", as Henry Lorimer of J&B explained! Some of us, myself

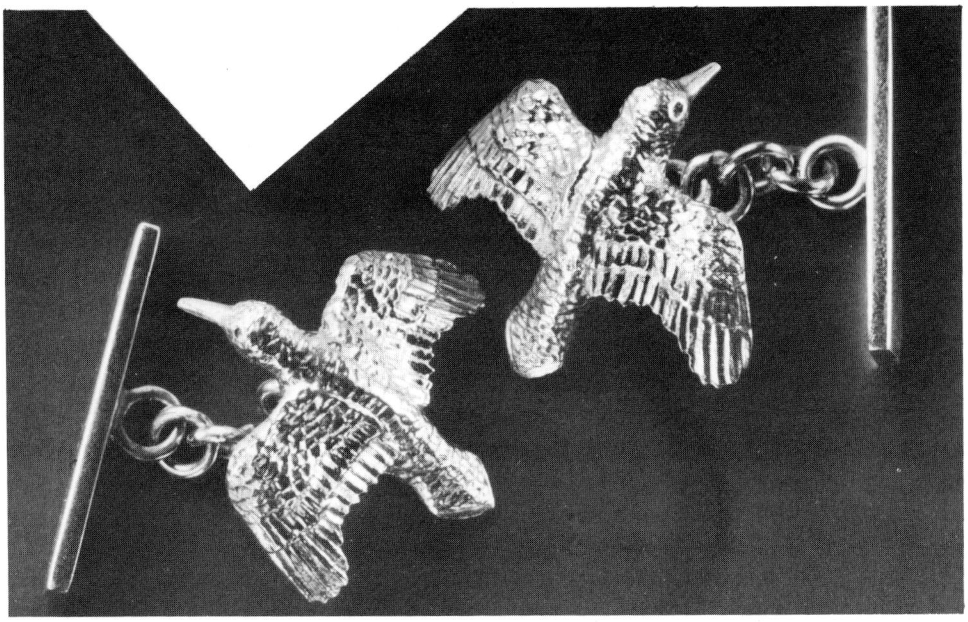

Another type of right-and-left – one on each sleeve! A pair of finely-modelled woodcock cufflinks, the work of Ian Ruff of Ruffs (Jewellers) Ltd. of Gosport in Hampshire.

included, felt decidedly fraudulent, not yet having scored our first.

It was a wise man who first observed that "there is no such thing as a free meal". The truth of that remark was evident to me that night since, after all that wonderful food and wine, I was expected to get to my feet and (metaphorically) sing for my supper. "Just give them a speech which is witty, amusing and informative about woodcock," said the Club's founding Chairman, Tony Jackson, with a grin. It was rather daunting.

Facing me at the other end of the great banqueting hall was a life-size portrait of Queen Victoria shortly after her accession, and around the walls were other portraits of successive British sovereigns, most of whom had considerable reputations as keen and successful shots. It seemed appropriate at a gathering of people who had shot a right-and-left at woodcock to refer to a celebrated incident involving two woodcock which took place just a few years before the young Princess Victoria became Queen.

On 20 November, 1829, a shoot took place on the estate of the Coke family, Earls of Leicester, at Holkham in Norfolk. It was, and still is, a notable shoot, and among the guests was the fashionable sculptor Sir Francis Chantrey. On one of the beats two woodcock were flushed and Chantrey bagged them both with a single shot. This freak achievement – for, remarkable though it was and celebrated though it was to become, it was still a matter of pure chance rather than skill – was regarded as even more noteworthy since Chantrey was blind in his right eye. He shot from the right shoulder, however, and his flintlock gun had a special "cross-eyed" stock to enable him to align the barrels with his good left eye. One classically minded contemporary remarked that Chantrey's gun, like the bow of Ulysses, could only be used by its true owner.

The event caused a great deal of comment at the time, was duly entered in the Holkham game book, and Chantrey commemorated it by making a monumental sculpture in white marble, showing the two birds tumbling down and bearing a grateful inscription to his host, Thomas Coke. Curiously, Chantrey's inscription gives the year of this remarkable double as 1830, although the written record in the Holkham game-book clearly shows 20 November, 1829. The monument still remains at Holkham, though it was taken briefly to London for the British Field Sports Society's loan exhibition of sporting art and artefacts at Sotheby's in December, 1984. Later it was taken to America as a feature of the "Treasure Houses of Britain" exhibition held in the National Gallery in Washington in 1986.

A famous monument to commemorate a famous event – Sir Francis Chantrey's marble monument at Holkham to celebrate his two woodcock killed by one shot in 1829. Although the Holkham game book clearly records the event in 1829, Chantrey's sculpture gives 1830 as the date. The famous shot and the subsequent sculpture were the occasion for many witty verses and epigrams.

Word of Chantrey's extraordinary 'double' spread, and led to a very unusual phenomenon in the sporting world. For some years afterwards a long succession of contemporary sportsmen, academics, public figures, men of letters and wits wrote little poems and epigrams about it, many of them in Latin couplets and Greek hexameters. The manuscripts of these verses are preserved in the library at Holkham, and in 1857 they were published in what is now a very rare little book, entitled *Winged Words on Chantrey's Woodcock,* edited by James Patrick Muirhead.

Most of the contributors to this sporting *festschrift* in Chantrey's honour were struck not only by the freak event but by the way the marksmanship of a professional sculptor had bagged the birds, and the same sportsman's artistic skills had immortalized the birds in sculptured marble. One contribution – by a bishop – sets the tone:

Life in death, a mystic lot,
Dealt thou to the winged band:
Death – from thine unerring shot;
Life – from thine undying hand.

Muirhead, who later edited the verses and made an elegant translation of a long Latin poem written by the then Marquess of Wellesley, made several contributions of his own, of which this is one:

The hand of Chantrey by a single blow
At once laid these united woodcocks low;
But the same hand (its double skill so great),
By single blow their life did re-create.

Another couplet takes the same theme:

He hit the birds: and with an aim as true
And hand as skilful, hit their likeness too!

Others indulged in a little play on words, in the slightly ponderous wit of the period:

Chantrey invented the best of gun locks,
Which cocks one hammer and hammers two cocks.

or:

The 'cocks are two: the shot was one:
Chantrey had ***double-cocked*** *his gun.*

And a final couplet, from the pen of one Joseph Jekyll, summed up the wit the freak event and the unusual memorial:

Two birds with one stone – but the proverb has wit;
If one stone revives both the birds it has hit.

Although Chantrey's feat, his marble monument and some of the curious versifying which followed are quite well known, it is not generally realized that those two most celebrated woodcock were recorded in another artistic form, in a painting by the aspiring sporting and wildlife artist Edwin Landseer.

In 1836, at the age of 34, Landseer was commissioned by Chantrey to paint his favourite gundog "Mustard" and to include in the composition the two Holkham woodcock which had been shot seven years previously. Perhaps "Mustard" was with his master when the event happened: perhaps he even retrieved the birds. At all events, Landseer duly produced the painting, entitled "Mustard, son of Pepper", and sent it to the dog's delighted master. *Blackwood's Magazine* called it "an immortal picture", something of an overstatement perhaps, and public interest seems, predictably, to have focused less on the dog than the woodcock and Chantrey's much-discussed "double". There was no mistaking the client's pleasure. "I am more than satisfied that you have produced a picture of my favourite dog Mustard that stands without a rival."

Landseer, too much the gentleman and with a lifelong ineptitude for the business side of his painting, apparently did not submit any charges for his work. Chantrey wrote a jovial but firm letter to his young friend, demanding a bill for a realistic fee – "Now, on the score of money... I have to request that you will do yourself and your profession justice without one word about friendship.... This I insist upon and with this you must comply or I no longer remain, Yours sincerely, F. Chantrey. Mark this, Mister Landseer!"

Reluctantly, Landseer asked for 150 guineas for a painting which his client valued at 200 guineas. Chantrey paid Landseer's fee but added that "either I

must feel obligated to you for 50 guineas or you will feel under obligation to me for the same sum. I remain your Debtor."

Landseer, who was offered a knighthood six years later but refused, eventually accepting only in 1850, remained a close friend of Chantrey. He later depicted him in a delightful series of sporting cartoons, tussling up to his waist in water with a mighty salmon and sitting disconsolately in his shirt-tails while his clothes dried out. A gifted mimic, Landseer could impersonate Chantrey's voice, and once did so at a dinner party, much to the confusion of Chantrey's servants and the mirth of the other guests.

Although what Chantrey did is remarkable, and his skill as a sculptor perpetuated the event, it has also happened to others. Several Guns have actually killed two 'cock with their first barrel and a third with the second shot. In the enlarged edition of his compendious *Record Bags and Shooting Records* (1930) Hugh Gladstone lists 23 instances of two woodcock to one shot, and five cases of three 'cock to two barrels. Two of the two-for-one incidents happened to a father and his son, and another also involved the death of an unfortuate blackbird which chanced to get in the way of the same shot as killed the two 'cock. Predictably, almost all of these events took place in parts of the country where woodcock are numerous in winter, including Cornwall, Scotland, Northumberland, Norfolk and Ireland.

Most remarkable of all – a "double-decker" – is the story of Lord Balfour of Burleigh. Shooting in Clackmannanshire in the 1890s, he had four woodcock flush together from an oak wood and come over his peg. He shot all four with two barrels. Had the *Shooting Times* Woodcock Club existed in those days, Lord Balfour would presumably have been made life president and given a whole distillery all to himself.

CHAPTER VIII

WOODCOCK – SPRINGES, COCK-SHUTS AND FALCONS

"Fowling is much more troublesome, but all out as delightsome to some sorts of men, be it with guns, lime, nets, glades, gins, strings, baits, pitfalls, pipes, calls, stalking-horses, setting dogs, decoy ducks &... an ornament and a recreation."

Robert Burton *The Anatomy of Melancholy* (1621)

"Springes to catch woodcocks!" is the contemptuous comment of Polonius, the worldly-wise and cynical father of Ophelia in *Hamlet*, when he hears his daughter tell of Hamlet's declarations of love towards her. Quite simply, he means "traps to catch stupid people". A springe is a noose or snare, traditionally made of horsehair, and the woodcock was proverbially regarded as an especially stupid bird and very easy to catch in snares, nooses and traps. In medieval and Elizabethan English literature the woodcock is almost always mentioned as a symbol of stupidity and artlessness. In Beaumont and Fletcher's play *Wit Without Money* (1639) Isabella exclaims:

O Cupid!
What pretty gins thou hast to halter woodcocks!

and later in the same play says:

If I loved you not, I would laugh at you, and see you
Run your neck into the noose, and cry – "A woodcock!"

In France it is still a term of contempt to call someone a *bécasse* or a *"grand bec"*, and the expression *"sourde comme une bécasse"* ("as deaf as a woodcock") continues the traditional view of the bird as stupid, unresponsive and dim-witted. The old English and French idea of crediting woodcock with the very minimum of brains is found in other countries too.

A crude woodcut illustration of the sixteenth century, when woodcock were pursued by falconers, and trapped by the "fowler" with his springes and cock-shut nets.

Not too much noise! Charles Whymper's engraving shows a cautionary signal from an experienced beater on an Irish covert shoot. Opinions are divided on how best to drive woodcock. Some like nothing more than a gentle tapping of sticks, with dogs working quietly and closely to the beating line, while others favour lots of noise and disturbance by beaters and dogs alike.

The Spanish are scarcely less dismissive; to them the woodcock is *el sordo*, "the deaf one", for deafness has tended, unkindly but traditionally, to be associated with dullness and stupidity. In fact, the specific allegation of deafness almost certainly arose from an interpretation of the way in which woodcock will often lie very tight and flush only at the last minute, with dogs or beaters almost on top of them, however much noise is made, unlike many other woodland species which move off as soon as they hear danger approaching. (It is interesting, however, to note that driven woodcock afficionados are often sharply divided over the question of noise in the coverts. Some like lots of shouting, whistling, flailing with sticks and general hullaballoo, and lots of wild spaniels crashing about and giving tongue, to add to the general *mêlée*. Others favour a slow, restrained approach, with nothing more than a gentle tapping of sticks and dogs working silently and close to the beating line.)

"Fowling" or the art of taking wild birds with nets, traps, snares and various other mean is a very ancient art. For some species, especially small passerines, it also extended to concoctions such as birdlime, but this would not normally have been used specifically to take the non-perching woodcock. These methods were familiar to the Egyptians and other early civilizations of the Middle East, as well as to later generations of European bird catchers like Mozart's Pappageno, and, quite illegally, to a good many modern-day poachers too. Some of the oldest identifiable illustrations of our familiar gamebird species, including woodcock, come from the tomb carvings of ancient Egypt.

Ancient Egyptian carvings like this one are some of the earliest depictions of woodcock. The early civilisations of the Mediterranean knew about woodcock, which are winter visitors there, and caught them with nets, springs and foot-snares.

The Greeks also knew about the taking of birds on the ground with snares, nooses and springes, and an early Greek poem refers to "the triple twisted foot-snare; the springes of stretched sinew... and running neck nooses". In the Art Museum of the University of Pennsylvania there is a fine vase from the south of Italy in the fourth century B.C. depicting the god Eros holding a bird snare which is shown in some detail. It is not very different in style and construction from the woodcock traps and springes which were familiar to Shakespeare and were still used in Britain less than a century ago. You can still find countrymen, mainly in Cornwall, Devon and parts of Wales, who know how to set a snare for a woodcock.

The poet William Wordsworth also knew how to snare woodcock, and did it often during his childhood in the Lake District. In his long poetic biography *The Prelude* he describes how he and his school-fellows would set springes on the hill pastures to catch the woodcock which flighted out to feed there by night:

... 'twas my joy
With store of springes o'er my shoulder hung
To range the open heights where woodcocks run
Among the smooth green turf. Through half the night,
Scudding away from snare to snare, I plied
My anxious visitation.

This was enterprising and skilful work for a little boy who, he tells us, had not yet "told ten birthdays", and apparently an innocent enough activity. There would be birds for the table or, more probably, additional pocket-money when they were sold to a local game dealer, to become part of the regular consignment of Cumbrian woodcock sent on the Kendal stagecoach to the London market each week during the late autumn and winter.

Wordsworth's account confirms what the late eighteenth-century naturalist Thomas Pennant wrote about the extensive snaring of 'cock in Cumbria. "On the plain part of the hills, near Winander water [i.e. Windermere], he saw numbers of springes for woodcocks set between tufts of heath, with avenues of small stones on each side, to direct these foolish birds into the snares.... Multitudes are taken in this manner in the open weather, are sold on the spot for sixteen or twenty pence a couple [in the 1760s the price was six or seven pence a couple] and sent to the all-devouring Capital by the Kendal stage." W.H. Scott in *British Field Sports* (1820) also wrote of the large numbers of woodcock taken in springes and nets in Cumberland and Westmorland each winter and sent to London, but he quotes a very much higher price: "At particular seasons, as high as sixteen shillings the couple." This is an exceptionally large sum of money for that period. Quite probably the local boys like Wordsworth made some useful additions to their pocket money by selling snared woodcock at sixteen or eighteen pence a couple, while the dealers make a real financial killing by selling the birds in London for ten times as much or more.

Perhaps those high prices and the chance to supplement his pocket money occasionally led to temptation, for Wordsworth admits that his night-time round of his 'cock snares was not always totally innocent. He had occasionally been tempted to take a woodcock from another boy's springe, and tells of the sense of guilt he felt afterwards:

Sometimes it befell
In these night wanderings, that a strong desire
O'erpowered my better reason, and the bird
Which was the captive of another's toil
Became my prey; and when the deed was done
I heard among the solitary hills
Low breathings coming after me.

In snaring and other forms of trapping, the woodcock was a comparatively easy prey, owing to its predictable habits, especially in winter. Once its night-time feeding grounds were located, usually by the tell-tale marks left by the birds' probing in mud and ooze, it became a simple matter to set a springe or other trap, with a high probability of success. One of the very best descriptions of woodcock snaring and trapping and the use of old-style springes is given by A.E. Knox, in his *Game Birds and Wild Fowl* (1850). As a boy, and without any expert guidance from an old hand, he made his first attempts to catch woodcock and found it quite easy. The birds' feeding grounds and runs were very obvious, as they had been a generation earlier to the youthful Wordsworth and his Cumbrian schoolmates, and all he needed was a well-placed trap with a funnelled approach to guide the feeding bird into it.

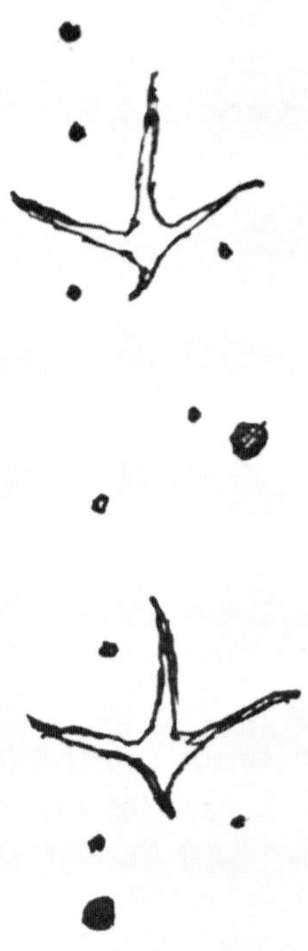

Woodcock tracks in the snow. Note the imprint left by the short hind toe, and the difference between the tentative shallow probings of the bill and the larger holes made where the bird has probed deeply.

"When quite a boy, I once availed myself of this habit to catch a woodcock, which I fondly imagined I could successfully rear in confinement. The scene was a small dell of birch and alder. A common box trap, such as is used for taking rats and stoats or weasels alive, was the instrument that I thought most likely to suit my purpose. This I placed exactly in the middle of the run, where the tracks and perforations were most numerous, but without taking the precaution of screening it from observation. On visiting the spot next morning I found that my first essay had been unsuccessful: and a short examination sufficed to show the cause. There were traces of at least one or two woodcocks close to the trap; but instead of attempting to pass through it, they had inclined a little out of the direct line, and, apparently without evincing any other symptom of alarm, had, after passing the obstacle, resumed their course through the swamp." Evidently woodcock, for all their proverbial stupidity and susceptibility to trapping, were not going to walk into a trap set so ingenuously in the open. But young Knox refined his tactics, and hit on the traditional 'cock-trappers' technique of funnelling the feeding birds into the trap.

"I now placed a few boughs on both sides so as to prevent a recurrence of this mishap, but not without sundry misgivings that my rude fence might cause the birds to take flight, and prehaps scare them from their feeding places. My apprehensions, however, were groundless, for on the following morning I found a woodcock safely incarcerated, which, as a faithful chronicler of facts, I am bound to confess soon died under my fostering care."

The use of the springe to catch woodcock and snipe began with a simple running noose of cord, twine or animal sinew attached to a whippy twig. If correctly placed on the feeding grounds and on a clearly identified run, with some method of guiding the walking bird into the desired position, the slightest contact of the bird with the horizontal trigger-twig would release the spring of the snare and the noose would snap closed around the 'cock's neck and jerk it into the air. Later refinements resulted in another design of springe, which used a finely plaited length of horsehair. This was looped into a noose, and a whippy rod was once again used as the snare's power source, but the running of the noose was reversed so that the snared bird was not pulled into the air, to dangle and strangle slowly like a hanged man on a gallows. Birds might be held alive like this for some time, and the old-style springe often meant that in the morning the trapper checking his snares might find a proportion of his catch still alive, and sometimes relatively undamaged. By contrast, the "improved" model closed tightly around the woodcock's neck and pulled its head and neck sharply downwards and against a transverse peg or twig at ground level. A cleaner kill was much more likely.

But the ancient type of springe remained in regular use in many country areas of Britain, and Knox described how, in the 1840s, he saw an old-style woodcock trapper going about his craft "in one of the most picturesque tracts of the forest range of Sussex".

"Suspended like a felon on a gibbet" – Joseph Wolf's engraving shows a woodcock taken in a springe – a noose, usually of horsehair, sprung on a wand of willow.

"We soon found many tracks of the woodcock on the black mud; and on one spot these, as well as the borings of his beak, were very numerous. Here my companion halted, and pulling out his knife, cut down a tall willow rod, which he stuck firmly into the ground in nearly an upright position, or perhaps rather inclining backwards. On the opposite side of the run he fixed a peg, so as to project only a few inches above the surface: to this he fastened a slight stick about a foot long, attached loosely with a tough string, much as the swingel of a flail is to its hand-staff: another branch of willow was bent into an arch, and both ends driven into the soft ground to a considerable depth on the opposite side of the track, and nearer to the tall upright wand. To the tip of the latter a string was now fastened, the end of which was formed into a noose; while, about half-way down, another piece of stick, about six inches long, was tied by its middle. The flexible wand was then bent forcibly downwards, one end of the little stick overhead was passed under the arch, while it was retained in this position, and at the same time the bow prevented from springing upwards, by its extremity being placed against a notch at the end of the stick which had been fastened to the peg on the other side of the run, across which it now lay, two or three inches from the ground, and supported the noose. This, in fact, constituted the trigger, which was to be released when struck by the breast of the woodcock.

"The old man constructed the trap in much less time than I have taken – and how imperfectly – to describe it.... His last care was to weave the sedges on either side of the run into a kind of screen so as to *weir* the woodcock into the snare, and this he accomplished with much skill and expedition."

Knox arranged to meet his old trapper friend at daybreak next morning, but his impatience to see the outcome took him to the spot before the old man. He was not disappointed. "On emerging from the sedges, there hung dangling before my eyes, suspended like a gibbeted felon in mid-air – a woodcock. He

Sir Ralph Payne-Gallwey Bt, was one of the keenest and best informed nineteenth century writers on woodcock – and many other forms of game shooting and wildfowling. Here he is depicted in his gunroom at Thirkleby Hall. His many conventional sporting guns are shown alongside his famous collection of punt-guns, and the many forms of bows and crossbows with which he also experimented. He was a keen fisherman, as his rack of rods shows, and a hooded goshawk denotes his enthusiasm for falconry. (Photo: Sothebys)

was noosed round the neck, and although still warm was quite dead; and as I smoothed down his ruffled, though bloodless feathers, and admired the exquisite arrangement of his plumage, I thought he was worthy of a place in my collection. There he now occupies a conspicuous niche, and I never look at him without thinking of bygone days, the swamp in the glen, and the old poacher and his springe."

Sir Ralph Payne-Gallwey had a particular interest in woodcock and a typically Victorian fascination with the mechanical workings of sporting implements and equipment of all kinds, from punt guns to crossbows. On his trips to Ireland in pursuit of wildfowl, snipe and woodcock he often came across the use of the springe to take woodcock and waterfowl of various species, and notes that modified forms of springe were also used in eastern and southern England to take game of all sorts, including partridges and hares.

"A springe for taking snipe, woodcock, and other wildfowl, often used in Ireland, though scarcely lawful to describe, is not only a very effective means of capture, but is extremely simple in its construction. It is made as follows:

"Stick a pliant wand of a yard and a half in length firmly into the earth; bend it down till the ends of a short cross-stick attached to it, and which may be four inches long, catch (as shown in the woodcut) in the notches cut to receive them in two stout pegs driven firmly into the ground, and showing a couple of inches above the surface. Pass the fine wires that are attached to the cross-stick over a slight nick in the top of each peg, and place the running nooses flat on the soil.... When a bird is snared, the little stick between the upright is freed at once, the wand flies upwards, and the victim is strangled. This is all done so quickly and quietly that the captive is not missed by his companions, though he dangle above them."

A springe for taking woodcock or snipe. Here Charles Whymper has shown a snipe taken in the traditional horsehair snare used since ancient times.

Springes might be set in ones and twos, especially if the snarer only wanted one for the pot. But large-scale snaring to supply the market was also practised, and the snarer would set a line consisting perhaps of dozens of springes, rather like a rabbit trapper, though the woodcock springes required much more care and time to set properly. These commercial snarers set off well before nightfall, like young Wordsworth, "with store of springes", and might set two or three dozen in a boggy field or marsh which was known to attract numbers of woodcock at night. Just as a single springe would probably be set with turves or lengths of wood to guide the feeding 'cock towards the noose, the larger-scale operation involved exploiting the woodcocks' tendency to walk about while feeding, and to wander around obstacles rather than hop or fly over them. Banks of earth, low thorn hedges and ridges of turf and sods of earth would be set across a pasture or bog, with gaps here and there to let woodcock through, and these were the snaring points. De Visme Shaw had seen this done in the 1860s, but knew that the practice was dying out in all but the remotest areas, where there were few vigilant gamekeepers likely to see it.

"On coming to the hedge or ridge, a woodcock, according to its habit, instead of flying over, walked along the side till it reached the first opening, and attempting to pass through, it was almost inevitably made a captive. Where woodcock were plentiful, the results must have amply repaid the trouble of erecting the ridge or hedge and keeping it patched up year after year. Possibly this plan is still in vogue on a small scale in some of the wilder parts of this kingdom, but the modern poacher, in England at least, would have a small chance of pursuing a system that entailed the construction of so conspicuous an object as an artificial ridge or a low hedge across the marshland."

That "triple twisted foot-snare" known to the ancient Greeks was also used to catch woodcock, but it seems to have been much more widely used in France and other Mediterannean countries than in the British Isles. It was a less skilful form of snaring woodcock, and consisted of setting a large number of free-running nooses lying on the ground more or less at random across areas where woodcock were known to feed at night. The system worked on the assumption that, if enough small nooses were set out, 'cock would be bound to step into some of them as they walked about and probed for food, and would thus be caught and held by the legs. A favourite place to set a series of these nooses was around the fringes of a muddy pool or along the edges of a drain or spring which woodcock visited regularly at night, especially if such places remained unfrozen when other feeding grounds were frozen too hard to be probed for food. This method, though effective, is crude when compared with the artistry of the well-made and cunningly set springe. Though its use is illegal, we may still admire the skill needed to make, position

and use a springe effectively. But ground nooses are unacceptable, though unfortunately they are still in use in some parts of the world, to catch various species of ground-feeding birds. Modern monofilament nylon nooses are easy to make, long-lasting and almost invisible to birds and other creatures, even in daylight, and their use is as much to be deplored as the illegal use of monofilament netting to take salmon.

The springe or snare was one of the commonest methods of taking both woodcock and snipe, but 'cock were often caught in other ways. The "cock-shut" or flight net was widely used in medieval and more modern times, and is frequently referred to by Shakespeare and other writers of Elizabethan times. It consisted of a fine net set up on poles or hung between trees, usually along forest rides or in gaps at the edges of coverts and other areas where woodcock were known to roost during the daytime. Flight netting succeeded because it was known that woodcock tend to follow the same regular flightlines to and from their night-time feeding grounds, leaving and returning to their roosts along the same flight paths and through the same gaps night after night. Once the birds' flightlines had been established it was a simple matter to set nets in the critical positions and wait for the flighting 'cock to fly into them and become entangled.

Often the birds' routes and the rides and gaps they favoured in particular coverts were known and continued unchanged for decades. Brian Vesey-Fitzgerald, formerly Editor of *The Field*, wrote in 1946 of how "the birds in my wood all use the same feeding grounds, and they all fly to these grounds by the same route and return by the same route, but they fly independently. They come flying down the ride – usually at a height of about five feet – one behind the other with an interval of a minute or so between each.... Bird after bird does exactly the same thing, and bird after bird has done exactly the same thing evening after evening for all the twenty and more years that I have known them in the wood. The return flight is exactly the same, and entrance to the wood is made in exactly the same place, and a similar flighting movement takes place at dawn."

The effectiveness of this method of taking woodcock when conditions were right is shown by a very early account, in George Owen's *Description of Pembrokshire* (1602) which speaks of "marvellous plentie" of 'cock in that area between Michaelmas and Christmas, when the birds were caught "in cock shoote tyme (as yt is tearmed) wch is the twylight.... Yt is no strange thing to take a hundred or sixe score in one woodd in XXIIII houres". This must have indicated not only a tremendously high density of woodcock but also some very intensive netting. Another old account tells of one wood where thirteen cock-shuts were regularly set.

De Visme Shaw gives a good description of cock-shut netting. "The arrangements for netting 'cock were simple. A net of requisite length and breadth was suspended across the glade or opening used by the birds leaving the covert.... The moment the bird struck the net, the fowler, crouching in the undergrowth or hidden by an artificial screen, released or pulled the line he held, the result being that the net dropped and the 'cock found itself captive."

Netting of flighting woodcock seems generally to have declined during the nineteenth century, by which time the sporting gun was the principal means of taking woodcock, both by legitimate sportsmen and poachers. Snaring and netting did continue, however, especially in western parts of Britain and Ireland where numbers of wintering woodcock have always tended to be higher than elsewhere in the country. P.D. Williams, with long experience of woodcock shooting, especially in Cornwall, described in 1929 how he had once seen the gamebook of a West Country squire who, with his keeper, regularly shot three or four days each week in the period 1802-1817.

Setting a "cock-shut net". A party of authorised bird ringers and helpers set up mist nets in a woodcock breeding area in early spring, to catch and ring roding birds. This scene would have been recognisable to the glade-netters of medieval times, who caught woodcock for the table by the same methods.

Woodcock and snipe were his principal game, with pheasants a rarity, which is still true of many western parts of Britian and Ireland today, and that old gamebook also had a special column to record woodcock "taken in the net".

The Rev W.B. Daniel, writing in 1801, said that although springes were widely used in Cumbria, "glade netting" was particularly prevalent in the West Country, and he condemned it as an over-exploitation of the species. "The greatest havock is made in Cornwall and Devonshire, by glade nets hung in the woods. The Exeter coach has brought thirty dozen in a week up to the London markets, where the price is now so exorbitant that they sometimes sell from ten to sixteen shillings the couple.... It is well known they leave their retreats on the approach of eve, and spread among the glades, always keeping the little paths; by which means the nets are so destructive."

Most flight or glade netting was a twilight activity, but it was also used as a way of taking woodcock in daylight in coverts which were known to hold large numbers of roosting 'cock on winter days. On the Glynllivon estate of the Wynn family in North Wales a special area of covert was laid out in the last century specifically for netting rather than shooting. "Woodcock Hill" was an old plantation maintained so as to have a central clearing and a series of rides radiating outwards through it in a pattern of long, thin glades, like the spokes of a wheel. The rides were each netted where they converged at the central clearing, and parties of beaters drove the segments of covert inwards, flushing the 'cock and driving them towards the hanging nets. This is one of the few detailed surviving records of formal woodcock netting in the daytime using beaters.

Today's scientists and authorized bird ringers use mist nets which are fundamentally the same as those used by centuries of fowlers and poachers, but today's mist net has a series of "shelves" or pockets woven into the design, so that it is no longer necessary to "shut" the net manually to be sure of entangling your bird. The woodcock strikes the fine net and drops to become firmly but gently entangled in the mesh of one of the ledges, from which it can then be carefully removed for measuring, weighing, ringing and perhaps also to have a radio-tag fitted, before it is released. Stress is minimal and is reduced still further by the fact that this all takes place in virtual darkness, which has a calming effect on wild creatures. Instead of simply pulling the bird's neck and consigning it to the larder or the game dealer, today's mist-netter releases his woodcock. If radio-tagged, its transmissions will add to the scientists' data, while the eventual recovery of a ringed bird contributes further to what we know about the movements, migration patterns and longevity of the species. But I can't help feeling that the cock-shut fowlers of Shakespeare's time would feel quite at home on a modern mist netting operation, and would see little difference between their hides and screens of brambles and those in which Graham Hirons and other scientists have hidden to watch roding 'cock and to use their bantams and ducks to lure birds down and into the nets.

Since woodcock flight out to feed at dusk and are thus susceptible to netting at last light, Tudor and Elizabethan English derived from the fowlers' art a special term to describe that particular time of evening – "cock-shut time". There is a reference in Ben Jonson:

Mistress, this is only spite –
For you would not yesternight
Kiss him in the cockshut light.

while Shakespeare, referring to King Richard III's twilight inspection of his troops before the battle of Bosworth Field, describes how

Thomas, the Earl of Surrey, and himself
Much about cockshut time went through the army.

"Cock-shut time" is still a term known and used by some country people, but it has been changed subtly in certain instances into "cock-*shoot* time". This might seem to be nothing more than a simple corruption of an old term, as netting gave way to the use of guns to take woodcock. But the cock-shooting referred to is not the straightforward pursuit of woodcock with dogs and guns on a normal shooting day. Quite specifically it means the shooting of flighting woodcock at dusk in the winter months, as the birds fly out to feed along the rides and through the gaps where cock-shut nets might once have been placed.

This is a well-established and specialized form of woodcock shooting, which is still widely practiced in many countries across the woodcock's wintering areas in western Europe. Often a solitary Gun will round off his day's rough shooting by waiting by a clearing or gap at the edge of woodland,

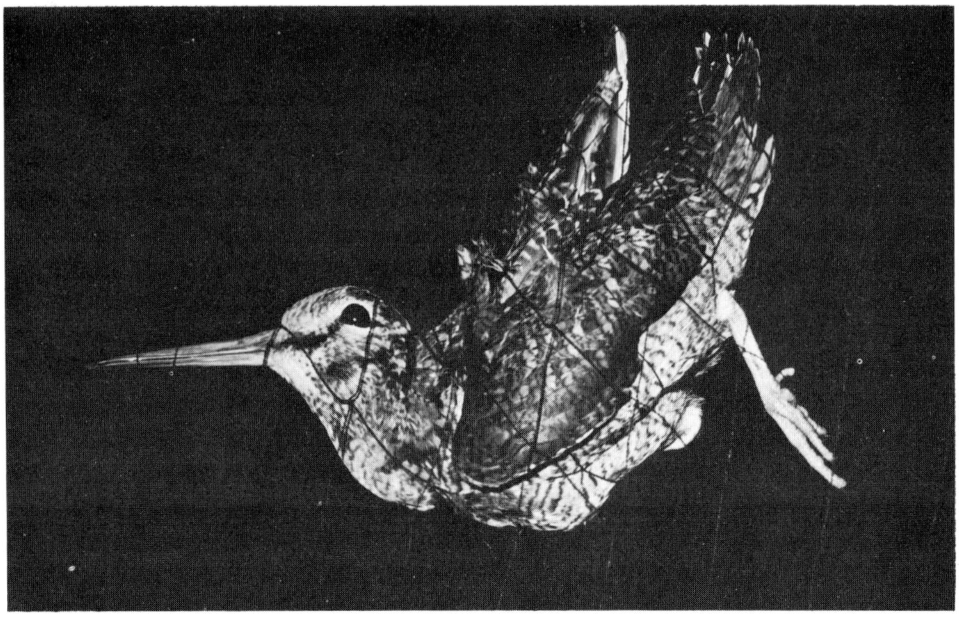

The "cock-shut" netter's work is rewarded, and a flighting woodcock is enmeshed in a mist net set across a clearing or gap. This bird did not end up on the dinner table, but was weighed, measured and ringed before being released with a tiny radio transmitter on his back, as part of a scientific study of woodcock behaviour.

usually positioning himself so that any bird flighting out in the half-light will be silhouetted against the sky. If a hot spot has been chosen – and these flight lines are often immemorially well established – the Gun may have four or five chances of a shot at single birds flighting out over a brief period of perhaps fifteen or twenty minutes. The poor light and the woodcock's deceptive wingbeat and speed make for difficult shooting, and a retriever with a good nose is absolutely essential if any shot birds are to be retrieved.

It is exciting and testing shooting, and requires a good deal of practice and some extensive twilight reconnaissance of the area, perhaps over several seasons, if it is to be really successful, and I have never heard of anyone making a large bag on a dusk flight. Three or four 'cock would be an extremely unusual total. Anyone unfamiliar with flighting woodcock, even if he is taken to a known flight line and put in position, will find it a sobering experience to see how many apparently easy shots he misses, regardless of how good a shot he may be at duck or other twilight birds. When tracer-type shotgun cartridges became readily available in Britain and Ireland in the 1960s and 1970s there was a brief vogue for using them when flighting 'cock at dusk, and it was quite a revelation to see how badly one could misjudge the birds' speed. Apart from dispelling any feelings of hubris on the part of a sportsman who fancied himself as a good shot, tracer cartridges conferred no other benefits for flight shooting. Rather the reverse, indeed, for the bright flash of each shot destroyed the acuteness of one's twilight vision and made it even more difficult to see the next bird. Muzzle flash from conventional cartridges can have a similar effect, but to a lesser extent.

The French, with their rich sporting vocabulary, have a special term for woodcock flighting – *le tir à la passée* (literally "pass-shooting", which is what sportsmen in the USA call flight shooting of duck and other species). Traditionally this has been a favourite form of woodcock shooting in France, especially in France's maritime *départements* along the English Channel and the Atlantic seaboard. Rough shooters in these areas had depended heavily upon rabbits for their sport, until myxomatosis devastated the population in 1952–53. Shooters turned their attentions to other quarry and woodcock shooting pressure, especially of birds flighting at dawn and dusk, increased greatly. Devoted as they are to woodcock shooting over pointing dogs only, the *Club National des Bécassiers* deplored it in the same way as driving woodcock or walking them up in cover over spaniels. "It is tantamount to murder, objectionable to all ethical sporting principles, and to be condemned from every point of view," wrote Dante Fraguglione in a recent French book on woodcock.

This is a very extreme view to take and an unfair one, I believe, at least as regards the shooting of flighting woodcock in the British Isles. However, the French National Woodcock Club (CNB) remains implacably opposed to it, and continues to advocate woodcock shooting over a pointing dog as the only acceptable method. But modern conditions and historical precedents in France are not necessarily to be applied universally. In Britain and Ireland only comparatively few woodcock are shot in this way, and flight shooting has never contributed more than a very small proportion of the total numbers of woodcock shot annually in these islands. In France, however, it was estimated in 1967 that some 75% of the total national woodcock bag each season were birds shot *à la passée*. In actual numbers this represents 1,125,000 woodcock out of a total annual bag of about 1.5 million. This probably explains the French policy on flight shooting. Quite simply, many felt guilty. Others suspected that they might be overdoing things, and thus risking putting too much shooting pressure on their wintering population, especially in the Atlantic provinces. But the assessment of the effects of shooting pressure on any species is always difficult, and exceptionally so with woodcock, so it would be unwise to be dogmatic without much more research and sound evidence. Nevertheless, strong representations were made to the French Government by the CNB, with the result that a ban on shooting flighting woodcock was introduced by ministerial order in 1963. In practice, however, this decree remains more honoured in the breach than the observance, and is virtually impossible to oversee and enforce.

In the Irish Republic the Wildlife Act of 1976 sought, among many other provisions concerning game, to put an end to the practice of shooting flighting woodcock at dusk. In the United Kingdom, however, woodcock flighting at dusk has, strictly speaking, always been on the fringes of legality, since the law forbids the pursuit of game before one hour prior to sunrise and later than one hour after sunset. Official sunset time comes long before the last of the light has gone, and when woodcock begin to flight out to feed on winter evenings they may do so just as the clock should be telling the punctiliously law-abiding sportsman that they are no longer "fair game". Effective enforcement of this law is quite another matter, however.

There does not seem to be any evidence to suggest that dusk flighting of woodcock has had any detrimental effects on total woodcock numbers in the past, or that more than a tiny proportion of shooters, even the real woodcock enthusiasts, have ever bothered to do it. It is difficult to believe that such flight shooting as does go on today constitutes any threat to woodcock numbers. Much more serious is the problem of shooting duck at night in areas where the birds are silhouetted against the night-long glow of city lights and oil refinery flares. This is potentially very damaging to wildfowl, which can be subjected to disturbance throughout the night, and night after night, when they should be left to feed and rest. It is unethical, illegal, and should not be confused with the perfectly respectable and very skilful tradition of flighting wigeon under the moon – a true fowling art, and one for which the combined conditions of tide, moon, cloud and wind will probably only be right on a very few nights each season.

"Firing for 'cock" is an old poachers' practice, comparable in some ways to "burning the water" or "leistering" for salmon, which used to be practised on the Tweed and other Scottish rivers, as described by Sir Walter Scott and William Scrope early last century. It involved two men, one carrying a brightly burning brand or flare and the other a gun, working slowly and quietly across marshes, bogs and wet pastures where woodcock were known to feed by night. Woodcock are reluctant to fly off under these conditions and were often shot on the ground. The modern equivalent of the poacher's blazing brand is the high-powered lamp, as used for lamping foxes and rabbits.

There have been recent reports that woodcock shooting at night with lamps is still carried on in Corsica where larger numbers of 'cock are allegedly taken in this way, even though it is quite illegal. In 1975 a correspondent wrote in some distress to a Corsican newspaper, describing how he had seen areas of low-lying marsh lit nightly by the lamps of many illegal woodcock shooters, whose shots could clearly be heard.

This seems to be a modern and potentially much more destructive development of another old form of "firing for 'cock", which involved not guns but hand-nets. The procedure was for two poachers – often a man and a boy – to walk slowly and carefully through areas where woodcock were known to feed by night, the man carrying a lantern and armed with a round net on a long pole, rather like a fisherman's long-handled landing net. The boy walked behind, steadily ringing a small bell. Apparently the combination of the dazzling light and the tinkling of the little bell had a mesmerising effect on the woodcock, and it was possible to get close enough to bring the net down over the bird on the ground. One imagines this required a good deal of skill and fieldcraft, and the old descriptions and illustrations conjure up a rather charming picture of what must have gone on. This is one especially delightful seventeenth-century account:

"This sport we call in England, most commonly bird-batting, and some call it low-belling; and the use of it is to go with a great light of cressets, or rags of linen dipped in tallow, which will make a good light; and you must have a pan or plate made like a lanthorn, to carry your light in, which must have a great socket to hold the light, and carry it before you on your breast, with a bell in your other hand, and of a great bigness, made in the manner of a cow-bell, but still larger; and you must ring it always after one order. If you carry the bell, you must have two companions with nets, one on each side of you; and what with the bell, and what with the light, the birds will be so amazed, that when you come near them, they will turn up their white bellies: your companions shall then lay their nets quietly upon them, and take them. But you must continue to ring the bell; for, if the sound shall cease, the other birds, if there be any more near at hand, will rise up and fly away.... This is an excellent method to catch larks, woodcocks, partridges, and all other land birds."

Another, rather more modern example of taking woodcock with a light at night was described in the 1890s in a letter to the English sporting press, by a sportsman who signed himself "Moorman". He told how he was having a look around his coverts at night, suspecting poachers to be at work, and accompanied by one of his gamekeepers, who carried a "dark lantern", a lamp with a sliding or hinged section to cover the light. In a plantation of fir trees he could hear occasional sounds of woodcock calling, and it was apparent that a migratory call of 'cock was coming into the covert. Some birds were seen to alight on the ground, and while "Moorman" shone his lantern on the birds, his keeper made a headlong grab at one of the birds which lay along a hedgerow. "'I've got 'im, Master!' he cried, breathlessly, and sure enough he had, the bird being more frightened than hurt."

"Firing for 'cock" was an old way of taking woodcock by night, using a bright light to dazzle birds on the ground. Charles Whymper's picture shows the chance capture of a woodcock by a landowner and his keeper patrolling the coverts on a night in late autumn when a "fall" of 'cock came in.

As if catching woodcock with one's bare hands at night were not skilful enough, there are various accounts of roosting woodcock being caught by hand in broad daylight. This has usually been achieved by gamekeepers, whose work in winter often takes them into the coverts and other daytime roosting habitat. Sharp eyes are needed to spot a squatting 'cock, and a very stealthy approach if the bird is not to flush. Those large eyes with their all-round field of view will certainly have seen your approach before you have spotted the bird. Dugald MacIntyre describes how, as a highland keeper, he knew of regular daytime roosting spots for woodcock in the heather of the open moors, in mild winters. He describes stalking towards these "known seats", spotting the roosting 'cock, and "by moving as if to pass them, could pick them up". His description of picking up woodcock as "rather a fine art" is an understatement! It evidently has something in common with the poacher's trick of picking up squatting hares, as described so beautifully by Richard Jefferies in his classic *The Gamekeeper at Home* (1878) and illustrated in an engraving by Charles Whymper: "You must persuade the hare that he is unseen; and so long as he notices no start or sign of recognition... he will remain still, believing you will pass."

Woodcock have been caught in the hand while flying, especially in thick cover, and I know several sportsmen in the West Country and Ireland who have caught birds by flinging out a hand and catching the passing woodcock with the same sort of instinctive action as a good slip-fielder taking a catch in cricket. Good reflexes and co-ordination of eye and hand are needed here, but to stalk and catch a woodcock on the ground must be as difficult an achievement as one could attempt. Yet Dugald MacIntyre did it almost twenty times, and other sportsmen and ornithologists have described how they have been able to get close enough actually to stroke a bird on the ground. This may be marginally easier if the woodcock is a hen sitting tight on a clutch of eggs, but some people have even been able to do this with roosting birds. William Hollywood, the wildlife artist, told me of how he was able to approach and stroke a woodcock squatting to rest in the sunshine among some rough grasses in a meadow near Lough Neagh in central Ulster. The bird did not fly off and appeared quite unalarmed, but when its resting place was revisited some twenty minutes or so later the bird was found to have gone.

Much more distasteful than these tales and practices of many generations of old sportsmen, ornithologists and poachers are the reports one hears occasionally of numbers of woodcock being lamped and shot at night, especially in severe weather. When conditions are extreme, numbers of woodcock will concentrate at whatever unfrozen feeding points they can find. A small rivulet or spring which somehow remains unfrozen when everywhere else is frozen solid can draw in large numbers of 'cock, even in broad daylight and especially at night.

I knew of one such spot in the west of Ireland in the very severe weather of January, 1982. Unfortunately, it was also known to one of the local poachers. On several successive nights he went there, swinging his car round on the track so that the headlights shone on the little pond and revealed the woodcock which were feeding there, probing in the mud around the water's edge. One or two shots with a twelve-bore from the car window meant a bag of several 'cock, and this was sometimes repeated later the same night, when more hard-pressed birds had come in to feed.

But Ireland is a sporting country, and news spreads quickly in rural areas. Such was the contempt of the local people for this individual and his unsporting slaughter of woodcock – allegedly as many as fourteen with two shots on one occasion – that he found himself unable to find a buyer for his ill-gotten birds, even among those who might not normally have inquired too closely about the origins of a salmon or a brace of pheasants offered for sale at the back door. With no market for his woodcock, that particular poacher left the birds in peace.

Before it was finally made illegal in England on 1 August, 1958, the gin trap was probably the most widely used spring trap in Britain. In various forms, sizes and designs it had been used for more than two centuries as one of the major aids to gamekeepering and the control of farmland pests. In its largest and most powerful form it was used to trap bears in the forests of North America and poachers in the game coverts of Britain, until an Act of 1827 made that particular form of poacher-catching illegal.

Gins were an effective, if cruel, means of catching mammals like foxes, and sometimes also badgers and otters, as well as the smaller objects of the gamekeeper's antipathy, like stoats and weasels, and the gin trap was also used extensively to catch the ubiquitous rabbit in those pre-myxomatosis days. Wire snares were preferred by most warreners who wanted to be able to offer a clean, uncrushed rabbit for sale, but gins were widely used too, especially where the soil was sandy and a snare more difficult to set and peg down securely. Woodcock frequently fell victims to these gins.

A large seaside rabbit warren near Ballintoy in County Antrim, on the estate of the Herdman family, was regularly trapped with gins in the last century. R. Lloyd Patterson, writing in 1880, described the severity of the winter of 1878-79, when extremely cold conditions meant that woodcock and snipe were driven in large numbers to the seashore near this warren. "There is an

extensive warren there; and these rabbits are regularly caught for the market. The warrener sets his trap at the mouth of a burrow, and spreads a little fresh sand over the trap to conceal it. When the surface of the ground was frozen so hard that the snipes and woodcocks could not probe into it with their bills, they thrust them into the fresh and unfrozen sand concealing the traps, and many of them were thus caught" – presumably by the bill or head in this instance, but often by one or both feet.

There are a good many scattered records of woodcock caught in gin traps by the legs, and quite a few birds have been shot and found on examination to be missing one or both lower legs, in a way that suggests that gins or other spring traps were to blame. Two of the woodcock ringed and later recovered in the 1920s in County Fermanagh by Sir Basil Brooke were recovered in "rabbit traps" (ie gins), and Colebrooke estate used gin traps extensively in a concerted attempt to limit the huge rabbit population there. Thirty years earlier his grandfather, Sir Victor Brooke, regularly achieved bags of over 1000 rabbits per day to five or six Guns, and on two days in 1890 four Guns shot 2011 rabbits and one solitary woodcock. Sir Basil believed that the rabbits caused undue disturbance in the coverts, thus reducing the numbers both of wintering woodcock and of breeding birds.

Seigne describes how in December, 1926, he shot a woodcock in County Tipperary "which had both legs severed just above the claws, probably the work of one of these cruel gin traps. The curious point about it was that the bird was in quite good condition. The stumps had healed over perfectly, and it could evidently manage to stand and even get about a little on the ground. I am afraid that spring traps are still used extensively in Ireland, and, I am told, in Devon and Cornwall, and must account for a good many 'cock and other birds, the lives of which are spent so largely on the ground." In 1945 he was shown another recently shot woodcock "with both feet severed just below the knee-joint. The wounds had healed over and the bird had evidently been able to get about on its stumps. But it was in poor condition and could not have lived long. This was undoubtedly the work of a gin set for rabbits.... One Irish farmer told me that he had found three woodcock in his traps last season."

Pole traps, variations of the gin-type spring trap, were designed to be set up on prominent points such as fence posts, rock outcrops and the plucking points of birds of prey so as to catch crows and hawks. But apart from their cruelty they were also indiscriminate, and were even known to take the occasional woodcock, although 'cock are not normally perching birds. Happily, pole traps are now quite illegal, and no spring trap of any sort may be set in the open or used to catch any bird.

Finally, to end this consideration of some of the odd, often illegal and sometimes very ancient methods by which woodcock have been taken, one must not forget falconry.

The art of flying hawks and falcons at live quarry, for food and sport is, jointly with coursing, probably the most ancient field sport still practised. Its history in the East goes back at least 3000 years, and in Europe it came to prominence in the early Middle Ages.

Medieval and later French falconers flew their peregrines at herons, and British falconry has always concentrated on the partridge, the grouse and the rook as quarry for falcons. A few falconers, however, have specialized in woodcock.

Cranbourne Chase, the area near where Dorset, Hampshire and Wiltshire converge and only a few miles from where this is written, used to be the scene of woodcock hawking, according to William Chafin in his *Anecdotes and History of Cranbourn Chase* (1816). An area known locally as "the hawking downs" had woods close by "that produced woodcocks which came to a flight for the hawks in the open glades when disturbed from the woods, and shewed great sport".

At the end of the eighteenth century, the famous Colonel Thomas Thornton (1747-1823), who founded the Falconry Club in 1772, killed the remarkable total of forty-nine woodcock in one week with his falcons on one of his many sporting trips to Scotland. Also in Scotland, the Renfrewshire Subscription Club led by a Renfrewshire laird, Mr Fleming of Barrochan, kept a team of falcons specially to be flown at partidges in the early autumn and then at woodcock later in the winter.

In Ireland in the 1820s John Sinclair of the Falls near Belfast kept falcons and flew them frequently and with great success at woodcock, both in Ireland and also in Scotland, which he visited regularly to join forces with the 'cock-hawking members of the Renfrewshire Club. In his best season in Scotland he took fifty-seven woodcock with falcons.

Sinclair flew his woodcock hawks on a number of the best Irish woodcock estates too, including Rossmore Park, the seat of the Westenra family, Earls of Rossmore, in County Monaghan. One particular flight at woodcock here had a remarkable ending. One of the Westenra family slipped a peregrine at a woodcock on a very windy day, with a strong south-westerly blowing. The woodcock and the pursuing falcon climbed higher and higher, as the 'cock tried to prevent the falcon from getting above it and into a position from which to launch a stoop. Both birds were soon lost to sight and there was no further sign of the falcon. She was presumed simply to have raked off downwind and been lost, until the end of the story was revealed by the arrival of a letter.

It bore a Scottish postmark and enclosed with it were the falcon's varvels, metal rings fitted to the leather jesses or leg-straps and engraved with Westenra's name and address. Within a day and a half of being slipped at that woodcock in central Ulster, the falcon had been seen in a farmyard ten miles from Aberdeen, attacking domestic pigeons. The farmer, not surprisingly, promptly shot the marauder, only to find that she was a falconer's escapee. The fate of the woodcock is unknown, but the falcon, undoubtedly assisted by that strong wind, had travelled from Monaghan to the north-west coast of Scotland in less than two days.

Those who specialized in woodcock hawking generally considered that the woodcock was a risky flight, with the quarry tending to rise higher and higher, and the falconer was quite likely to lose his bird. In the mid-seventeenth century Sir Thomas Browne of Norwich told of a falcon flown at a woodcock in Norfolk which disappeared and the chase was calculated to have covered a distance of over thirty miles in an hour. An earlier falconers' tale from Germany tells of a falcon which was slipped at a woodcock and chased it non-stop from Prussia far into Westphalia.

Thomas Nash, in his curious and very rare little book entitled *Quaternio, or the Foure-fold Way to a Happy Life* (1632) tells of how a falconer went out "early on a winter's morning, to the woody fields and pastures to flie the Cocke, where having by the little white feather in his tayle discovered him in a brake, he cast off a tassel gentle [i.e. a male peregrine], and how he never ceased in his circular motion until he had recovered his place, how suddenly upon the flushing of the Cocke he came downe, and missing of it in the downecome what working there was on both sides, how the Cocke mounted as if he would have pierced the skies; how the Hawke flew the contrarie way, untill he had made the winde his friend, how then by degrees he got up, yet never offered to come in untill he had got the advantage of the higher ground, and then he made in, what speed the Cocke made to save himselfe, and what hasty pursuit the Hawke made, and how after two long miles flight killed it, yet in killing of it killed himselfe."

And Nash adds, with a delicacy of feeling unusual for the period, "I must confesse it hath often gone againste my stomacke...yet I must likewise confesse I have beene sometimes for societies sake, a spectator of such a tragedie."

Early last century a certain Colonel Bonham of the 10th Hussars was a keen falconer, with a particular interest in grouse hawking, for which he took a moor at Scardroy in Scotland, and also in woodcock hawking, for which he travelled to Ireland. He described one peregrine's flight at an Irish 'cock, which eluded the falcon across an open moor but pitched into cover in a small area of bushes. Bonham and his falconers reached the copse and saw the woodcock rise, slowly and with apparent exhaustion, its bill open with breathlessness, to be struck dead by the falcon which hit its quarry in typical fashion, striking the bird's back with its hind talons.

Another military man with a penchant for falconry was Major Charles Hawkins Fisher who, in a talk to the Cotswold Naturalists' Field Club in 1889, gave a stirring account of a falcon's flight at a woodcock. This was in Argyllshire, on Fassfern estate on the northern shores of Loch Eil, west of Fort William. A woodcock was flushed by beaters from an area of withered bracken, and Fisher slipped a female peregrine called "Taillie", which had been taken as an eyass (nestling) from an eyrie on the Worm's Head cliffs of the Gower peninsula in Pembrokeshire.

" Up and up the woodcock went in long zig-zags, with precisely the style and action of her smaller relative the common snipe, but mute. The falcon mounted rapidly in her train, though at a considerable disadvantage at first. I saw it was going to be a long affair, got out my glasses, and lay down on the heather. On one side of me was my falconer, Jamie Barr, one of the well-known family of Scotch falconers; on the other side my ghillie, Sandy Kennedy, the proud possessor of the best pair of eyes in all Argyll....

"The woodcock, with the falcon below and behind her, did not dare to come down or return... and soon a pair of dots were high over the sea loch (there a mile wide), the cock's point being evidently Morven, on the other side of the strait.... But finding herself over the water and unable to shake off her pursuer or gain the distant haven of Morven, she had no alternative but to seek

A close shave! George Lodge's spirited engraving shows a woodcock narrowly escaping the stoop of a peregrine tiercel. Some falconers like the famous Colonel Thornton specialised in woodcock hawking, usually with peregrines. Flights at woodcock can be very high and cover long distances, and often meant the loss of the falcon.

the shelter of the bracken on our side, from whence she sprang; so the poor fowl turned tail and 'went for it' in a long slanting descent from an incredible altitude.

"As they both neared us, they presented the appearance of two little balls falling out of the sky right towards us, and quite straight, with the difference (fatal to the poor woodcock) that 'Taillie', who began below her, was now well above. The hawk was evidently unwilling or afraid to stoop over the water, but the moment the 'cock was over the land, she shot herself forward and straight in the air, instead of slanting, half perpendicularly down, like her quarry, (both moving with incredible speed), turned over and stooped....

"It was fatal this time to the woodcock, for leaving a cloud of feathers behind, she tumbled head from heels before leaving us, into the very bank of bracken she came from, and meeting there with an old anthill, bounded off it many a yard, and lay still. The hawk soon recovered herself, and dashed onto her well-earned quarry. Needless to say I did not disturb her thereon, but served out the whisky, and drank her health all round."

CHAPTER IX

WOODCOCK AND GUNDOGS

"Cocking spaniels are unquestionably the best dogs for cock shooting, and with them the sport is most animating. A very steady brace of setters or pointers, one having a deep-toned, the other a lighter toned bell, hung around the neck, suit also the taste of some sportsmen."

D.P. Blaine: *Rural Sports* (1858)

As you might expect, cocker spaniels are so called because the breed was developed specifically for flushing woodcock in the days when sportsmen in November forsook the stubbles and their partridge shooting, left their pointers and setters in the kennels, and wanted dogs to beat out thick coverts for woodcock and perhaps the occasional pheasant. You often see 'cocking spaniels in old sporting engravings and prints, and there are still some excellent strains of true working cockers today, although the spaniel world is now dominated by the English Springer. A good springer is a superb dog for woodcock shooting, and for shooting of all kinds. (A bad springer – and they are far too common – is a canine catastrophe, a misery to its owner and a disgrace to the breed.)

Then there are the setter breeds and the English Pointer, with a long tradition as 'cock shooters' dogs of a rather specialized sort; and also the multi-purpose breeds which have a well-established role in European woodcock shooting and are increasingly popular as gundogs in the British Isles. It is impossible to single out one breed and say it is the ideal 'cock shooter's dog. So much depends on where and how you shoot, on personal preferences and your "feel" for how a dog works – and of course on the abilities and character of the individual dog.

Shooting dogs and woodcock have a relationship which is somewhat less than straightforward – rather like their masters. In discussing how sporting

With decorous poise a woodcock flushes ahead of an unusually fierce looking spaniel in this engraving after Samuel Howitt, from the *Sporting Magazine* (1810).

Woodcock retrieved by a Brittany spaniel, engraved on the floor-plate of a side-by-side gun by Zoli; and by a setter on a Beretta over-and-under gun. Both are the work of Caesare Giovanelli's team of fine engravers. (Photo: Gunmark)

breeds of dog behave towards woodcock it is convenient to divide them into two broad categories – the flushing and retrieving breeds like spaniels and labradors; and the pointers and setters which seek game by its air scent, but which are not normally used to retrieve shot 'cock. There is, of course, a grey area between these two groups, occupied principally by the "all-purpose" gundogs, especially the European hunt-point-and-retrieve breeds like the GSP, the Vizsla and the Münsterlander, but these two general categories are nevertheless useful in discussing how dogs behave towards woodcock.

Among trainers and handlers of retrievers and spaniels it is well known that certain individual dogs can show a definite aversion to picking up woodcock, and to a rather lesser extent snipe, in their mouths. Nor is this distaste for woodcock confined to gundogs. Lurchers often encounter night-feeding woodcock while lamping for rabbits, and I have heard some accounts of lurchers picking up feeding woodcock and spitting the birds out with obvious disgust, instantly and unharmed. This reaction seems to crop up out of the blue, and I do not know of any particular tendency for the trait to be inherited among gundogs, although a hard mouth or various other undesirable traits can be handed on. Sometimes the offspring of a dog and bitch which are both keen and reliable retrievers of woodcock may show a definite distaste for them, especially in the early stages when they are first introduced to the birds. It may first be noticed when a young dog in training is asked to pick up its first cold woodcock, or perhaps one which has been shot in the open and has fallen quite dead, in clear view of the dog.

Usually this dislike of woodcock is apparent from the way in which the young dog runs out and picks up the shot bird readily enough, only to spit it out almost immediately. Others will hover rather undecidedly over the bird, sniffing at it with evident distrust and clearly reluctant to take it in the mouth. Some will actually roll on the bird, much as they would with a piece of carrion, a fox dropping or one of those forms of foul-smelling debris which seem to have a fatal attraction for some dogs, making them unbearable in house or car.

Sometimes there is a sort of compromise reaction, where a young dog is keen to please its master and the instinct to pick up and carry is very strong, but the youngster is still unwilling to commit itself to a proper, full-mouthed retrieve of something it obviously finds rather unpleasant. In such a case you may see your woodcock or snipe retrieved very tentatively, often held only by an extremity such as a wing-tip, a leg or even the bill. The dog's lips may be curled back in evident distaste and its unsavoury mouthful will probably be dropped quickly at the handler's feet, if not before. Clearly there is something very disagreeable to the dog, but this is not always the case, and even when this problem does occur it should not be insoluble.

It is a common enough reaction among young dogs, and it can usually be cured by plenty of praise and encouragement, and lots of practice with these problem species. Many trainers start a young dog off on a retrieving dummy with snipe or woodcock wings tied to it, and a policy of "constructive jealousy" can work wonders too. If a cold woodcock is thrown and the youngster is made to wait while an older, proven dog is sent to retrieve it in full view of the puppy, it can often induce a much more positive and spirited retrieve the next time. Whatever the trainer's favourite tricks may be, the young dog can almost be persuaded to retrieve woodcock and snipe without undue difficulty, and eventually to do it with as much zest and efficiency as any other form of game. A few, a very few, dogs retain a lifelong reluctance to retrieve these species except under protest. Practice normally makes perfect, however, and lots of woodcock and snipe experience will usually turn most retrievers and spaniels into willing and efficient finders of these birds.

Sir Ralph Payne-Gallwey, no mean authority both on dogs and woodcock,

A woodcock neatly retrieved by a springer spaniel, in a watercolour by John Paley. Springers and cockers were originally bred with woodcock shooting in mind. Initial reluctance to retrieve woodcock and snipe is not unusual, but perseverance should overcome it.

suggested another and rather harsher Victorian remedy to persuade a young retriever to pick up woodcock or snipe: "Starve such a dog till he will munch the bones of Cock or Snipe for his dinner, and he will, for the rest of his life, never afterwards refuse to retrieve these birds when you shoot them." Perhaps this was an effective method, but one suspects that it might have caused other problems. I wonder how many birds were slightly munched by the time they were brought to hand, or whether it would ever have been wise to leave such a dog unattended with the day's bag.

Perhaps certain dogs are incurable, even by Payne-Gallwey's technique of appealing to their appetite. A very worried correspondent to *The Field* in 1936 described how her otherwise omnivorous collie refused to eat even the smallest morsels of snipe or woodcock, though fond of all other game. The writer wondered whether a dog, with its "more unblunted instinct", might be aware of "some unwholesome or even noxious principle" in these birds, perhaps even making them unfit for human consumption! I'm afraid this good lady was talking nonsense. Canine aversion is more than offset by human delight in eating both snipe and woodcock – really delicious morsels, fit for any gourmet, and as wholesome as one could wish. I tend to agree with William Daniel who wrote in 1801 that "as to the flesh [of woodcock], the compiler being rather an admirer of it himself, does not recollect ever giving it to a dog."

The Rev William Daniel is an important figure in the history of British sporting literature. The first volume of his massive *Rural Sports* appeared in 1801 and began to bridge the gaps between ancient traditions of the chase and recognizably modern field sports. Delabere Blaine, who wrote an even longer sporting encyclopedia in 1858, shot with Daniel and described him as "a sporting trump", an outstanding dog handler – "they seemed to live only to obey him" – and especially fond of woodcock shooting over his team of cocker spaniels. "If a pheasant got up when he was engaged in 'cock shooting, he would not willingly fire at it, and if killed by any one of his party he would express his regrets; putting his disapprobation on the supposition that it unsteadied his dogs."

Steady or not, a dog which retrieves reliably is essential if you shoot woodcock or snipe regularly. Losses and unnecessary suffering to wounded

A woodcock down and dead among fallen leaves. With natural camouflage like this, a good retriever is vital if shot birds are not to be lost.

and unpicked birds is the inevitable alternative. It is not even essential to have a dog which thrashes its way through cover and flushes woodcock for you, desirable though that obviously is if you shoot 'cock by walking up in rough country. After all, you may be able to arrange to go woodcock shooting with another Gun who has a good beating dog. But it is absolute folly not to have a reliable dog to seek for and pick up your shot woodcock. Anyone who relies on picking up his own birds is bound to miss a good many, a wasteful and frustrating business.

There are some dogs, however, which just refuse to retrieve woodcock. Happily, this is very uncommon, and careful training and lots of encouragement will usually induce even the most reluctant dog to take to woodcock eventually. Most become as enthusiastic and efficient on woodcock and snipe as on any other species. But there are a few exceptions, which will perform impeccably on pheasants, partridge, grouse and pigeons – even when the latter's loose feathers clog its throat and make it cough and sneeze – but which retain a lifelong dislike of woodcock. If you find yourself saddled with one of these you are unfortunate indeed, but if he is an otherwise good dog do not get rid of him. Good dogs do not grow on trees! Keep him for your general game shooting and get another dog as your woodcock and snipe specialist.

The shooter who relies on woodcock as his principal winter quarry will simply not tolerate a dog which, despite the trainer's best endeavours, refuses to take to woodcock and retrieve them unhesitatingly and reliably. For that reason you will not find many 'cock-shy dogs in Cornwall, Ireland, the Hebrides or west Wales, and a puppy bred from proven woodcock-finding stock in those parts of the country may be your best choice if you want a dog for woodcock shooting.

Reluctance to retrieve woodcock is only one of the various ways in which 'cock-shyness can manifest itself. Spaniels, the traditional dogs for beating out cover in search of woodcock, will sometimes show their dislike of this bird by deliberately avoiding them – "blinking their birds", as it is called. This is unusual but it can occur, and it is obviously a major disadvantage for the woodcock shooter. Unfortunately, this fault can be present in a dog, usually a spaniel but also in other breeds including labradors and the HPR breeds when they are used in dense cover, without its master being aware of it. A dog may appear to be finding and flushing woodcock without any reluctance when in fact the birds are merely being dislodged from cover by the presence of the dog and the noise and disturbance of its approach and that of the Guns. But an efficient cover-working dog should not merely create a general disturbance in the undergrowth but should quest intelligently and purposefully, using its nose to find the squatting 'cock and pushing on to flush the bird from its seat. Occasionally one finds a dog which, if it gets a whiff of live scent from a woodcock, will try to avoid the bird. This undesirable trait will inevitably mean that a great many woodcock will go unflushed in the course of that dog's working career.

This can be an insoluble problem. It does not arise from an aversion to the dead scent or the taste of the shot bird in the dog's mouth. Here we are dealing with the dog's negative reaction to the air-scent given off by the live bird. Curing this may simply be impossible.

Spaniels are closely related to the various breeds of setter, and certain individual spaniels and setters will persist in "blinking" their woodcock all their lives. In my experience this fault seems to be much less common among English pointers, and comparatively rare in labradors and retrievers in general. Encouragement by the handler, and an element of competition and jealousy induced by other dogs, may bring about a cure, but there are occasional "hard cases" which resist all attempts to rectify this flaw. As with a problem retriever, you have two choices: you can keep an otherwise sound dog for use principally on other game (and he may be a star performer on pheasants or rabbits), using him only as a general beater and to swell the pack on a woodcock day, or you can replace him with another. Once again, however, it is good to be able to report that this is an unusual problem in a gundog, and one which most sportsmen will be very unlucky to encounter.

If, like most woodcock shooters, you have a sound and keen dog with a good record as a finder and retriever of woodcock, you may still encounter some other strange finding and retrieving problems from time to time. In particular, many dogs will find the greatest difficulty in locating and picking up a woodcock if it comes down in a face-down, belly-flop position, with its wings partly extended.

Time and again I have seen woodcock shot and fall in this way, and the fall of the bird has in many cases been clearly marked by an experienced woodcock dog. The handler has sent the dog out for what should have been a perfectly elementary retrieve and the dog has proved to be utterly at a loss. It will usually run out keenly, right on the line of the fallen bird and, if it's a good marker, stopping almost at the point of fall. But, extraordinarily, the dog may then find itself quite baffled, unless it can actually see the bird on the ground. Even on a good scenting day it clearly shows it is not getting even a whiff or hint of scent from the dead bird, which may be only a few yards or feet away from it. I have even seen some superb woodcock-finding dogs, including more than one Field Trial Champion, actually standing right on top of the bird and looking back at their masters in total bewilderment, asking for further instructions.

Clearly this particular type of retrieve poses some sort of special problem, and I have been relieved to have my own observations confirmed in many letters and comments from other woodcock shooters.

From what I have seen, and from others' accounts, the key to this mystery seems to lie in the position of the dead bird. If it falls on its back or on its side, or in the usual rather untidy sprawl of a cleanly shot bird, the problem seems not to arise. The dog will run out to the mark, or can be manoeuvred into position by its handler in the case of a blind retrieve, and it will either see the bird or scent it and complete the retrieve in a perfectly straightforward way. But a bird which falls flat on its face with outspread wings seems to give off

A woodcock which falls in this position, belly-flat with wings slightly spread, can be an impossible retrieve for even the best of woodcock dogs. A dead or wounded woodcock in this position seems to give off virtually no scent.

little or no scent and a top-class dog can be right on top of it and yet remain quite oblivious of it.

In the absence of any tell-tale scent the dog may be able to see the bird which has fallen in full view, perhaps on short grass or on the bare soil of a ploughed field, in which case it will rely wholly on sight and complete the retrieve promptly. But if the dog is unsighted, or if the 'cock falls into long grass, brambles, heather or other cover where its plumage makes it difficult for the dog to see it, then there may be major difficulties with the retrieve. For the woodcock, unlike most other sporting birds, seems to emit no perceptible scent if it is lying in this position.

We have all seen pheasants, grouse, partridge, duck and snipe come down and lie in the same position, and they all appear to give off much less scent than if they fell in some other posture, and it may take even a very good dog a few moments longer than normal to locate it. But the outcome is usually successful, and these birds have clearly been giving off some degree of scent to help the questing retriever. The woodcock, however, seems to present a much more extreme case, where scent is simply imperceptible. The result can be both frustrating and rather comic, as one watches a really good dog baffled and unable to locate a bird which you yourself may be able to see quite clearly.

Information from others over the years has confirmed that this is not an uncommon experience among woodcock shooters, both in Europe and North America. I have a particularly interesting account from Colonel Glenn Baker of Woodcock Hill, Pennsylvania, whose very experienced and reliable German short-haired pointer "General" failed on several occasions to find a woodcock (*Philohela minor* in these instances, of course) which was lying literally at the dog's feet. Yet this dog was an efficient finder and retriever of woodcock, with hundreds of birds to his credit over a long working life of thirteen seasons. All of this shows yet another unusual facet of the woodcock and its ways, and confirms the old huntsman's adage that "there's nowt so queer as scent 'cept a woman".

No mention of shooting woodcock over retrieving and spaniel breeds would be complete without mentioning the Irish Water Spaniel, a unique breed which combines some of the characteristics of retriever and spaniel, to which is added a very great deal of its own inimitable character and a very distinctive appearance – like "a bundle of rags in a cyclone" according to Somerville and Ross. Their long-suffering and very sporting Irish Resident Magistrate, Major Sinclair Yeats, was keen on his woodcock shooting and possessed the inimitable and incorrigible "Maria", although he also pursued what he described as "the hermit woodcock" by shooting over an Irish setter on the open hills, a traditional Irish form of 'cock shooting, especially in mild weather.

The Irish water spaniel is particularly associated with the Barrington family, formerly of Glenstal Abbey in County Limerick, one of the very finest Irish woodcock shoots of Victorian and Edwardian times. An invitation to one of the Glenstal 'cock shoots was a coveted honour in the fiercely competitive world of top-flight game shooting a century or so ago. Bags were consistently high, with the two best beats regularly producing 50-80 woodcock each on a driven day.

Sir Charles Burton Barrington Bt. (right) of Glenstal Abbey, County Limerick, with his son and "Grouse", the most famous of their kennel of Irish Water Spaniels. Glenstal was one of Europe's finest woodcock shoots and the Barrington spaniels were all expert woodcock finders and retrievers.

Sir Charles Burton Barrington and later his son, Sir Charles Bacon Barrington, carried on the shoots and maintained their famous kennel of Irish Water Spaniels through the First World War and up to the 1920s, when "the troubles" in Ireland put an end to it all. Despite the dogs' thick, curly coats, which seemed designed to catch on any bramble, thorns or other cover, the Glenstal water spaniels were used extensively to beat out the coverts, which were specially maintained with woodcock shooting in mind. They also retrieved the shot birds, and guest Guns were expressly requested not to bring their own retrievers to the shoots. All dog-work was to be left to the Barringtons' kennel of spaniels. Perhaps the most famous of many outstanding water spaniels at Glenstal was a dog called "Grouse", one of the breed's most celebrated stud dogs of all time, and a superb working gundog, especially on woodcock. He continued his sporting work in the summer months too, accompanying members of the family on fishing days and regularly retrieving trout and salmon. With "Grouse" in attendance, a landing net or gaff was apparently superfluous.

The second broad category of woodcock shooters' dogs comprises the pointers and setters, specialized and attractive working dogs. Like individual retrievers and spaniels, they also can have their strengths and weaknesses with woodcock. Setters and pointers – usually the "pure" setting breeds like the Irish, English and Gordon setters, rather than the multi-purpose HPR breeds – will occasionally "blink" their woodcock, while proving perfectly staunch and reliable on other game, including snipe. This was allegedly the case with the most brilliantly successful Irish setter of the post-war era, International Field Trial Champion Ballymac Eagle, a dog which remains a legend among "bird dog" enthusiasts for his supremacy on a grouse moor, and whose blood can be found in the breeding of almost every true working Irish setter in Britain and Ireland. Like some other setters, and more rarely with English pointers, Ballymac Eagle was said to be oblivious of woodcock, running over them and flushing them as he quartered in search of something more interesting. Yet he was a superbly stylish, fast and clever grouse dog, who carried off all the top honours in the trialling world and passed on his outstanding talents to many generations of his progeny. I once owned and shot over two Irish setter bitches, both of which had Ballymac Eagle blood on sire's and dam's side. They worked well on woodcock and set them staunchly, and as they got older I also allowed them both to retrieve woodcock, which they did with enthusiasm.

If a pointing or setting dog either fails to acknowledge and point woodcock,

The effectiveness of good pointers and setters – in November 1944 in northern Spain these two "bird-doggers" made a total bag of 78 woodcock in a day and a half.

or blinks them when he does wind them, it is probably an incurable defect, and the shooter who wants a woodcock dog had better look elsewhere. If there is a cure for this I have yet to hear of it, but luckily it seems to be a very uncommon problem. Most pointers and setters will stand as firmly on the scent of a squatting woodcock as any other game, and practice improves their performance.

This is especially true of setters, which seem often to become more and more clever with experience, to the point where they display an uncanny ability to find woodcock, and other game too. Setters display this ability to learn and to benefit from experience much more than English pointers, though they often take longer to train and to settle down to steady work than pointers. These are often comparatively straightforward and quick to train, working well and with a very specially stylish action as only an English pointer can, at the age of eighteen months or less. But they reach their peak early and, as the seasons pass, will seldom if ever develop that educated and crafty gamefinding ability which one so often finds in the slower-developing and psychologically more complex setter breeds.

Nowadays fewer woodcock are deliberately shot over pointers and setters

An early Victorian sportsman shooting woodcock over two wild-looking "setting spaniels", and accompanied by his man who carries the second muzzle-loader, ready loaded. Both wear the beaver hats, cutaway coats and leggings typical of the period.

in Britain and Ireland than by the other, more widely practiced methods of working cover with beating dogs, or driving 'cock from coverts over standing or slowly walking Guns. But there are a great many sportsmen in parts of Wales, Scotland and, above all, in Ireland who rely on bird-dogs, chiefly setters, to find their woodcock, especially when the birds lie out in heather and lighter cover in mild weather. That is how earlier generations used to do it, and very successful they were too.

It is an effective and attractive way to pursue woodcock, with the day-long pleasure of watching a stylish breed of dog at work, and that unique and indescribable surge of excitement which comes when the dog stops and sets. Who knows what lies ahead of that sensitive nose? Perhaps a hesitant twitch of the tip of the tail or a half-cocking of the ears may hint to you that a rabbit or a hare is about to dash out of cover, for both these creatures seem often to induce a rather distinctive reaction in pointers and setters, quite different from the way they point gamebirds like grouse, pheasants or woodcock. A good dog will hold its point until the Guns are in position and a click of the fingers or a quick command sends it roading in to flush its game, which may be a single bird like the solitary daytime-roosting woodcock, or a covey of grouse or partridges. The cover and the general habitat is, of course, an excellent general clue to what you are likely to find in any given area, but always with bird-dogging there remains this exciting uncertainty.

This goes a long way to offset one of the most important advantages of shooting over a setter or pointer, which is your preparedness for the shot and your comparative certainty about the position of the game and its likely direction of flight when flushed. In theory, a woodcock or any other game pointed and flushed in relatively open ground should be a simple shot – in fact, no half-decent Gun should ever miss. But the reality is often very different, and many an apparently straightforward shot is missed clean with both barrels. We have all done it. Excitement and adrenalin can do strange things and cause even the most reliable of shots to bungle occasionally, and it is just as well that this is so. If shooting was always easy there would be no point!

Shooting over setters and pointers can, when conditions are right, be a very

A nice day's bag of woodcock made in Hungary over that country's native breed, the Vizsla. The various multi-purpose hunt-point-and-retrieve breeds from Europe are increasingly favoured by the British and Irish woodcock shooter.

deadly way of making a bag of woodcock. The Guns have important advance warning of a bird's presence before it takes wing, and if they are well-positioned and can mount their guns and fire with deft but unhasty accuracy when the 'cock flushes the odds are decidedly in favour of the Gun – an unusual thing in woodcock shooting. In walked-up or driven shooting, especially in close cover, the 'cock almost always has a better than evens chance of getting away.

If you are shooting woodcock in thickish cover a setter, and more especially a pointer, may not be the best choice of dog. The English pointer is fairly thin-skinned and suffers severely in thorn and bramble scrub, much more so than the various setter breeds with their thicker skins and denser coats. Setters' feet are better protected, too, with ample hair between the toes and they are much less likely to become footsore, an important consideration when the going is tough and when the ground is hard, flinty or icy. The English pointer was not bred to face thick cover and those which are plucky enough to do so can cut themselves badly. In particular the thin skin of the tail makes it especially vulnerable to severe lacerations and profuse bleeding from the blood vessels which are very close to the surface there. This problem can become chronic, calling for cauterization or even slight docking in extreme cases. The lovely whippy tail action of an English pointer is one of the breed's most delightful features, and a pointer with a badly scarred or docked tail is a very sorry sight.

A setter, especially a spirited Irish or Gordon setter, often hunts well in cover, quartering close and working rather like a spaniel, but its real *forte* is game-finding on more open ground. This is how Edward Laverack, whose name is synonymous with good working English setters, went about his woodcock shooting in the Hebrides, and especially on Islay. There he hunted the fringes of the open hill and the sparsely wooded glens near Ardimersay, shooting alone over a brace of setters and accompanied by a boy who led a second brace of dogs and carried the bag and cartridges.

Well-thinned plantations of hardwoods and very young blocks of coniferous woodland can often suit setters quite well, and it is usually possible to keep the dog in sight in places like this. Nothing is more frustrating than to know

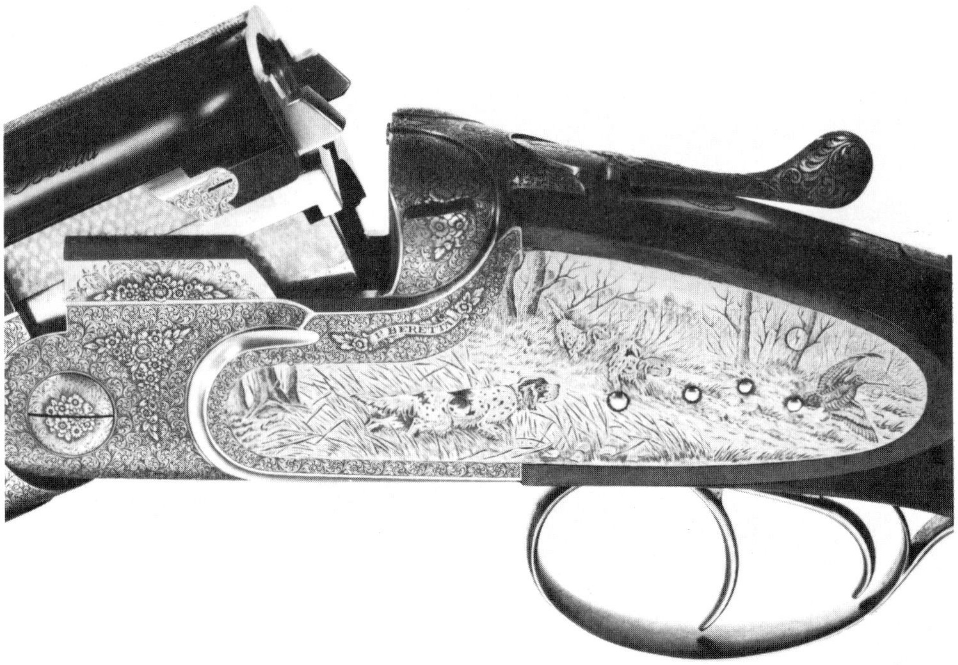

A trio of English setters have just found and flushed a woodcock in this finely engraved scene on the lock-plate of a Beretta over-and-under gun. The engraving is from the celebrated *atelier* of Caesare Giovanelli at Brescia in northern Italy.
(Photo: Gunmark)

that your dog is probably on point somewhere, and not to be able to find him! A light-coloured dog, such as an English setter, is naturally easier to see than the dark black and tan of the Gordon or the rich russet of the Irish red setter, but even a pure white dog can disappear from sight and find a point in fairly open woodland, and then you may have quite a search to find him before he comes off point, or runs in and flushes in frustration, or the bird eventually flies off of its own accord before you get there. Only the very cleverest and most obliging of dogs will leave its point to come and look for you, to lead you back to the bird – though it can happen. Osgood MacKenzie, who shot large bags of woodcock on the islands in Loch Maree in Wester Ross in the 1860s, told of a very talented setter bitch which would find a bird and, if need be, come off her point to find him and lead him back to the spot. This paragon was bred in the kennels of the Gordon-Cumming family at Altyre in the Findhorn valley of Morayshire.

"They order this matter better in France" – or, if not better, at least rather differently, and this applies in many other European countries, too. In France and Belgium, and in most of Europe south of the Alps, the pursuit of the woodcock with pointing and setting dogs is regarded as the *crème de la crème* of small game shooting, the champagne of sport, rather as we in Britain and Ireland reserve a very special place of honour for top-quality driven woodcock and snipe shooting. But while we are probably equally delighted to get any chance of a shot at a woodcock, whether walked-up, driven, over setters or just as an occasional exciting extra on a pheasant covert shoot, the European purist tends to regard the pursuit of woodcock as something which is only properly to be conducted by one or at most two Guns shooting over a steady pointer or one of the setter breeds. The real woodcock enthusiast revels in his solitary outings, accompanied only by his faithful *chien d'arrêt*. He disdains any other form of woodcock shooting as vaguely disreputable, and certainly not an honourable and worthy way to pursue his *belle mordorée*, the "beautiful russet-coloured queen of the woodlands". (It is interesting to note in passing that, to the French sportsman, a woodcock is always "she": this is in contrast to the curious old British and Irish belief, formerly widely held, that only *male* woodcock migrated to winter here.)

Walked-up shooting, with a pack of assorted spaniels and retrievers beating out the cover in an apparently random but probably very effective sort of way, and flushing woodcock unexpectedly and very excitingly into view of the Guns, is far too unscientific and haphazard for the organized, logical Gallic mind. For him this approach is totally lacking in the systematic, scientific finesse of the setter handler, who works his dog among his favourite woodcock spots through acres of woodlands, always waiting for that heart-stopping thump of excitement when his dog comes on point. Then it is a matter of manoeuvring into the best possible position for the shot, bearing in mind the likely direction in which the woodcock is likely to rise and his probable escape route through the trees. If all goes well the dog flushes his 'cock on command and the Gun should have a comparatively simple shot. In woodland the classic French style is to shoot your bird cleanly just as he reaches the zenith of his upward spring and begins to level out as he clears the woodland canopy – the consummation of an exercise in *la chasse* which is a curious combination of calculated planning and romantic questing. The French have a rich sporting vocabulary and use two vivid terms to describe the near vertical rise of a flushed woodcock – a *chandelle* or a *cheminée:* like a rocket or flare; and like going straight up a chimney.

It is a splendid business when it all goes according to plan, but woodcock shooting is seldom quite as straightforward as that. The eighteenth-century writer John Acton, if indeed he was the anonymous author of the influential and popular *An Essay on Shooting* (1789), clearly knew all about the problems of working bird dogs in cover. He uses the term "pointer" as a generic term for both pointers and setters, but distinguishes between the "smooth pointer... active and lively enough in his range, but in general proper only for an open country", and the "rough pointer... to range the woods and rough places, as well as the plain". Clearly Acton's "rough pointer" is what we would call a setter. He describes the vexations of bird-dogging in cover with evident feeling:

Italy has its own club of woodcock shooting enthusiasts.

"Pointers, in general, stand at the cock, which is oftentimes very inconvenient; because it cannot be known what is become of the dogs, or whereabouts they are; and as they will not come away when they are sett, on being called or whistled to, the shooter has frequently to wait for them until his patience is exhausted."

Two centuries after Acton's time this remains a very major problem, unless you are blessed with a really special dog like one remarkable old pointer bitch I used to shoot over in the west of Ireland. She would range at will and in what looked like a very haphazard way over vast areas, out of sight of the Guns for much of the time, but she would leave her point and come looking for us and lead us back to where the bird was sitting! Unfortunately, that is a canine talent you don't come across every day. For most bird dogs, however, the problem of finding a dog which has come on point out of sight can be largely overcome by an arrangement whereby, if you cannot *see* your dog, you can at least *hear* him. Acton goes on to explain:

"To obviate this inconvenience in shooting cocks with pointers, some sportsmen fasten a small bell about the neck or the tail of each dog, by the sound of which he may be followed in the wood, and when the sound ceases, the shooter knows that the dog is on a point, and is thereby enabled to guess the place where the dog is."

A woodcock's pin-feather and a *grelot* or traditional collar bell for a pointer or setter comprise the emblem of France's flourishing National Woodcock Club (CNB). It criticises any form of woodcock shooting other than a solitary sportsman shooting over a pointing dog.

Belling the dog is part and parcel of the French *bécassier's* traditional and approved technique, and it is widely used in other Mediterranean countries, and also among the quail hunters of the southern States of the USA. The French woodcock enthusiasts' association, the *Club National des Bécassiers* (CNB), has as its emblem the woodcock's pin-feather and the *grelot* or oblong-sectioned bell which is fastened to the dog's collar. This is an essential item of equipment for the *bécassier*.

Many French woodcock experts have put their thoughts and experiences on paper and contributed to the considerable mass of writings about woodcock hunting which have been published in French. (This is in marked contrast to the relative paucity of woodcock material in English sporting literature, with no substantial book hitherto devoted exclusively to this species.) Edouard Demole was one of those devotees, and his *Subtilities de la Chasse à la Bécasse* is a classic of Continental small game sporting literature. First published in 1943, when France was an occupied country and a small edition on poor quality economy-standard paper was the best that could be produced, this was reprinted in a suitably handsome edition in 1964 with the help of the author's widow.

In a detailed discussion of *chiens d'arrêt* and the use of the *grelot*, Demole explains how this should be designed so as to give a clear, ringing tone which will make the dog's whereabouts evident to his master but will not deafen the dog to whistled or shouted commands, and not so loud as to frighten game. Demole believed that the best bells were made from thin sheet metal rather than cast iron, which he judged to be too resonant. The key-shaped clapper should give a regular, rhythmic sound as the dog quarters his ground, but should be sensitive enough to respond to the changes in the dog's movements as he senses a touch of scent, its ringing becoming irregular as the dog draws on the scent or pauses to test the wind, and stopping altogether when the dog sets firmly on the squatting bird. The bell should, he says, be fixed rigidly to the dog's collar with a metal clasp to allow for easy attachment and removal as required, and to associate the bell and its clapper closely with the dog's every movement, however slight. As a final but important refinement he tells us that the bell, oblong in section, should be attached so as to allow the clapper to swing to and fro across the short axis, giving maximum sensitivity.

These exacting criteria for the sportsman's design and attachment of the bell to his dog are apparently matched only by the subtle abilities of some dogs when they become accustomed to working with a bell on their collar. A crafty and experienced setter can move with such care when drawing on a scent, or moving slowly on the track of a woodcock moving away ahead of it, that the bell gives nothing more than the occasional slight tinkle. This means a minimum of disturbance for the bird, which may be very jumpy and on the point of flushing wild, and calls for attentiveness from the Gun, who must keep an ear cocked for these sounds. It is not a simple case of "bell ringing = dog running: bell silent = dog setting". The art of bird-dogging for woodcock with a *grelot* on the dog's collar is subtler and more sophisticated than that, and it is a complex and infinitely varied form of dog work, in which the French take particular delight, and about which they have written and argued a great deal.

Here in Britain and Ireland belling a bird dog is still fairly uncommon, although it has been tried with some success by shooters who have seen the practice in other countries. As we can see from the accounts given by Acton and other early writers, it has been known to British sportsmen for centuries, and one occasionally comes across old setter bells in the gunrooms of shooting lodges and at auction sales in country houses. They are worth collecting, either for practical use or as interesting examples of sporting history.

Bells are used more and more by the woodland deer stalker in lowland Britain, who may occasionally have to use a dog to find a dead or wounded deer in thick cover. Here almost any breed may be pressed into service, the only criterion being its ability to follow a blood trail or the deer's scent steadily and reliably. But the deer stalker must move about with silence and stealth, and the last thing he wants is a constantly tinkling bell in his pocket or rucksack. The bell will therefore often be left in the car until it is needed, or its inside is stuffed with cloth or tissue to silence the clapper.

Lionel Currie, who has shot woodcock in Ireland for about thirty-seven seasons over bird dogs, mostly English setters, tells me that he used collar bells with great success, but with the added refinement that his setters remained on point and were not encouraged to road in and flush the 'cock themselves. "As my setters generally worked out of sight I had a bell attached to their collars... and it was the cessation of the 'music' which indicated to me that the dog had found a bird. As the setter did not flush the birds I used a retriever for this purpose."

For anyone who has not tried belling his bird dog, it is a technique worth trying. The dog may take a little time to get used to the bell, but that will depend to a great extent upon the individual dog's temperament. A keen working dog waved off into woodlands where it has previously found game will usually set off with undiminished enthusiasm. It may take the handler considerably longer to get accustomed to following the bell, and to listening carefully for those subtle but telling changes in rhythm which let you know what your dog is doing. Despite the French woodcock hunters' exacting criteria about what constitutes a good bell, you need not be unduly choosy, although experiments and experience invariably mean that you will develop your own preferences. Old harness bells of the type formerly fitted to many sets of coaching and driving harness are very good, and have a long slot through which a wide leather collar can be slipped easily. This holds the bell rigidly in place so that it responds quite directly to the dog's movements and does not flop about and distract its wearer. The tone is normally good enough for this purpose, and these bells are not hard to come by in junk shops and on bric-a-brac stalls in markets, expecially in country areas.

An excellent alternative to the harness bell is a large version of the falconers' hawk bell. When made properly from well-worked brass these bells give a sweetness of tone which carries long distances without ever being excessively loud for either the dog or the game it seeks. Makers and suppliers of good hawk bells can probably supply something ideal for the setter handler, and the result should be attractive to listen to and highly effective under field conditions. It will cost considerably more than a harness bell, but we are still only talking about a few pounds.

One final point should not be overlooked. Most pointer and setter handlers – and most gundog owners – run their dogs on shooting days without a collar. Indeed, many such dogs never wear a collar at all. You may therefore have to get your dog accustomed to a collar, which he may find uncomfortable to begin with. You will also have to remember that, when belled, your dog's collar may add to the risks of its getting hung up on wire or on a branch in dense cover. Don't overlook this possibility.

One last and very intriguing aspect of woodcock and the behaviour of dogs towards them is the business of whether or not woodcock can suppress their scent, to put the dog off its point. This is a quite separate matter from the question, discussed earlier, of the way in which a shot woodcock landing in a belly-flat position can present problems for a retriever.

The European hunting literature contains many discussions of the alleged phenomenon of scent suppression in woodcock, and the subject has been

aired at great length in *La Mordorée,* the quarterly magazine of the French National Woodcock Club (the CNB). Invariably the topic arises from experiences with pointing and setting dogs, including not only the "classic" breeds but also the HPR breeds of Europe and the "setting spaniels" like the Brittany and the Small Münsterlander.

Most reported incidents follow this pattern: the dog is questing in the normal way, invariably in woodland and light cover, and comes to a sudden and steady point. For whatever reason, perhaps distance or awkward terrain, it takes the Guns some time to get up close behind the dog. It holds its point firmly enough to begin with but as time goes by the dog seems to become unsteady, first moving its head slightly forwards or sideways and then taking a few uncertain paces forward. It seems puzzled by the situation and acts as though it is no longer sure of the bird's scent, and may start casting about, very slowly and quietly at first, in search of a surer scent. Then a woodcock flushes without warning from the place where the dog first pointed. Not surprisingly the Guns are usually taken by surprise and the bird excapes unshot at, or at best saluted hastily and ineffectively.

There are many slight variations on that outline description, but it seems fairly typical of what has been reported on many occasions, verbally and in written accounts in the sporting press and in books.

Incidents like this have led many woodcock shooters to the conclusion that these birds can, on certain occasions, somehow suppress their scent to the extent that the dog becomes uncertain of the woodcock's presence and exact whereabouts. It has been argued that this is a defence mechanism against predatory mammals like the fox and the shooter's dog, whereby the squatting bird succeeds in "turning off" its characteristic scent so as literally to throw its enemy off the scent.

In many ways it would seem to make sense for a bird like the woodcock, with its highly cryptic camouflaged plumage and its need to hide its presence from potential predators, to have some physiological mechanism enabling it to reduce its tell-tale scent when danger threatens. Predators like the fox rely on their noses, and share that whole subtle and complex world of scent which our dogs so obviously know – a sensory dimension largely denied to man with his relatively primitive olfactory sense. A ground-nesting and ground-roosting bird like the woodcock must be at risk if its scent is perceptible to predatory mammals.

Recent research in Scandinavia has shown that the willow grouse, a close relative of our native red grouse, can reduce its scent, both when it is incubating its eggs in the breeding season and when it is crouching on the ground and aware of a potential predatory threat. Its heartbeat rate drops and its whole metabolism slows down, resulting in a much-reduced emission of bodily scent, making it less easily detected by the sensitive nose of the questing predator. This is an interesting contrast to the human response to a similar sort of threat, when the heartbeat and breathing rate rises, the individual perspires more freely and the whole metabolism speeds up under the stimulus of adrenalin, in preparation for one or other of the so-called "flight-or-fight options" when danger is imminent. It is a well-known phenomenon of nesting gamebirds like the pheasant, and more particularly the partridge, that the hen bird on its nest gives off little or no scent, and can be missed by even the most reliable pointer or setter when the keeper is trying to locate and count nests in the spring. (Research in the 1980s by scientists of The Game Conservancy on grousemoors in the north of England has shown that grouse with *strongylosis,* a heavy infestation of the strongyle threadworm, give off more scent and are therefore presumably more vulnerable to predation than uninfected grouse.)

Perhaps the woodcock, like the willow grouse, can respond by suppressing its scent in some way which we do not as yet understand, when it realizes that it is in danger. Once again, only scientific research can provide the real answer: meanwhile it remains a fascinating topic for discussion and conjecture. The anecdotal literature of woodcock shooting in Europe, especially over the pointing breeds of dog, is full of accounts of woodcock allegedly throwing a dog off its point by the suppression of scent. However, as with so many other aspects of sporting lore, it needs to be explored and confirmed by thorough scientific study. Fascinating though the *après chasse* tales and discussions are – and who would miss them? – only the rigorously objective methods of the research biologist can resolve this puzzle and tell us what actually happens and why.

CHAPTER X

SHORT-BILLED WOODCOCK AND OTHER ODDITIES

"I've got a couple of queer-looking woodcock here, with short bills. You'd better come and have a look at them."

James Hamilton – January 1982

A "short-billed woodcock" sounds like a contradiction in terms. The woodcock's long and prominent bill is its most obvious physical feature. British sporting literature is full of affectionate references to "sport with the longbills"; doggerel poets have punned on the word "bill"; and most European terms for the bird have to do with its bill – *bécasse* or *grand bec* in France, *bekas* in Bulgaria, *becada* in Spain, and so on. Ornithologists who have made a special study of birds' bills have frequently looked in detail at the woodcock, and there are many scientific papers which discuss the woodcock's long and very specialized probing and feeding device.

But what are we to make of woodcock with bills half or little more than a third of the normal length? They have occurred throughout the woodcock's winter range in Europe, and they are being reported by sportsmen from many countries more frequently each season.

Although the woodcock is a bird which can exhibit enormous individual variations in coloration, size and weight, its bill length has always been regarded as fairly constant, within certain limits. Several scientists have carefully measured large samples of shot birds over many years and have agreed that normal woodcock bill lengths fall within the range 67–81 millimetres – approximately 2¾–3¼ inches. Those have been the findings of scientists who have looked at woodcock throughout central and western Europe, Scandinavia and the British Isles, and as far away as the Azores, the most westerly breeding point for the species.

The short-billed woodcock saga seems to have begun on 26 December, 1933, when a sportsman living in Brittany went out shooting, like a great many other sportsmen throughout the world who traditionally regard Boxing Day as

A short-billed woodcock shot in South Uist in 1985. Its 33-millimetre bill is less than half the species' average and shows a wrinkling of the upper mandible found in many short-billed woodcock, but there is no evidence of physical damage or injury.

important in the shooting calendar. Near the village of Plougasnou he shot a woodcock with a bill 51 millimetres long, almost three-quarters of an inch shorter than the normal average. In 1946 another woodcock was shot in north-western France, near Cape Finistere, and found to have a bill measuring only 36mm (about 1⅜ inches) – just half the approximate average length for the species.

Neither of these oddities seems to have caused much of a stir at the time, but it is significant that they were noticed and recorded. Woodcock shooters in general tend to look carefully at the birds they shoot. This is part of the special pleasure of woodcock shooting. The bag is usually small, each 'cock shot is a special event, and the Gun has time to look and admire his birds individually as his dog retrieves them, and probably to look at others' woodcock at the end of the day. Such personal attention would simply not be possible on a large-scale driven day at pheasants, partidges or grouse, when the shot birds tend to be consigned quickly to the game cart and the Guns move briskly on to the next drive.

This short-billed woodcock, shot by Lionel Currie in County Fermanagh in January 1986, has a bill length of 46mm. The pointing finger indicates a rather slight lump on the upper mandible, which seems to occur in quite a high proportion of short-billed birds.

In 1948 the third known example of a short-billed woodcock, a Danish-shot bird this time, was reported. This received rather more publicity and began to alert a few of the keener European woodcock enthusiasts to the existence of these variants. But British and Irish shooters seem to have remained unaware of them, even after the first British-shot short-bill appeared in 1972.

By 1979 the European woodcock enthusiast Dante Fraguglione was able to list seventy-eight records of shortbilled woodcock, beginning with the Danish recovery of 1948, and these came from the Netherlands, Belgium, Italy, Sweden, Switzerland, and from Britain and the Channel Islands (four birds). France yielded over half of these records, with a total of forty-two birds, including one quite extraordinary report of seven short-billed birds allegedly being shot in one day at Sallen, in the Calvados region of north-western France, on 20 November, 1978.

Fraguglione's article in *La Mordorée* (issue 132), the quarterly magazine of the French National Woodcock Club (CNB), is a lengthy and detailed discussion of the phenomenon. More importantly, however, it gave real prominence to short-billed woodcock for the first time. Woodcock enthusiasts and sportsmen with inquiring minds started talking and writing about it. Popular articles, notes and photographs showing short-billed woodcock began to appear in the sporting magazines, from Ireland to Rumania. The result has been that more and more information, records, photographs and specimens have come to light. Woodcock enthusiasts and most game shooters now know of the phenomenon and keep their eyes open, examing woodcock in the bag on shooting days with greater attention than before.

By 1983 Fraguglione was able to list 134 recorded examples of short-billed birds, with bill lengths ranging from 28mm upwards. Records came from all over western Europe, and Fraguglione's list showed these numbers for the following countries:

Belgium	6	Italy	7
Britain	4	Netherlands	5
Denmark	10	Spain	1
France	97	Sweden	2
Ireland	1	Switzerland	1

A high proportion of these birds had bill lengths in the range 35–45mm, and once again this mysterious and perennially fascinating bird has presented biologists and sportsmen with another intriguing puzzle. The overwhelming preponderance of French short-bills is probably partly explained by the fact that *La Mordorée* had alerted French sportsmen to the phenomenon, and they were probably more on the lookout for these individuals than sportsmen elsewhere. In addition, French sportsmen are very woodcock-minded, shooting pressure on the species there is relatively high, and France's estimated annual bag of 1.5 million woodcock is by far the largest in western Europe, and probably in the world.

This short-billed woodcock was shot in Norfolk in 1984. The upper mandible measures 44mm and displays the crinkling seen in many short-billed specimens. Yet there are no signs of physical damage to the mandible.

Some obvious questions come to mind immediately. Are these deformed or injured birds, whose bills have not developed normally? Are they young birds with a retarded bill growth? Could they belong to a race or sub-species of the woodcock not previously recorded? If so, and since they must be migrants, with individuals cropping up all across western Europe, where are the breeding grounds of this short-billed variant race? If this is not a hitherto unidentified race, has it only evolved recently? If so, what has caused such a large jump? Is it an example of an evolutionary leap, rather than a progressive development? Could it be caused by pollution, chemicals in the environment or radioactivity?

These and many other questions still remain largely unanswered. But discussion really began in 1976 when the matter was put into sharp focus in three basic questions put forward by the eminent Belgian ornithologist and

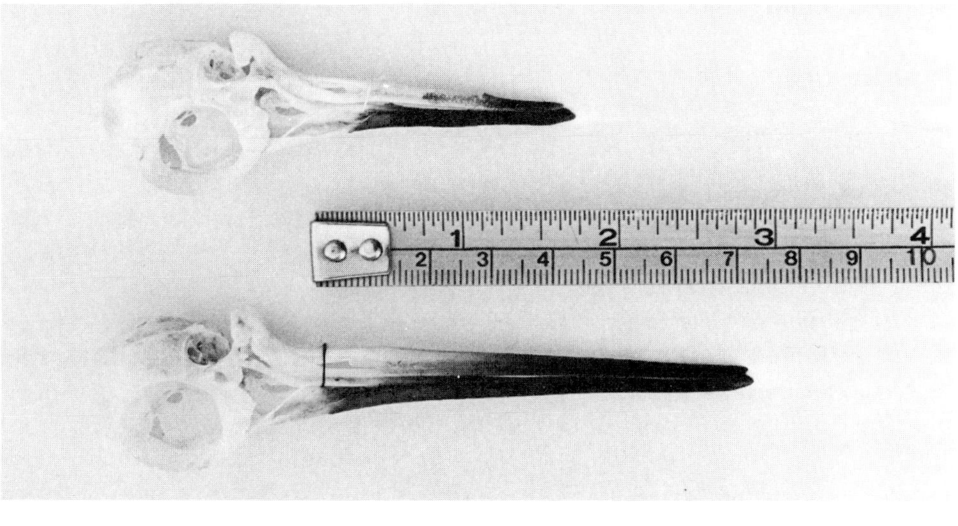

These two skulls show the clear difference between an average normal bill (68mm) and a short bill (40mm). We seem to be dealing with a definite "jump" rather than a gradual shortening of bill length.

sportsman Count Léon Lippens. Writing for the magazine of the Royal St Hubert Club of Belgium, he asked:

1. Is this a mutation caused by woodcock eating earthworms contaminated with chemicals?
2. Are we dealing with an unknown local subspecies which has extended its wintering range and changed its migration routes?
3. Are we witnessing a physical change in the species *Scolopax rusticola* in general?

Fraguglione addressed himself to the problem under these three general headings in his article published in *La Mordorée* in 1979, and concluded that the existence of short-billed woodcock was not attributable to chemical or other toxins, or to the effects of radioactivity. Nor was he able, on the basis of comparatively few reports from a wide area of western Europe, to suggest that the short-billed birds might belong to some hitherto unknown sub-species or race of woodcock. European woodcock cannot be divided into any apparent races anywhere in their wide range across Europe, North Africa and Asia. In technical terms they are "monotypic", although the woodcock displays a great degree of individual variation in size, weight and colour of plumage. There is

Richard Robjent's comparative sketch of the heads of a short-billed woodcock and a normal example, showing a hint of the distortion found on the upper mandibles of some short-billed 'cock.

only one species of *Scolopax rusticola*, and even the sedentary and little-known woodcock of south-east Asia, like the Amami woodcock and the Dusky woodcock, might only be local representatives of this monotypic species, and not separate species. Finally, Fraguglione cautiously suggested that the evidence might point to the beginnings of an important evolutionary mutation or adaptation, by which the European woodcock was adapting to changed and changing habitat and feeding conditions.

British and Irish woodcock enthusiasts have become increasingly aware of the short-billed phenomenon since 1982. The winter of 1981–82 was notable in Britain for the severe weather which struck in December and, after a short reprieve around New Year, returned with more low temperatures in January. There were two temporary hard-weather shooting bans in Britain, and woodcock shooting was also briefly suspended in the Irish Republic. True to historical form, hard weather in continental Europe brought a vast influx of woodcock to the British Isles, and everyone who shot game that winter will remember having seen (and, except during the ban periods, shot) more woodcock than for many years previously, the last really bumper woodcock invasion having occurred in the bitter winter of 1963. Among sportsmen everywhere the talk was of weather, wildfowl, shooting bans – and lots of woodcock. Guns for whom the bird was only a rare sight found they were suddenly seeing lots of them. Many younger shooters were able to enter their very first woodcock in their gamebooks, while older or more woodcock-minded Guns got the sort of opportunity to see, study and shoot woodcock which only comes perhaps once or twice in a sporting lifetime.

My own direct introduction to examples of short-billed woodcock came in January, 1982. On the last Saturday of the season I was shooting in Donegal, and after getting back and changing for supper I received an unexpected telephone call from Captain James Hamilton of Brownhall in south Donegal. He had been on a woodcock shoot that day near Killybegs, west of Donegal town, and two short-billed woodcock had been bagged. These were actually first noticed by another of the Guns, who chanced to see that two of the birds laid out at the end of the day had bills noticeably shorter than the rest of the bag. The "queer birds" were at Brownhall, only a twenty-minute drive away for me.

In every other respect these birds were perfectly normal woodcock, both in good physical condition, weighing about 10½–11 ounces, and with perfectly normal plumage. But their bills were noticeably shorter than the 67–81mm range which is usually expected. These were about 45mm and 53mm, both ¾–1″ shorter than the average for the rest of the day's bag of 'cock. The birds were destined to be sent to the National Museum in Dublin, and I was also leaving next morning, so there was barely time for some rough-and-ready measuring and a hasty snapshot by the light of a table lamp. Alice Hamilton, indulgent as ever to the foibles of Irish sporting life, kindly let me purloin the measuring tape from her sewing basket to give an indication of the relative lengths of the bills of these two woodcock compared with a third "normal" specimen placed alongside.

News travels fast in any sporting community, and nowhere faster than in Ireland. Within a day I heard from another shooting friend, Mervyn Archdale

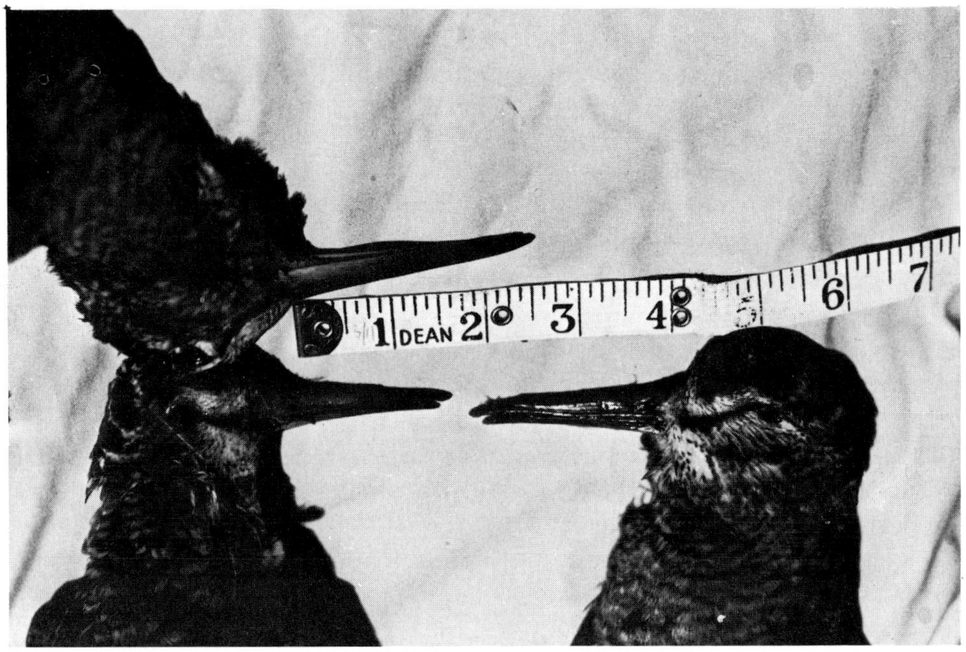

An impromptu snapshot of two short-billed woodcock shot in south Donegal in late January 1982. The difference between these and the "normal" specimen is very obvious.

of Omagh, that a short-billed woodcock had been shot the previous week in County Tyrone, and that specimen had been sent off to the Ulster Museum in Belfast. So at the very end of a long shooting season and a year of quite fantastic woodcock numbers in many western parts of Britain and in most of Ireland, three short-billed examples had been bagged in west Ulster. Happily, all three had been noted and preserved. We will never know how many others may have gone un-noticed, then or in previous or subsequent seasons.

In fact, I believe comparatively few would have been overlooked. Woodcock are an important quarry species in Ireland, where they tend to represent a high proportion of the average local shooter's bag. This is also true of Cornwall, parts of Wales and the Hebrides, and woodcock are prized by sportsmen everywhere. Consequently they tend to be given more than a passing glance, and I believe that anything unusual about a woodcock is more likely to be noticed than with most other game species. Certainly our ancestors had an almost obsessive interest in spotting, recording and preserving oddities, and sent every unusual, memorable or freakish bird down to the local "stuffer". The literature and the old game books and diaries are full of references to albino or semi-albino woodcock and many other variations of colour, size and weight.

I therefore find it hard to believe that short-billed woodcock would have escaped the notice and the comment of Victorian and Edwardian woodcock shooters. Landowners and the elite band of woodcock keepers on the premier woodcock shooting estates like Ashford Castle, Glenstal Abbey and Muckross in Ireland; Lanarth and Tresco in Cornwall and the Isles of Scilly; the great woodcock estates of the Hebrides, especially Islay, Raasay and Mull; and Alnwick in Northumberland – all ran their woodcock shoots with the greatest care, meticulous documentation and great attention to detail. They knew they had some of the finest and most coveted covert shooting in the world, and when a bag of 80 or 100 'cock was laid out at the end of one of their big days, a short-billed bird would have stood out conspicuously from the rest. There would probably have been an excited letter to *Land and Water* or *The Field*, or even *The Times*. There would certainly have been a mounted specimen for the gunroom, perhaps a photograph, or at the very least an entry in the gamebook to record such an event.

We also know that rarity-spotters like Mr Whitaker of Nottinghamshire and the artist F.W. Frowhawk, with their obsessive interest in unusual plumage variations among woodcock, had agents scouring the game-dealers' stores and the racks of birds at poultry markets in Britain and Europe. These men wanted to find oddities for their collections, and they did succeed in spotting and preserving many interesting colour variants, and wrote about them to the sporting and wildlife press. But there is not one word about short-billed birds.

The only hint I can find – and it is a very tenuous one – is a small watercolour by Charles St John in one of his sketch-books, now in the private collection of Captain Charles Moncrieff. This picture consists of two head studies of woodcock, and is captioned in St John's writing "Different woodcocks". It shows two birds, one of which appears to have a bill which is very marginally shorter and stouter looking than the other's. The difference is slight and these may well have been birds with a slight difference in bill length but still well within the normal range of about 68–81mm. There are other differences as well, for one bird's head is much more darkly marked than the other, and the eye-stripe of one bird is also much darker and more prominent. St John did not go into further detail, either in his sketch books, his notes or in his published writings, and I do not think this can be regarded as a proper record of a short-billed woodcock.

Despite many personal inquiries over several years, and extensive

An overhead shot of two woodcock heads and bills. The bird on the right was shot in Gloucestershire in 1972 and was the first recorded from Britain. The short-billed bird's upper mandible shows the crinkling characteristic of many such birds. (Photo: T.H.Blank)

correpondence, both privately and in the sporting press, I have not been able to uncover a single instance of a short-billed woodcock in Britain or Ireland prior to 1972, when a bird with a bill measuring 33.5mm was shot in Gloucestershire. This was recorded and preserved in the collection of the late Dr Jeffrey Harrison, one of Britain's foremost authorities on wetland birds.

The first short-billed woodcock to be shot in Ireland of which I have been able to find a record was actually bagged by the man who has been most prominent in bringing the short-billed phenomenon to sportsmen's notice. Dante Fraguglione visited Ireland on a shooting trip in 1980 and on 10 January he shot a female woodcock with a bill measuring 46mm. For once the Irish sporting grapevine seems to have failed, for this incident was not generally known until details were published the following year in *La Mordorée* – which is not widely read in Ireland!

After the shooting of the Donegal and Tyrone short-bills in January, 1982, I had an opportunity to alert the British and Irish shooting fraternity to these variants by the publication of a feature article in *Shooting Times and Country Magazine* on 30 September, 1982. This seemed a good time of year to mention the phenomenon, with another shooting season under way, the first migrants due and the first serious woodcock shoots taking place within a few weeks.

The response to that article and a request for more information and specimens was remarkable, and has grown steadily ever since. I received a total of about 26 reports of short-billed birds shot in 1981-82, and the information came from shooters as far apart as Cornwall, Cheshire, Lincolnshire and Scotland, in addition to the three Irish birds already noted. One keen Cornish woodcock shooter had records of five birds shot there between 19 December, 1981, and 9 January, 1982, with bills measuring between 29mm and 54mm. Four of these were first-year birds, which is in keeping with the West Country's relatively high proportion of young birds to old in the bag.

To date I have over 130 reliable reports of short-billed woodcock shot in Britain and Ireland during the period 1981–86. Thirty-one such birds have been sent to me, from places as widely scattered as Orkney, Cornwall, the

Outer Hebrides, Norfolk, the Midlands, Inverness-shire, west Wales and all four provinces of Ireland. Some have been complete specimens, some were heads only, and those I have examined have had bills which measure from 32mm to 54mm. (It is perhaps worth mentioning that the method I have adopted as standard is to take the measurement from the tip of the upper mandible to the rear edge of the bird's nostril opening.)

My collection of reports of short-bills is drawn from a widely scattered range, and there is no reliable indication that they are more likely to be found in one part of the country than another. Many more examples must come to light before a pattern emerges and can be identified with any certainty. However, in 1985–86 one small area of Britain yielded some extraordinary information.

Compare the 44mm bill length of this adult woodcock with that of the 12 day old chick shown below it.

Islay, in the Inner Hebrides and part of the Highland county of Argyllshire, has always been one of Britain's premier woodcock areas. In particular the southern parts of the island, on the estates of the Campbell and latterly the Morrison families, have afforded some of the highest densities of wintering woodcock and some of the largest bags ever found in Britain or Ireland. Islay and woodcock are almost synonymous.

Ken Aldridge organizes small parties of visiting Guns to shoot woodcock on Islay, usually by walking up over spaniels, over many thousands of acres of rough hill land, in the little glens and on the fringes of the open hill. In the course of 57 shooting days during the period 28 October, 1985, to 30 January, 1986, 133 woodcock were shot. Of these no fewer than 20 had bills measuring less than 51mm, and 13 less than 45mm. The shortest individual bill measured 1¼″ or 32mm.

This presents an extraordinary picture, with one bird in six falling well below what is taken as the normal range of bill length, and one bird in ten having a bill an inch or more shorter than the average. It is too soon to know whether this is typical of Islay in general, or of the Hebrides and nearby parts of mainland Scotland. We will have to await measurements in future seasons, by Ken Aldridge, other Islay sportsmen and those who shoot woodcock in the west Highlands, and indeed throughout Britain, Ireland and the woodcock's entire range. But these Islay data are the most singular example I know of numbers of short-billed woodcock being shot in one small area. The only other published example which is remotely comparable are the seven short-billed birds recorded by Fraguglione from Sallen, in the Calvados area of France, but those were apparently all shot on the same day in November, 1978.

All the published references to short-billed woodcock, and all the photographs and measurements have, not surprisingly, been taken from dead birds bagged on shooting days. But a clear sighting of a *live* short-billed woodcock is a real rarity, and quite the most interesting reports of short-billed birds which have come to me concern close and unmistakable sightings of live short-bills. One very detailed description came to me from Arthur Cadman. On a dark night in late November 1984 he was driving down the track from his house high on the ridge to the north-west of Inverness city when he saw a squatting woodcock in the car headlights. It did not move and he was able to drive within a few feet of it. Every detail was visible in the bright lights of the car, and the bird had a very short bill. Arthur's sighting was confirmed by two other people in the car with him, and this is the first sighting of a live short-billed woodcock to come to my attention.

Another sighting, under very different circumstances, was sent to me by a keen and experienced bird watcher who flushed a woodcock from among some sand dunes on the Welsh coast. It flew within a few feet of him and was seen clearly to have a much shorter bill than the normal woodcock.

Comparison was made easier by the fact that the same observer flushed several other woodcock on the same piece of ground, and all had bills of the length one normally expects to see.

On the face of it, the short-billed phenomenon seems to be both widespread and increasingly frequent. I believe this is so, but one must remember that other factors can creep into one's calculations. When more people know about a phenomenon and start to talk about it and look for it with new interest, as was certainly the case here, more examples are likely to be spotted and reported. Thus one must allow for a certain amount of "observer factor" in assessing the total number of reports.

In addition, there is a natural tendency for people to spot and report the obvious short-billed woodcock. It is very important to know more about the "intermediate" birds. What proportion of woodcock have bills within the approximate range 50–65mm? This roughly spans the gap which seems to exist between the generally accepted range of "normal" bills (approximately 67–81mm) and the obvious short-bills (say 28–50mm). It is vitally important that we collect much more evidence about woodcock bill lengths, based on measurements taken from a very much larger sample of birds than has ever been examined before.

If a co-ordinated and widespread measuring programme could be arranged throughout the woodcock's range it would help enormously towards a proper understanding of the problem. Most woodcock recovered are shot, but mist-netted birds can yield information too. More ringing of woodcock, especially of young broods, will help also, for not one of the short-billed birds recorded to date has borne a ring. Consequently there is no evidence to show where these birds have come from, if in fact there is any tendency for short-billed birds to originate in any specific areas.

The evidence of general ringing data on woodcock in Europe suggests that the Finnish birds spread more widely across Europe during the following winter than birds bred in other regions. Short-billed woodcock have been shot in almost every country in Europe, and this may provide some grounds for thinking that they may perhaps come from Finland. But that is pure conjecture. If all short-billed woodcock had leg-bands showing they came from Finland, one would be on much firmer ground! There may also be scope for other ways of determining these birds' origins, if techniques can be

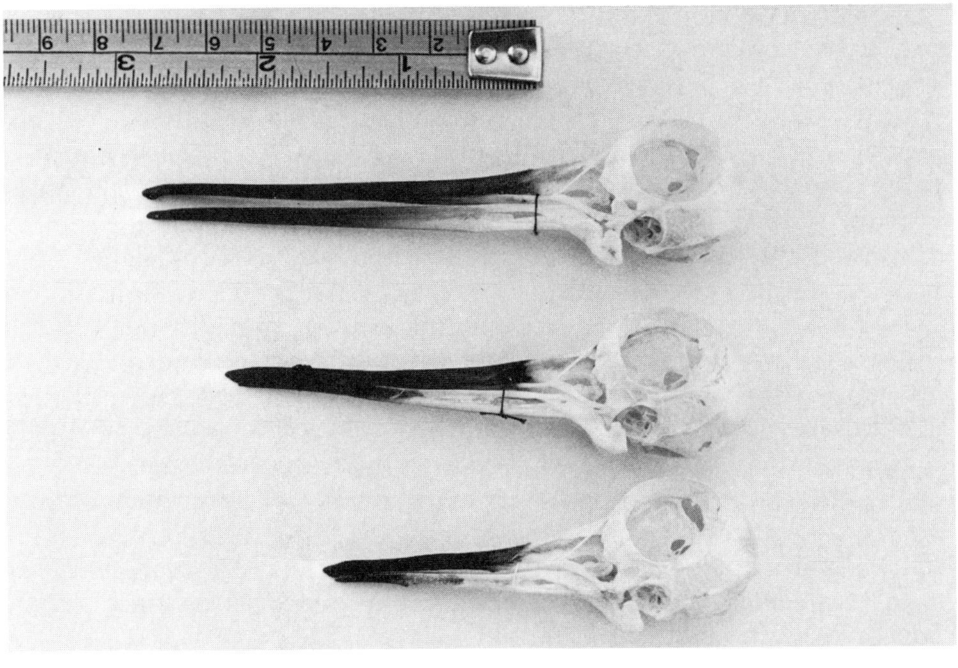

Three woodcock skulls from the writer's collection. The top bill, measuring 68mm, is a good normal example, while the bottom bill measures a mere 35mm. But are we missing woodcock with bills of intermediate length, like the middle one here? At 54mm, is it a "short long-bill" or a "long short-bill"? If more sportsmen measured all the woodcock they shoot and pooled the results we would know much more about this phenomenon.

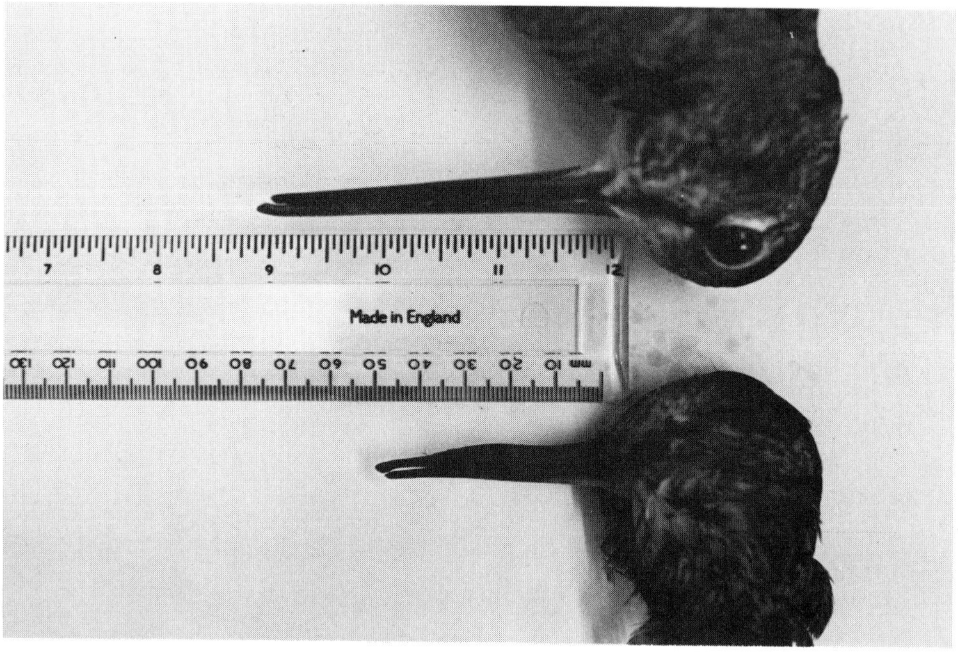

At 51mm, this English-shot short-billed woodcock shows a clear difference when placed alongside a normal example. Although the upper mandible shows the bump or crinkle found on many (but not all) short-billed birds, there are no signs of injury or physical damage to the bill.

developed to use the chemical trace elements in plumage and the birds' burdens of internal parasites to show where they have come from.

Nevertheless, whatever their geographical origins, these birds are occurring more and more often in the British Isles and Europe. How and why this is happening remains a puzzle. We need lots more information, more specimens of such birds, and a large measure of co-operation among sportsmen and biologists throughout the woodcock's range. Since woodcock are widely shot, sportsmen everywhere can play a vital role in helping unravel this mystery. If every woodcock shot was carefully examined and measured, one wing from each bird retained and examined for ageing, and if short-billed and other unusual specimens were preserved and forwarded to a co-ordinating biologist in each country or region, such as the BASC and The Game Conservancy in Britain and Ireland, much would be achieved. It would help illuminate not only the short-billed phenomenon but our whole understanding of the species in general – a bird which fascinates sportsmen and biologists alike, but remains in so many respects a bird of mystery.

Whatever evolutionary, genetic or environmental factor or combination of factors has brought about the emergence of this short-billed bird, it shows that woodcock need not necessarily be at any disadvantage with a bill which perhaps only allows them to probe half as deeply as other birds with bills the normal length. The essential earthworms and other invertebrate creatures which comprise the woodcock's diet must be available in sufficient abundance within 1½–2 inches of the surface of the ground, and even less with some of the very short-billed birds. If this is the case, the woodcock's specialized long bill may actually be longer than is strictly necessary for adequate feeding, at least in some parts of the birds' breeding and wintering range.

When we saw those first Irish short-bills in the bitter winter of 1981–82 inevitably there were plenty of jokes about the poor birds having worn down their bills on the frozen earth. In fact, these short-billed birds may well be a signal indicating either that the woodcocks' feeding habits are somehow different, or that its environment is changing in some way, or a combination of the two. In particular, a shorter bill would indicate that deep probing in soft soil and mud is not how these birds feed. More surface feeding and drier conditions seem to be indicated. The French woodcock biologist Vincent Bouckaert has suggested that shorter bills mean important changes in the woodcocks' breeding habitat, and in the patterns of forestry and woodland management. He points to drainage and increasingly dry conditions in the birds' nesting habitat as particularly significant and potentially serious for the species.

On the other hand, if these habitat changes are happening, the emergence of the short-billed form may be an encouraging sign, demonstrating that the woodcock is a resilient and adaptable species, capable of making the physical changes necessary to cope with a changed environment. Bouckaert has nevertheless argued that the short-billed phenomenon should be seen as a warning that the ecology of traditional temperate woodlands throughout the species' range may be threatened.

Following his seminal paper in *La Mordorée* in 1979, Dante Fraguglione devoted a special chapter of his *La Bécasse des Bois* (Bordeaux, 1983) to the short-billed phenomenon, in which he reviewed the evidence available to him. This was drawn chiefly from continental Europe, and he concluded that the short-billed woodcock must now be considered as a definite sub-species of *Scolopax rusticola*, interbreeding with it but fundamentally different in bill-length. From this he goes on to suggest that the European woodcock must henceforth be regarded as "polytypic", and not as universally monotypic throughout his range, which was how the species has always been regarded. This view is a personal one, and has not been arrived at without a lot of thought and study, but I believe it is still much too early to draw such firm conclusions. More samples, more evidence and much more research will be needed before this puzzle is clarified and explained.

When a sudden variation like this occurs it can be a sign that some latent genetic tendency in the species, hitherto suppressed, is making itself evident, perhaps because the species as a whole is under less pressure. Perhaps – and it is an encouraging speculation – the woodcock is finding conditions more conducive to survival and the production of young. In Britain and Ireland woodcock have expanded their breeding range and numbers significantly over the last century, and there are much larger areas of wintering habitat nowadays, chiefly owing to afforestation. Biologists and sportsmen throughout Europe are generally agreed that woodcock numbers are increasing. So whatever the reasons for the appearance and proliferation of these short-billed birds, it is almost certainly a sign that the species in general is flourishing.

Although the short-billed woodcock seems to be a very new phenomenon, some very unusual and often very attractive colour variations among woodcock have been reported over hundreds of years. They are very unusual, although the woodcock does show quite a range of "standard" colorations in its plumage, and these have caused a lot of interest and comment among sportsmen and ornithologists.

James Latham, in his great *A General Synopsis of Birds* (1781–87) said there were three varieties of woodcock, which he described respectively as "pale red", "dun or rather cream", and "of a pure white". The coloration of woodcock has always interested sportsmen, especially in the last century. "Bird stuffing" was in vogue and there was a tendency automatically to have any odd or unusual specimen or any memorable trophy sent to the nearest stuffers, which were to be found in most towns. Thus a good many unusual memorable woodcock were preserved, and a special study of woodcock colouring was made by Joseph Whitaker of Rainsworth Lodge in Nottinghamshire. He was a keen student and writer on the natural history of his native Nottinghamshire, a Fellow of the Zoological Society, and he is best remembered for his two important books, *The Deer-Parks and Paddocks of England* (1892) and *British Duck Decoys of Today* (1918).

In a letter to *The Field* in July, 1931, he mentioned his collection of mounted and cased woodcock, "which contain 24 British varieties of woodcocks – I fancy a world's record". He was certainly proud of his collection, which he built up with great enthusiasm in his later years. Whitaker's friend and contemporary, the ornithologist and bird artist F.W. Frowhawk, wrote in *The Field* in 1916 that the British Museum's collection of bird skins at Tring contained "no fewer than fifteen varieties of the woodcock", while Whitaker's private collection comprised "six varieties". Frowhawk went through all the unusually coloured specimens he could find and describes a number of plumage colour variations, including "entirely or partially white, cinnamon, ashy-grey, variegated, pied, and even melanic. The most frequent variety is probably the fawn or cinnamon type."

Here Frowhawk has singled out a colour type which biologists call "flavistic" and which the French refer to as "*isabellisme*", an unusually pale, semi-albino form but retaining some coloration and pigments, unlike the true albino which, by its total and striking whiteness and its distinctively reddish eyes, is quite devoid of any pigment. Flavism is a familiar matter for the pheasant shooter, who often encounters the so-called "white pheasant", which can occur in both cocks and hens but is perhaps slightly commoner in hens. Perhaps one in a thousand reared and released pheasants is of this near-white type. Indeed, it is sufficiently common for an experimental poultry husbandry unit in Northern Ireland to have experimented recently with line-breeding of flavistics. (This was done in an attempt to produce a strain of "white pheasants" for rearing on a broiler basis for commercial marketing, on the questionable assumption that the paler bird, which plucks cleaner and whiter, would appeal to those housewives who do not normally buy game.) Flavism is very much rarer in woodcock than among pheasants, however. Although Latham was confident enough to list the pale and white birds as regular categories, their occurrence is extremely infrequent and certainly unusual enough to be noticed and recorded by sportsmen since the eighteenth century.

On 7 November, 1748, the Earl of Gainsborough had a shooting party on his

A delicately coloured pale woodcock with markings in cinnamon, gingers and buffs, shot in County Donegal in 1984.

estate at Exton Hall, in what was then Rutlandshire. While beating out the coverts of Lunnerley Wood, in the estate's deer park, a quite remarkable woodcock was shot. Its head, neck and breast were white and the plumage of its back was described as greyish rather than the usual reddish-brown. Its tail was not the rich chestnut red of most woodcock, but a pale sandy colour, and its wings were quite white, except for two brown feathers on the right wing. This event evidently caused quite a stir among the guests and their host, and Lord Gainsborough later commissioned the artist Godwin, who had his studio nearby at Oakham, to paint the bird. A copy of the painting was given to each of the guest Guns, as a memento of their sport and the remarkable bird it had produced. By 1931 Whitaker, in his ceaseless search for everything relating to odd-coloured woodcock, had managed to trace three of those copies. I wonder how many of those paintings still survive today?

In 1791 a pure white woodcock was seen in the coverts at Penrice Castle in Glamorganshire, and it re-appeared the following season, and again in 1793. By this time one imagines it must have become something of a legend among local sportsmen, probably with a price on its head. It eluded the Guns to the last, however, and was found dead along with many other woodcock on the estate in the exceptionally severe winter weather of 1793.

Four years later, on 15 November, 1797, the Duke of Gordon's gamekeeper shot a woodcock with white primaries and primary covert feathers, but with the first three primaries and the rest of its plumage otherwise quite normal in colour. Another 'cock, totally white, was shot in March, 1798, by Sir John Lade's gamekeeper at Salehurst in Sussex, while in November, 1798, a partial albino woodcock with white wings was shot at Box in Somerset. A year or two later a quite remarkable "double" was achieved by a sportsman at Wadebridge in Cornwall, who bagged a pale bird, probably of the flavistic type, and another with white wings and an albino breast feather.

These were unusual enough to be recorded and noted by later sporting writers, like the Rev W.B. Daniel in his compendious *Rural Sports* (1801). But Frowhawk and Whitaker went into much greater detail in their studies earlier this century. Frowhawk considered the flavistic or cinnamon-coloured variant the most common, but drew attention to other types including near-albinos with subtle hints of grey or silver on a white ground, occasionally with black barring or patching. One of these was shot at Thoresby in Nottinghamshire in 1861 and inevitably found its way into the collection of Whitaker, a few miles away at Rainsworth. On 24 November, 1924, the Marquis of Headfort shot a white woodcock in Littleport Wood on the Oakport estate in County Roscommon. Frowhawk illustrated it and it was duly reported in *The Field* in the following February.

Frowhawk describes other, still rarer woodcock which seemed to him to combine some of the characteristics of both albino and melanistic birds. Whitaker had a specimen of one of these, which Frowhawk painted and described as a "pied" woodcock. This very striking-looking example was shot near Belfast in County Down in 1872, and has dark, almost black markings on the head, back and throat. These give way to occasional dark flecks and patches on the upper wings and along the flanks, against a white ground. The bird's eyes were apparently conventionally dark, but its bill was yellowish rather than the normal olive greenish-brown, and the legs and feet were very pale.

Complete melanism (i.e. unusually dark colouring, such as we find in the "black" or dark green types of pheasant) is very rare, but Frowhawk describes an example spotted in Leadenhall poultry market in London in November, 1903, and later taken to the Tring collection. Its upper parts were an almost blackish shade of chestnut with solid black barring, with a very dark coloured

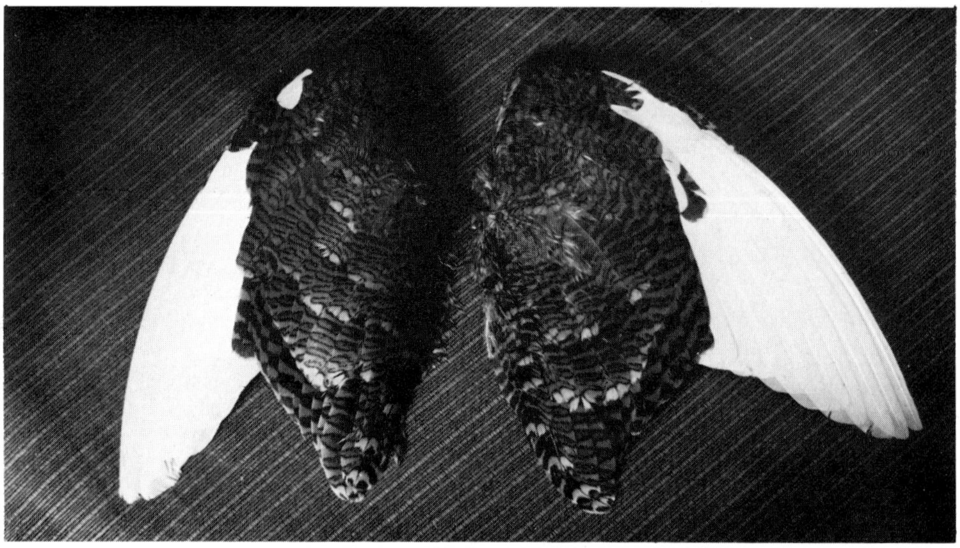

Pure white primary feathers on both wings of a woodcock shot in Dorset in 1984.

head, nape and throat, and another melanistic example, though not quite so heavily marked, was also in the British Museum's Tring collection.

Perhaps today's sportsmen are less ready to take up their pens and write to the sporting magazines and report these unusual-looking woodcock. I don't believe we are any less observant than our ancestors, although we do not automatically send every oddity to the taxidermist. Since the early 1980s, when I started to ask regularly for details of woodcock oddities through feature articles and letters in the shooting magazines, I have received quite a few reports. These included the wings of a partially albino bird shot in Dorset in 1984 and also the complete body of a very delicately marked pale cinnamon woodcock, shot in south Donegal in the same season. This has been superbly preserved and set up by Christopher Stoate, Honorary Secretary of the Guild of Taxidermists.

Another unusually pale-coloured bird was reported in 1984 from the Burgenland area of eastern Austria. Spring shooting of woodcock is permitted there, and on 27 March, 1984, a first-year female woodcock was shot, with its underparts, neck, flanks and the underside of the tail marked a bright rusty yellow colour. There were no other abnormalities, and the bird proved on dissection to be a female of the previous year, smallish but in good condition with a weight of 295 grams, a good average when compared with other recorded weights for female woodcock in March in Austria. This specimen has been mounted for the Steiermark hunting museum in Graz.

To end this consideration of some of the various oddities which crop up among woodcock – can the woodcock tend and help cure its wounds and injuries? In various parts of Europe the woodcock is sometimes known as "the surgeon bird" or "the nurse". This arises from the belief that an injured or wounded woodcock can patch up its wounds, help broken bones to mend, and even minister to the needs of other injured woodcock.

The literature of woodcock, especially in France and Italy, has repeated references to woodcock being shot and found on examination to have a plaster, splint or poultice on some part of its body. This is most commonly a broken leg, but may extend to a thigh or body wound, an injured wing or a damaged or broken bill.

If you have been brought up in the old, romantic European traditions of woodcock shooting it is tempting to think of the woodcock as able to tend its injuries. But what is the evidence for this? There are innumerable accounts of woodcock with hardened pieces of mud, grasses and feathers surrounding a wound, often old and well healed. This includes the feet and lower leg, and

Despite severe deformity of its left wing, probably the result of injury, this woodcock flew strongly when flushed and shot by Howard Cutliffe of Swansea, during a rough shooting day on the Gower peninsula in Pembrokeshire in January 1974.

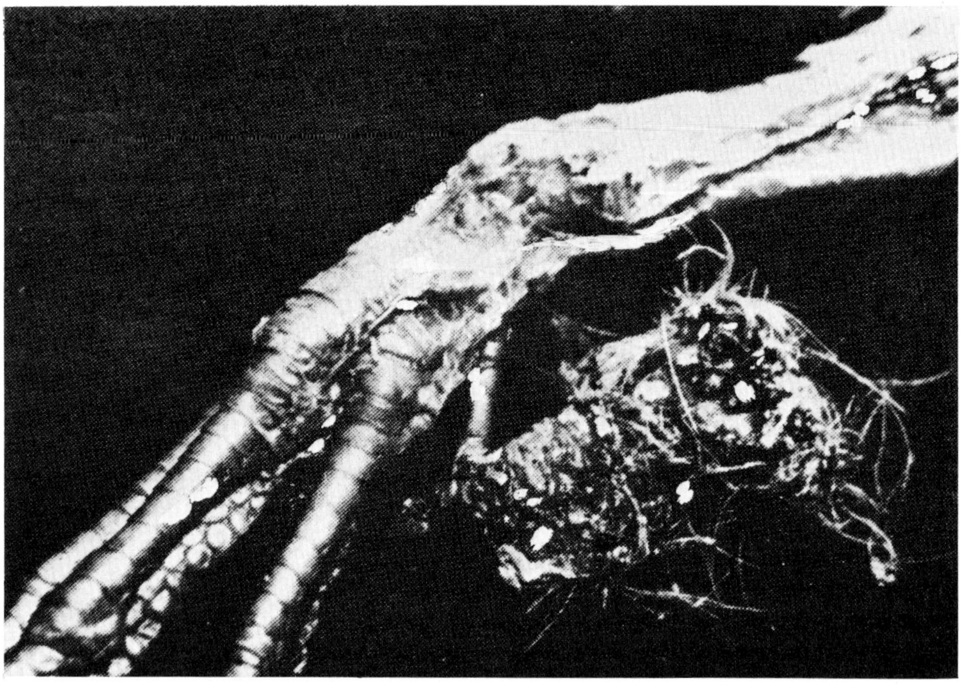

Can injured or wounded woodcock bind up their injuries? This specimen reveals a well healed wound caused by a shot pellet. The injured part was surrounded by a plaster consisting of mud, grasses and downy feathers plucked from the bird's belly and breast.

also the bill. This seems extraordinary, since anything which prevents the bird from opening its bill would seem to constitute a sentence of death by starvation for the bird. But such cases have been reported and sometimes photographed, and the question needs to be investigated and explained.

Woodcock spend a lot of time on the ground, often walking through loose grass and leaf litter and on muddy ground. If it has an open wound on its foot or leg, caused perhaps by hitting an obstacle in flight or being struck by a stray pellet from a shooter's cartridge, you might expect mud and various pieces of vegetation to stick to the open, bleeding spot. But how do we explain the presence in these dried plasters of woodcock feathers, usually small, downy feathers from the bird's lower breast and belly? These cannot have been picked up by chance as the bird dragged its wound along: they are more likely to have been plucked by the woodcock from its own body and placed on or around the damaged spot.

Can it be that woodcock will deliberately mix a combination of mud, leaf fragments, grass and its own feathers to place around the wound? Many European sportsmen are convinced that woodcock do this. It is still unexplained, yet another woodcock mystery, and another good reason for looking very carefully at every woodcock you shoot. The sportsman has a special role to play in helping the biologist to unravel these mysteries, for he sees more woodcock in the hand than anyone else. Close co-operation between the shooting communities and game biologists throughout the woodcock's range is the only way to find out more about a bird which everyone finds unusual, interesting and often downright baffling in its ways.

CHAPTER XI

WOODCOCK AROUND THE WORLD

"Our species of woodcock is unknown in that country: a kind is there found that has the general appearance of it ..."

Rev. W.B. Daniel: *Rural Sports* (1801)

This book is primarily about *Scolopax rusticola*, the European woodcock familiar to British and Irish sportsmen, but it is worth looking for a moment at the other closely related woodcock species which occur elsewhere.

The American woodcock is a well known and thoroughly studied bird, a close relation of our European woodcock but belonging to a quite distinct species, and it is discussed later. But there are other species and sub-species of woodcock which are not so widely known, have not so far been easy to categorize and classify, and in most cases are virtually unknown.

Taxonomists, those painstaking scientists who undertake the complex business of assigning living things to their particular pigeon-holes like families, species, sub-species and races, and then designating them by appropriate and precise Latin names, are still in some disagreement about the various types of woodcock to be found in south-east Asia and Indonesia. However, I have tried here to give an outline picture of the position for the

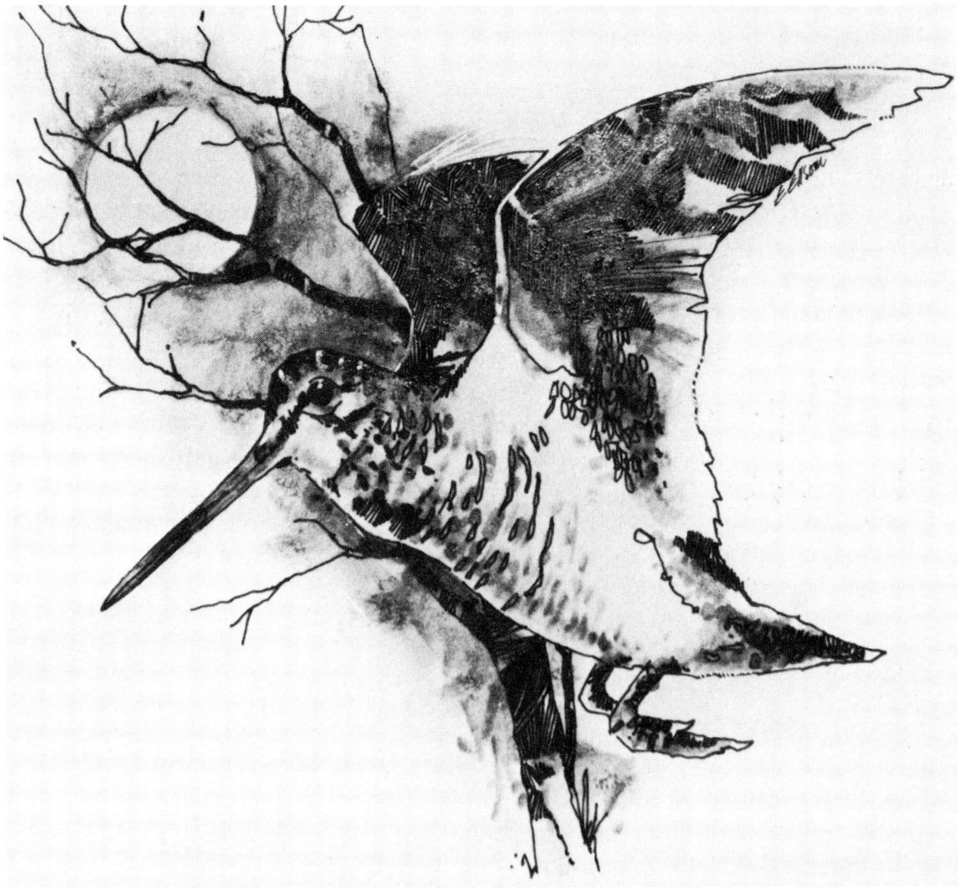

There are other woodcock species in southeast Asia, whose appearance is similar to the familiar European woodcock, but we still know very little about their ways.

layman, based on the most recently published material. In fairness to the taxonomists, theirs is not an easy task, for these races and species are virtually unstudied and some are only represented by a handful of specimens in museum collections, mostly collected many years ago.

The islands of Indonesia, the Celebes and the Moluccas, and the southern islands of Japan are home to four species of woodcock which, while very similar to *S. rusticola*, also display important differences. The Amami woodcock (*S. mira*) belongs to the Ryukyu group of islands to the south of Japan. This area is also visited by migrant European woodcock, and it is probably impossible to distinguish between them accurately under field conditions. Like the European woodcock, its plumage is subject to a wide range of individual variation, making positive identification of birds in the hand even more difficult. In general it differs from the European woodcock in plumage, with a predominant colouration which is olive rather than russet, with bolder black markings, although its chicks are noticeably reddish in colour when they get their first feathers. Other distinguishing points are the Amami woodcock's larger feet and longer toes, and its bigger, more powerful bill, which forms a shallower angle with the bird's forehead, which is rather flatter than in *S. rusticola*. There is a distinctly pink area of skin around and behind the eye which helps to separate Amami woodcock from European birds. Its underparts are paler than the European woodcock, and the wings are more rounded. Observant sportsmen, with an eye to the pinfeathers as a trophy, have noticed that these are rather larger in the Amami woodcock.

Java, Sumatra and New Guinea have their own resident species, the Dusky woodcock (*S. saturata*). This occurs chiefly along the southern and south-western parts of Sumatra and Java and in east New Guinea. However, it has been argued that the New Guinea bird is actually a separate subspecies or race, *Scolopax saturata rosenbergii*, and the New Guinea bird is often referred to as "Rosenberg's Woodcock" and the Sumatra and Java bird as "Horsefield's Woodcock". The Berau peninsula in western New Guinea, part of the adjacent hill country and the Huon peninsula in the east of the island are three areas known to hold a resident woodcock first described in 1871 and formally named *Scolopax saturata rosenbergii*, after the collector Von Rosenberg, who was one of the first to collect and report a specimen of this bird. In appearance it is similar in many respects to the closely related subspecies, the Javanese and Sumatran woodcock, rather smaller overall than the European woodcock but with a generally longer bill, some 5mm longer than the European average. Like the other woodcock species of the Far East its feet are larger and its legs longer. It is dark in colour, the darkest of all the woodcocks in the colouring of its upper parts, but it lacks the very heavy, dark barring of the breast and underparts of the Javanese race of *S. saturata* and the feathers of the breast and the lower underparts are a lighter creamy white. It has not been extensively studied but it seems to frequent the tropical forest, especially where conditions are damp and swampy.

Like the Amami woodcock, the Dusky woodcock has a more rounded wing and a bigger, stronger bill than our familiar European woodcock, but it is a rather smaller bird. Some recent measurements give an average bill length between 74–84mm, rather longer than the average range in *S. rusticola*, but in other respects it is about 30% smaller.

Skins in museum collections reveal a bird which is much darker than the European woodcock, with a deeper, less variegated range of brownish-red colour tones on its upper plumage, and the head is not so prominently barred as in the European woodcock. Its underparts are much darker, too, with broader and more mottled barring than the delicate horizontal markings of *S. rusticola*, and there is a prominent whitish patch on the bird's upper belly. In flight it gives the impression of a much darker bird than the European woodcock.

Studies of woodcock in Java and Sumatra early this century showed that they favour the cooler, more temperate areas where broken margins of forest give way to more open upland regions, usually around 4000–9000 feet. A nest has been found in the crater of a volcano at about 5500 feet.

This species undertakes a breeding season roding display which is rather similar to the European woodcock, and the male likewise has two principal roding calls. But these differ in tone from *S. rusticola* and may be given while the bird is perching. This is not unknown in the European species but it is very rare. Most interesting of all, perhaps, in distinguishing *S. saturata* from our own woodcock is that it is not always a ground nester. The nests, which tend to be close to a forest edge, consist of beds of mosses and are sometimes raised above the forest floor, in trees and bushes at a height of up to 3–7 feet above the ground.

In the Celebes archipelago another woodcock is resident in the central and northern parts of the main island. Or perhaps one should actually say there are two types of Celebes or Sulawesi woodcock, for it is claimed that two quite distinct subspecies exist, *S. celebensis heinrichi* in the north-eastern tip of Sulawesi, and *S. celebensis celebensis* in the central parts of the island. It may be that these are merely two distinct populations of the same bird, and the picture is made even more complicated by some claims that the Celebes woodcock is actually the same species as the Moluccan or Obi woodcock, which we come to later.

The behaviour of these two races or populations is rather similar, and they are apparently furtive and secretive to an even greater degree than the European woodcock, which makes them quite exceptionally difficult to find and to study adequately. Their behaviour has been described as skulking and shy, reminiscent in some ways of the water rail and the corncrake in that they often lurk undetectably in thick undergrowth, squatting almost invisibly, sitting very tight or scuttling off quietly at high speed at the approach of danger, and most reluctant to fly except when very hard pressed. When they do take to the wing their flight is slow, low and laboured and the bird will pitch down again within a short distance. *S.c. celebensis* is said to be confined to the central part of the island, in the hills north of Lake Poso and found at heights of around 6–7000 feet.

The Sulawesi woodcock is larger than the Amami or the Dusky woodcock, but those rounded wings which it is so reluctant to use are about the same length as the European woodcock. However, its legs are longer by an average of about 10 millimetres. Longer and stronger also is the bill, which is described as set rather higher on the bird's head, and of a greyish-blue colour, in contrast to the more or less uniform olive green-brown of the European species. The legs and feet are the same greyish-blue, quite unlike *S. rusticola*, whose feet colouring can vary considerably but usually varies between a light fleshy-grey hue through various roseate and reddish tones. *S. celebensis* differs also in the remarkable size of its feet. Taking the measurement of the middle toe of captured specimens showed an average length of 45–48mm, while the European bird's average is about 38mm. We therefore have here a woodcock which, although roughly the same size as the European bird, has distinctly larger feet, a much longer bill and longer legs.

The other Celebes race or population, *S.c. heinrichi* was first identified when a male was captured in November 1930 in the Matinang Hills. Studies of this and two other birds, all males, has revealed a similar wing length to the birds of the central part of the island and also to the European woodcock, and with the same large feet of the other Celebes subspecies, but with a much

Woodcock have always been favourite subjects for sporting gun engravers, especially in Europe. Here are six engravings of woodcock on the action plates and top levers of Beretta guns. Some are shown in pairs and others as single birds, and all are the work of master engraver Caesare Giovanelli and his colleagues at Brescia in northern Italy. (Photos: Gunmark)

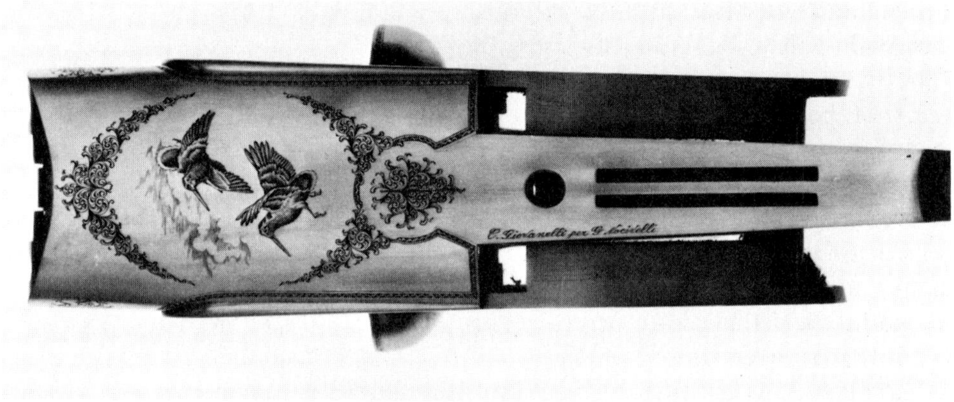

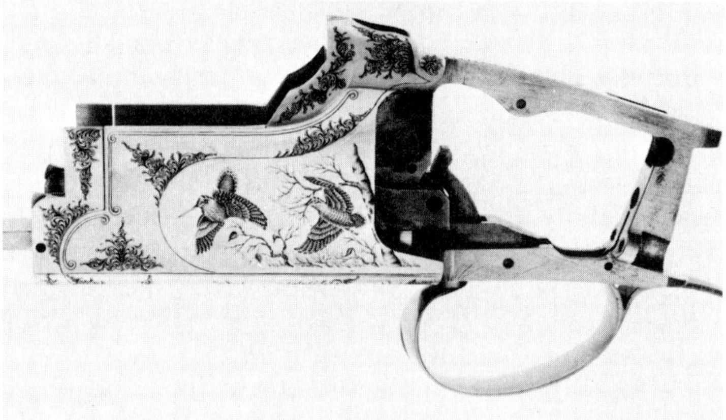

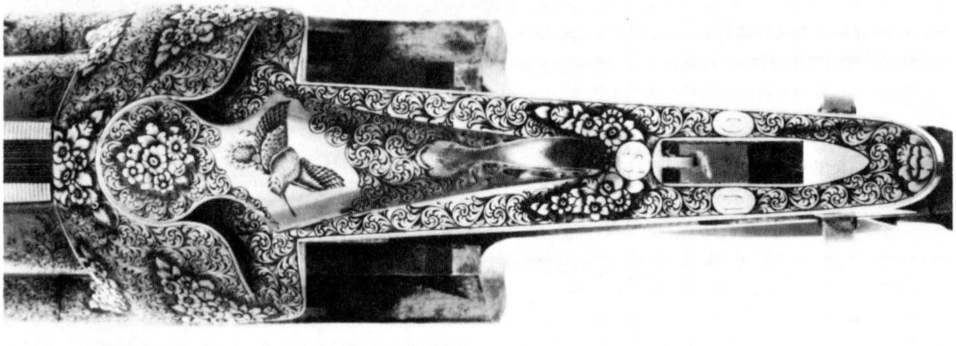

shorter and rather finer bill. At 76–80mm this is much closer to the European bird, falling just within the top end of the spectrum for the European woodcock. However, the woodcock of Sulawesi remain very little known, and the *heinrichi* race or population cannot be clearly understood from the total evidence of a mere three specimens.

The Celebes woodcock is found in dense woodland among the hill forests above 3500 feet and up to 7500 feet where the vegetation progressively gives way to low scrub and mosses, and its preferred habitat seems to be much the same as the Dusky woodcock of Sumatra and Java.

Last of the Old World species is the Obi or Moluccan species, found only on the islands of Obi and Batjan in the Molucca Islands to the west of New Guinea. This was first formally described in 1866 and named *Scolopax rochussenii* by the taxonomist Schlegel, who named it after the then governor of the Dutch East Indies, M. Rochussen. It has not been seen since 1902, and is apparently only known from five specimens. In general shape it resembles the European woodcock but is much larger, perhaps 25% bigger, and quite the largest of the woodcocks. It has larger feet and longer legs, and the bill is also much longer than *S. rusticola*, between 90–100mm. The underparts are uniformly pale, though darker than the European bird and with none of its transverse black markings. The upper parts have large and striking ochre-buff spots, unlike any other woodcock and much more prominent than the smaller, more reddish speckling of the Sulawesi woodcock. Its predominantly pale and rather uniformly coloured underparts have been compared with the very much smaller American woodcock, which is the next and last of the woodcock species on our list.

"It should be recollected, that our species of woodcock is unknown in that country: a kind is there found that has the general appearance of it, but which is scarce half the size, and wants the bars on the breast and belly." So much for the woodcock of North America, according to the Rev William Daniel in his *Rural Sports* (1801).

The American woodcock (*Scolopax minor*) is by far the smallest of all the woodcocks, barely half the size of its cousin in Europe and Asia, but in its appearance, flight and habits it has many very close similarities. The first settlers of North America knew they were dealing with a miniature form of the bird they had known in Europe, and in the French-speaking areas of Louisiana and the Cajun country of the Deep South, the bird is known as *bécasse*, just like *S. rusticola* in France. The Americans also have a wide range of other regional and colloquial terms for their woodcock. The timberdoodle and the hokumpoke are perhaps the most vivid of these. Bog-borer, bog-sucker and siphon-snipe all reveal some understanding of how the bird feeds, although the last name is reminiscent of the old myth of the woodcock as "the bird of suction" which never ate solid food but somehow managed to suck liquid nourishment out of the soil. But surely no woodcock ever deserved to be called a mudbat!

The emblem of the Quebec Woodcock Club. French-Canadian sportsmen retain much of the traditional enthusiasm of the European *bécassiers*, but their quarry is the smaller North American woodcock.

The American woodcock has a greyish head usually with a single blackish bar, and lacks the very distinct multiple barring on the head of the European bird. The feathers of the back are mottled with blacks and buffs, but with an overall hue which is much more greyish than the European bird. The American and European birds share a prominent blackish stripe running from the eye to the base of the bill, but the American 'cock has none of the barred underparts markings of our woodcock. Its throat, breast and belly are a virtually uniform orange-buff or cinnamon colour, and the primary feathers of the wing are slaty grey, in contrast to the rich browns, russets and buffs of the European woodcock. During the autumn and winter months the American woodcock is at its peak weight, like its European counterpart, unless hard

Richard Robjent's watercolour of an American woodcock in winter shows a bird which is strikingly similar in general shape to our European bird, but there are important differences in size, plumage and some aspects of behaviour.

frosts prevent adequate feeding. During the shooting season a male American woodcock will probably weigh about five or six ounces, and a female between seven and eight. This reveals a marked difference in weight and therefore in size between males and females, something which does not happen to anything like the same extent in the European woodcock.

No American "woodcock hunter" claims to be able to distinguish males from females when the birds are flushed on shooting days. Once in the hand, however, whether they have been shot or caught alive for banding, the birds can be sexed accurately. Apart from the fact that females are invariably larger and heavier than males, though there is some degree of overlap, the birds can be sexed fairly precisely by looking at bill lengths. The American woodcock's bill length lies within the range 62–73mm, shorter than the average for the European bird, but relatively rather longer for what is a significantly smaller and lighter bird. Any bird with a bill of 72mm or over is always female: a length of 64mm or less always means a male. The 70–72mm range is 95% female, and 64–66mm bills mean 95% males. This still leaves some degree of doubt about a small proportion of American woodcock, but a further examination of the first three primary feathers of the wintg makes it possible to sex precisely without dissection in over 99.6% of cases.

Uniquely among woodcock, the American bird has three very narrow outer primaries, extremely slender by comparison with the broad knife-blade shape of the European bird's primaries. If the total width of these three feathers comes to 12.4mm or less, the bird is male; 12.6mm or more means it's a female. Any uncertainties around the 12.5mm mark can be resolved by taking the bird's weight and bill length into account.

The development of these accurate sexing techniques for American woodcock is something which has so far been denied to those interested in the European woodcock, for which dissection remains the only certain method. Ageing the birds of both species involves an examination of the wing feathers, though the colouration of the tips of the secondary feathers is of primary importance in ageing the American bird, while the degree of wear on the tips of the outer primaries is the main thing to look at in European woodcock.

This diminutive cousin of the European woodcock has been very extensively studied, and several major scientific symposia have been devoted to the species. Without going into too much detail, it is worth mentioning some of the main ways in which the American timberdoodle compares and contrasts with the European woodcock.

Both birds share a fondness for moist areas, rich in worms and other invertebrate foods, and they are active mainly at dawn and dusk, and during the hours of darkness when they feed. Mixed woodlands with a dense understorey broken up by clearings, rides and glades are a favourite habitat for both birds, and the American woodcock is also very migratory in its ways, though there are sedentary populations too, as with *S. rusticola*. Its range extends across the eastern United States and in spring and summer breeding migrants are found north of the Great Lakes and into New Brunswick and Nova Scotia in north-east Canada. Parts of Canada and the New England states are important breeding areas, and woodcock also breed abundantly down through the long line of the Appalachian Mountains.

The winter range of the American woodcock is much more restricted, owing to the severe frosty weather which prevails for months on end in many northern areas where it breeds in spring. The southern Atlantic coastal areas as far south as Florida are major wintering grounds, as are the coasts of the Gulf of Mexico as far as eastern Texas. But Louisiana seems to be by far the most important single wintering area for the species in the whole of North America.

The breeding behaviour of the American woodcock has attracted a lot of attention from naturalists and scientists, and some writers have become almost as lyrical and fulsome in their descriptions of the "sky-dancer" on its "singing

The American woodcock is not only smaller than the European bird, but the difference in plumage is immediately obvious. In particular there is no barring or flecking on the flanks and underparts.

grounds" as European sportsmen in extolling the unique mystery and delights of woodcock shooting at roding time.

Like the European bird, the American woodcock is rarely heard to make any sounds in winter but the male is highly vocal in spring and early summer. He does not undertake regular roding flights over an area of nesting habitat in the same way as our woodcock, but adopts another method of advertising his presence to receptive females in the vicinity.

At dawn and dusk the male flies out from his roosting spot to his chosen singing ground, usually a distance of not more than a few hundred yards, and begins a display which may last about three-quarters of an hour. A low gurgling sound is given while the bird is on the ground, followed by a series of high, nasal sounds, usually rendered as *peents*. After a few minutes of calling like this on the ground, the male flies up in a spiraling flight to a height of perhaps 300–400 feet, making a twittering sound with his wings and giving a liquid, chirping call. After a minute or so he drops again, usually almost at the spot where he began his singing, and he may make fifteen or twenty such flights in the course of a display session.

Often a female will fly in quickly and silently, and mating will take place immediately. Singing males have been found to mate readily with mounted decoy specimens of female woodcock, something which has also been achieved experimentally by scientists studying the roding behaviour of woodcock in Europe. Other males venturing into the singing ground are repulsed with harsh, angry cries, and it is thought that dominant male woodcock select regular, favourite singing grounds. If the dominant bird is removed or disappears for any reason, such as an accident, shooting or live-trapping, it is quickly replaced by another bird, just as dominant roding European woodcock are replaced from the reservoir of sub-dominant males.

The American woodcock is a well studied species, much more so than the European woodcock. The USA has a tradition of well-funded and thorough research into wildlife, and game in particular. Tens of thousands of American woodcock have been ringed and released, several times the total numbers of woodcock ringed throughout the British Isles and Europe. The species has been the subject of a series of important scientific symposia in post-war years, and has attracted particular interest as an indicator species for the environmental well-being of woodland habitats throughout eastern regions of North America. Aldo Leopold, that most eminent of American ecologists, had a particular affection for the timberdoodle and its ways. His enthusiasm for woodcock and his determination that the spring sky-dancer on his singing grounds should remain part of the natural scene in the eastern USA was perhaps the most important single influence in focusing the interest and concern of American game conservationists and biologists on the woodcock. Aldo Leopold's work, his inspiring writing, and the studies of other woodcock biologists who have followed him set an example to those of us, sportsmen and scientists, in the Old World who want to know more about the American woodcock's larger cousin and help to conserve it as a renewable sporting asset for future generations.